BLAZE OF COURAGE

THE PESHTIGO FIRE CHRONICLES

BOOK TWO

AVRIE SWAN

WILD HEART
BOOKS

To Evie,
My sister, best friend, and adventure buddy

ACKNOWLEDGMENTS

To begin, I would like to thank my family for their amazing help. Thank you to my mother, both for your valuable advice and for your infinite patience. Thank you to Teddy for always being willing to listen to my rambling and brainstorming sessions. Thanks also to Evie, who has been my biggest fan from the start. Love you!

Thanks to my Illinois family and Wisconsin friends for always advocating for me. You're the best! I'm also incredibly thankful for the community of authors I've met over the past year. I've learned so much from you all, and I can't wait to see what the next chapter brings.

Shout out to my fellow employees at the library. I wouldn't be able to write without the encouragement of people like you! Thanks also to the awesome team at Wild Heart Books, including Denise, Sarah, Sherri, and so many others. I couldn't have asked for a better support system.

As always, thanks to God for all that He has done and all the opportunities He has given me. This book never would have existed had He not surrounded me with such wonderful people and given me such gracious opportunities. To Him be the glory, always and forever.

Last but not least, thank you, dear reader, for taking the time to read my stories. God bless!

CHAPTER 1

The letter was like a boulder in Charlotte Clarke's hand, pressing down with an unbearable weight and making her wish she could drop it into the fireplace and watch it burn. Could what the words shouted at her in bold black strokes be true? She never should have picked the paper up from her sister Carina's drawer, but the temptation to read it had been too great. And now a terrible knowledge burdened her. *We're going to lose everything.*

Her heart beating unsteadily, Charlotte folded the past-due notice and placed it back in Carina's drawer. There wasn't much time before her sister returned home from the laundry, and she would wait until later to ask about the letter. But why did Carina even have it? Their mother was the one who dealt with financial affairs, including rent.

Charlotte sank onto Carina's bed and buried her head in her hands. *If only Father was here.* Things hadn't been the same since he had gotten lost in a blizzard and died all those years ago. They had barely scraped by, and now it looked as though their fragile peace was going to be uprooted once more. Mother said it was God's grace that had kept them alive, but that couldn't be true. No loving God would put them through such suffering. In reality, they were alone—alone and nearing destitution.

"Lottie, where are you?"

Mother.

Charlotte leaped to her feet and straightened the folds of her plain dress. She couldn't let Mother see anything was amiss. Not until she had a chance to speak to Carina and figure out whether their mother knew of the rent notice.

Mother's cheery face appeared in the doorway. "There you are!" Her russet brows furrowed in confusion. "What are you doing in Carina's room?"

Charlotte ran a hand over her chestnut-brown braid. "Looking for hairpins before I go on my walk. I lost most of mine, and with Carina's wild tresses, I figured she would have a couple extra I could borrow." It wasn't a lie. She *had* opened Carina's dresser drawer to look for hairpins. She had simply gotten distracted after discovering the letter at the bottom.

Mother shook her head, a slight smile on her face. While she was as beautiful as ever, age had begun showing in her appearance, from the silver threads in her russet hair to the fine wrinkles around her eyes and mouth. Yet, through it all, the dear woman always seemed to radiate the same warmth and kindness that she had since Charlotte was a child. "You really need to be more careful with your things, Lottie." Her chastisement was gentle despite the serious words. "You're twenty-two years of age. Young ladies such as yourself should know to keep track of their belongings." Mother leaned against the doorframe and tapped a finger beneath her chin. "But I suppose it doesn't matter now. I was going to suggest you help me clean, but if you were planning on taking a walk, I won't stop you. It's a beautiful day, and the warmth isn't going to last much longer."

Charlotte inclined her head. "Wonderful. I'll be back soon." She brushed past Mother and scurried down the hall before the tears building at the back of her eyes could spill over. There would be no explaining her sudden change in mood, not without revealing the contents of the note.

Charlotte left the back door and plunged into the woods, tugging anxiously at her braid as she walked. What were they going to do if they lost the house? Where would they go? They had nobody to turn to, no family to ask for support. Mother was an only child, and her parents had passed on long ago. Perhaps she could take up work. But would that be enough? Her meager wages likely wouldn't make a dent in the money they owed. Despair filled Charlotte as she trekked between the trees. The way she saw it, there was no way for them to save the house. They were bound to lose it all.

Charlotte was so engrossed in her worry that she completely missed the large thorn bush in front of her until it was too late. "Ouch!" She winced as the thick branches ensnared her dress and scraped her hands. She attempted to back away but quickly found she was trapped. "Oh, no."

Colorful leaves drifted to the ground and swirled around Charlotte as she struggled to free her skirt from the bush. She tugged fruitlessly at her hem, willing the fabric to untangle from the thorns. Tears welled in her eyes and spilled down her cheeks as the dress remained firmly stuck. It felt as though the prickly plant was mocking her, grabbing on harder the more she tried to get free. "Why did this have to happen now?"

"Thorn bushes do have a tendency to arrive at the worst of times."

The deep voice sounded from somewhere behind her. Charlotte twisted to see over her shoulder, blinking away tears as a familiar face came into view. "Edwin!"

Edwin sketched a mock bow, his white sleeves billowing around him like wings. "My lady. Would you like some help in getting free of this dastardly bush?"

"Yes, please." Charlotte stepped as far back as she could and allowed Edwin to take a look at her ensnared skirt. While he snapped branches and yanked thorns from the fabric, she wiped the tears from her cheeks. There was no need to make her best friend think she was crying over a plant, though it was likely too late for that.

After a moment, her skirt dropped free of the bush. Charlotte fixed what she hoped to be a convincing smile on her face as Edwin straightened with a triumphant grin. "Thank you, kind sir. My day would have been a lot worse if I had to walk home with a ripped dress."

"I imagine so." Edwin tipped his head, causing a strand of thick black hair to fall over his eye. "What're you doing out here, Lottie? You look... well..."

Charlotte pursed her lips. She imagined she looked quite a sight after having spent the last two minutes crying. "I could ask you the same thing. What brings you out here at this time of day? Shouldn't you be working? Your father wouldn't be happy to know you snuck away from the dairy farm." Mr. Deeran had never been fond of lax workers, and that included his own son.

Edwin shook his head, a twinkle in his eye. "It's nearly four-thirty, Lottie. You know I only work till three." He raised a brow. "How long have you been wandering around out here, exactly?"

"Not long. I suppose I didn't think of the time." She had been too distracted by the letter and the implications it held to consider the time of day. "I wanted to get outside while it was still light out."

"That's understandable. Mind if I walk with you?"

Charlotte shook her head and accepted Edwin's proffered arm. "Not at all." She enjoyed his company. They had been friends for as long as she could remember, after all, and he had been her companion on many escapades.

After a few minutes of strolling in silence, Charlotte released a breath. The tension inside her was rapidly approaching a breaking point, and she couldn't contain it any longer. "To tell the truth, I didn't come out here simply to walk. I was going to, originally, but then I discovered something that required thought." Charlotte bit the inside of the cheek. Did she dare tell Edwin? Perhaps he could help her plan a solution. Yes, it was better to tell him than try and conceal the truth. "Mr. Howard is going to evict us," she admitted, her shoulders slumping. "We don't have the money to cover rent. I could take a job to help, but I don't think that would be enough."

The corners of Edwin's mouth drooped, and he patted Charlotte's arm. "I'm sorry to hear that, Lottie. I know how much you love that house." He stared thoughtfully at the tree-tops. "I doubt that you taking up work would be enough. Perhaps... well..." He tilted his head. "No, it's probably a foolish idea. On the other hand, perhaps it isn't."

"What is it?" Charlotte drew to a halt and turned to face her friend. "Please, Edwin. We have so little time left to save our home. Any idea is worth consideration."

Edwin's cheeks bloomed red. "Well, I was going to suggest that you marry me."

"I beg your pardon?" Charlotte's mouth ran dry. "Edwin, I couldn't marry you. That wouldn't be fair."

"In what way would it not be fair? We certainly don't despise each other, and my family has been telling me to find a woman to settle down with for months now. The two of us get along well. Why not pair together? It would benefit us both."

Charlotte released Edwin's arm and took a step back.

"Edwin, I don't believe it would be enough to save the house. Even if it was, it wouldn't be fair for me to put you in debt on account of us. It would take you hours of work and a large chunk of wages to cover our rent, and I couldn't possibly expect you to give away your hard-earned money."

"It would be worth it to see you and your family happily settled. With your father gone, I couldn't stand to see you ladies on the street."

Charlotte shuddered, a throbbing ache building at the back of her head. Too much was happening all at once. "Please, Edwin, let us put this matter aside for now. It makes me so anxious." She rubbed her temples.

Edwin's lips parted, words clearly on the tip of his tongue, but he was quick to clamp them shut again with a slight shake of his head. At length, he shrugged. "As you wish."

Charlotte resumed walking as she tried to clear her thoughts. While she got along with Edwin, something inside her recoiled at the thought of joining him in matrimony. Perhaps it was the flippant way he had courted other girls...or perhaps it was the fact that Charlotte didn't love him. *Yes.* In the end, that was the simple truth. While Edwin was her best friend, that was all he was and all he ever would be. She felt no real love or affection for him—at least, not the sort that would lead to marriage.

Charlotte touched the trunk of one of the trees beside her. Before long, the woods would be covered in snow, and it would be far less pleasant to stroll here. No longer would a warm breeze blow through the autumn-toned leaves, sending them floating noiselessly to the ground, nor would little songbirds twitter joyfully as they flitted from branch to branch. The world would fall into a season of hibernation, when everything became draped in a cold blanket of white.

Normally, the thought of the winter season brought Charlotte joy. Now she could think only of their present problem.

What would happen if they lost their home before winter? A chill ran up her spine. Would they be forced to wander about in the snow, fighting desperately to survive? Would they end up like Father?

Perhaps Edwin's idea was worth considering, after all.

CHAPTER 2

She was dreaming. Charlotte had always been able to tell when she was sleeping, and this time was no different. She stood at the edge of the forest, facing the only home she had known. The sun blazed down with an abnormal amount of heat as she walked toward the house. The long grass crunched under her feet, the brittle blades swishing against the hem of her nightgown. Hot wind blew through the clearing, whispering in Charlotte's ear and tugging strands of hair free from her braid as she came to the door. She reached out to turn the knob but froze when a scream sounded from somewhere in the distance.

Charlotte spun on her heel with a gasp and gazed out into the clearing, the grass swaying in the breeze. There was no further sign that anyone was in trouble. Everything appeared normal, apart from the strange, steady heat burning her face and hands.

So why was her head shouting a warning? And what was that feeling creeping up the back of her neck?

The wind picked up, swirling around Charlotte with a growing cacophony until it tore at her skirts and screamed with the force of a gale. The door at her back shuddered under the power of the gusts, shaking so violently that Charlotte feared it would break. The wind hurled out cinder and ash from the forest, lighting fire to everything Charlotte knew and loved.

"What's happening?" she cried.

"Charlotte!"

Charlotte sucked in a startled breath and opened her eyes, her heart thundering in her chest.

"Charlotte, fire!" Carina stood in the doorway of Charlotte's bedroom, face pale and feet bare. She wore a white nightgown, the color a stark contrast to her vibrant hair. What was she doing there? Carina almost never awoke in the middle of the night. "Wake up. We have to get out of the house before it reaches us!"

Charlotte pushed herself to her elbows as her sister's words registered. She wasn't dreaming. This was real. "Are you certain?"

Carina nodded. The rest of her sister's words were lost on Charlotte as she got to her feet and stared out the window. *No, it cannot be!*

And yet a sickly orange tint lit the sky, illuminating the horrible scene unfolding outside. A blaze far taller than Charlotte could have ever imagined ate its way through the town, drawing closer and closer to the house. Trees groaned and fell in the flames as they snaked through the dry grass like lightning. The wind only fueled the blaze, making it grow larger and more menacing the closer it came.

When Charlotte looked around, Carina had fled, most likely to warn their mother of the oncoming danger. What should she do? *My things!* Upon collecting the blanket from her bed, Charlotte ran to the closet and started to stuff her dresses into it. Smoke began to filter into the room, making her cough and wipe her eyes as she continued gathering her belongings. Her bare feet were cold on the hardwood floor, a strange sensation compared with the raging fire drawing closer and closer outside.

"There's no time, Charlotte!" Carina spoke from the bedroom door. She grabbed Charlotte's hands, causing the blanket to spill to the ground. Before she could blink, her sister had pushed her through the hallway and out the front door, into the burning night.

Terror seemed to fill the air in a riot of wind and screaming as people dashed by, running from the flaming town. Charlotte winced as a fleeing woman slammed into her side, the force of the blow nearly knocking her to the ground. She wrapped her arms around her stomach and wiped at her eyes with the other, glancing around. Relief rushed through her as she spotted her sister only a few feet away. Their mother couldn't be far behind. She would know to leave the house before it caught on fire. Wouldn't she?

A sudden cry pierced the air, this one distinctly animal in nature.

Charlotte's heart skipped a beat. "Trudy!"

The cow was still in the shed. They always kept the front gate closed during the night, which meant Gertrude would have no way to escape. *I can't leave her to die.* Charlotte dashed from the yard without looking back to see whether or not Carina had noticed her leaving. If she hadn't, Charlotte would simply have to rejoin her after the cow was freed. There was no time to waste.

Sharp grass pricked Charlotte's bare feet, a chilling reminder of her dream. Soon they were scratched and scraped from the rough ground, sending pain shooting upward as she sprinted across the yard. By the time she caught sight of the cowshed, the blaze already licked at the little building, attacking the wooden beams and climbing the sides. Trudy's frantic cries bellowed from inside.

Charlotte picked up speed, her heart pounding. "I'm

coming!" She jumped burning fence posts that lay like matchsticks on the ground and ran the last few feet before drawing to a halt in front of the building.

Clearly, the cow was nearing hysteria as she kicked at the walls of the shed and mooed loudly. The wood shuddered and groaned with the force of the animal's fright, though it didn't collapse. However, it was only a matter of time before the fire and winds weakened the building.

"Hang on, Trudy!" Charlotte tugged at the thick rope that held the shed doors shut, breaking off in a cough as she inhaled a lungful of smoke. After a moment, she managed to unravel the rope and fling the doors wide open.

The air seemed to grow even heavier as she entered the tiny building. Darting flames seared Charlotte's cheeks as she plastered herself against the wall and shimmied past Trudy to the other side of the shed, putting her in front of the cow. Flames singed the hair that clung to her sweat-soaked face as she moved, and heat crawled up her back. Trying to ignore the fact that her face was surely burned, Charlotte grasped the cow's rope halter, pushing hard on the animal's chest. "Back up, Trudy! Back up!"

The cow began reluctantly following Charlotte's directive, taking one step at a time until her hind end was outside of the shed. Just as her front legs reached the doorway, a large portion of the shed's ceiling came crashing to the ground. Charlotte screamed as chunks of burning wood landed on her outstretched arms. She dropped Gertrude's halter and struggled to brush them off. She managed to remove the wood and beat the fire out, but not before her arms had turned nearly numb with pain.

Startled by Charlotte's outburst, Gertrude let out a cry and jumped backward, her eyes rolling in fear. Unwilling to let the cow run into the fire, Charlotte grabbed Gertrude's halter despite the pain that shot like lightning through her arms. "It's all right, Trudy." The harsh wind ripped the words from her mouth almost instantly.

Charlotte moved to the cow's back and used every ounce of energy she had left to heft herself up and over Gertrude. She splayed across the middle of the anxious cow like a sack of potatoes. "Go, Trudy, go!" Charlotte slapped the bovine's rump, sending her running into the clearing.

Sounds and sights filtered through the smoke as Gertrude lumbered through the burning wind, images flickering in the orange haze—a mother calling desperately for her missing child, a screaming horse with a flaming tail, and a building collapsing with a thunderous crash. Whether they ran toward safety or more danger, Charlotte didn't know. She could only hope the cow had some instinct that would lead them through the flames. Whether a few minutes or a few hours passed was impossible to tell, as she could see only the same glowing smoke and the occasional outline of a figure running past.

At last, Trudy halted, leading Charlotte to raise her head. The sound of splashing and calling meant they must have reached the edge of the riverbank. Charlotte squinted into the flaming night. Unfortunately, the haze was so thick that she couldn't even make out the ground beneath her.

Without any warning, Gertrude plunged into the river. Charlotte could only hang on and hope she wouldn't fall off and be kicked under as the cow swam away from the bank. Frigid water bit her legs and arms, providing a small amount of relief to her burns. Soon, however, the cold went from relieving to painful, crawling up her limbs and sending icy shards ricocheting through her spine. Shivering, Charlotte struggled to push herself into a sitting position. Unfortunately, her energy was spent, and she only wriggled a bit before drooping farther over the cow's back.

Gertrude slowed, growing lethargic in the cold water. The poor creature wasn't meant to swim for long periods of time, especially not with a person on her back. The cow would perish if they had to stay in the river much longer, and Charlotte would most likely follow suit.

"Please," she whispered, her voice hoarse. "God, help us."

It was the last thing she managed to say before she knew no more.

❧

Fog obscured Charlotte's vision, thick and black. Her arms and legs drooped, far too heavy to move. Was she trapped in river mud? It had been her greatest fear as a child, though her mother had told her that being afraid of mud was foolish. Perhaps she was drowning. Charlotte had always imagined drowning would be...well, a bit more frightening. This was peaceful and warm, as if she was covered by a thick blanket.

Voices pierced the edge of Charlotte's conscience, a low murmuring that she couldn't decipher. They sounded far away, as if from the next room over. She strained to listen, to get closer to the comforting sound. If she really was drowning, they could help her. Surely, they would see her beneath the surface of the water and pull her up.

One of the voices became clearer. "...too many for me to treat." It sounded ragged and tired, as though the emotions of the person it belonged to were stretched thin. "I'm not certain what we should do. This is terrible, just terrible. It all happened so quickly. They say it was the farmers that caused it, you know. Burning the fields. All it took was one strong wind to blow the whole thing out of control. I heard some say the gale was powerful enough to form a cyclone. Can you believe it? A cyclone of fire."

"I know." The other voice was deep and comforting, with a

hint of an accent that Charlotte couldn't quite place. "Is there anyone close by that could help us?"

"I'm afraid not. This fire displaced far too many. The doctors in the neighboring towns are busy assisting patients of their own. I couldn't send more work to them, not when they're as overwhelmed as we are."

The fire. Charlotte recalled everything now—the terror, the towering flames, the howling wind. How had she survived? *Trudy.* Where was the cow? Had she perished in the river? Or was she wandering about alone?

Charlotte struggled to open her eyes, frustration building within her when they remained glued shut. She had to ask the speakers if they had seen her mother and sister, had to know if they knew what happened to Trudy. Yet, despite her attempts, her body was stubbornly still, as if Charlotte was trapped inside her own skin, unable to move.

A third voice spoke up. "What about Milwaukee? Could we not send them there on one of the ships? There are hospitals in the city, and plenty of churches that would be willing to take them in."

If Charlotte had the ability to gasp, she would have. South to Milwaukee? She couldn't go to the city, not when her mother and sister were surely looking for her. How would they ever find her?

"That's a fair idea. The best one we have, at any rate," the tired voice conceded. "A few boats survived the blaze. We'll prepare some of the patients for transport and send them to Green Bay. They can take however many they can manage into the hospitals there and send the rest to Milwaukee. The telegraph wires are down, so I won't be able to warn them of the incoming fire victims. I can only hope they'll have room. There's so many. So, so many."

"Aye," the accented voice said. "I'll go with and make sure the poor souls get help."

"Good man. Now, Dr. Hall and I must get back to the waiting room. There's hundreds of people awaiting treatment. Start moving the worst of the victims closer to the door, please. I'll ask the boys to run down to the docks. Once they find a willing captain, we can have them carry these unfortunate folks outside."

Footsteps marked the departure of the man whom Charlotte guessed to be the doctor. There was a moment of silence, and then a sigh echoed through the room.

"Well, I suppose I'd better get started," the third man said softly.

Charlotte made one last attempt to open her eyes. Triumph jolted through her when the blackness finally faded from her vision, replaced by blurry light. Opening her mouth, she drew breath to speak but instead broke into a coughing fit.

A shadow crossed her vision, and someone held a glass of water to her lips. Charlotte took a few sips of the cool liquid, the tension in her lungs easing as she did. "Thank you," she whispered. The pillows propped beneath her allowed her to look at the man by her side without moving her head, which was a relief considering the throbbing pain in her head.

A smile crossed the man's face, an expression that was difficult to make out beneath his thick beard. "But of course. How do you feel?"

"I...I can't move my arms or legs despite my best attempts," Charlotte admitted. "However, my legs have begun to tingle a bit."

The man hummed. "That's good. It means you might yet recover from the frostbite in your limbs."

Charlotte winced. "Frostbite? Are you a doctor?" *The river.*

"Not a doctor, but a volunteer. And yes, you are suffering from frostbite, along with burns on your arms and a few lesser ones on your face. However, you need not worry. We'll have you on a boat south shortly, where they'll see that you're well cared for. I fear we have no room left here. The doctor's office is over-flowing, which is why many patients, like you, have been brought here to await treatment."

"Where is here? Peshtigo?" Try as she might, with her blurry vision, she couldn't make out anything beyond the foot of her bed.

"Marinette. We've taken over as many buildings as we can to use as relief centers. There's not enough space in the hospital for all of you."

Charlotte shifted, trying and failing to lift her arms above the blankets. "I appreciate why you want to send me to Milwau-kee, but I can't go. How will my family find me if I'm in a different city? I need to look for them."

The man folded his arms across his chest, his brown eyes patient. "I understand, Miss Clarke, but you won't be able to look for them at all in your current state. Besides, there are no guarantees that they are alive. Hard as it is to believe, hundreds, maybe even thousands of people died last night. While I know you want to hold on to your hope, who is to say they aren't among that number?"

Charlotte swallowed. "Until I know for certain that they are...gone...I refuse to leave. I must look for them. Searching for them is the only way to find peace of mind."

"Don't you think they would prefer for you to heal? Miss Clarke, if you do not get treatment soon, you'll be in danger of losing one or both of your legs and arms. If that happens, you'll be doing no searching at all."

"L-lose my legs?" Some of Charlotte's resolve fell away, replaced by something much colder—fear.

"Indeed. Miss Clarke, I have no desire to separate you from your family. I simply want to help you before it is too late," the man said gently.

Charlotte bit her lip, fighting tears. Oh, how she missed her mother's warm arms and comforting words. Where was she?

Where was Carina? "Well...I suppose so. I really must go, then?"

"Yes. There is no other way." The man tucked his hands into the pockets of his black jacket, gazing at Charlotte with eyes full of sympathy. "Take heart, Miss Clarke. I'll pray for you. I have a feeling we could all use it right about now."

Charlotte's expression must have changed to mirror her distaste at the statement, for the man raised his brow.

"Not a God-fearing woman, are you?"

Charlotte shrugged, trying to appear unbothered. "It's...a complicated matter. You can hardly blame me for having doubts."

"Well, a bit of prayer never hurt anyone." The kind man gestured toward the pillow behind her head. "Now, get some rest. The boat will be ready soon, and you're going to be on it. With luck, you'll be able to return up the lake in a few months, healthy and whole. You and your family could even rebuild your house if you were so inclined." He turned and left Charlotte's bedside, moving to rest a hand on the forehead of the man lying on another cot.

Charlotte blinked. Rebuild their home? No. She would find her sister and mother, and they would move far, far away, to a place where they would never have to think of the fire again.

She wanted nothing more to do with Peshtigo.

CHAPTER 3

The blast of a train horn pierced through the fog in Charlotte's brain, drawing her slowly from her slumber. Boarding a locomotive after spending hours on a boat had drained the last of her energy, and she had fallen asleep shortly after two men had carried her to a cot inside one of the train cars. She had to have slept the trip away, for now the train was slowing, signaling their arrival in Milwaukee. Tilting her head, Charlotte struggled to see out one of the train car's dingy windows. Unfortunately, the only thing that she could make out was the faint outline of a small building, most likely the depot.

The door creaked open, allowing cold air to flood the car. Footsteps reached Charlotte's ears, followed by the sound of soft voices. Despite trying as hard as she could to stay awake, her eyes grew heavier and heavier as the voices drew closer. She must have fallen asleep before they reached her, for the next time she opened her eyes, she was in a large room. It was plain white from ceiling to floor and covered from front to back with cots. Each bed held a different patient—men, women, and even a few children. Many of them seemed to be fast asleep, but a few were reading and talking to each other. Where was she?

Squeaking metal drew Charlotte's attention to the brown-haired woman in the cot beside her, who was shifting around and pulling the blankets tighter around herself. She must have sensed Charlotte's attention, for she glanced up with a slight smile. "I'm sorry to have woken you. These cots are awfully loud." She brushed a strand of hair from her eyes and tilted her head. "My name is Flora. What's yours?"

"Charlotte." Looking down at her arms, she found they were bound with clean cloth. Pushing the blankets back a fraction revealed that her legs were bandaged in a similar fashion. How long would they be that way? What did they look like underneath? She was afraid to know.

Heavy footsteps brought an end to her worried assessment. A doctor spoke as he halted at the foot of her bed in a flurry of his white coat and black shoes. "Good afternoon, Miss Clarke. My name is Dr. Hart." His wavy gray hair and neatly trimmed beard reminded Charlotte of the grandfather she had visited occasionally as a child, as did the wrinkles fanning around his mouth and eyes. Overall, he seemed a kind man. He studied her bandaged arms with a serious expression. "How do your arms feel? The medicine I gave you should have numbed them, but I fear it won't take away the pain completely."

"My arms feel far better than before, Doctor. It is not them that concern me." Charlotte tried and failed to smile. "I was hoping you could tell me if you or anyone else has heard from my family. I haven't seen them since the fire began." A shiver ran down Charlotte's spine, and the tingling in her arms increased at the mention of the word. "Their names are Carina and Mary Clarke."

"I'm afraid I haven't. However, the medical staff in Marinette assured me they would do their best to reunite every patient and family they could. If they get word of your mother or sister, I'm certain they'll send a letter."

"Oh." Charlotte frowned, trying to contain her disappointment. "In that case, how long am I required to stay here? I must get back to Marinette and look for them. My poor sister is probably worried sick about me."

Dr. Hart's lips pressed into a solemn line. "No doubt. Assuming they made it through the night, I'm sure they'll find you. I encourage you to wait and let them come to you rather than going out to look for them yourself. With your arms and legs in their present condition, I estimate you'll be here for at least a month. Those burns are small but severe and will take time to heal."

Charlotte winced. "A month? Will there be scars?" She reached up to touch the tender skin on her cheeks, surprised by how smooth it felt. "What about my face?" Her hand moved to a strand of hair, the ends of which had been singed completely off. "And my hair?"

"Your hair will grow back. Your face, too, should heal with very little scarring. As for your arms, I'm afraid there may be more lasting damage." The doctor leaned forward, his eyes earnest. "But scars are nothing to be ashamed of. In your case, they will be a mark of bravery. A sign that you survived what many others did not."

"I was lucky," Charlotte admitted softly. "Do you know how many...perished?"

Dr. Hart sighed, running a hand through his hair. "No, I'm afraid not. Most of the town is still too hot to access, so the initial number is certain to grow. The survivors are combing the wreckage in search of those they lost."

"How terrible." Fear wrapped around Charlotte, obscuring all other thoughts like a black storm cloud. What if her mother and sister were among that number? What would she do? Where would she go?

Charlotte attempted to take a breath, and when her lungs refused to accept the air, she brought a hand to her throat. Pressure built in her ears, as though a rope had tightened around her neck. She dropped her hand to her chest and felt her heart pounding a rapid beat. What was happening?

"Miss Clarke, breathe slowly." Dr. Hart's voice echoed from beside her. "You're having an anxiety attack."

Charlotte struggled to draw air into her rapidly constricting lungs. As she forced herself to take deep breaths, the darkness began to disappear from the corners of her vision, and her shoulders slowly relaxed. The smell of antiseptic and linens reached her nose first. Then the room came back into focus, along with Dr. Hart's concerned gaze.

"There you are, Miss Clarke. Keep breathing nice and slow."

"I'm sorry. I don't know what came over me just now. I've never had an anxiety attack before," Charlotte whispered, trying to keep from crying. "I was once friends with a woman who was prone to fainting spells. I never knew it felt so awful."

The corners of the doctor's mouth rose ever so slightly. He leaned forward and rested a gentle hand on her shoulder, giving her a view of the circles beneath his eyes. He was surely as tired as she was, perhaps even more so. "In your situation, it's to be expected. Take my advice, Miss Clarke, and get some rest. It will take time to come to grips with all that has occurred in the past three days." He straightened. "For now, it would be better for you to rest and let your body heal."

Charlotte nodded shakily. "All right. Thank you, Dr. Hart."

"Of course. If I could offer you a suggestion, it would be to put this catastrophe far from your mind. I know it sounds impossible, but you must try. Talk, sleep, look out the window —just leave thinking about the fire for a different day." Dr. Hart turned away from the bed, then spoke over his shoulder. "You will make it through this, Miss Clarke. I know you will."

Charlotte bit her lip, willing the tears from her eyes. She wanted to believe that forgetting the fire would be possible, but how could it be when the only things running through her mind were her sister's terrified face as they escaped the house and her mother's smile when Charlotte bid her good night?

Was it even worth it to go on if it meant living without her family?

~

November 1871

"Vincent, do you know where Flora has gone?" Charlotte planted her hands on her hips. "She isn't in her bed as she was when I left an hour ago."

The tall, dark-haired record keeper tossed Charlotte an annoyed look. He was the least sociable man she knew, but he had an incredibly good memory and usually recalled the status of each and every patient. Sure enough, he replied without even bothering to look at the papers clutched beneath his elbow. "She was moved to the second room."

Charlotte bit the inside of her cheek. Despite having been at the hospital for only a few weeks, she knew what the second room was for. It was reserved for unfortunate souls that were nearing the end of their life. At length, she murmured, "I see. Thank you."

Turning, she hastened down the corridor, rubbing the scars on her arms in a habit that was rapidly becoming familiar. While the skin was mostly healed, the whitish-pink lines were an ugly reminder of the night that had forever changed her life. The night when it seemed God had looked away from the city of Peshtigo. *Not that He ever bothered with me, anyway.*

Coming to a halt in front of the doorway marked *1-A*, Charlotte peered inside and searched the rows of cots for her friend.

At the back of the room, a head of dark hair peeked from atop a crisp hospital blanket.

"Flora?" Charlotte crept into the room, which remained eerily silent despite the fact that there were at least six people beneath the shroud-like covers of the cots. They all had the look and smell of death about them, making Charlotte shudder as she snuck past. She remained quiet until she drew to a halt in front of the last cot, where she cleared her throat. "Flora? Are you awake?"

"Charlotte? Is that you?" The voice was faint, so faint Charlotte could have easily mistaken it for the rustling of blankets.

"I'm here, Flora." Charlotte moved to her friend's side and gazed down at the young woman's pale, sunken face. Her lovely cheeks had grown paper-thin, and deep circles ringed her eyes. Her appearance was a far cry from the once-vivacious woman who had encouraged Charlotte to get out of bed, even though she herself could not do so.

Flora had already been ill when Charlotte met her a month ago, and her sickness had progressed to the point where she could no longer find the strength to sit up in bed. Nobody, not even the doctor, seemed to know what was destroying her health—however, they all knew it was only a matter of time before it overcame her. But she wouldn't die alone. Charlotte had determined to make sure of that.

"I guess this ceiling will be the last thing I ever see, won't it?" A smile crossed Flora's cracked lips. "It's a true shame, that. I always hoped I would die in a field, surrounded by sweet-smelling flowers and the endless sky above. It would have been far more poetic." She coughed, the sound rattling from somewhere deep in her chest. "Ah, but I suppose we all have our own foolish wishes. What about you? What is your most foolish wish, Lottie?"

Besides that you would get out of bed and be healthy once more? Charlotte gazed out the window at the tall buildings that blocked her view of the sky. They were ugly, those buildings—not at all inspiring to those who were trapped inside with nothing else to look at. Certainly not suitable for one so close to death. She would have to do something to remedy the situation.

"Well," she said at length, "I suppose a foolish wish of mine would be to find my mother and sister and live happily for the rest of our lives. I dream of a day when they walk through the door and hug me as if nothing ever happened. Then, once we're finished hugging and talking, we find a new place to live, somewhere where we'll never have to worry about bank notices or fires ever again."

Flora locked eyes with Charlotte, her gaze kind and knowing. "That's not a foolish wish, Charlotte Clarke. It's a real wish, and I believe it will come true. I'm certain they're searching for you. It's only been a month, after all. Give it some time."

Charlotte exhaled, a smile teasing the corners of her mouth. "I know. If they don't get here soon, though, I'm going to go and look for them myself. It's high time I left this place, anyway."

Flora laughed, the sound a mere shadow of what it had once been. "You say that as if you're a nuisance. You know the doctor would let you stay as long as you need. He's too nice to put anyone out on the streets."

"So you say," Charlotte said with a wry chuckle. "At any rate, I can't stay here much longer. I found a boardinghouse when I went out earlier. The proprietress is a bit snippy, but she agreed to take me if I had the money. With my new position at the tailor, I should be able to afford rent." And the rest of her money would be saved for the return trip to Marinette. Once there, she would find Carina and Mother, and they would move somewhere warm and sunny.

"Well, then, what's stopping you? You don't need to wait for me. You know I'll never make it out of this bed. You could come and visit me, if you really wanted to. I would appreciate the company."

"I suppose so. The idea of moving on is rather nerve-wracking, that's all." Charlotte perked up, an idea springing to her mind. "Say, Flora, I have a wonderful idea. I'll be back in a bit."

"Changing the topic, are we? Well, all right. Hurry back." Flora broke into another coughing fit, the sound fading as Charlotte left the room.

Charlotte hastened through the hall and burst into the church's front room. After gathering the sketchbook and chalk pastels a kind soul had donated a few days ago, she ripped a piece of large, thick paper from the sketchbook and got to work sketching a blue sky filled with white clouds. Though the blue was a bit dull and the clouds looked like blobs, it would serve her purpose well enough. She blew on the artwork to remove the excess chalk before putting a bit of paste on the back of the painting and lifting it carefully to avoid getting the glue on her hands. Charlotte ran as quickly as her legs could carry her to the second room and stopped beside Flora's bed. "Flora, look what I have!"

"What is that?" Flora asked with a frown. "I can't see when you keep moving from side to side like that."

"Just wait." Snatching a chair from the back of the room, Charlotte placed it at the foot of the bed and clambered atop. She raised the drawing over her head and stuck it firmly to the ceiling, where the paste held it in place. "Hurrah! What do you think? A sight better than those buildings, isn't it?" She hopped down from the chair.

Flora laughed weakly, her brown eyes sparkling with joy. "Why, Lottie, you brought the sky to me! You made my wish come true. If only I could do the same for you." She tilted her head. "It seems as though you got a bit of sky on your arms, by the way."

Charlotte glanced at her forearms, where the pink scars had

been covered in part by blue chalk. "Well, would you look at that? It would appear I did." She removed a handkerchief from her pocket and scrubbed at the offending smudges before rolling her sleeves down. She then moved to the side of the bed so she could take her friend's hand. "As for granting my wish, you have nothing to worry about. I would never expect anything of you, Flora. I only hope I brought you a small dose of joy. We could all use it in a place like this."

"Yes, that's true," Flora agreed, her breath rattling in her throat. "I've had a hard time finding it as of late."

Charlotte smiled, though it faded quickly. "Joy will come again, Flora. I'm sure of it."

Oh, how she despised lying. But what truth could she say that wouldn't make the situation seem worse? What could a person possibly have to look forward to when all that waited for them after death was aloneness? No. She couldn't tell Flora that. She had to keep the hope alive, small as it was.

Especially when there were still people who needed her.

~

"Miss Clarke? Is that you?"

Charlotte glanced up from the book she had laid open on her cot, squinting into the dimly lit room as she tried to catch sight of the person who had said her name. "Yes. Who's asking?"

The speaker stepped forward, her face becoming visible in the soft light of Charlotte's candle. "It's Sister Anderson," the nun said, her habit glowing white against the blackness around her. She was a familiar sight, having brought Charlotte her meals on multiple occasions. Charlotte had even helped her out in the kitchen a few times. "I have something for you. This was delivered to the hospital earlier today. I tried to give it to you, but you weren't here at the time." She lifted her hand, revealing a small white envelope clutched in her palm.

Charlotte frowned and leaned forward to accept the missive. The paper crinkled in her hand as she sat back and held it close to the light of her candle. She studied the address for a moment before releasing a soft gasp. "It's from Marinette! I think I know what this is." Excitement built in her chest. Had they found her family? The nun cleared her throat, and Charlotte jolted slightly. "I'm sorry. Thank you."

The nun inclined her head, her eyes twinkling. "I expect you want to read it in private. Have a good evening." She turned, leaving Charlotte alone.

Releasing a nervous breath, Charlotte carefully slid a finger underneath the flap and freed the letter. She opened the folded paper and studied the inked words with an anxious gaze.

Dear Miss Clarke,

You may recall me from the time we spoke in Marinette. I was the man who conversed with you after you first awoke, before you boarded the ship to Green Bay. It is with the utmost regret, Miss Clarke, that I must inform you that your mother and sister were discovered deceased in the ruins of your home two days ago. Please accept my sincerest condolences on your loss. I pray that you will have comfort and healing during this difficult time.

Sincerely,

L.P.

Charlotte lowered the letter slowly to the cot, trying and failing to process the awful words. Carina and her mother, dead? But that couldn't be. She had seen Carina outside the house. And yet, if the man who wrote the official letter said so...

One tear fell onto her hand, the impact sending goosebumps racing over her arm. The second landed on the letter itself, and from then on, Charlotte lost count of how many tears she shed. Emotions raced through her chest like a train off the tracks. She had known it was a possibility, had known there was a chance that they wouldn't be coming to find her. And yet she had desperately hoped it wasn't so. But now there was no disguising the truth.

Charlotte Clarke was completely, undeniably alone.

~

The next morning, the frigid sort that would keep most individuals tucked under the warm comfort of their blankets, Charlotte rose and made her cot quickly, keeping her gaze far from the envelope that lay on the floor beside the bed. Though she knew in her heart that she wouldn't be able to avoid processing the letter's contents forever, for the time being, it was easier to pretend it didn't exist.

Miss Anderson appeared at the foot of the cot, her face red. Her dress was slightly askew, as though she had run at a considerable speed to fetch Charlotte. "Miss Clarke? Miss Flora is requesting your presence. I'm sorry to be bothering you so early in the morning, but it really is urgent." Her voice dropped. "It won't be long now."

Charlotte's heart jolted painfully in her chest. *Oh, Flora.* She bent down and collected the envelope to avoid any chance of the nurse accidentally reading it or tossing it out, slipping it into the pocket of her gown. She had planned on telling Flora about it, but that wouldn't happen now.

Charlotte soon stood at Flora's bedside and stared at her friend's pale face with apprehension. "Flora?" she whispered, afraid of raising her voice lest she cause the dear woman any distress.

Shifting under the covers, Flora released a soft breath. "Lottie, I need to ask something of you." Her voice was brittle and tired, as though the effort cost her a great deal. "I hate to do it, but I have so little time left." She waved off Charlotte's protests with a skeletal hand. "It's true, Charlotte."

Charlotte bit her lip. "I'm your friend, Flora. You can ask anything of me."

"I fear you won't be nearly as willing when you hear what I'm asking." Reaching beneath the bedcovers, Flora withdrew a locket on a necklace chain and placed it in Charlotte's palm with trembling fingers. It was golden, with an ornate leaf design on the front reminiscent of ivy on a garden wall. It was a beautiful piece of jewelry—one Charlotte never would have been able to afford, not even when her father was still alive. An heirloom, perhaps?

Charlotte clicked the locket open and discovered a small piece of paper inside. "What's this?"

"That locket was given to me by my mother when I was a young girl," Flora murmured, looking fondly at the necklace. "I kept it with me for years, even when an argument ripped my family apart and drew me far from my parents. I regret my angry words now, but I fear it is too late to make amends in person. That is why I need you, Charlotte. The paper in that locket is an apology to my mother. My fondest wish is for you to deliver it to her—and the locket too." She broke off into a coughing fit, and when she lowered her sleeve, there were a few specks of red on the fabric.

"Deliver it? Where does she live?"

"Albany, Kentucky. Once you got there, you would have to ask for the Aspens. Their residence isn't hard to find. You're one of the only people I trust with this, Lottie. I may be able to ask someone else, but by then, it could be too late." Flora sniffed. "I want to be certain that it gets into my mother's hands."

Charlotte clutched the locket to her chest. Her, go to Kentucky? But at least that was far from Wisconsin. Would it be far enough to make her forget? To give her a chance to start over? Maybe. It was worth the journey if she could begin again.

"All right," Charlotte said slowly, warming to the idea. "I'll do it." Both to fulfill her friend's wish and to escape the memories of that horrible night.

Flora beamed, causing some of the color to return briefly to her cheeks. "You will? Oh, thank you, Lottie. Thank you so much. I can die in peace knowing my mother won't be angry with me any longer. You must leave as soon as you have enough funds for travel." She raised a trembling finger and shook it at Charlotte. "And make sure you keep the locket on at all times so you don't lose it. I know how easily you misplace things. You told me yourself." She let her arm drop back to the bed and released a contented sigh. "I need Mother to have it no matter what."

Charlotte inclined her head and tucked her hand into her pocket, crushing the letter in her palm until it was nothing more than a wad of paper. She wouldn't look at the awful thing again. Not when she had a new goal in mind. "I'll get it to her, Flora. I promise."

CHAPTER 4

Sycamore, Illinois
April 1872

Thundering hoofbeats drowned out all other noises, rising and swelling like a tidal wave as the horse drew closer to where Stefan Roberts stood at the racetrack fence.

"Come on, Lake. You have to move faster," Stefan whispered, leaning his elbows against the rough wood of the fence. His heartbeat accelerated in time to the horse's hooves, pounding in his chest as the dark bay flew past and headed for the far end of the track. The stallion's strides lengthened, its legs stretching farther and farther as it galloped down the final stretch. Then, with one last burst of energy, it crossed the imaginary finish line.

"Time!" a voice called from down the track. The stable hand holding the stopwatch released a laugh and shook his head. "Well, I'll be. Lake beat his old record by a full three seconds!"

Stefan let out a breath of relief as whoops and cheers filled the air from the other stable hands. A few of them sauntered up to clap him on the back, offering congratulations with wide smiles on their faces. Ignoring their incessant chatter, Stefan remained transfixed by the horse as it slowed to a walk. The jockey patted the gelding's heaving sides as they made their way around the track, cooling him down after the intense run. Sweat drenched the bay's hindquarters, evidence that the gallop had cost him more than his seemingly effortless performance led them to believe.

"Excuse me, gentlemen. I need to speak with Blake." Stefan left the stable hands by the fence, crossed to the track gate, and slid inside. After closing it behind him, he headed for the horse on the other side of the field. Unfortunately, the uneven, footprint-pocked ground made Stefan's limp more and more pronounced the closer he drew to the animal. He winced as he stumbled into a divot, causing pain to shoot up his leg. It took a moment to free the mutinous foot from the hole.

The jockey must have noticed Stefan's struggle, for he led the horse across the field. "Mr. Roberts, what are you doing out here? You should have waited for me to come to you." Blake's face creased in concern as he drew to a halt in front of Stefan. While the man kept his eyes on Stefan's face, Stefan didn't miss the momentary glance he cast downward.

Embarrassment flooded Stefan, for while he wore his customary navy trousers, there was no disguising the ugly truth that lay beneath. Even the long months of therapy hadn't been enough to give him back the strength and agility he had once possessed. He had become a broken shell of his former self.

To make matters worse, nearly everyone knew it.

Stefan kept his face expressionless as he gestured toward the thoroughbred behind Blake. "Lake ran exceptionally well. I expect my father will want to send him to Kentucky soon. He'll have a buyer before the first race is over."

Blake grinned, tipping his cap back. "It's all thanks to you,

Mr. Roberts. Lake never would have recovered from that injury without your expert care."

Stefan walked over to Lake's Luck, running his hands over the thoroughbred's hocks. A few months ago, they had thought the horse would never race again. A torn ligament had pulled the gelding from the tracks, forcing them to keep him stabled while Stefan's father decided whether or not his career was salvageable. Luckily, Father had allowed Stefan to take over Lake's recovery, and now his hard work was paying off.

"You know, you should talk to your father about taking over more of the business. You'd make a fine manager." Blake crossed his thin arms. While young, the lad had opinions and certainly wasn't afraid to voice them. "He has to step down sooner or later. Why won't he allow you to take over? You have a way with animals, as is clearly seen by Lake. Why ignore it?"

Stefan looked at the ground, working hard to keep his jaw from clenching. The boy had a point. "While I appreciate that, my father wishes to remain in control of his business, and I can understand why. We've had enough upheaval in our lives."

"Franz, you mean?" Blake asked softly.

Stefan took a deep breath and drew himself up. "Take Lake to the stables and make sure he's properly rubbed down. I'll speak with my father to see if he's ready for Kentucky."

Blake shrugged and turned to Lake, brushing the sweat-slicked hair on the horse's neck. "If you say so, sir."

As the jockey led the racehorse from the track, Stefan turned his sights toward the house that sat behind the stables. It took a considerable amount of effort to reach the building, but he managed it in a relatively short time. Silently congratulating himself for improving his pace, Stefan pushed the front door open and limped inside. "*Vater*?"

"Your father is in his study, sir," the housemaid, Priscilla, called from the top of the stairs. She held a feather duster in one hand, evidence that the furniture on the second floor had most likely been in need of attention. Stefan wouldn't know, for he rarely set foot in the upstairs rooms. Nobody did. Not anymore.

"Thank you." Stefan made his way down the hall to his father's office. Inside, the warm scents of wood smoke and tobacco, along with the faint smell of leather, surrounded him. Books covered every square inch of the walls, their spines so clean they practically sparkled. At the back of the room lay an oak writing desk from which Stefan's father looked up.

Now in his late sixties, Johann Roberts didn't visit the stables as often as he once did. Age and grief had turned his hair white as snow and slowed his movements. Yet despite the arthritis in his joints and the wrinkles around his eyes, Stefan's father continued to run the horse stables from his office with the same amount of vigor as before. No doubt he would continue to do so until the day the good Lord took him home.

"Vater?" Stefan stepped farther into the office and removed his bowler hat.

"Stefan, my boy." Vater's thick German accent, followed by a sharp cough, pierced the space between them. "What brings you here? Interesting things happening out at the stables, eh?"

Stefan nodded, shifting from one foot to the other. "Indeed. Lake's Luck just beat his previous record by three seconds. That means he's improved past where he was before the injury." He tucked his hands behind his back so his father wouldn't see him fidgeting with the cuffs of his coat. "I was hoping you'll send Lake to the Kentucky races since he's now in proper form. We'd get a fine sum for him once the buyers see how he runs, maybe even enough to expand the barn as you wanted to." *And we'd be able to cover the doctor's visits.*

Stefan's father hummed beneath his breath. "Three seconds, you say? Good. That makes him one of the fastest horses I've ever bred. A fine turnaround considering his condition a few months ago." He leaned back, steepling his fingers on the desk. "There's only one problem. None of the hands are available to go to Kentucky. We're already short with the absences of Tucker, Will, and Horace. I need the rest of the hands to focus on the mares which are about to foal. I've decided we will not be attending races until next year."

"Not attend the races?" Stefan didn't bother to mask his surprise. "But Vater, how do you intend to cover taxes? How do you intend to pay our stable hands? Our horses won't sell unless we exhibit their skills on the racetrack." And Kentucky was undoubtedly the place to do so.

Vater huffed a sigh. "We should be able to make it through the year if we are frugal, especially with the additional money from the new foals. It will mean holding back on some things, certainly, but those things will simply have to wait. Until then, the horses will remain here."

Stefan drew himself up, trying to ignore the spike of fear that shot through his heart at the thought of what he was about to say. "Let me go. I know the way well enough, and I know the horses you want at the races. They could get injured—or worse, stolen—if we sent them to Kentucky by train, so we'll go the old-fashioned way. I'll take the wagon and Orion with me. All I'll need are funds for room and board, in addition to supplies for the horses. We'll be at the Monticello stables before the races begin."

"*Absolut nicht.* That's not a possibility, Stefan. I need you here. I'll not let you leave so soon after the war." His father's accent always grew thicker with worry. "I won't allow you to go back to that wretched state."

Stefan clenched his fists. "Vater, that blasted war ended seven years ago. And I can certainly handle Kentucky. I'm more than capable of leaving the stables and traveling, and I'm as able a horseman as any of our employees. Let me do this."

"Stefan, it is too much of a risk." Vater pleaded, slipping

momentarily into German. "I cannot lose you. You're too young."

Panic stabbed Stefan as he recognized the blank look filtering into his father's eyes. *Not now.* "Vater, I am nearly twenty-seven years old. I'm no longer the young, foolish lad I once was." *Nor am I the person I was when I last left Kentucky.*

Vater blinked, the look receding. "Twenty-seven, are you? Oh, *ja.* Well, I suppose there's no harm in you taking the horses. But be careful, and hurry home."

Stefan's shoulders relaxed. "Thank you, Vater. I will."

As he crossed the room, his father called out. "Stefan? Do me a favor, will you? Tell Katherine I'd like the pork for dinner and not the turkey."

Stefan paused at the door. "Her name is Priscilla, Vater. Priscilla is the maid."

"Oh. Well, tell Priscilla that I want the pork."

Stefan hummed his agreement and exited, running shaking fingers through his hair. Kate was not the name of the maid, but the name of his mother—who had been deceased for seven years. That Vater didn't recognize the magnitude of his mistake was yet another sign of his fading memory. It was only a matter of time before he became a shell of a person, without memory of his family or identity. *That,* even more than taxes and stable hands, was the main reason they needed the money from selling the horses. Vater was only getting worse, though Stefan didn't have the heart to tell him. The doctor's bills continued to grow with each visit, and it was only a matter of time before they would have to start cutting costs elsewhere to pay for Vater's care. The races were essential—not only to keep the stables running, but also to ensure Vater was safe and healthy.

And that was why Stefan was going to get the horses to Kentucky. There was no time for doubt, no time for hesitation. The clock was ticking, and his father's legacy...his legacy...hung in the balance.

"Ladies and gentlemen, we are approaching the Chicago depot. Please gather your belongings and prepare to depart, as this is our final stop."

Charlotte clutched her worn carpetbag tightly in her lap as she gazed out the window. Much like Milwaukee, Chicago appeared to be a place of constant movement. Buildings stretched far overhead, so tall it looked as if they almost touched the sky. The sun glinted off their many windows, reminding her of diamonds. People bustled along the sidewalks, striding determinedly as if they each had an important destination in mind. While it was spring and the weather was relatively warm, many still wore thick coats and capes.

As the train came to a stop with a screech and hiss of steam, Charlotte quickly stood and hurried from the train car before she could change her mind. She felt the few remaining coins in her dress pocket with a sigh. The cost of surviving was high, especially when the only work one could find was at a tailor shop. Most of her pay had gone straight to room and board. Now, having spent the majority of her remaining money on the train ticket to Chicago, it seemed as though she would be walking the rest of the way to Kentucky. It was a dismal thought, to be sure, but she had promised Flora she would get the locket to Kentucky, and Charlotte Clarke was not one to break a promise.

So focused was Charlotte on her thoughts that she nearly ran headfirst into a group of frilly taffeta- and silk-covered women that stood in a cluster near the edge of the platform.

"Goodness gracious. Watch where you're going, clumsy girl!" One of the brightly colored socialites waved her lace fan at Charlotte like a fretting bird. A mink stole adorned her shoulders, and the animal's fake eyes stared at Charlotte as though beseeching her for help.

"Sorry, miss." Charlotte moved aside and made an effort not to look at the unfortunate mink. For the poor thing to be killed was one thing, but to be turned into clothing for a haughty woman seemed a fate even worse. As she continued down the boardwalk with her carpetbag in hand, the finely dressed women began talking about her.

"What a strange young woman. Where do you think she got that dress?" one wondered aloud.

"A charity bin, most likely," another said amid a flurry of titters from the group.

Charlotte's cheeks heated. She *had* gotten the dress from a donation bin. Truly, when she had first selected the dress, she had thought it quite pretty. The top layer of the garment was a soft blue, while the bottom layer was white cotton. The sleeves draped long and loose about the elbows before tapering to a cuff at the wrist. Charlotte had even found a cheery yellow sash and a pair of white gloves to complete the ensemble. She had felt quite clever and elegant—but it seemed as though she had been sadly mistaken.

She paused in front of the depot map and traced the path she would have to take to reach Kentucky. It seemed small on paper, but on foot, it could take weeks or even months. She would have to rely on the hospitality of farmers in order to find shelter for the night. Staying at an inn every evening would cost too much. She worried her lip. Hopefully, she would be able to find enough people willing to help a stranger. Traveling alone wouldn't help her cause either.

"Now, where on earth did you acquire a necklace like that?"

Charlotte flinched at the sound of the socialite's high-pitched voice. Whirling, she put a protective hand over the locket at her throat. "It's hardly your business to know where my jewelry came from, miss. You clearly don't enjoy conversing with my sort, anyway."

The socialite harrumphed and crossed her arms. "On the

contrary, it certainly is. What if you stole it? Why, I bet you did, didn't you? You're nothing more than a common thief! Were you hoping to steal from me when you bumped into me earlier?" She opened her reticule as though ensuring Charlotte hadn't taken anything.

"Thief? Goodness, no! My friend gave me this locket. I would never steal!"

"That's precisely what a thief would say. Police! I found a thief!" the woman called, waving her closed fan at Charlotte's face.

Charlotte let out a gasp of dismay when an officer at the edge of the platform looked their way. Turning, she hitched her carpetbag under one arm and darted away amid shouts and screeches from the socialites. She clamped her free hand over her hat and hopped off the depot platform to head south. Or, at least, what she hoped was south. Truthfully, she had no clue. Carina had always been the one to keep track of where they were. Without her, Charlotte was lost.

Once she was a safe distance from the depot, Charlotte slowed to a walk and took a few deep breaths. Several strands of hair had come free from beneath her shepherdess hat and frizzed around her face in what was certainly a harried look. In addition, a thin layer of mud coated her hem, but no one paid attention to her. Good. She was tired of having eyes on her.

It looked as though she'd run directly into a farmer's market. Brightly colored stands lined both sides of the street, each displaying a variety of goods that ranged from food to brass trinkets. Charlotte made her way to the nearest booth and paid for an apple, chewing it contentedly as she moved down the aisle. It was the first thing she had eaten all day, making the crisp fruit taste all the sweeter. As she walked, she searched the area for someone she could ask for directions. While there were many pedestrians wandering about, most looked as though they would be more likely to make off with her bag than give her instructions. What were they all doing in a market?

Charlotte released a breath, realization washing over her. *The fire.* The Chicago Fire had displaced as many people as the Peshtigo Fire, if not more. And on the same day, no less! Perhaps they were wandering around in search of a few coins or a fresh-cooked meal. She would have been forced to do the same had she not been transferred to the hospital.

A police officer—a different one, thankfully—leaned against a lamppost, overseeing the market. His shiny badge and black revolver threatened punishment for anyone who dared try to steal from the shopkeepers. He was Charlotte's best option for directions, and so she took a deep breath and approached the man, clearing her throat. "Excuse me. Sir?"

The officer glanced at her and raised a blond eyebrow. "What can I do for you, miss?"

"I was wondering if you might direct me toward the southern side of Chicago. I got a bit turned around in all the hubbub," Charlotte said with an apologetic smile.

The officer hummed in sympathy. "It's a mess around here." He pointed down the road, the badge on his chest flashing in the sun. "If you're looking to head south, all you have to do is remain on this road for two miles, and you'll reach the lower half of Chicago before long. Just stay clear of the burned area to the east. There's plenty of marauders around there that would be quick to take advantage of a young lady such as yourself."

"I will. Thank you, sir," Charlotte said gratefully, leaving the officer to his work. The thought of marauders made her shudder. What lengths would they go to get her belongings? She didn't want her journey to end before it had even begun. No. Charlotte wouldn't let herself be cowed by any vagrants. Even if she was beginning to wish she could go back to her boarding-house in Milwaukee and hide beneath the covers of her cot.

After finishing her apple, Charlotte gave the core to a gray horse that stood beside the road with an empty wagon and two thoroughbreds tethered behind it. She then turned her focus to steering clear of the people that bustled along the sidewalk around her, making sure to keep her carpetbag tightly in hand. Several times, someone bumped into her, though the pickpockets would find no reticule dangling from her wrist. She had sewn hidden pockets into her dresses to keep her meager earnings safe.

Another person jostled her from the side, causing the carpetbag to tumble from Charlotte's hands. "No!" She gasped as she crouched down to try and snatch the bag from between the legs of the passerby. Just as her fingers brushed the fabric, it was ripped from the ground by a tall figure in a ragged coat, who took off running the instant the bag was in his hands.

"Hey! That's mine!" Charlotte straightened and pushed her way through the crowd in an attempt to reach the man.

The thief tossed a grin over his shoulder and continued his dash down the road. Charlotte gave chase, elbowing people as she struggled to keep up with the man. She dodged a valet with a large trunk and ducked under two men carrying a wooden beam, all while keeping her eyes on the thief. She couldn't afford to lose what few belongings she had, even if her head was warning her that chasing after him was a terrible idea. "Drop that bag! That is my luggage!"

The thief, of course, offered no response, and instead whipped around a side alley with such speed that Charlotte suspected it was not the first time he had used the inconspicuous passage to make a getaway. Though her instincts continued to scream a warning, she darted around the corner and followed the man into the alley. What she was not expecting was to run smack dab into his large, stale-smelling chest, bringing her to an abrupt halt.

"Well, now, what have we here? A little lady who's wanting to take my bag. That's called stealin', miss. Why, I might just have to call for the police. You wouldn't want that, would you?" The man sneered, revealing a set of yellowed teeth behind his cracked lips. He held Charlotte's bag behind his back.

Charlotte took a large step back and drew in a breath. "Well, if that isn't the pot calling the kettle black. I'll thank you to give *my* bag back before *I* call for the police." She slid her arms behind her back to hide how they trembled. *Don't lose your nerve now, Lottie.* "I honestly don't see why you want it, anyway. There's nothing valuable in there. I only have a few second-hand dresses."

The man narrowed his eyes as though assessing the truth of her words. He must have found her expression telling, for he opened the carpetbag and began riffling through the clothes inside. Charlotte nearly gasped in protest but managed to hold her tongue, as it was most likely the only chance she had of getting her belongings back.

After a few moments, the thief tossed her bag down with an annoyed grunt. He turned his red-rimmed glare on Charlotte. "You're just as poor as the rest of us, aren't ya? You don't look like it in that fancy garb. Steal it, did ya?"

"I may be poor, sir, but I would never steal, even if I was desperate. Unlike some. I got my belongings from a charity bin, like most decent folk would." Charlotte bent to pick up her tattered bag. As she did, the locket slid free from beneath her collar and dangled in the air, the sun reflecting off the gold.

The thief's watery eyes fixed on the jewelry. "Now, then, what's a poor gal like you doing with a necklace like that?" He took a step forward, stretching out his hand.

Jerking upright, Charlotte held the carpetbag up to her chest like a shield. "Stay away." Was there a policeman close enough to hear if she screamed? Would anyone even care?

The man sneered. He grabbed for the locket, causing Charlotte to cry out and whirl. Running as fast as she could, she had nearly reached the end of the alley before she was yanked back by her dress collar.

"Not so fast," the thief hissed in her ear, the smell of chewing tobacco heavy on his breath. "You have something of mine. Hand it over, and I'll let you go without an issue."

"Get off of me." Charlotte struggled to wriggle free. "I'll never give you my locket."

"You heard the woman. Let go at once."

A new voice pierced the air, this one deep and laced with a faint German accent. Looking up, Charlotte nearly choked at the sight of a gun—inches from her head.

CHAPTER 5

Stefan aimed the revolver steadily at the vagrant who held the young woman captive. Though he kept a straight face, his heart raced. If the thief didn't believe his bluff and flee, Stefan wouldn't be able to give chase. He could only hope the man would let the lady go without a fuss.

Stefan had heard the woman scream from a food vendor's stand at the end of the road, and judging by their current situation, it was a good thing he had. Although she didn't look like a woman of wealth. Her straw shepherdess hat and dress were simple in design, even with the fancy sash and gloves. So why had the rabble-rouser targeted her? Perhaps it was the locket about her neck, gold with an intricate leaf design around the edges. It certainly would have caught the eye of many a person wandering around the market, especially those with less than honorable intentions.

The woman's wide eyes, a strange shade of murky blue, caught Stefan's attention. She gave him a pleading look, and he realized the thief hadn't responded to his previous words. "You have five seconds to let her go, or I'll fire." He kept his voice low and serious.

The thief hesitated for a moment, clearly weighing his options. Then, flaring his nostrils, he let go of his captive and took off down the alley.

Stefan lowered the gun and studied the woman, who was rubbing at her forehead with trembling fingers. "Are you all right?" he asked, though he wished he could take the words back almost immediately. Of course, she wasn't all right—she had just been attacked! *Stefan, you fool.*

"I'll be fine. I must thank you, sir, for your gallant rescue. I doubt I would have gotten free of that villain had you not arrived." The lady straightened and took a deep breath. "I must say, this was not how I was expecting my first day away from Milwaukee to turn out."

Stefan placed the revolver back in his pocket and glanced back over his shoulder. He needed to get back to the horses. There were undoubtedly more people wandering the streets who would take anything they could get their hands on, and he wouldn't let his prized animals be their next target. "I doubt anyone, including myself, would expect such a thing to occur. Do you have an escort whom I can see you back to?"

The young woman shook her head. "No, I am passing through the city on my own. I suppose I should introduce myself. My name is Charlotte. Charlotte Clarke, that is. And yourself?"

"Stefan Roberts. Well, Miss Clarke, if you have nobody to return to, I would be most grateful if you would allow me to accompany you back to the main sidewalk. You're less likely to be accosted there."

"That would be splendid. Let me fetch my bag, please."

Stefan waited while the rather harried Miss Clarke collected her worn carpetbag from the ground, and once she returned, they set off. As they walked, a multitude of questions raced through his mind. Why was a young woman such as herself traveling alone? What was she doing with such an expensive locket? Where was she going? While all the questions likely had interesting answers, he knew better than to ask. Stefan instead chose to remain silent, allowing Miss Clarke to catch her breath as they walked along. He could tell that she had noticed his limp, which was pronounced even when he was well-rested. Luckily, the young woman didn't ask about it.

Miss Clarke finally broke the silence by lightly clearing her throat. "What brings you to Chicago, Mr. Roberts? Do you live here?"

"No. I hail from Sycamore, which is to the west of Chicago. I've been tasked with delivering two of my father's racehorses to our stable in Kentucky, and the city was simply a stop on the way." Stefan glanced down the road, relief filling his chest when he spied the horses waiting next to the wagon. "I plan to be back on the road within an hour. I must be at the stables by June in order to compete in the spring races."

Miss Clarke drew to a halt. "Kentucky, you say? I'm also going that way. Where are your father's stables?"

"Monticello, at the bottom of the state."

The young woman bit her lip, her brows furrowing as she gazed at the crowd they had emerged into. "I don't suppose you have room for an extra traveler, do you?"

Stefan frowned. "I'm afraid that wouldn't be plausible, Miss Clarke. For the two of us to travel together would be incredibly unseemly." Not to mention, he hadn't planned on enduring company.

"Oh, but I wouldn't be much trouble! I only have one luggage bag, and I could even walk if necessary. I couldn't pay you, but I could help wherever you needed—"

"Miss Clarke." His sharply spoken words brought the woman's rambling to a halt. Stefan fixed her with a stern look. "I understand that you are alone, but there are plenty of women traveling through this area. If you ask, I'm certain you will be able to find a proper companion to accompany you. I'm afraid I cannot afford to deviate from my path for even a moment, and you would slow me down considerably." The words were harsher than he had intended, but there was no taking them back now. Stefan relaxed by a fraction and tried a softer approach. "I am sorry, Miss Clarke, but the answer is no. Good day." With that said, he turned and walked with as much confidence as he could muster to his wagon, releasing a sigh as he went. While he took no pleasure in hurting a young woman's feelings, he also needed to stand firm in his decision.

Lake and the other thoroughbred Stefan had been charged with delivering were secured at the back of the wagon using a length of loose rope he'd threaded through their bridles. While at first the racehorses had balked at being relegated to the back of a moving vehicle, they were quick to adapt and had soon proven to be easy traveling companions.

Stefan gave Lake a pat on the nose before moving to the front of the wagon, where Orion, his dapple gray Percheron, stood tall and proud, his eyes alert as he waited patiently for Stefan's arrival. The horse had been with him for years, and there was no animal that Stefan trusted more to get him safely to Kentucky.

Orion pricked his ears and snuffled at Stefan's outstretched palm, searching for treats. Upon seeing that there was nothing to eat, he threw his head up in protest and released an irritated snort.

"Sorry, my friend. I couldn't find any apples," Stefan said by way of apology, scratching the horse beneath his thick mane. "It's too crowded here. We'll have to check some of the stands outside of town and see what we can find."

Orion let out a loud whinny of protest, making Stefan chuckle as he untied the horse's reins from the hitching post and lifted himself onto the wagon bench. "I know. If it's any consolation, I couldn't find lunch either." Clucking his tongue, he flicked the reins and set Orion into motion. As they moved along the crowded street, he couldn't resist glancing at where he had left Miss Clarke. She was nowhere to be found, most likely having moved off to find someone else to take her to Kentucky. While Stefan was glad she had listened to him, he couldn't help but feel a tiny pang of guilt at having left her in such a brusque manner. He cast one last look around the market before directing the wagon down a side street that would take him south.

~

The air was far fresher outside the city, free of the smoke and noise of a hundred voices and clacking wheels. The road Stefan had chosen was narrow and little-traveled, leaving the thoroughbreds plenty of room to walk alongside the wagon. Tiny flower buds were just beginning to peep their heads up along the sides of the path, creating flashes of purple and white in the thick spring grass. Songbirds announced their return in the trees, flying above the horses' heads as they searched for nesting materials.

Stefan relaxed against the back of the wagon seat and released a long breath. "Orion, I don't believe I'll ever move to the city. There's too much noise in a place like that. This is far superior."

Orion let out a whinny of agreement, swishing his tail back and forth to ward off stray flies. His head bobbed up and down with each clomp of his hooves, and every so often, he glanced off to the side, watching a stray butterfly or bird in the trees.

Stefan twisted in his seat to assess the condition of the thoroughbreds. As he did, a familiar flash of blue caught his eye. A young woman was slowly but steadily making her way closer to the wagon—a woman who was carrying a very familiar carpetbag.

"I don't believe it," Stefan mumbled, turning back to the

front. She must've taken a shortcut. "I don't suppose we could hide in that stand of trees, could we?"

Orion remained silent and continued walking, apparently not deeming the question worthy of a response.

Stefan would not look behind him again. Neither could he spur his horses faster without being quite a cad. There would be no ignoring the headstrong Miss Clarke once she caught up, but for now, he would enjoy a few more minutes of silence.

Unfortunately, his momentary peace was soon shattered by a voice. "Mr. Roberts?"

Sighing, Stefan glanced down at the young woman who now kept pace by the side of his wagon. "Hello again, Miss Clarke. Can I help you?"

"Well, if it isn't too much trouble, I was wondering if I could walk alongside you. I won't be a bother, and I'll leave as soon as you arrive at an inn for the night. Why, you won't even know I'm here. It's simply that, well..." Miss Clarke released a nervous chuckle before continuing. "You seem to know where you're going, and I'm afraid I haven't the faintest clue."

Stefan narrowed his eyes, trying to discern whether or not the woman had an ulterior motive. Despite her continual request to follow him, Miss Clarke didn't exhibit malice or another nefarious intention. On the contrary, she reminded him of a lost puppy. Shaking his head, he gave in. "I suppose that would be all right. But be warned that you are putting your reputation on the line by accompanying a man, even if it's only for a short while."

"Oh, thank you! I promise I won't be any trouble," Miss Clarke exclaimed with a smile.

Stefan fought a grimace, focusing back on the road. *This is only going to cause trouble.* "We shall see about that."

For a time, they continued on in silence, the only sound the plodding of the horses' hooves in the dirt. Though Stefan tried to keep his eyes on the road, he couldn't help but glance at the young woman walking beside the wagon. The hem of her dress had become coated in dust, and it was clear that she was getting tired, for her carpetbag was drooping lower and lower in her arms. For her to make it so far without complaining was truly a show of determination.

Something in Stefan's chest loosened. While he didn't want Miss Clarke to join him, he also wasn't a heathen. "Miss Clarke, if you are getting tired, you are welcome to sit beside me on the wagon bench. There's room enough for both of us."

Miss Clarke looked up at him, squinting from beneath the short brim of her hat. "Are you certain? I don't want to impose on you, especially when you've been so kind. You've already done more than enough."

Stefan drew the wagon to a halt and leaned forward, resting his elbows on his knees. "I can't tell if you're being serious or sarcastic. At any rate, you're allowed to join me." He held out a hand in a peace offering. "I promise to keep at least a foot of space between us."

Miss Clarke grinned. "Mr. Roberts, I do not suspect you of the intention of misconduct. You proved your honor to me the first time we met." Moving to the opposite side of the wagon, she tossed her luggage onto the bench and used his hand to lift herself up, keeping the bag between them as she settled her skirts around her ankles. "I must admit, this is quite nice. I haven't had a chance to sit since I arrived on the train this morning."

Stefan clicked his tongue, causing the wagon to jolt back into motion. "I apologize for making you walk for such a long time. You simply caught me off guard. I wasn't expecting to travel with anyone other than the horses."

Miss Clarke lifted a hand to her mouth to conceal her soft laugh. "That's quite fair, especially considering the fact that I've been rather obnoxious. For that, *I* must apologize. I would hire a female companion or take a coach, but I don't have the funds for either. I'm afraid I don't even have the money for another train ticket—hence, the reason I was going to walk from Chicago."

Stefan lifted a brow. What on earth had made this woman desperate enough to *walk* from Chicago to Kentucky? "That will take an incredibly long time. Where are you headed?"

"Albany. Do you know of it?"

Stefan adjusted the reins in his hands, memories of thick trees and rolling hills coming to mind. "Yes. It's just a bit past Monticello, at the bottom of the state. If you take the right roads, you should be able to make it there in good time."

"I see." Miss Clarke stared out at the scenery as though in contemplation. After a moment, she released a heavy sigh. Perhaps thoughts of the long walk ahead of her had proved to be too much. "That's a lovely horse you have, Mr. Roberts. As a matter of fact, they're all wonderful. Your father's stables must have quite a few customers. Do all of his horses race?"

Stefan hummed and adjusted his cap. "The thoroughbreds do, but not Orion. He's my horse." He gestured to the Percheron. "I've owned him since he was a foal. We've seen quite a few years together, he and I."

"Orion. That's a fine name for a fine horse," Miss Clarke said approvingly. "What of the others?" She swiveled, looking at the thoroughbreds. "What are their names?"

"Lake's Luck and Persnickety. My father named them." Stefan allowed himself a small smile. "The one and only time he let me name a racehorse was when I was four. I feel sorry for the beast that was saddled with 'Sunshine' its entire life."

Miss Clarke laughed again, her cheeks glowing pink with merriment. "Oh, but that isn't bad at all! Sunny is a perfectly acceptable name for a horse."

"I suppose so, but I think my father was looking for something more...powerful." His father had been a different man back then—cheerful, happy, and unbothered by the troubles and stress of the world. There had certainly been times of struggle on the farm, but Vater had always seemed to find a way to rise above them. As a child, Stefan had regarded his father as a hero. When had it all changed? An overcast day, when rain flooded down in sheets and open doors banged in the wind…

"Mr. Roberts, are you all right?" Miss Clarke's query jolted him back into reality.

"I'm perfectly well. Got a bit lost in my thoughts, that's all." Stefan's own brusque tone startled him. He cleared his throat and shifted, uncomfortable with his involuntary reaction to the question. As they lapsed into silence once more, he resolved not to sink back into negative memories again.

There were many secrets best left buried.

Charlotte glanced at her traveling companion out of the corner of her eye, for he had gone quiet once again. So far the only thing she knew about him was that his father bred racehorses. Mr. Roberts had offered no explanation for his limp or his moment of melancholy, and Charlotte was far too polite to inquire about either. Even if she was incredibly curious.

From a glance, it was impossible to tell the cause of the man's lopsided gait. He wore dark-brown trousers and a navy jacket, with a tan-colored waistcoat beneath. Dark-brown hair peeked from under a wide-brimmed felt hat, along with blue eyes that reminded her of forget-me-nots. While he had glanced at Charlotte only a few times, a depth of emotion lay behind his gaze. The man had a story—of that, Charlotte was certain. If Carina was traveling alongside them, she would have tried to puzzle out the man. *If only she was here.* Perhaps Charlotte would pretend to be Carina for a day and see if she could unearth the man's secrets.

"We are approaching an inn, Miss Clarke. I plan to stay there for the evening. You're more than welcome to make arrangements to do so as well, if you'd like." Mr. Roberts pointed toward a small group of buildings farther down the lane.

Charlotte felt the coins in her pocket. She had enough for perhaps one night, but nothing more. And if she stayed at the inn, she would have no money left for food. It was a rather depressing situation. "Well, all right. I'll see what they have," she finally settled on saying, pasting a shaky smile on her face. If they didn't have any rooms she could afford, she would have to find a barn to sleep in.

Mr. Roberts drew the wagon to a halt in front of the inn and dropped the reins, clearly trusting that Orion would stay in place. The man favored his left leg, leaning almost all of his weight on his right as he lowered himself to the ground and crossed to Charlotte's side of the wagon. She gathered her luggage and accepted his proffered hand with a smile, jumping down from the bench. "My thanks, Mr. Roberts. You've been more than kind to me today."

Mr. Roberts nodded solemnly as he collected his satchel from the wagon bed. "Of course, Miss Clarke. In the event that we do not meet again, I wish you safe travels to Kentucky."

Charlotte clutched her carpetbag to her chest, trying to prevent her panic from showing on her face. She had only just met the man, for goodness' sake. So why, then, did a spike of fear run through her at the thought of parting ways? Perhaps there had been something comforting in having a companion, even if said companion had been rather unsociable. "Thank you. I wish the same for you."

Mr. Roberts gestured toward the inn and lifted the reins over Orion's head with the other, not bothering to look at her. "I'm going to see that the horses are safely settled in the stable. Why don't you go inside and inquire about a room for yourself?"

"Very well." Charlotte waved halfheartedly in farewell. "Goodbye, Mr. Roberts." She made her way toward the door, though she had a feeling she already knew what the nature of the answer to her query about the price of a room would be. Sure enough, a quick talk with the young man standing behind the front desk confirmed that a room at the inn was far beyond her meager funds.

"I really am sorry, miss. I wish we could do more for you," the clerk said with an apologetic smile.

Charlotte shrugged, trying not to let her dejection show. "That's quite all right. I understand."

He leaned over the counter, peering toward a door with a sign on it that read, *Manager*. "You know, if you just so happen to take a little walk to the left of the building, you'd find yourself at the barn. You might slip inside—completely by accident, of course—and head for the loft. The staff has a tendency to overlook it most days. It's foolish of them, really. A person could stay there for quite a while and avoid notice."

Charlotte released her tight hold on the carpetbag as relief expanded in her chest. "You're too kind, sir. You have my thanks. I do believe I will take a walk."

The clerk grinned. "The weather is perfect for it. Have a good evening, miss."

Poking her head back outside, Charlotte made sure that Mr. Roberts had left the clearing before she ventured out the door. The last thing she wanted was for him to see her sorry state of affairs, even though the opinion of a stranger shouldn't have mattered that much to her. She had a sneaking suspicion the man would feel obligated to pay for her stay, a thing she couldn't stomach the idea of. Charity in the form of money was something she had never been able to accept.

With her carpetbag tucked underneath one arm, Charlotte made her way toward a brown building that appeared to be the barn. She slid the heavy door open and slipped inside, smiling as the familiar scent of hay surrounded her. Dust motes swirled through the air, dancing in and out of the fading light that came from the doorway and windows. From somewhere within the building, a cow lowed and a bell clanged. The scene reminded Charlotte of home, of Gertrude and the little cow shed and cold nights surrounded by warm hay. Oh, how she missed it.

After climbing the ladder into the hayloft, Charlotte found a place to set her bag and gathered a pile of hay to create a bed of sorts. She unpinned her hair and plaited it into a thick braid. With that accomplished, she sat down on the hay and dragged her bag over to use as a pillow. While it wasn't necessarily the most comfortable bed, it would do for the night.

Charlotte laid her head on the bag, looking up at the ceiling for a moment before shivering. Who knew it would get so cold? She sat up and reached into her bag, pulling her thin blanket from within. It was one of the few things she had purchased before leaving Milwaukee, along with a hairbrush and a few other necessities.

"To think I considered myself poor before the fire," Charlotte muttered as she spread the blanket over herself. While it had been a number of weeks since she received that terrible letter telling of the loss of her family, sometimes she felt as though the shock from learning the news had never fully worn off. How could her sister, with her sparkling eyes and secret collection of romance novels, have disappeared forever? How could her mother, with her soft smile and callused hands, be gone? And then, as if the fire hadn't been terrible enough, Flora had died a few days before she departed for Chicago.

Charlotte tugged one of her gloves off and pulled her sleeve back, revealing the pale scars that crisscrossed like spider webs along the back of her forearm and hand. She had thought she was mature before the fire, that she knew what it meant to be an adult. "How wrong I was."

She could only hope that she would be able to start a new

life once she reached Kentucky. If she couldn't, what else would she do?

~

The barn door slid open with a thunderous *clang*. Charlotte bolted upright and pulled the blanket tightly around her, her heart beating a rapid tempo in her chest. After wiping the vestiges of sleep from her eyes, she crept to the edge of the loft so she could peer down at the intruder. A man wearing a familiar felt hat stood in the doorway, a plate balanced in one hand. What was Mr. Roberts doing in the barn?

"Miss Clarke? Are you in there?" The man glanced back and forth, then released a sigh, as though coming to the barn had been the last thing on his mind. "I brought some bread and fruit."

He brought me breakfast? Charlotte's stomach rumbled at the mention of food, reminding her of the measly apple she had eaten yesterday. Grimacing, she gave in to her hunger. "I'm up here, Mr. Roberts. Give me a moment to collect my things."

Mr. Roberts looked up at the loft, his gaze spearing her a moment later. He frowned and tipped his hat back with his free hand. "There you are. Aren't you cold?"

Charlotte snorted as she reached back to grab her carpetbag. "Goodness, no. I'm practically roasting." At Mr. Roberts's confused expression, she laughed and began climbing down the ladder. "Of course, I'm cold. Sleeping with hay as a bed does not exactly provide one with an incredible amount of warmth."

"You should have told me you were sleeping in the barn. I know I haven't been all that friendly, but I wouldn't deny you the funds for a room—or at the very least, a proper blanket."

Charlotte stepped off the ladder and turned to face Mr.

Roberts, though she had to look up a considerable distance to meet his eyes. The man stood at least a full head above her, though she was by no means a tall woman. "That is precisely why I didn't tell you. I wouldn't have wanted to impose on your kindness. Besides, it wasn't all that difficult to sleep in the hayloft. How did you find me?"

"The desk clerk informed me of your whereabouts when I asked him what became of you this morning. I figured I should check on you and ensure that you didn't freeze to death overnight." Mr. Roberts handed her the plate of toast and strawberries.

"Well, thank you very much for caring." Charlotte accepted the plate and devoured the slice of bread without any decorum whatsoever.

"Forgive me for asking, but when was the last time you ate?"

Charlotte finished the last strawberry and patted her lips dry with the handkerchief she kept tucked in her dress pocket. She wasn't completely uncivilized, after all. "I had an apple yesterday, and the day before that, I ate two meals. I simply didn't have time to stop for a full meal while we were traveling." She cleared her throat. "Still, that doesn't excuse my behavior. For that, I apologize."

Mr. Roberts waved off her words, his expression softening. "I'm not bothered about that. Be honest. Do you have money for food? If not, I can certainly assist."

Charlotte's cheeks heated. "I have the necessary funds, though I need to save them if I'm going to reach Kentucky with a full stomach."

"Miss Clarke, if you don't mind me asking, why exactly are you going to Kentucky?" Mr. Roberts moved to sit on a nearby barrel. "Your situation is more than strange."

Charlotte pursed her lips and took a seat on the crate opposite him. "Trust me when I say I'm well aware of that. As I mentioned yesterday, I'm going to Kentucky to deliver a locket for my friend. It was her final wish that it be returned to her mother. I was not going to turn her down, not when she looked so desperate." She stuffed the handkerchief back up her sleeve. "And believe me when I say I will get to Kentucky. No shortage of money will stop me."

Mr. Roberts looked at the locket hanging from her neck, his brows furrowing. "My condolences for your loss. In that case, why are you traveling alone? I can understand going to Kentucky, but surely, you had someone else who could make the journey with you. Traveling such a great distance on your own is incredibly dangerous."

Charlotte took great interest in the hay on the floor. "I have no one. My father has been dead for years, and my sister and mother were separated from me during a fire that destroyed our town. I...I received confirmation a month later that they did not survive the night. And so, in the end, I decided to leave for Kentucky by myself. There was no use waiting around for someone who would never come."

For a moment, the barn was silent. Then, Mr. Roberts cleared his throat, looking suitably apologetic. "I apologize for prying, Miss Clarke. I didn't mean to make you relive bad memories."

"It wasn't your fault. You hardly could have known," Charlotte said with a soft smile. "Do you understand now why I am here and why I must complete this trip?"

Mr. Roberts's jaw twitched, and he shifted uncomfortably on the barrel. "I suppose, though it doesn't necessarily make me feel any better. Young ladies shouldn't be left to traverse country roads on their own, especially when they cannot afford to stay at an inn."

"I'm not all that young." Charlotte tried to keep the disgruntlement from her face. "I turned twenty-three this April. That's a perfectly reasonable age for traveling. I made it this far, after all."

"Regardless of your age, it isn't safe." Mr. Roberts crossed his arms and rolled his shoulders back, causing the thick fabric of his jacket to stretch across his broad frame. "You'll have to continue traveling with me."

"I beg your pardon?" Charlotte halted in the process of lifting an accusing finger, thrown off guard by the sudden statement. "I thought you didn't want me to come along with you. If I recall correctly, you considered it highly improper for an unmarried lady to be traveling with a man."

Mr. Roberts blinked, the stern look fleeing from his face. "I did say that, didn't I?" To Charlotte's surprise, he shook his head and chuckled. "Ah, well. I suppose it isn't a bad idea, especially considering the fact that we're heading in the same direction. You would get your locket to your friend, and I would get the horses to my father's stables." He stood and brushed the hay from his jacket. "The more I consider it, the more I find that I have no objections. In that case, would you care to join me on my trip to Kentucky? Purely as acquaintances, of course," he hurriedly added, the tips of his ears reddening.

Charlotte collected her bag from the floor and straightened, the corners of her mouth lifting. "Wonderful! Since we're going to be traveling together, I think it only right that you call me Charlotte."

"Very well." Mr. Roberts cleared his throat and adjusted his hat. "Then you can call me Stefan."

"Well, Stefan, I'm glad you came around to the idea." The trip was sure to go much faster and safer with a companion—even if she couldn't make heads or tails of the man.

CHAPTER 7

$\mathcal{A}$s they pulled away from the inn, Stefan couldn't help but look at Charlotte. Up until their last conversation, he had assumed her to be a naïve young woman who was traveling to Kentucky to visit a friend or perhaps some family. However, after hearing her story, it was clear he had been incorrect. Shame twinged in his stomach at the memory of abandoning her in Chicago. She was a bit foolhardy, but admirable, nonetheless.

Stefan considered Charlotte's rumpled dress and hat. She had insisted upon repinning the squashed thing on her head before they left, though Stefan wasn't certain whether or not it actually protected her from anything. Women's fashion was somewhat of a mystery to him, with all the frills and bows and useless little decorations that seemed to be involved. He had always been of the opinion that the best clothing was practical clothing. That being said, Charlotte's current dress seemed to have pockets, which even he knew was unusual. "How exactly did you acquire pockets in your dress, Charlotte?"

She grinned and adjusted the folds of her skirt, revealing a small pocket near her left side. "I sewed them into the dress myself. I discovered that keeping my money on my person was safer than keeping it in a reticule." She rolled her shoulders back with pride. "Pickpockets generally don't expect a lady to keep her change in the folds of her dress."

Stefan blinked. "Well, that's quite resourceful of you. You seem to know how to make the best out of a poor situation."

"I do try." Charlotte released her dress with a laugh.

A sudden lurch brought the wagon to a halt. Orion whinnied and tossed his head, straining hard to pull the vehicle forward. Unfortunately, it remained firmly lodged in place. A glance over the edge revealed that the left side of the wagon had become stuck in a muddy rut—a rut that had avoided his notice because he had been looking at Charlotte. "Stupid mud," Stefan muttered, removing his jacket and rolling up his sleeves.

"What happened?"

"We've fallen into a rut. I'm going to have to try and push us out," Stefan answered as he lowered himself carefully to the ground and moved to assess the condition of the back wheels. They wouldn't get free without a fight, for the back left wheel had sunk a full three inches into the muck.

"Charlotte, would you mind taking up the reins?" Stefan did his best to keep the irritation out of his voice. It wouldn't be fair to take his anger out on the innocent woman. "When I shout, tap them on Orion's back. I'll push from behind, and hopefully, our combined efforts will help the wheels to roll free. We'll go on the count of three."

"I have the reins. On your count, Stefan," Charlotte called from the wagon bench.

Stefan placed his right shoulder against the rough wood of the wagon. "One, two, three!" He threw his weight forward, ignoring the jolt of pain that ran through his left side. "Come on!" He ground out the words, hoping to feel the wheel moving even by an inch. Despite his efforts, it remained firmly stuck.

"Confound it." Stefan backed away and placed his hands on his knees, taking a few deep breaths. There had to be another way.

"Could we tie the thoroughbreds to the front? They might be able to help pull."

Stefan straightened, studying the racehorses that watched curiously from a safe spot beyond the mud. "We could tie the rope to the front of the wagon, but I have no harnesses for them. I fear what will happen if they try to pull the wagon from their bridles. It could cause damage to their necks."

Charlotte turned back to the front. "Very well. Shall we try again, then?"

Stefan's side protested the idea, but there was no other option. "Yes. One, two, and three!" He threw his weight back against the wagon. Again, the wheels refused to move, though the vehicle shuddered with the force of Orion tugging it forward.

"It's no use, Stefan. Orion just isn't strong enough by himself."

Stefan turned around and leaned back against the wagon as a drop of sweat ran down his cheek. "Confound it all!" Perhaps he could attach a rope to the back wheel and wiggle it in an attempt to loosen—

"Woah, there! Good afternoon, traveler! Having some troubles?"

Stefan's head snapped up in surprise. In front of him stood a white mare, and atop the mare was a man whose brown eyes peered curiously at Stefan from beneath a floppy hat. A thin layer of dust covered his neatly trimmed beard and gray jacket, a sign he had been on the road for some time.

Stefan pointed to the sunken wheels. "I'm afraid we've become stuck in the mud. I don't suppose you could lend us a hand, could you?"

The stranger chuckled and maneuvered his horse closer to the wagon, carefully avoiding the patch of muck. "Well, it wouldn't be very kind of me to leave you here, would it? If you have some rope I can tie around my saddle, I'd be more than happy to help." The slight drawl to his words was enough to make Stefan tense, but he was hardly in a position to be choosy. Besides, there was no telling where the man had come from or who he was.

Stefan called to the front of the wagon. "Charlotte, could you get the extra length of rope that's underneath the bench?"

"Certainly." Charlotte ducked her head as she felt around beneath the wagon seat. A moment later, she straightened and held the length of rope up victoriously. "Here it is!"

The man moved to the front of the wagon and took the rope from Charlotte, tipping his hat. "Thank you, ma'am. We'll have you and your husband out in a jiffy."

"Oh, she's not—we're not..." Stefan began.

The man winked. "Ah, I see. Still sorting things through, are you?"

Stefan attempted a smile, though it turned to a grimace rather quickly. "In a manner of speaking."

The man tied one end of the rope to the pommel of his saddle and the other to the front of the wagon, fixing it just below the bench. Once that was accomplished, he directed his mare to stand next to Orion with the rope stretched taut between horse and wagon. He glanced over his shoulder at Stefan and gave him a reassuring nod. "All right. I'm ready whenever you are."

Stefan set his shoulder back against the wagon, shifting his weight onto his right leg to try and alleviate some of the pain shooting up his left side. "Here we go. Ready, set, pull!"

There was a sucking noise as the mud tore at the wheels, pulling at the wood in an attempt to keep them down. However, with the combined force of Orion, the white mare, and Stefan, the wagon finally rolled onto a dry slope.

Charlotte let out a cheer. "Wonderfully done, sirs! Good boy, Orion!"

Stefan straightened and rubbed his sore shoulder. "Thank the Lord." Walking around to the front, he nodded to the helpful rider. "You have my thanks, sir."

"No thanks necessary. My name is John," the man drawled, his accent becoming even more pronounced with the words.

Stefan blinked. "Stefan." His voice came out a bit harsher than he meant for it to. Something about the man made him uneasy, though he couldn't say for sure what it was. "We are in your debt, John."

The man leaned forward, patting the mare's side. "Oh, there's no need for that. I'm simply glad I could help. Where are you folks headed?"

The question was innocent enough, so Stefan answered it. "Kentucky." He stepped back to brush a hand across Orion's nose. The horse had been studying them with quiet intensity, his ears pricked forward in preparation for the next command. Did he have a strange feeling about John as well? Orion's instincts were rarely wrong. "My father owns stables at the bottom of the state."

John gestured to the open lane. "I happen to be heading to Kentucky as well, though my destination is in Lexington. I have an urgent meeting there, so I had best be on my way." He tipped his hat, his dark eyes assessing. "I wish you both safe travels and Godspeed."

Stefan raised a hand in farewell. "The same to you. Good day, John."

As the man rode away in a flurry of dust, Charlotte watched the retreating figure. Her prolonged silence stirred Stefan's unease. Did she, too, have a curious feeling about the man? He hadn't done anything wrong. On the contrary, without him, they would still be stuck. At length, Stefan asked, "Is everything all right?"

Charlotte hummed, rubbing at her sleeves. "Yes. Why don't you come and take a seat? You must be tired after that hard work."

What was running through her head? Clearly, more than she wished to tell him, but he could hardly force a confidence from her. Stefan hefted himself onto the wagon. After setting Orion into motion, he leaned back and wiggled his throbbing left leg ever so slightly. While he was proficient enough without the use of a cane, he had to rest frequently, or his leg became stiff and sore. He would pay for his overexertion later, but for now, he was glad that they were free and back on their way.

As they traveled, a tingle made its way up Stefan's spine. It was a feeling he hadn't experienced in years, one that instantly set him on edge—the feeling of being watched. Stefan half expected to see the John at the edge of the road. There was nobody in front of or behind them, but the hairs on the back of Stefan's neck stood at attention, every nerve on high alert. Something was wrong.

Charlotte was digging through her bag, clearly unbothered. What would she do if they were ambushed? Did her bravery extend to fighting off attackers?

Stefan moved his attention back to the grove of trees they were passing through, glancing through the trunks as though a black-clothed villain was lying in wait among the shadows. It certainly wasn't unheard of for robbers to wait by the side of the road, preying upon unsuspecting wagons. He reached by instinct for the revolver he kept tucked inside his jacket. Hopefully, if danger did befall them, he would be fast enough to stop it.

"Stefan, are you all right? You've looked on edge ever since we freed the wagon." Charlotte's voice caused Stefan to jump in his seat, every muscle tensing.

"Don't scare me like that!" When she shot him a glance with brows furrowed, Stefan forced himself to take a deep breath.

Calm yourself, Stefan. There's no reason to be so testy. Still, keeping himself from tensing was difficult when every nerve screamed a warning. "I'm sorry. It's hard to explain, but I feel as though we're being...watched."

Charlotte glanced behind them and tucked a loose strand of hair behind her ear. "I don't see anyone. Are you certain?"

"No, but I have a feeling, and that feeling isn't often wrong. I believe it would be wise for us to get off the road soon."

"Why would anyone follow us? We don't have anything valuable." Charlotte tilted her head. "Except the horses." She fisted a hand beneath her chin, looking Lake up and down. "Considering their fine breeding, it would make sense that someone would want to take them."

"Indeed." Whistling, Stefan flicked the reins and urged Orion into a trot. "We'll settle at Frankfort for the evening. I saw a sign not far back."

Charlotte studied him for a moment before settling back against the wagon bench. "If that's what you feel is best."

Stefan shuddered as the feeling intensified. "That I do."

After a few more miles, they entered Frankfort. It wasn't the booming metropolis of Chicago, but it was busy enough that they stood a chance of blending into the hubbub. Pulling the wagon to the side of the street, Stefan scanned the storefronts for an inn. A small building caught his attention, the shingle hanging from the wall proclaiming it to be a bed-and-breakfast.

Stefan directed Orion to the other side of the street and drew the wagon to a halt before turning to face his traveling companion. "Would you wait with the horses while I visit this inn? I'm going to inquire about rooms for the evening." Her expression grew dark in an instant, and he held up a hand. "I'll be paying for your room for this night and this night only. For safety purposes, of course. You can pay me later if it makes you feel better."

His words seemed to mollify her, for she crossed her arms with a dainty huff. "Very well."

Stefan lowered himself to the ground and made his way slowly up the steps to the inn, the heat of Charlotte's eyes burning a hole between his shoulder blades. He steeled his jaw and tried to walk as normally as he could with the pain in his leg, ignoring her gaze. He was all too used to looks of sympathy, and it was something he despised.

Inside, he managed to secure two rooms for a relatively low price, along with the promise of a warm breakfast before they set back off. Stefan's spirits lifted ever so slightly as he left the building and crossed the street. However, the smile quickly dropped from his face when he returned to the wagon and found Orion and the thoroughbreds standing by themselves, the wagon bench empty.

Charlotte was gone.

CHAPTER 8

A FEW MOMENTS EARLIER...

Charlotte watched as Stefan crossed the street, his limp more pronounced than before. She couldn't help but feel sorry for him, especially after he had been made to push the wagon out of the mud. Whatever it was that affected his left leg couldn't be pleasant to live with. Hopefully, they would be able to stay at the inn so the poor man could get some well-deserved rest.

From the front of the wagon, Orion let out a loud whinny, his ears pricked in the direction Stefan had gone. The horse seemed agitated in the absence of his owner, as though he feared something bad would occur. He pawed the ground and danced back and forth, the harness jangling.

"Not to worry, Orion. He'll be back shortly." Even as Charlotte reassured the horse, a trickle of fear ran through her. What if there was truth to Stefan's claim that they were being watched? At first, she hadn't believed him, but what if he was correct and Orion was sensing some sort of evil presence nearby? Charlotte had no weapons with which to protect herself. Hopefully, a thief would not be so foolish as to try and steal the horses from her in broad daylight. "Hurry, Stefan," she muttered, rubbing her arms.

A movement from the left drew her attention, followed by a shout. Charlotte gasped as the door to one of the shops across the street slammed open, and a person was tossed unceremoniously onto the wooden boardwalk.

"Don't come back, you hear? I've had enough with your lot!" the man who had done the tossing yelled, his face mottled red beneath his thick black beard. The door to the shop banged shut as the brawny fellow went back inside, leaving the unfortunate soul—merely a boy, it seemed—sprawled on the boards.

The lad picked himself off the ground. He couldn't have been older than twelve or thirteen, judging by his thin face and narrow shoulders. His red hair was ruffled and his worn jacket two sizes too big, the gray waistcoat underneath spotted with flecks of mud. His newsboy cap, at first affixed to his head, now lay on the ground a foot away. The young man brushed off his trousers and peered at the building as though considering going back in. He had a look of pure desperation on his face, a look that Charlotte knew well. It was the look of someone who was willing to try anything to survive.

Before she could stop herself, Charlotte clambered down from the wagon and hurried up behind the boy. She ducked to collect his cap before straightening and tugging gently on his sleeve. "Excuse me," she said quietly. "Are you all right?"

The boy whirled, his eyes widening. Charlotte froze and sucked in a breath, for one of his eyes was blue and the other was brown. How curious.

Before she could formulate a proper sentence, the lad took off, leaving Charlotte standing on the sidewalk.

"Wait! I mean no harm! You left your cap." Charlotte waved it in the air. When the boy continued to run, she picked up her skirts and darted after him. "Come back!"

The young man cut around a corner with such speed that Charlotte nearly ran straight past him. Luckily, she managed to turn at the last second. It was probably a foolish decision to be running into alleys, especially considering how her previous chase had ended, but it was too late to turn back. She was forced to skid to a stop regardless at a dead end. Standing at the back wall was the young man, his arm braced against the bricks. Only, he seemed to have multiplied.

Charlotte blinked and looked closer. Twins?

"Look." The young man she had been chasing gasped, bending over his knees. "That lady chased me all the way from the store. She's crazy!"

The other lad laughed, glancing over at Charlotte. Unlike his brother, both of his eyes were grayish-blue in color, and his clothing was much brighter, especially his green waistcoat and red bandanna. "Well, either she's too fast or you're too slow. Say, lady, what's the matter? We didn't take anything from you, if that's what you're worried about. Bas looks a little scruffy around the edges, but he would never steal."

Stepping closer, Charlotte held up her hands. "I mean no harm. I saw what happened at the drugstore and wanted to help. Besides, you forgot this." She tossed the boy's cap, and it landed at his feet.

The second lad whirled to face the first, his russet brows furrowing. "What exactly happened outside the drugstore?"

The first boy straightened, combing the curls off his forehead. "The same thing that's happened everywhere else. They won't give me a job. Said I looked like a street rat."

The second boy crossed his thin arms. Though he had no jacket, he wore a white dress shirt beneath his waistcoat, the sleeves rolled to his elbows. The cap on his head was similar to the one on the ground, though he had tilted it jauntily to one side. "I thought we already discussed the probability of that plan working and decided it wasn't worth it. They aren't going to give us jobs, Bas." Turning back to Charlotte, the boy grinned. "Thanks for returning the hat. I'm sorry you had to run all the way over here to give it back." He gestured between himself and his companion. "I'm Tom, and this fool is my brother, Sebastian." He bowed, revealing a banjo slung over his back. "As you can see, we do not need assistance. Thank you and good day."

Charlotte pursed her lips. Though her head told her she should walk away and leave them to their business, her heart told her to stay. Something had led her to the two boys, and she wasn't about to let the opportunity go to waste. "You haven't been able to find a job, you say?" she said, an idea beginning to take root.

Sebastian shook his head, the motion causing his hair to tumble back over his eyes. "I've searched everywhere. Either they have no need for another employee, or they take one look at us and believe we're tramps who want to take advantage of them." He combed his hair back with one hand, clearly agitated. "You must understand, we only want to make an honest living. We aren't thieves or anything of that sort."

Tom shrugged, tapping the shoulder strap that held his banjo on his back. "I say we keep playing music. At least we make a handful of coins by doing that. It's better than nothing."

"That won't last forever," Sebastian retorted.

Charlotte bit the inside of her cheek, recalling Sebastian's desperate expression. She knew what it felt like to want to earn a decent living, enough to put clothes on one's back and a roof over one's head. "I may have a job for the two of you." She drew the words out, trying to think.

The twins glanced up, their faces wearing identical expressions of surprise. "Truly?" Sebastian asked, his eyes shining with hope.

"How are you with animals?" Charlotte tilted her head. "Horses, specifically?"

"Our family used to own a horse named Rufus. We took care of him more often than not, so I'd say we're decent with horses." Tom uncrossed his arms and studied her with growing curiosity.

"Would you be all right traveling, or do you need a job here in town?"

Sebastian's shoulders slumped. "Miss, we don't really care where we go so long as we have food to eat and somewhere to sleep at night. Living in an alley isn't easy, especially in this weather."

Charlotte held a hand to her heart. "Please, call me Charlotte. How would you two feel about accompanying me to Kentucky? My friend and I are traveling there with two race-horses, and we could use some extra hands to care for them." While Stefan hadn't seemed to struggle with the horses, he would surely appreciate the help. Wouldn't he? "I can't promise you pay...or anything, really, but I can put in a good word with my traveling companion. I could probably convince him to let you share a room at the inn with him or at least sleep in the wagon."

She wasn't entirely sure how Stefan would react to the addition of two hungry boys to their traveling party, but if his treatment of her was any indication, he had a good heart beneath his surly demeanor. Surely, he would be willing to help the two children once he saw how dire their situation was. Assuming he had the money. Did he? His father owned stables, so he must have had at least a moderate salary. In that case, a few extra coins on food for the twins wouldn't affect his purse by much.

Sebastian and Tom glanced at each other through some silent form of communication. They must have reached a decision, for Tom took a hesitant step forward. "I suppose we'll join you, Miss Charlotte."

Charlotte clasped her hands together. "Wonderful! We

should go tell my friend, Mr. Stefan Roberts. The poor man is probably wondering where I've gone."

Sebastian snatched his cap from the ground and fell in step beside her as they left the alley, fixing it back on his head. "You're traveling with a man? Is he old?"

Charlotte couldn't help the smile that spread across her face. "Well, I haven't asked. However, I would guess him to be somewhere around my age, if not a bit older."

Sebastian's eyes narrowed, the contrasting colors standing out even more in the light of the sun. "You aren't married? Isn't it considered wrong for a man and single lady to travel together?"

Charlotte coughed and adjusted the tie keeping her hat attached to the back of her head in an effort to conceal her burning cheeks. "Stefan has gone to great lengths to ensure that we obey the rules of proper society."

"How do you know him?" Tom piped up from Charlotte's other side. "Since you aren't married."

"We met in Chicago and agreed to travel together since we're both going to Kentucky." Charlotte tugged her skirts up to avoid a pile of horse droppings. "I needed an escort, and he was gallant enough to accept."

Tom raised an eyebrow. "Why are you going to Kentucky, then?"

"Full of questions, aren't we? I'm traveling there because I have to deliver a special gift to someone." Charlotte interlaced her fingers in front of her. "My friend requested that I take it to her mother, as she was too ill to do so herself."

Sebastian quirked his brow. "Does it have anything to do with that fancy necklace around your neck, or is that yours? It's very pretty."

Charlotte gasped, her hand flying up to the locket. *Drat!* It must have come loose during her chase. "This...well..." She tucked the necklace back under her collar. "This is nothing."

Sebastian's stare only intensified, and her shoulders slumped by a fraction. "Oh, all right. Yes, it is the locket. But you mustn't go talking about it. I've already gotten into trouble because of the silly thing once."

Sebastian bounced on his heels with a satisfied smile. "Don't worry, miss. I won't say a word. I'm certain she'll be glad to have it back."

"So I hope. Ah, there's Stefan." He was standing at the wagon with a look of bewilderment on his face, as well as... panic? "Stefan, over here!" Charlotte called, waving her hand. Before he could turn their way, she provided a quick warning to the boys. "I should mention that Stefan has an impaired left leg. I do not know why, but I would caution you not to ask about it. I would hate to damage his pride."

The twins murmured their agreement, their expressions turning apprehensive as Stefan's gaze landed on Charlotte, going from relief to dark anger in a mere second. "Charlotte!" His voice boomed across the clearing. "Get over here this instant!"

"Cheery, isn't he?" Charlotte crossed the street with the twins trailing behind. "Stefan, you'll never believe—"

"Where have you been?" Stefan cut her off, his eyes spearing into her like ice. "I thought thieves made off with you, and here you come, waltzing up the street as if you didn't just nearly put me in my grave!" He gestured to the twins, who looked as though they were reconsidering Charlotte's offer. "And who are these two? I suppose they rescued you after you got yourself into another situation?"

Charlotte released an irritated huff. "First, you grouchy man, I try not to make a habit of getting myself into *situations*. Second, I saw Sebastian getting thrown from the drugstore across the street and went after him to ensure that he was all right. As it turns out, these two boys are in need of a job, which is what the drugstore owner so rudely denied them. I thought it might be worth it to offer them a position caring for your horses in exchange for food and board."

It hadn't seemed possible, but somehow Stefan's expression grew even darker. "Am I to assume that you want me to pay these two people, boys you picked off the street, to watch my horses? Charlotte, you don't even know them!"

Charlotte tugged on Stefan's sleeve, instructing the boys to stay put. After leading him around to the other side of the wagon, she released him and stepped back. "Look... While I don't know those boys, I know their situation very well. They are alone and looking for an honest way to survive. Can you begrudge them that?" Seeing his conflicted expression, she pressed on. "They cannot be more than thirteen years old. They need someone to look after them. They are currently living in an alley and making money by playing music on the sidewalk. That's no life for anyone, as I think you would agree. Please, give them a chance, and I'm sure you'll find them worthwhile. They don't need much, just food and a place to sleep."

Stefan took a deep breath and glanced over the wagon at where the boys still stood, scuffing the toes of their boots on the ground. "You are certain they are alone?" he asked, his voice low and considerably gentler.

Charlotte inclined her head. "There was nobody with them."

Stefan studied her for a moment before folding his arms across his chest, his face relaxing into something softer. "Fine. I will give them a chance, but if something goes wrong, they must leave."

Charlotte grinned, causing Stefan to blink. "Oh, how wonderful!" She nearly pulled the prickly man into a hug before thinking better of it and taking a step back. "Thank you so much." She sobered slightly. "I'm terribly sorry for frightening you. I never meant to cause you grief."

Stefan straightened and raised one brow. "Just don't do it

again." He glanced at the twins. "Well, then, I suppose we should put them out of their misery."

Charlotte clasped her hands together as he walked around the wagon to greet the boys. While he spoke to each of them in turn, determination took hold in her chest. There was indeed a soft heart beneath Stefan's stoic exterior, and she intended to unearth it.

CHAPTER 9

he cold morning air bit Stefan's cheeks as he pushed his way out the door and ambled toward the stables across the street from the inn. Though the sun had risen over an hour ago, the air was still, undisturbed by talk or hoofbeats, and the boardwalks were free of people. The only sign of life was the faint cooing of doves from the trees lining the sides of the road. It filled Stefan with a sense of peace knowing that, for a while at least, he could be alone.

Pushing the stable door open, Stefan entered the building and moved to the stalls that housed the thoroughbreds. "*Guten Morgen,*" he whispered, stroking Lake's nose when the curious horse poked his head over the stall door. "How are you today, my friend? Hungry?"

Lake bobbed his head in agreement and pulled his upper lip back in a grin, making Stefan laugh as he moved toward the barrel of oats at the back of the room. "Well, then, you are in luck. I have a fine scoop of oats waiting for you."

As he reached the barrel, a shadow fell across the doorway. Stefan looked up and was surprised to see one of the twins entering the barn. It was hard to tell which of them it was in the dim light, though he guessed it to be the quieter of the two judging by his softer approach. "You're up early. What brings you to the barn?"

The boy's brows furrowed with obvious anxiety. Now that he was closer, Stefan could see he was most definitely the quieter twin—Sebastian, if he recalled correctly. His different-colored eyes were very recognizable. "I saw you leave the room and thought you might need help with the horses." Sebastian twisted the bottom of his jacket in one hand. "That's my job, isn't it? I have to repay you for our food and lodging somehow."

Stefan inclined his head. While he was sorry for the loss of his solitude, he couldn't be angry at the lad for wanting to help. "Fair enough. Where's your brother?"

"Still sleeping, I'm afraid. Do you want me to wake him?" Sebastian took a step back and glanced over his shoulder. He still fidgeted with his jacket. "He doesn't always sleep this late, I promise. It's just been so long since we've had a proper place to rest."

Sebastian was clearly eager to please, most likely still nervous that Stefan would put the twins back on the streets. It was not wrong to assume, considering the rather brutish way he had treated the boys the previous evening. The pain in his leg had made him especially snappish, something Stefan had regretted the instant he woke the following morning. It was the main reason he hadn't woken them up, even though they had been sleeping on a pallet near the foot of his bed.

Stefan waved Sebastian's suggestion off with one hand. "There's no need for that. Tom—his name is Tom, correct?—Tom can sleep in for today. I'll expect him to be up bright and early the following morning, however. The horses don't wait for us to wake, even if I sometimes wish they would." He turned to the barrel of oats behind him. "Could you help me feed them? The oats are in this barrel."

"Of course." Sebastian sprang forward, reaching for the

metal scoop that sat atop the barrel. "What are their names?" He nodded at the thoroughbreds as he gathered oats into the scoop.

"Lake's Luck and Persnickety. Two finer horses you'll never find in this part of the States." Pride filled Stefan as he studied the thoroughbreds. "With proper care, they'll do quite well at the races. It's important for us to ensure that they don't get injured or sick on the way. That's why I chose to transport them on foot as opposed to train. There's too big a risk of illness, injury, and theft on the railways."

"I see." Sebastian dumped the scoop of oats into Lake's feeding trough. "Only one scoop?"

Stefan leaned against the wall so he could watch the lad. "Correct. Where are you from, Sebastian?"

"You can call me Bastian. Almost everyone that knows me does, with the exception of Tom," Sebastian said, dumping the oats into Lake's feeding trough. "My brother and I are from Chicago. We came here a few months ago to look for work. There wasn't anything left for us in the city, so we decided to leave and find a smaller town to live in. Our Chicago flat was getting too crowded, anyway."

Stefan caught the hidden meaning behind the boy's words. The pain reflected in Bastian's gaze solidified his suspicions. "The fire?"

Bastian's jaw tightened, and he didn't say more. He didn't have to.

Bastian was solemn for a young man—more solemn than Tom, it seemed. Stefan had spoken to the brothers for only a few moments the previous evening, but it had been enough for him to get a sense of just how different in personality the two were. The doctor that cared for Vater had told him that each person handled grief in their own way, and it seemed as though the twins were no different.

"I'm sorry," Stefan murmured. "It must have been hard to leave."

Bastian bowed his head, stroking Lake softly behind the ear as the horse munched on its breakfast. "It was. I stopped speaking of it for that very reason. I figure it's best to look ahead and not behind."

"I understand." Stefan pushed off the wall and moved to stand next to the boy. "In that case, let's speak of this no longer. Why don't you help me get the harness on Orion?" He gestured in the horse's direction.

Bastian looked up, his gaze shining with silent gratitude. "Of course."

Stefan tucked his hands behind his back, watching as the boy went to greet the Percheron. He knew all too well what it was like to want to run from the past. And he knew that, no matter how hard he tried, he couldn't escape it forever. Nobody could. It had a funny way of coming back to haunt a person.

As they hefted the harness onto Orion's back, a sound at the front of the barn drew Stefan's attention. Charlotte stood near the doorway in a plain brown dress that ran a few sizes too large, making her look as though she was drowning in the fabric folds. Her gloves and hat were the same. Did she have any others? Probably not.

"Good morning!" She ambled over, her head tilting slightly as she studied the two of them. "How are you two getting along?"

Stefan finished fastening the harness and turned, folding his arms across his chest. "Well enough. Are you prepared to leave? The sun rose over an hour ago, you know."

Charlotte pursed her lips. "Yes. There's no need to be snippy. I'm not all that late."

Stefan winced, guilt flashing through him. *There you go again with your big mouth.* "I'm sorry. I didn't mean to sound rude."

Charlotte smiled, her expression bright as sunshine. Well, not quite. There was something hiding behind her eyes that, to Stefan, seemed to block out the light. Perhaps she hadn't gotten a proper amount of sleep. "How do you fare? Was the room suitable?" He blurted out the query, surprising himself with his own impulsiveness.

Charlotte blinked, clearly caught off guard by the rather improper question. "I'm well, thank you. The room was lovely. It was a whole lot better than sleeping in a barn, anyway." She chuckled. "I was glad to wake up without hay in my hair."

Stefan hummed, his brain failing to come up with a response. "*G-gut*," he eventually stuttered, mentally cursing himself for the silence that followed. If only he could think of something eloquent to say. Why did his tongue remain so stubbornly tied?

Bastian broke the quiet. "You know German?"

"A bit, thanks to my father." Stefan grabbed hold of Orion's halter and led the horse toward the wagon at the center of the barn, grateful for the change of topic. "He emigrated here from Germany when he was just a bit younger than I am now. Twenty-four, I believe."

"That's interesting. How old are you, then?" Bastian trailed after Stefan with Charlotte close behind, tucking his arms behind his back.

A snort escaped Stefan as he hitched Orion to the wagon. "Curious, aren't you? Twenty-seven." He led Orion out of the barn and into the morning light, bringing him to a halt just outside the building. Turning to Bastian, he fixed the boy with a stern eye. "Now, go and wake your brother. Once the thoroughbreds have been tied to the wagon, we'll set off."

"Yes, sir." Bastian straightened and took off toward the inn, leaving Stefan alone with Charlotte.

"I must admit, I didn't expect you to be as young as you are." Charlotte accepted Stefan's hand, hefting herself and her bag onto the wagon bench. "That's not meant to be an insult," she quickly added. "You surprised me, that's all."

Stefan joined her on the bench, though her bag was once again positioned between them. "Do I really seem older than I am?" Yet, even as he voiced the question, he already knew the answer. He wasn't eighteen anymore. He had become worn and tired, with a gait more suited to a man of eighty than one in his mid-twenties. *Confounded leg.* Stefan adjusted the offending limb. He envied the twins, who ran back across the street with ease and tossed their few belongings into the wagon. Their agility was the main reason he had chosen to climb into the wagon instead of retrieving the thoroughbreds. It would save his limb a lot of pain.

"Sorry for my tardiness, lady and gentleman. I will endeavor to awake at an earlier hour in the future," Tom announced, pausing near Stefan's side of the wagon with a grin on his face. The young man's hair was disheveled, with red curls falling onto his forehead and tumbling over his eyes. His clothing was wrinkled in a similar manner, making Stefan wonder if Charlotte's statement that the boys needed someone to watch over them wasn't entirely incorrect. Should he try and find them some new clothing? Where would he even do such a thing? They didn't have time to get anything made, and he didn't know of any shops along the way.

"What's the first thing you need me to do, Mr. Roberts?" Tom's question brought an abrupt end to Stefan's perusal. He tucked the thought about clothing away for the time being. It was an issue he would consider later on.

"I need you two to fetch the thoroughbreds from the stable and tie a length of rope to each of their harnesses. From there, bring them here and use the rope to attach them to the back of the wagon," he instructed, pointing toward the stalls.

Tom shoved his cap on his head. "Right. Back in a jiffy." The rambunctious lad darted toward the barn, followed closely by his less enthusiastic brother.

Charlotte tilted her head. "What a curious boy. Quite a showman, no?"

Stefan leaned back on the bench. "Indeed. I don't believe I'll have a quiet moment again."

The smile fell from Charlotte's face as she watched the twins disappear into the stable. "I know you didn't want the twins to come with us, but I'm grateful that you allowed it. I fear what would have happened to them if they were left to fend for themselves." She turned to Stefan, her gaze serious. "Nobody deserves to be left alone, Stefan, especially not at their age. Thank you for allowing them to come along. I'm sorry to have foisted so much on you in such a short time."

Stefan sighed as the boys reemerged with the horses in hand. "What's done is done. I hope they'll be able to keep up. Traveling for days on end on my schedule won't be leisurely."

"Neither is sleeping on the ground. You're doing a fine thing, Stefan. Even if they don't stay for the entire journey, they'll remember your kindness for a very long time."

Was it kindness if Stefan was simply allowing them to come with? Or was he putting them in a life far harsher than the one they were already living? And why did it matter to him whether Charlotte thought he was doing the right thing? The more she spoke to Stefan, the more confused he became. On one hand, he enjoyed her company. But on the other hand, her words tended to make him jumpy. But why did her cheerful demeanor grate so much on his nerves?

Stefan's shoulders drooped. He knew why, though he had been dodging the answer. He was afraid of what would happen if Charlotte and the boys learned about his mistake. The one that had cost him so much and destroyed his home.

Why would they want anything to do with a man who couldn't save his own family?

~

"Say, it's a bit quiet around here. Do you mind if I play a song or two on my banjo?" Tom leaned his elbows on the back of the wagon bench in order to glance between Stefan and Charlotte.

"I'm not opposed," Charlotte replied, turning to Stefan as though for confirmation.

Stefan rolled his shoulders back, mentally preparing his ears for whatever lay ahead. He had been enjoying the silence, but he wasn't about to turn the boy down. "Go on."

Tom whooped and reached for the instrument he had set near his feet. A few moments later, a cheerful tune echoed through the clearing. Surprisingly, the young man was quite proficient at playing the banjo. Notes danced and sang through the air as the strings plucked out a jaunty song Stefan could have sworn he recognized. If he remembered correctly, the words that went with it were about two young lovers.

The music brought back faint memories of a different time. A piano had rendered the tune then, but the cheerful melody had been the same. And the person who had played the song had been, like Tom—young, innocent, and carefree.

Suddenly, in his mind, blue and gray on the ground mixed with screaming that cut off all music and joy. Red on whitish-gold, two colors that never should have mixed. He was falling, falling...

"Stop." Stefan twisted in his seat. "Stop!"

Tom froze, his left hand poised over the neck of the banjo. He stared at Stefan in wide-eyed fear. "Sorry, sir. I didn't mean to make you angry."

Stefan forced himself to let go of the reins, which had become tangled in his hands. *Get your head back in the present, Stefan. You're scaring him.* "It's fine. Just leave the banjo alone for the time being. Please," he muttered, turning back to the front. "It's distracting."

Charlotte frowned and cast a concerned look in his direction. "I, for one, thought it was very nice. Where did you learn to play so well, Tom?"

Tom remained silent a moment before answering, as though assessing what Stefan's reaction to the question might be. "My grandfather and father were excellent musicians. They taught Bastian and I how to play so we could continue the family tradition. I can only hope to someday be as good as they were."

"That's lovely, Tom." Charlotte turned to look at Bastian, who sat beside Tom in the wagon bed. "And what instrument do you play, Sebastian?"

"You can call me Bastian, miss. I used to play the bodhrán, a sort of drum you hold in your hand. My pa brought it from Ireland back when he first came to America."

"'Used to'? Did you stop playing?"

"Yes." The word was soft, low enough that for a moment Stefan wasn't certain he had heard it. "I don't play anymore. Music never was my strong suit."

Stefan didn't miss the emotion that colored the boy's voice. It seemed as though music held dark memories for both of them.

CHAPTER 10

The chirping of a bird in distress was the first indication that something was wrong. Stefan glanced between the trees, searching in vain for the little creature that was making such a harsh noise. Finding none, he turned his gaze back toward the road and attempted to focus on driving. Yet, no matter how hard he tried, he couldn't ignore the bird's warning cries. They were unsettling, a clear indicator that something dangerous lurked nearby.

Stefan blinked and rolled his shoulders, trying to shake the feeling of unease. "It's only a bird," he murmured, shifting in his seat. "It's probably angry at a hawk or some other creature."

"Did you say something, Stefan?" Charlotte had been silent ever since speaking with Bastian, making Stefan wonder if she was thinking about his strange outburst.

He swallowed, the tips of his ears warming. *What a wonderful first impression I've made. I probably seem like a madman.* "I was just considering the bird in the trees over that way. It sounds distressed, and I was wondering what's frightening it."

Charlotte glanced toward the trees. "It is quite loud, isn't it? I suppose a predator must have gotten too close to its nest."

Stefan opened his mouth to respond, but faint hoofbeats cut him off. Every one of his nerves flew into alert, and a horrible feeling crawled like a spider down his spine. Despite the logical voice in his head that told him he was probably overreacting, he rotated quickly in his seat, scouring the road for the source of the sound.

In the distance, a rider thundered down the lane. A hat hung low on the person's head, hiding the face, and a black cape billowed around broad shoulders. Something inside Stefan shouted a loud and clear warning.

"Hang on, everyone." Stefan gave a sharp whistle. Orion jolted forward at the signal, making the wagon jump and bounce as they raced at breakneck speed for a nearby side path.

"Goodness! Where are we going?" Charlotte cried, clasping the brim of her hat with one hand and the edge of the wooden bench with the other. She was jostled to and fro as the wagon rolled over a divot in the road and released a small "oof."

"Off the road before that rider passes." Stefan steered Orion deftly onto the side path and behind a thick stand of maple and birch trees. Drawing the horse to a halt, he tried to calm his racing heart as the hoofbeats drew nearer.

"Stefan? What is it?" Charlotte whispered, her gaze worried. Clearly, she could see his distress. "Do you know that man?"

"No, but I have a bad feeling. Please, trust me and stay silent until he goes by."

Charlotte pressed her lips together, and they fell into an uneasy silence as the rider closed in on their position.

Stefan caught a glimpse of the man and his horse through the trees. They had slowed to a walk, and the rider was glancing around as though looking for something—or someone. Stefan's throat ran dry. Dust from the wagon still hung in the air where he had spurred Orion into a run, which was likely what made the stranger slow. Had he seen them turn onto the path? Would he come after them?

For a moment, the man's gaze seemed to pass over the very spot where the wagon was hidden. Stefan held his breath, not willing to move even an inch lest he give their position away. Charlotte sat stiffly beside him, mimicking his frozen posture, and the lack of noise from the back of the wagon indicated the twins were doing the same. Then, to his immense relief, the rider let out a sharp whistle, and the horse leaped back into motion. Within a few seconds, they had galloped away, leaving the road in silence once more.

Stefan let out a loud breath and sagged against the wagon bench, raking his hair under his hat with trembling fingers. *Thank goodness.*

"Who was that?" Tom's curious voice hissed from behind Stefan's ear.

Stefan shook his head. "I don't know, but he was looking for someone. I fear what would have happened if he had overtaken us." There was something very wrong about the stranger.

Charlotte blinked at him. "A highwayman?"

"Most likely." Stefan steered Orion back onto the main road, trying to calm his racing heart. "We need to be careful from now on. There's no telling who or what is waiting for us around the corner."

The man's search hadn't seemed random. It was as if he'd been looking for something. Stefan glanced at Charlotte, the thought deepening into suspicion. *Or someone.*

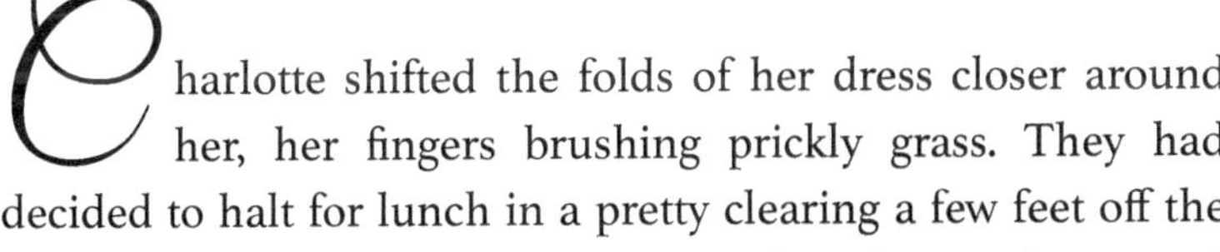

*C*harlotte shifted the folds of her dress closer around her, her fingers brushing prickly grass. They had decided to halt for lunch in a pretty clearing a few feet off the road. Stefan had parked the wagon under a large oak tree and left the horses to graze in the field, which provided Charlotte the perfect place to eat her meal. She had selected one of the wheels to lean against, allowing her to rest while also keeping an eye on the surrounding area. The apple in her hand glistened in the sun as she tilted it to and fro, her thoughts darting between Stefan and the strange man from the road.

"This Mr. Roberts of yours is quite a strange fellow, don't you think?" Tom mused from behind Charlotte's head. He had hopped aboard the wagon and perched on the edge of the vehicle, leaving his scuffed boots to dangle in the corner of her vision. A moment later, the boy's shoes hit the ground with a soft thump, and he sat down beside her, clearly dissatisfied with her lack of response. "Do you really think that horseman was following us?"

Charlotte considered her words a moment before opening her mouth. "Stefan...is a bit odd, I'll admit. However, I don't think his fears are entirely unwarranted." She smiled as Lake and Persnickety playfully tossed their heads. "There could very well have been a thief following us."

Tom shrugged his thin shoulders. "I suppose. Regardless, I'm not afraid of any old highwayman. I think we should stay and confront him. We could fend him off."

Charlotte laughed before taking a bite of her apple. She chewed for a second before answering. "Well, that's very brave of you." She swiped juice from her face with the back of one hand. "However, I still believe Stefan's plan was safer."

Tom glanced across the clearing. "He seems a bit paranoid to me. Did you see how he reacted to my banjo playing? Who doesn't like music?" He drew his knees to his chest and set his elbows atop them, resting his chin on his hand. "Bas seems to like him, though. I wonder why." With his free hand, he gestured to his brother, who was currently helping Stefan carry buckets of water up to the horses from the nearby creek.

Charlotte rested her cheek in her hand as Stefan placed a

bucket before Persnickety and began scratching the horse's neck, causing the animal to bob its head up and down. A gentle look adorned his face as he ran a hand over the horse's back, brushing some of the dust from Persnickety's fur. Clearly, he cared very deeply for the horses. "I imagine Sebastian sees what's beneath all of that surliness, as I do. Stefan is a kind man. I'm sure of it. He's simply a little harsh around the edges." Why, she didn't know. The man had put up walls of stone and evidently wasn't eager to let her in.

"I can't help but wonder what happened to his leg. Do you think he was in the war? Maybe he got shot by a Rebel bullet." Tom mimicked holding up a rifle and squinted as though sighting an enemy. "I'll bet he did. That would account for the way he jumps at every sound. I've heard loads of stories about men who stayed angry and afraid after going to battle." He brightened, lowering the imaginary rifle. "Do you think he would tell us stories about the battles he was in?"

Charlotte shook her head. "I'm not certain, but even if he would, I wouldn't care to hear. That war was an awful thing. It very nearly took my father's life. He came back just as paranoid as Stefan, if not more." Which was why she hadn't been entirely frightened by his outburst on the road. It was clear that the man was struggling with something, and while it would have been easy to dismiss him as having lost his senses, Charlotte knew there was a different reason for Stefan's snappish attitude. He was suffering in the same way her father had suffered, and it only made her feel sorrier for the man.

Tom straightened with a regretful expression. "Oh. I'm sorry, Miss Charlotte. I shouldn't have brought it up."

"No, no. There's no harm in speaking about it. However, considering the pain it brings me, I don't think it wise to ask Stefan. He's already on edge, and we don't need to make things worse."

Tom stretched his legs out, crossing one over the other.

"True. He asked me to guard the horses. As if anyone would try to take them with the whole lot of us here." The boy folded his arms. "No matter. If anyone did try, I'd stop him before he could blink."

Charlotte couldn't help but smile. "And how do you intend to do that? Hit him over the head with your banjo?"

"I would never waste my banjo on a thief. I'd rather pop him on the nose and risk bruising my knuckles." Tom took a few swings at the air in demonstration.

"Well, I think you had better go and help Bastian before *you're* on the receiving end of some violence." Charlotte pointed to where Bastian stood a few feet away with a dark look on his face, Lake drinking from the bucket on the ground beside him. "I get the impression that you were meant to be bringing water up from the creek with your brother."

Tom hopped to his feet, brushing the dirt from his trousers. "Guilty as charged, but Mr. Roberts did say I should keep an eye on the horses. I simply chose the more fun job." He grinned impishly and darted across the field to his brother, who pushed him on the shoulder.

Charlotte watched in bemusement as the twins raced each other to the river. "Silly boys," she murmured, turning back to look for Stefan. He was making his way up the hill in her direction, his limp more pronounced with the sharp incline. Charlotte averted her eyes to avoid causing him any embarrassment.

Luckily, Orion was only a foot from where she sat, so she called his name. To her surprise, the horse looked up and ambled over, ears pricked and eyes wide. "Well, hello, there. You listen very well for a horse." She laughed, stroking the Percheron's soft nose as he snuffled the remains of her apple "Hungry, aren't you? You can have it."

The horse munched contentedly on the apple, his gray ears flicking back and forth and his nostrils quivering.

A dark shadow crossed Charlotte's vision. Looking up, she

found Stefan standing in front of her with his arms crossed over his chest. "Spoiling my horse, are you?"

Charlotte was about to apologize when she noticed the humorous glint in his eyes. "Perhaps. After pulling the wagon for hours on end, he deserves a treat." The corners of her mouth tugged up against her will.

"Fair enough." Stefan leaned against the side of the wagon. For a time, they rested in silence, watching as the twins refilled both buckets and brought them back up from the creek. They set one in front of the thoroughbreds and the other in front of Orion, who had wandered over to see what they were doing.

"I'm a bit worried." Stefan's voice broke the stillness, soft but honest, and Charlotte tipped her head back to observe him. A thick lock of hair had escaped his hat to drape over his forehead, nearly covering his eyes. His furrowed brows formed deep grooves in a forehead that should have been smooth with youth. His frown, too, seemed deeply etched on his face. Stefan did not look like a man of only twenty-seven. Had he fought like Tom guessed? It wasn't hard to imagine. So many had left their homes to serve in the war, and he was likely one of that number.

"About what?" Charlotte pulled a blade of grass to roll between her fingers.

Stefan shifted from one foot to the other. "That we won't make it to Kentucky on time. We were on a tight schedule to begin with, but with the addition of the twins and this matter of the horseman, we've slowed considerably. If anything else should occur, we'll miss the races, and I'll have let my father down." He hefted a sigh. "I would hate to do that."

Charlotte sat up a bit straighter and discarded the grass. "I doubt your father will be disappointed, especially once you tell him how much you helped me and the twins. I should think he would be more pleased to know you did a good deed."

"You don't know the man. He would be glad to know I

helped you, but his livelihood depends on my getting the horses to Kentucky. If we cannot sell them, we won't have enough to live by."

Charlotte swallowed, guilt draping her chest and heart. She had assumed that Stefan would be able to care for the twins without even asking if he had enough money to do so.

"I'm sorry, Stefan. I wouldn't have suggested the twins come with us if I knew you were in such a difficult place."

Stefan lifted a shoulder, his eyes crinkling at the corners. "I might have minded at first, but they shouldn't be forced to live on the streets. Besides, all will be well if we can get to the races on time." He tilted his head. "The horses should both sell without a problem. They're the only ones ready to race this season, unfortunately. Lake very nearly wasn't."

"What happened to him?" Charlotte turned, studying the racehorse.

"His leg was injured while our jockey was working with him." Stefan gestured to one of the thoroughbred's back legs. "We feared it would never heal. I worked with Lake for months to get him back in shape."

"Months? I imagine that took a lot of work. You must love the horses and the stables very much."

"Yes." Stefan gazed at the horses, his eyes softening. "They've helped me a great deal."

"Perhaps you should eventually take over for your father, then. I'm sure you'd do a fine job." Charlotte fiddled with the brim of her hat. "It seems as though you have a fair idea of the way your father likes his business run. You'd be the next logical successor, wouldn't you? Unless you have siblings, of course."

A grimace crossed Stefan's face, as though her words pained him. "I was meant to take over his position, and I've wanted to relieve my father of his workload for a very long time. However, he refuses to relinquish any of it. It makes me sad, seeing how taxing it is on him, but there's little I can do without his permission. I can only wait and hope that at some point, he'll realize I can be trusted to run the business."

"And what of your mother? Does she have much to say on the matter?"

Stefan's face twisted, and he ducked his head. "No. She passed on long ago. It is one of the reasons I allowed Vater to retain full control over the stables. He needed the work to distract him."

"I'm sorry. It seems we have one thing in common, then," Charlotte said quietly.

"More than you think, Charlotte. Some of the things I have witnessed do not bear describing." Stefan lifted his head and looked out into the clearing, his voice so sad that Charlotte couldn't help but say something to try and comfort him.

"But we are here now, aren't we? Surrounded by blue skies and a newly awakened forest. It's certainly worth appreciating."

"That is true. If only it could all be like the present," Stefan muttered. "But the future is too uncertain."

Charlotte rested a hand on the locket at her throat and watched the twins, who were in the midst of a friendly tussle. Tom had tipped a bucket of water over Bastian's head and was fleeing his soaked brother, who chased after him with a vengeful expression. "It can't be all that bad—not if those two are in it." She laughed. "Had we not detoured to stop at the inn, we never would have discovered them."

Stefan studied the twins with a glint in his eye. "Yes, indeed. They're interesting boys. Tom seems like a bit of an imp, doesn't he?"

Charlotte tilted her head. "A prankster, yes, but he means no harm. He simply wants a bit of attention. As he's been on his own for what I assume to be a long time, he needs someone to look up to. Someone who will be proud of him. All children do, really."

"You're more perceptive than you let on. Tell me, what do you see when you look at Bastian?"

Charlotte bit the inside of her cheek to prevent herself from giggling as Bastian finally managed to tackle his brother from behind, bringing them both tumbling to the ground. "When I speak with Bastian, I see a boy who is eager to please and terribly uncertain about himself. A boy who's too shy to speak up to his brother."

"You discovered all that from talking with them?"

Charlotte dropped her hands to her lap and fiddled with the folds of her dress. "No. It's also in the way they act and the manner in which they speak. It's in the way they pretend to be brave, even though they are nothing more than boys."

"And what do you see when you look at me, Charlotte?"

Charlotte turned to look into eyes that gazed back at her with an intensity that put her in mind of a clear sky on bitterly cold day. Something fluttered in her stomach as she stared into those eyes, and she swallowed. "I see sadness," she whispered. "Deep, tired sadness, though you cover it with a blanket of thorns."

Stefan averted his gaze, looking back out at the clearing. For a moment, he said nothing, letting a heavy silence settle between them. And then he spoke. "It's funny you should say that, Charlotte. I see the same thing in you."

~

As the sun sank low in the sky, the wagon came to a stop in front of a small inn. Charlotte didn't know the name of the town they were in, but it was small and homey, with a restaurant that smelled of enticing food and a few small businesses along the road. The waning daylight cast a warm glow over the buildings, throwing shades of yellow and purple on the faded boards. Chatter echoed from somewhere in the town, though the streets were bare of all but a few individuals. It was enough to make Charlotte want to fall asleep right then and there. However, the promise of a roof over her head kept her going.

"Ladies and gentlemen, we have arrived at our final stop for the evening," she said in an imitation of a train conductor, lowering herself to the ground. "All passengers must disembark."

The twins laughed as they joined her, racing into the inn a moment later. Left alone with Stefan, Charlotte pulled her carpetbag from the wagon bench and took a step toward the barn at the back of the inn.

"Charlotte." Stefan's voice sounded from over her shoulder, deep and knowing.

Charlotte froze. "Yes?"

"You don't need to sleep in the barn. I'll pay for your stay." He moved to stand beside her. "Go inside and find rooms for us."

"Are you certain? I hate to take money from you." Charlotte hefted her bag higher in her arms. "It feels so...low of me. Especially after what I did with the twins."

Stefan set a hand on the wagon, a smile appearing on his face for a moment despite the circles beneath his eyes. Clearly, the long, stressful day of travel had worn him out. "I assure you, it was not low in the least. If you take a room at the inn, it will give me peace of mind. So, really, you're doing me a favor by accepting my offer."

Charlotte huffed a quiet laugh and turned toward the inn. "Very well."

As small as the town was, it wasn't hard to secure two vacant rooms. Charlotte sent the twins off to the one they would share with Stefan with the promise to meet them early the next morning. Then she made her way over to the inn's warm fireplace, where she waited for Stefan to return from the stables.

After a long few minutes, Stefan trudged in, his face weary. "Ah, Charlotte. Why aren't you in your room?"

"I wanted to ensure that you...well, that you made it in safely. Thank you once again for paying for our lodgings. It is incredibly kind of you." Charlotte plucked a piece of hay from the man's shoulder, her gloved fingers brushing the fabric of his coat. "Will you be all right?" she added softly.

Stefan looked up, his gaze softening. "Yes, Charlotte, I will be all right. And it truly is no trouble to pay for your room." He jerked his head in the direction of the hall. "Now, go and get some rest. We have another long day tomorrow."

Charlotte found her room at the end of the hallway. Just before she unlocked the door, she paused and faced Stefan, who appeared to be waiting for the twins to open the door. "Good night, Stefan," she murmured.

He glanced at her, his eyes shining in the dim lamplight. "Good night, Charlotte. Rest well."

She quickly turned away so he wouldn't see the blush spreading across her face. It was only due to his kindness that her heart had begun to pick up in speed. Wasn't it?

CHAPTER 11

lond hair matched gold buttons flashing on a navy uniform. "Stefan, now I can join you in the cavalry. We'll go to war together. As brothers should."

Stefan rolled over in bed, releasing a harsh breath.

Cannons rumbled, a deep thrumming that mixed with the galloping of horses' hooves. His saber clashed against his side and Orion's muscles stretched beneath him as the horse plunged into the chaos. Gunfire echoed in the clearing and felled the man riding in front of him.

He shoved the blankets away, heart pounding.

Crushed beneath a dead horse lay his brother's broken body, that same blond hair stained with red. More gunshots, and then—

Boom. A crash of thunder brought Stefan upright in bed, sweat running down his temple. He snapped his head back and forth, taking in the unfamiliar surroundings. It took a moment to remember he was at the inn, far in distance and time from the memories still flooding his mind. He swiped at his forehead with a trembling hand, his heart still beating wildly from the all-too-familiar dream. A dream that haunted him whenever he managed to fall into a deep sleep.

Outside, rain battered the windows in a relentless torrent, flinging droplets against the glass with a sound like bullets. Every few seconds, the flash of lightning warned of an oncoming crash of thunder, loud enough to make Stefan jump. He swung his legs over the side of the bed, searching in the dark for the box of matches he had set on the nightstand. Finding it, he hurriedly lit the lamp at the side of the bed. Warm light illuminated the room, and relief flooded him.

Stefan let out a shuddering breath and ran a hand through his hair, pushing it off his forehead. He studied the faces of the twins, who slept peacefully on their pallet near the back of the room. Luckily, his outburst hadn't awakened them. What would he have done if it had? There was no easy way to explain the memories that dogged his every moment of sleep.

Once Stefan's heart had slowed, he reached for the Bible on the nightstand. He opened the cracked leather cover and traced Mother's name on the inside page, studying her elegant handwriting next to the sharp, choppy strokes of Vater's. "I'm sorry," he whispered. "I'm sorry I failed you both. I should have tried harder to keep Franz from joining up."

His little brother had been so proud to help Stefan fight, so eager, that he hadn't fully considered the consequences. But Stefan had. He had known full well what it meant to go to battle, and he had let Franz enlist without revealing the boy's age. The day of his brother's first and only skirmish had haunted him since.

Yet once the enlistment paper was signed, he couldn't really have stopped his brother. To not appear for duty would have resulted in Franz being labeled a deserter, an insult that his brother never would have forgiven him for. Franz had chosen to fight, even though he knew it might end in his demise.

If Stefan were an optimist, he might have said that Franz's death was a kind one, quick and most likely painless. But he couldn't find anything good about it, not with his brother's pale, frozen face permanently etched in his mind. On the trip back to Kentucky, with the simple wooden coffin in the back of the wagon, it had haunted him. While he told his parents their son wasn't coming home, it had hung over his head like a dark cloud.

War was a cruel thing. It had ended long ago, and yet Stefan still awoke with every storm and dreaded every sudden noise. He was plagued by the same terrible dream, over and over.

Stefan slid the Bible shut. Could there ever be an end to the torment? Was it true what Miss Clarke said, that he was holding onto a bitter sadness? If so, how could he let go of it?

For he had to let go of it. If Stefan didn't find a way to overcome the darkness inside him, it would very likely consume him. He could hide it away and cover it up, but there was no escaping it. His nightmares were proof that his despair had not gone far.

Stefan looked at the Bible in his lap. "Help me," he whispered. "If You're listening, please give me the peace I need. I know there must be something better than this. This...this isn't living. Please, help me." *Please.*

❧

*M*orning dawned soggy and cold, the gray sky doing nothing to improve Charlotte's mood as she trudged across the street to the stables. "Silly mud," she grumbled, shaking her skirts in a fruitless attempt to clear some of the muck from the hem. Once she reached the stable door, she wasted no time in pushing it open and hurrying out of the thick fog.

Inside the stable, it was a bit drier, but no less cold. Quiet rustling echoed through the building as horses shifted in their stalls, their soft nickers filling the air. A few of the animals studied Charlotte as she wandered into the middle of the aisle and glanced around, their brown eyes blinking. She smiled. She couldn't blame Stefan for being drawn to the stables, not when it was so peaceful and inviting. That being said, she couldn't see where he had gone. "Stefan? Are you there?" she called, glancing into the stall closest to her as she moved farther into the building.

"I'm here, Charlotte."

The response came from the last stall, followed by the appearance of Stefan. *Oh dear.* Dark circles ringed the man's eyes, a sure sign of a poor night's sleep. His disheveled hair and rumpled shirt only added to the image. Had the storm contributed to his state? It had certainly woken Charlotte up a time or two, but she had fallen back asleep.

"Ah, there you are! Good morning, Stefan. I was hoping to find you at the inn, but the clerk told me that you had already left." Charlotte spoke with an excess of cheer, attempting to disguise her shock at his appearance. "How long have you been out here, exactly?"

Stefan winced, turning away from Charlotte to stroke Orion's nose. "Do I really look that bad?" Her expression must have betrayed her, for he released a long breath. "I've been here for a while. I had a rough evening, as I'm sure you can tell. That storm was exceptionally loud, and I awoke the instant it began. In the end, I couldn't fall back asleep and decided to come to the stables."

Charlotte could sense that there was more to his sleeplessness than just the storm, but she would not press for details. "I never liked storms either. It always frightened our cow, Gertrude, too. She kicked a hole in our shed during a particularly noisy thunderstorm. It took me a whole day to repair. Then again, I was never particularly good at that sort of thing."

Stefan remained with his back turned toward her. "Was she always so ornery?"

"Goodness, no. Trudy was as sweet as a cow could be. Why, she even saved my life."

This seemed to get Stefan's attention, for he swiveled around to face her. "In what way?"

"During the fire, I jumped on her back, and she carried me to the safety of the river. I held onto her all through the night, until I finally passed out from exhaustion. Why, had it not been for Trudy, I doubt I would have even reached the river. She was a very intelligent creature to have found the water through the smoke and flames. I do hope someone took her in after the fire died down." Charlotte tapped a finger against her cheek. "I didn't have a chance to take her with me. When I awoke, I was in a makeshift hospital a whole town over."

"Animals are incredible, aren't they?" Stefan turned a fond smile on Orion, and the horse whinnied softly in response.

Charlotte hummed. "That they are." She let silence settle over them for a moment before speaking again. "Are you truly all right, Stefan? If you need someone to talk to, I'm here."

Stefan's shoulders drooped ever so slightly, and for a moment, Charlotte feared she had gone too far. However, his next words proved her wrong. "Thank you, Charlotte. To tell the truth, I am not entirely certain. But I believe things will improve with time. At least, I hope they will." His voice held a thinly veiled note of desperation that tugged at Charlotte's heart.

"I'm certain they will. Things will turn out just fine."

If only she could believe her own words. But it was proving to be difficult when her own future hung in the balance.

~

A drizzle descended upon the wagon as they plodded along the road, permeating Charlotte's dress despite the umbrella that Stefan had wedged between them. She had no coat, and instead had settled for pulling her blanket around her. The thin material did little to shield her from the poor weather. Stefan and the twins seemed equally miserable, for all three of them sat with hunched shoulders and sagging hats.

Stefan focused on the road, clearly determined to keep the wagon from sinking into another patch of mud. It was working, for the wheels remained free of muck and Orion had no trouble finding steady footing. The downside was they were moving at a snail's pace. By the time Tom checked his pocket watch and announced that it was noon, they had traveled only a few miles, which Stefan didn't seem pleased about.

"We'll stop here for a bit," he stated, removing his hat and banging it against the wagon bench to rid it of water. "There's no point in continuing on when I can hardly see the road. Hopefully, the mist will clear up soon. In the meantime, I'm going to check the horses' hooves. It's easy for them to step on sharp stones in the mud." He set the hat back on his head and grimaced when a few droplets of water splattered onto his face.

Tom hopped down from the wagon, landing in a water puddle. "Good grief, it's cold. Blasted spring storms," the boy grumbled, moving toward the back of the wagon.

Charlotte followed suit, lowering herself cautiously to the ground and searching for a place to sit and eat the sliced ham she had bought before they left.

A few feet from the wagon, she discovered a small river, its dark waters barely visible through the fog. The recent rain had caused the current to swell, eating away at the dirt on the river-bank. "I suppose this is as good a spot as any," Charlotte murmured, looking for a relatively dry spot on which to sit. Finding none, she resigned herself to standing while she munched on her ham.

While it was undoubtedly cold and wet, she couldn't help but feel content as she gazed through the mist at the river. After living in the city for so many months, she had nearly forgotten how quiet it was in the country. The only sounds she could hear were the tapping of rain on tree leaves and the quiet shushing of the river. In Peshtigo, she had often walked down to the river for one reason or another. There was something wonderful about the pure peace that came from being surrounded by nature, left alone to sort through one's thoughts. Charlotte had nearly forgotten how much she had enjoyed her nature walks. Had it really been so long since she had last ambled through a forest, with nobody but the birds in the trees for company? The last time she had gone on a walk through the woods had been with Edwin. She gazed down at her rain-soaked skirts, guilt overwhelming her. The last conversation she had held with her friend had been an argument. Had he even survived the fire?

"Not exactly perfect weather for a picnic, is it?" a familiar voice said from behind her.

Charlotte half smiled and replied without turning around. "No, but there's something enjoyable about it all the same. It's quiet, for one."

Stefan hummed, coming to stand beside her. He held the umbrella in one hand and moved it over Charlotte so they were both safe beneath the oiled black canvas. When she gave him a questioning look, he explained, "It wouldn't do for you to catch cold."

"Thank you." Charlotte cleared her throat, trying to ignore the way her heart was speeding up at his closeness. "It is a bit chilly for April, isn't it?"

"That it is. Hopefully, it will clear up within the next day or so. I wouldn't want to continue traveling in this weather, not when I could run us off the road. I don't feel like pushing the wagon free again. We may not be able to find another good Samaritan like John either."

"I agree."

For a moment, they stood in silence, listening to the pitter-patter of raindrops on the umbrella.

"You know, before you came up behind me, I was just thinking of how much this reminds me of Peshtigo." Charlotte pursed her lips. "Or, at least, what it was like before the fire."

Stefan shifted beside her. "What was it like? Did you live there your whole life?"

"Yes, I was born and raised there. There was a river quite like this one that ran through the middle of town. I mostly went there on sunny afternoons, but sometimes I journeyed through the rain to see what I could find on the shore. Oftentimes, the storms would stir things up from the riverbed and toss them onto the beach. My sister, Carina, and I thought of it as a treasure hunt and ran up and down the riverbank in search of glass bottles and the like." Charlotte sniffed, the corners of her mouth twitching up. "We never found anything that could even remotely be considered treasure, but that didn't curb our enthusiasm in the least."

Stefan inclined his head. "I don't doubt it. Your sister seems as though she was a good person."

"She was." Charlotte shivered as if a gust of wind had brushed past her, though none had. "The day I learned she was gone was the darkest day of my life. I was so lost. I didn't know what I was going to do or where I would go." And to some extent, she still didn't. But that was a problem for another time. Getting to Kentucky and delivering the locket took precedence.

Stefan gazed at the dark river, clearly lost in his own thoughts. "I understand the feeling. Did they have a proper burial, at least?"

"I...I don't know." A pinprick of shame ran through Charlotte as she spoke the words. "The letter never said anything about a burial." And she hadn't been willing to find out. Her family was gone, and that was all she needed to know.

"Will you ever go back? To Peshtigo, I mean."

There it was. The question she had been dreading for months. *Will you go back?* Charlotte hesitated a moment, trying to find the words that would explain her feelings, before shaking her head. "I don't believe so. There can be nothing good gained from traveling back to that horrible place. It will only remind me of all that I've lost."

Stefan looked as though he was about to respond, but before he got the chance, a loud splash caused them both to whirl around.

"Tom!" Bastian cried. The boy was standing at the edge of the riverbank, near a dropoff a full foot above the water.

Tracking his frightened gaze, Charlotte spotted a familiar head of red hair in the middle of the river, followed by a flailing arm. "Good heavens. Tom fell in the river!" She gathered her skirts in one hand and ran toward Bastian, her heart thudding in her chest. The sound of footsteps behind her offered reassurance that Stefan wasn't far behind.

"What happened?" Stefan demanded as they drew abreast of Bastian.

"We were walking along the edge of the river, and the ground caved in. Tom slid in before I could grab him. Mr. Roberts, you have to help him! He can't swim!" Worry wreathed Bastian's pale face.

"Hold this." Stefan shoved the umbrella at Charlotte before diving straight into the water and swimming with choppy strokes toward the hand sticking up in the river. After a moment, he reached Tom and attempted to haul the boy's head above the water.

Watching them struggle, Charlotte gasped. "Stefan has a bad leg! He can't hold both Tom and himself up. Bastian, we have to do something. They'll drown!"

Bastian whirled around, panic evident on his face. "I can't swim either!"

Darkness surrounded Charlotte's vision, followed by the

familiar sensation of her chest tightening. *They'll drown. They'll sink beneath the waves, and I'll never see them again.* She forced herself to breathe, willing herself to calm down. "You can't panic now, Charlotte Clarke," she whispered. "Think." After a moment, she snapped her fingers. "The horses! Follow me."

They raced from the riverbank, heading straight for the thoroughbreds. Moving quickly, Charlotte untied Lake's rope from the back of the wagon and grabbed the horse's halter, urging him forward. "Come on, Lake! Bastian, get that long rope from the wagon bed. The one Mr. Roberts keeps as an extra."

As the boy lurched into action, Charlotte struggled to get the thoroughbred moving. "Go, Lake!" Clearly alarmed by her raised voice, the horse pinned its ears back and dug its hooves into the ground, refusing to budge. "Lake, please!" She tugged on the halter and tried to ignore the panic again rising in her chest.

Finally, the thoroughbred took a single step, and then another. Charlotte led him as quickly as she was able to the riverbank, Bastian following close behind with the rope. Searching the water frantically, she spotted Stefan in the midst of the current. He had managed to lift Tom's head above the water, but the two were clearly struggling to stay afloat.

"Bastian, tie that rope to Lake's halter and toss it out to Stefan," Charlotte instructed. "On my call, we'll push Lake from the front."

Bastian hurried to do as he was told. "Grab on!" he shouted, flinging the end of the rope out over the water. The other end he fastened securely under Lake's harness with nimble fingers. The horse balked slightly at the quick movements but thankfully remained in place.

Charlotte watched with growing anxiety as the rope drifted closer to where Stefan struggled to tread water. To her relief, he grabbed hold and looped the rope around his arm. "I've got it!"

"All right! Lake, back up!" Charlotte leaned her shoulder into the horse's chest. "Go on!"

With a loud neigh, the thoroughbred moved back, his front hooves digging into the mud. His head was pulled forward by the weight of the two people. *It's too much.* He wouldn't be able to get them free of the current on his own.

Charlotte whirled and grabbed the rope, pulling with all her might. "Come on, Bastian!"

Bastian grabbed hold of the rope and yanked, his thin arms straining against the weight. Between the three of them, Stefan and Tom began to move closer and closer to shore.

"That's it! Just a bit more!" Charlotte loosened her hold on the rope and guided Lake back farther. A few moments later, the man and boy were pulled onto the beach, flopping onto their stomachs. Tom immediately heaved a breath and coughed up a mouthful of water, his shoulders quaking with the effort.

Charlotte called Lake to a halt and stroked the agitated horse's nose. "You did it," she whispered, her voice raw. "We did it. Thank you."

On the riverbank, Stefan slowly unwound the rope from his arm and reached over to pat Tom on the back. "Are you all right?" His voice was a mere croak.

Tom sucked in a breath, propping himself up on his elbows. "I'll be fine. Thank you," he mumbled, breaking into a coughing fit directly after. The poor boy's lips were purple, and his shirt was drenched. "I knew I should have learned to swim." His eyes were downcast, fixed on the muddy earth below him.

Stefan shook his head. "What possessed you to walk on the edge of a riverbank if you can't swim?"

Tom shrugged. "How was I supposed to know the bank would collapse?" He reached up to his hair and grimaced. "My cap is gone."

"Bastian, take Lake back to the wagon and fetch all the blankets you can find. We need to get your brother and Stefan warm and dry." Charlotte handed the horse over to the boy before hurrying to the figures huddled on the riverbank and bending over them. "Goodness, you two gave us a fright. Are you both all right? It was very brave of you to go after Tom, Stefan."

Stefan pushed himself up to a kneeling position and gazed at her from beneath dripping locks. His shoulders trembled with shivers, or perhaps from the exertion of holding himself afloat. "I'm fine, thank you. Just cold. It was very smart of *you* to get the horse and pull us out. Your quick thinking saved us."

"It was nothing. I'm glad we were able to reach you in time. I feared you both would drown before we could pull you out."

"We are still here and in one piece," Stefan said with a slight smile. The smile fell from his face a moment later, and he shifted from one side to the other. "Well, mostly in one piece."

"Whatever do you mean?" Concern filled Charlotte as she looked him over.

Stefan released a sigh and straightened his legs, revealing that one of his pant legs was partially deflated. "It would appear as though I've lost my leg."

CHAPTER 12

In retrospect, there were probably a dozen more eloquent and informative responses Stefan could have chosen to tell the group that his wooden leg had gone missing. After all, how else would they have known it was a prosthetic? He certainly hadn't made mention of the fact that the bottom half of his left leg was wooden. Instead, three horrified faces now stared at him, including Bastian's, who had just returned with a pile of blankets in his arms. Poor Charlotte had turned so pale face that Stefan feared she would fall into a dead faint.

"Perhaps I should clarify. I never had a leg to begin with. Well, I did, but I lost the part below the knee years ago and have had a wooden one ever since." Stefan winced at the way he stumbled over his words. "So you see, I'm really quite all right."

There was a moment of silence as Charlotte and the twins seemed to process Stefan's words. Tom was the first to recover. "How did you lose it?" He stared up at Stefan from where he was still lying flat on the bank.

"Tom," Bastian hissed, dropping a blanket over his brother's head. "That's not polite."

Charlotte's face had softened into an expression of sadness. Surprising. Normally, when he explained about his leg, people responded with sympathy or disdain "I wish I had known," she whispered. "All this time, I assumed you merely had an old injury."

Stefan shrugged and struggled to rise, which was made far more difficult with only one leg. Luckily, Bastian was quick to come to his aid, looping Stefan's arm over his shoulder so they could both straighten. "Thank you, Bastian." Stefan glanced at Charlotte. "It *is* an old injury—only, a bit worse than you thought." He attempted to turn, wincing in embarrassment when all he managed was a small hop to the side. "Of all the humiliating things, it had to be this." He would have to add a new leg to the list of expenses back home.

Bastian offered Stefan support as they began a slow walk back to the wagon. Once there, Stefan hefted himself into the vehicle with some difficulty and held out a hand for Charlotte, accepting the blanket she offered him a moment later. He tucked away the umbrella she'd retrieved from the riverbank and unfolded the blanket to drape it around his shoulders, blocking out some of the cold. The boys clambered into the back.

Stefan twisted on his perch, eyeing the twins. "I think it would be wise for us to head for the town we just passed. Tom could use a warm fire."

"Me? I'm not the only one who nearly drowned. You must be cold as well." Tom's teeth chattered as he answered.

"True. I would not be opposed to a fire myself." Stefan tapped the reins on Orion's back and turned the wagon around, heading back in the direction they had come from.

As they traveled, he could sense Charlotte trying her hardest not to stare at his leg. Stefan could not deny her an explanation forever, but it was not a story he relished telling. However, Charlotte had saved his life as well as told him about one of the darkest nights in her past. Stefan owed her the same. Even if the thought terrified him more than an actual battle.

~

Thunder rolled as Stefan steered Orion into the warmth of the stables, reverberating in his chest and making his heart thump faster than normal. He pulled the harness off the Percheron's tall back and hefted it into the wagon bed before leading Orion awkwardly to the closest stall, his balance shifting with every step. Luckily, the horse was able to take his weight with ease and held his head relatively still as Stefan clutched his halter.

"Thank you, my friend. I am sorry for this. It's been a day, hasn't it?" Stefan guided Orion into the stall and resisted the urge to shudder. He had changed out of his clothes before getting the horses settled, but the fresh waistcoat, shirt, and trousers hadn't done much to warm him. Not to mention his leg was hurting even more than usual after having dove into the river. Had he considered the situation more, he might have tried to find another way to save Tom, perhaps throwing a rope as Charlotte had. But he hadn't hesitated to dive in after the boy. And how could he? Tom had nearly died, and it would have been Stefan's fault if he did.

Stefan stepped in after Orion and shut the stall door. He found a clean spot of ground to sit on and watched as the horse swished his tail and meandered over to chew on the pile of hay in the corner. The thoroughbreds were already settled in stalls farther down, which left him with nothing to do but go back in the inn. Dread rose in his chest at the mere thought. Charlotte had ushered the twins to sit in front of the inn's fireplace the moment they arrived and insisted he do the same once he was finished with the horses. The knowing look in her eyes had said she wanted to talk.

Laying his head back against the wooden boards of the stall, Stefan closed his eyes and took in a deep breath of woodchips and alfalfa. He would be covered in shavings by the time he rose, but he couldn't bring himself to care. It was a small price to pay for a moment of relaxation. Besides, he had often sat with the horses at home when he found the world was too much.

Voices echoed from the barn door, leading Stefan to open his eyes and straighten by a fraction. It was likely another group of travelers coming in for the evening. However, as they came closer, he recognized the twang in one of the man's voices. John? No. That couldn't be. But the man *had* said he was traveling to Kentucky. Had he also gotten stuck in the storm?

"I'm telling you, I don't think it's a good idea."

Stefan turned to peer between the slats of the stall, which revealed it *was* John speaking. Clearly, he had stopped to stay in the same town as them. He held his horse's reins in one hand and gestured with the other, speaking to the man beside him. Stefan couldn't make out the second traveler's face due to the limited view between the boards. Perhaps he should stand up and announce his presence before the men get too far into the building. He didn't want them to think he was spying on them. Before he could enact his plan, however, the second man spoke.

"I don't see what you mean. All we have to do is start pullin' people over and searching." The stranger released a dry laugh. "We'll find it a whole lot faster than your method."

Stefan frowned. Find what? John had said he was going to Lexington. Did he lose something on the way there? A tingle began at the back of his neck in the same way it had before, on the day he thought they were being watched.

"My method is safe." John's voice was clipped. "Your method is asking for trouble. You wanted us to get the package without causing a ruckus, and now you're practically advertising it to the world. What changed?"

"We're running out of time." Footsteps came closer to Orion's stall, and Stefan pushed himself farther into the corner. Something told him he didn't want to be caught listening in on this unusual conversation.

The boards shuddered as the man—whoever he was—leaned against the stall next to Orion, his back pressed to the wall. Stefan held his breath and forced himself to remain still as the stranger tipped his hat back and continued talking. "I'm telling you, John. I'm going to get what I came for, no matter what. Now, you haven't been around for all that long, so I'll give you a little grace. You don't fully know what bunch you're running with. But listen to me. You do things my way, or you don't do things at all. And you know what I mean by that." The dark tone of his voice left little to the imagination. "Now get your horse taken care of, and let's get out of here. I want to eat. That little restaurant down the way smelled awfully nice when we rode in."

Stefan released a breath as the man pushed off the stall and strode away, his footsteps fading a moment later. But John hadn't left.

After a few seconds, a stall door close to the stable entrance creaked open and shut. Stefan lifted himself enough to see John leading his horse inside before slumping back down. There was no way he would be able to sneak out before the man was finished—especially not when his lower leg was missing. He would simply have to wait for John to leave and hope the man didn't look too closely at the horses in the stalls farther down the aisle.

Several minutes passed in tense silence before the stall door opened once again. Stefan peered out in time to glimpse John exiting the stables, his shoulders hunched against the rain.

Luckily, it didn't look as though he was going in the direction of the inn.

Stefan hefted himself up and brushed his trousers off, casting a look around to make sure there was nobody else in the building. What was John looking for? And why did he have such a terrible feeling about the two men? They were planning something—that much was clear from their conversation. But what?

Stefan shook his head. For all he knew, they could be trying to retrieve something they had lost along the way. He huffed a sigh and pushed the stall door open, sliding out. No. That didn't account for their tone of voice. They were dangerous, and whatever they intended to do couldn't be good.

"Mr. Roberts?"

Stefan gasped and spun around, nearly elbowing Bastian in the face. "Bastian! What are you doing out here? I thought Charlotte was keeping you by the fire."

Bastian shrugged, his eyes glittering with amusement. "She was, but she told me to come out here and drag you in. She thought you were taking too long and started to worry that you needed help." He frowned. "I would have come out sooner if she hadn't insisted I change and warm up."

"That's all right." Stefan began a slow, unsteady walk toward the inn, using the stable wall for balance. "I don't suppose you saw a man walk out of here before you came in, did you?"

Bastian brushed a hand through his wet curls, sweeping them away from his eyes. "Yes, I did. He had a big hat on. Why? Did he talk to you?"

Stefan bit his lip, weighing the options. He could try to track John down and ask what he was doing. *Too dangerous.* He could also ask the town sheriff to keep an eye on the men. But what good would that do if he didn't have evidence of any wrongdoing? "It's nothing," he finally settled on saying.

It wasn't worth mentioning to Charlotte and the boys. John's business was his own. Stefan didn't know the man, and while he didn't have a good feeling about the interaction, it wasn't up to him to interfere. He had enough problems as it was. They would simply have to stay clear of John and hope they didn't have any further run-ins with him on the way to Kentucky.

"Okay." The corners of Bastian's mouth turned down. "Do you...need help?"

Stefan tilted his head, having reached the end of the stable wall. "Well...that would be nice, yes. Thank you." He set a hand on the boy's thin shoulder and tried his best not to put too much weight on Bastian as they walked forward. "Charlotte must have truly been worried to send you after me. She shouldn't be."

"I think she's like that with everyone." Bastian cast a quick glance down at Stefan's missing leg. "But especially you." He cleared his throat. "What with your leg and all."

Stefan grimaced. After overhearing John's conversation, he had nearly forgotten about the one waiting for him inside the inn. Charlotte was concerned over him now...and perhaps pitied him too. But would she still when she learned about his past? What questions would she have for him? And why did he care so much what she thought?

CHAPTER 13

Popping and crackling filled the room as the fire in the hearth slowly began to die down, the flames dwindling smaller and smaller as the logs beneath them turned to ash. Though the hour was growing late, Stefan remained in front of the inn's fireplace, soaking up the heat. The twins had gone to bed long ago, but Charlotte had decided to stay with him in the lobby. Despite his protests, she had insisted he not be alone, and even now sat quietly in the chair next to his. A few days ago, Stefan might have said that it was improper for them to be alone in the same room. After nearly drowning, however, it seemed of trivial importance.

Stefan had taken the liberty of pinning his left trouser up after returning from the stables so it wouldn't dangle uselessly at his side. It was something he hadn't done in a very long time, mostly because of the stares people aimed at the gap where his leg should have been. While their looks were only the result of simple curiosity, it didn't make it any less embarrassing. He would have to find a cane or crutch to use until they could secure a replacement leg. Then, at least, people wouldn't notice his unusual gait as much.

The sound of crinkling paper drew Stefan's attention back to Charlotte. She was rubbing her arms, something she seemed to do frequently, and flipping through the magazine on her lap. Though she appeared to be engrossed in the pages, Stefan didn't miss the occasional glances she sent his way. Curiously enough, they were directed at his face and not his leg.

"I can feel you watching me," Stefan murmured, keeping his eyes on the fire.

"O-oh. I didn't mean to be rude, honestly. It's simply that you've been so quiet, and...well..."

"You're curious to know what happened."

"You don't have to talk about it if you don't want to. I know some memories are too painful to speak of," Charlotte said quietly.

In reality, while he would rather talk about anything else, he couldn't run away from the conversation forever. Even if he did want to. After a moment, he released a long sigh. "I suppose I'm afraid to speak of it. Afraid it will make you see me differently."

Charlotte closed her magazine. "Stefan, you have proved you are an honorable man. Why, only a few hours ago, you risked your life over a boy you hardly know. Nothing you say could outweigh my opinion of you, not when I have seen first-hand how brave you truly are."

"I didn't feel brave. Not then." Stefan watched the flames as they danced over the blackened wood. "I joined the cavalry in the middle of the war, when I was eighteen. My father took great pride in the fact that his son was serving the Union. He bragged to his friends that I was a hero, off fighting for freedom and justice. Of course, he didn't know what I had done on the battlefield. How could he, when I never spoke of it? I would never have mentioned such horrors in front of my mother." He couldn't think of it even now—the men he had slain both with musket and saber. They hadn't deserved to die, but he'd had little choice.

Charlotte hummed, shifting closer to Stefan.

"One day, when I was on leave, my little brother, Franz, told me he had joined the cavalry. To fight alongside me, even though he was below the proper age. My father's tales of glory and heroism had gone to his head. Naturally, when he first told me, I was furious. But Franz would not be dissuaded." Stefan's hands started to shake, but he pressed on. "The next time I went into battle, he was at my side. The orderly line we formed didn't last once we heard the Rebel cry from across the field. I lost sight of him in the noise and haze. It was only by the time the gunfire slowed that I was able to finally locate him. He was lying in a ditch, shot in the chest and crushed beneath his horse." Stefan let out a shuddering breath.

Charlotte's glove-covered fingers drifted over his own, stopping the trembling. "Stefan, I'm so sorry you had to see that. That's terrible." Her voice was soft with sympathy. "That war took so much. Too many young, innocent men were sent to die. And those who didn't were left to pick up what remained."

Stefan nodded. "Franz was fifteen years old—far too young for a death so cruel. An instant after finding him, I was shot in the leg, shattering the bone. Orion carried me to the edge of the battlefield, where someone managed to drag me off my horse and get me to the field hospital." He gestured to his leg. "You can see the outcome of that for yourself. I was left without a brother and without the bottom of my leg."

The room fell silent as the fire sputtered and died, the last of the flames flickering and disappearing. Stefan tried hard not to fidget in his seat, his anxiety growing with every minute the room remained quiet. What was Charlotte thinking? That he should have tried harder to convince Franz to stay home? That it was his fault for not protecting his brother?

Finally, he could bear it no longer, and he looked at Charlotte. To Stefan's complete surprise, her eyes were large and sad, a tear rolling down her face. He instantly sat forward. He hadn't meant to make her cry, and consoling words rose to the forefront of his mind. "Charlotte, I—"

"I understand," she whispered. "I understand what it feels like to wish with everything in you that you had done things differently. To feel as though you did something cowardly or wrong." She drew her shoulders back. "Stefan, I would be lying if I said the pain goes away. Perhaps there's a way to be rid of it, but I certainly don't know how. All I know is that blaming yourself for something you can't change will never do any good. What matters is who you are now, and who you are now is a person anyone would be honored to know. I believe that if your brother was here, he would agree."

"What do you have to be ashamed of? You're be—" Stefan caught himself before the next words left his mouth. Beautiful? Where had that come from? "You're certainly no cripple." Oh, wonderful. *What a compliment.*

Charlotte seemed to gather herself for a moment before she tugged one of her gloves off and slowly rolled back her sleeve. Where he expected smooth skin were mottled scars that spread like a spider web across her forearm and hand. She rolled back her other sleeve, revealing a similar sight. "I know what it is like to be looked at and pitied. I know how difficult it is to recover. Most importantly, I know how much it hurts to know that you will never look the same again."

"The fire?" Stefan questioned gently.

"Yes. I ran into a flaming building to save the cow I told you about. The roof collapsed as I was leaving." Charlotte glanced up at him, face bright with understanding. "So you see, Stefan, you are not alone. I understand your struggle, and I think it is very brave of you to wear your wound with such strength."

Something warm bloomed within him. "I could say the same of you. The world can be a cruel place, can't it?"

Charlotte smiled, her eyes glistening with unshed tears. "Yes, but it can be wonderful, as well. We cannot allow the bad moments to destroy the good." She paused, seeming to let the gravity of her words sink in. Almost as if, in a way, she had surprised even herself. "It will always hurt a little, I think. But, in the end, things will get better. They have to."

"True. If only it did not take so long for happiness to come." Stefan leaned back in his chair, rubbing his temple.

"If you do not mind my asking, did your mother pass on before or after your brother?"

"There you go again with your strange, perceptive ways. She fell into a steep decline after my brother died and never recovered," Stefan admitted. "We buried them a few months apart. My father was never quite the same after that."

"I'm sorry. Losing two good people at the same time is an incredibly hard thing."

Stefan tilted his head ever so slightly. "You would know, wouldn't you? We really are quite alike in that regard. Two people, beaten and bruised, trying to start life anew."

Miss Clarke exhaled, the corners of her mouth turning up. "Oh, I don't think it's as grand as all that. Still, it does seem a bit strange that we found each other. Almost as if we were intended to help each other."

"Perhaps we were. God moves in mysterious ways."

Miss Clarke shrugged and turned away. "What God does or doesn't do is none of my concern."

"You aren't a Christian?" Stefan raised both brows. "That does come as a surprise."

"It's not that I'm not a Christian. I simply have a hard time understanding why someone would create us and leave us to live in such despair." Miss Clarke turned her hands palm up. "Why make us struggle to find the good? I'm glad we don't live in a world devoid of hope, but as you mentioned, it can be incredibly hard to find it."

"I once said something similar to my doctor." The man had put up with much of Stefan's complaining when he first got his prosthetic leg. He had also forced Stefan to get back on his feet —both figuratively and literally. "He told me that all things happen for good, regardless of how they may first appear."

Charlotte blinked. "Happen for good? I'm not sure I believe that, but I suppose it bears considering." She rose, causing the magazine to spill to the floor, and turned to Stefan with an apologetic frown. "I'm sorry. I meant to cheer you up, not drag you into my complicated relationship with God. Please, put all that from your mind and think only of what I said before. I do not see you differently because of your past, Stefan. In fact, it only makes me respect you more."

Stefan inclined his head and struggled to his feet. "I appreciate that." He lifted a hand in farewell. "Goodnight, Charlotte. I enjoyed our conversation."

"Goodnight, Stefan. I enjoyed speaking with you as well." She stooped to grab the magazine and placed it on the table in front of them before turning to leave.

Stefan drew a quick breath. "Oh, and Charlotte?"

She paused and glanced over her shoulder at him, the corners of her eyes crinkling. "Yes?"

Stefan swallowed. "I don't think your scars are anything to be pitied or hidden away. They prove you're brave, and they could never take away from your beauty."

"Oh." A soft blush stole across Charlotte's cheeks, and she smiled. "Well, thank you. I don't think you should be ashamed of your leg either." She coughed. "Goodnight, Stefan." She spun and hurried from the room, disappearing into the dim hallway.

A sense of calm lingered, mingled with newfound understanding. For so long, Stefan had dreaded speaking of his past to another person. Yet, in doing so, it was as if something inside him had lifted, an invisible curtain drawn back to reveal the pain inside. It should have hurt to have that pain revealed in such a frank manner. But Stefan couldn't bring himself to regret his conversation with Charlotte. In fact, as he gazed at the hallway where she had been, he found himself wishing she would come back. Very curious, indeed.

CHAPTER 14

"Psst, Miss Charlotte!"

Charlotte glanced around the empty court-yard, searching for the source of the whisper. The heavy morning air swirled around her, carrying the gentle scent of dew and fresh grass, and lifted a tendril of hair from behind her ear as she turned. The rising sun made the sky a hazy blue against the dark outlines of the inn and stables. The lanterns hanging from the porch shed some light on the scenery, but not enough to reveal who was calling her name.

The last thing she had expected was to be recognized while on her morning stroll. She had simply wanted to take some time before they left to sort through her thoughts. Unfortunately, the walk hadn't helped in the least. Questions and uncertainties continued to whirl through her mind with a vengeance.

"Miss Charlotte, over here!"

Charlotte followed the sound of the summons to a familiar plaid cap on a head peeking around the corner of the inn. "Why, Bastian! What are you doing awake at such an early hour?"

The lad smiled abashedly. "I was working on something for Mr. Roberts, and I was hoping you would tell me if you think he'll like it."

Charlotte cocked her head. What was this?

Bastian picked something up from the ground behind him. Turning around, he held the object out for inspection. It appeared to be a wooden crutch, fashioned from a thick oak branch and shaved smooth. A piece of wood had been attached to the top and padded with cloth, creating a place for a shoulder to comfortably rest. There was even a smooth beam jutting out of the middle, creating a handgrip. In short, the crutch was wonderfully crafted.

"Do you mean to tell me you made this?"

Bastian nodded, his eyes worried. "Do you think Mr. Roberts will like it? I noticed how much he was struggling to move around last night and thought I might be able to help. Tom and I certainly owe it to him after what happened at the river. We waited until he was asleep and snuck out to find the carpenter next to the inn, who was happy to let us borrow some tools once we told him what we were making. We got some branches from the forest and created this." He tilted the crutch, studying it with furrowed brows. "I hope Mr. Roberts won't be embarrassed. Perhaps I should forget about it."

"Slow down, Bastian. I'm certain Stefan will be grateful for it." Charlotte folded her arms across her chest. "He would be foolish not to."

"You were up awfully late yesterday. I nearly went out to see where Mr. Roberts went." Something mischievous flashed in Bastian's eyes. "I could hear bits and pieces of your conversation from our room, though. Did he call you beautiful?"

Charlotte narrowly avoided choking on air. Stefan hadn't exactly called her beautiful, but he had come close to it. However, that wasn't for Bastian to know. "What he did or did not call me is none of your concern. You shouldn't be listening in on other people's conversations, Sebastian. It isn't polite. Besides, he didn't call me beautiful."

"If you say so," Bastian said with a wry grin. "Just do me a favor and invite me to the wedding." He darted away before Charlotte could come up with a rebuttal, leaving her standing in the courtyard by herself.

"Silly boy." With a chuckle and an unexpected twinge of awareness, she headed back toward the inn. Would Stefan be up and tending to the horses? If the boys were awake, it was likely. If only he would take more time to rest, especially after their difficult conversation last night. Never in all her life had she been so sad to have one of her suspicions be proven correct. To think that the poor man had found his brother dead on the battlefield, and his mother died not long after! And on top of it, the loss of his leg.

Charlotte brushed a gloved hand against her sleeve, over the scars that lay beneath. Why she had shown them to Stefan was something of a mystery, for it was the first time she had revealed them to anyone. Perhaps in a way, selfish as it sounded, she had wanted to feel understood as well.

And she didn't regret her decision.

Hoofbeats echoed on the otherwise-empty street as a rider passed the inn. The white coat of the horse reminded her of the kind man's steed, the one who had pulled them from the mud. Could they be the same? It could be, but the likelihood of them choosing the same route was low. Or was it? Lexington was on the way to Monticello. Perhaps they would cross paths again before their travels were out, and they could find a way to repay Mr. John for his kindness.

Charlotte collected her bag from her room in the inn and made her way over to the stables. If Stefan was in fact there, she wanted to speak with him before they left. Not to mention she was eager to see how he reacted to the twin's creation.

As she reached the entrance, Charlotte drew to a halt as

Tom and Bastian handed the crutch to Stefan, whose wide eyes proved he had been caught off guard. He accepted the gift and fitted it beneath his left arm, revealing that it was close to perfect in length, if a bit large.

"I sanded the wood, and Tom stitched the cloth on. Does it work?" Bastian's hands were tucked behind his back, giving her a clear view of the way he fidgeted with the cuffs of his sleeves. *Poor boy. Always so eager to please.*

"It...it's wonderful. Thank you both. I never would have expected you two to be such fine craftsmen," Stefan replied, honesty in his tone.

"Oh, I'm not. Bas is the one who likes building things. He used to make little wooden things back home, like trinket boxes and figurines. Of course, none of them survived the fire." Tom lifted a shoulder. "A true shame. You should have seen the birds that he carved. They were so real, I nearly expected them to start singing."

Fire. So it seemed Stefan was not the only one who could relate to Charlotte's past.

Bastian's fidgeting stilled. "Tom is exaggerating. I simply enjoy whittling."

"And you've done a fine job. That crutch is splendid." Charlotte smiled as she entered the stable and patted the boy on the shoulder. "You both should be very proud."

Stefan took a few experimental steps, moving forward with relative ease. "Not bad. This will make traveling to Kentucky far simpler." He adjusted the crutch and straightened, a slight smile tugging at his lips. "Thank you again, Bastian. You should consider a future in carpentry."

"That would mean finding somewhere to live permanently." Tom frowned. "I much prefer the idea of staying on the road and taking our music around the country. Nowhere to belong and nothing to lose, I say."

Bastian looked ready to speak, but apparently thought

better of it. Instead, he leaned against the side of the wagon. "If you say so. Are we ready to leave?"

Charlotte met Stefan's gaze with a raised brow. Clearly, the matter of being a musician was a sore topic. She couldn't help but wonder why Bastian was so against his brother's passion. Jealousy, perhaps?

"If you boys would like to fetch your luggage from the inn, we can head out." Stefan pointed toward the door. "You as well, Charlotte."

Charlotte lifted her bag. "I have mine. I'll wait here with you." As the boys scurried away, she moved closer to Stefan. "It was kind of them to make that for you. Bastian was so afraid you wouldn't like it."

He twisted the bottom of the crutch, making a circular indent in the dirt. "I do like it, it's been a long time since I've had to use one of these."

"When did you first get your false leg?" Charlotte studied the pinned-up pant leg on Stefan's left side. After his revelation the previous day, his uneven gait made much more sense. And even then, she couldn't imagine the amount of practice it must have taken for him to be able to walk so efficiently.

"Around three months after I was injured. I first used crutches, then the prosthetic. I was less than enthralled when I first learned about it, but I became used to it. At least it reduced the number of people staring at me." Stefan chuckled. "And my doctor wouldn't have it any other way."

"I wear long sleeves and gloves for the same reason." Charlotte ducked her head. "I received too many curious looks for my liking, especially while I worked at the dress shop." She shivered and ran a hand over her arms. The stares of customers had made her wish she could drape herself in the cloth she was sewing, if only to hide the ugly skin from view. "It was awful."

"Perhaps they're simply looking because they enjoy your sense of fashion."

Charlotte couldn't help but laugh. "My sense of fashion, hmm? If I had one, it would be called 'The Charity Bin Extraordinaire.' I can't afford any frills or silk."

"I don't know much about women's fashion, but I think being practical is always fashionable. Especially when your dresses have pockets," Stefan said with a half smile.

Warmth blossomed in Charlotte's chest at the compliment. The easy conversation...the honest words between them...this camaraderie was so far from the harshness of the man she had first met in Chicago, though that hadn't been all that long ago. And the words were spoken regardless of her oversized dresses and scarred arms. How did he even find her worthy of the praise?

And yet...that he did find her worthy felt wonderful.

~

The rain and heavy clouds had dissipated overnight, leaving the sky clear and blue. Birds flitted over the horses as they plodded down the road, red-breasted robins and brown sparrows chirping at each other from the trees. It was, in short, a perfect spring day. The thoroughbreds seemed to agree, for it wasn't long before they were prancing alongside the wagon, tossing their heads and flicking their tails in a playful manner.

"Who will ride the horses at the races?" Tom asked from beside the wagon. Both of the twins had decided to walk rather than ride in the wagon so Orion could have a bit of a break. "It has to be someone small, correct?"

"Correct." Stefan shifted beside Charlotte, tilting his hat back with one hand. "We have several jockeys at the Kentucky stable who are well versed in horse racing. They'll ensure that our thoroughbreds race to the best of their abilities."

"And then what? Do you continue to race them for the rest of their life?" Tom moved closer, his face bright with curiosity.

"No. Not by our hand, anyway. We aim to sell the horses to reputable owners through the races. It gives us an excellent opportunity to showcase their skills." Stefan seemed a bit more relaxed today, though Charlotte didn't miss the way he continued to glance at the forest on either side of the lane. "My hope is that Lake and Persnickety will have new homes by the end of the season."

"Have you ever looked in on the horses you've sold?" Charlotte leaned forward, equally curious.

"Of course. My father often becomes good friends with his buyers and will visit on occasion to see how the horses are faring. So far, we haven't received a single complaint," Stefan said proudly. His gaze darted to the ground. "That being said, because my father is growing older, his visits have become few and far between."

Charlotte recalled Stefan's mention of his father the previous evening. The poor man had evidently not taken the loss of his wife and son well. "He seems like an excellent businessman."

"He is." Stefan lifted his head to meet her gaze. "I can only hope to someday be as good and honest as him. He will leave behind quite the legacy."

"And what of your dream to take over the stables? Will you ask him to relinquish some of his responsibilities?"

"I don't know. I'm afraid of what he'll say. He…he won't do so well if he doesn't have a distraction." Stefan fell silent, apparently unwilling to continue.

Luckily, Tom hastened to fill the silence. "Miss Charlotte, where does this friend of yours live? I know we're going to Kentucky, but where, exactly?"

"My friend's mother, you mean," Charlotte corrected. "She

lives in Albany. Flora told me to look for her at the Aspen residence."

"The Aspen residence? I know them. They're quite a nice family," Stefan said in surprise. "They've bought horses from us several times. They're very well off, if I'm not mistaken."

Charlotte sat back. "They're rich? Flora never spoke of having a wealthy background. I suppose it would make sense if she was estranged from her mother, but I would still think she would have had a bit of finery still with her. Yet she seemed as poor as I."

"Well, that locket she gave you isn't exactly inexpensive. It looks to me as though it's made of real gold," Bastian chimed in from Charlotte's right side. "Unless she stole it, I'd say it's perfectly reasonable to assume that she came from wealth."

Charlotte ran a hand over the collar of her dress, beneath which the locket was concealed. "I wish I had known about her background sooner. Flora was already very sick when I met her. She never really spoke of her past, or what led her to Milwaukee."

"And yet you chose to bring her locket all the way to Kentucky?" Bastian's voice was incredulous. "You're either awfully compassionate or awfully impulsive, don't you think?"

Charlotte released a short laugh. "Perhaps both. I couldn't deny fulfilling her final wish. She seemed so...desperate."

Bastian tucked his hands into his pockets. "Still, she told you nothing of her past?"

"Nothing beyond the fact that her mother had tossed her out years ago. I don't know why." Charlotte hugged her arms around her stomach, tapping her feet on the wagon floor. "It does make me wish I knew more. Perhaps Flora's mother will turn me away when I appear at their door. Perhaps she'll take one look at the locket and throw me straight out. I have no idea how big of a disagreement she had with her daughter, but I assume it must have been a great one to drive them so far apart."

Stefan clucked his tongue. "Not the Mrs. Aspen I know. She's a kind woman, always smiling. I've never heard a cross word from her or her husband."

Charlotte cast a sideways look at him. "What are they like?"

"They're among the most affluent members of society. I've never seen them in anything less than the finest state of dress, and their home is enormous. They have hundreds of acres and three carriage houses. They actually own two of our finest race-horses. As a matter of fact, they may even be attending the spring races in Lexington and Monticello."

"Good heavens." Anxiety jabbed Charlotte in the chest. "Perhaps I should check there first."

Stefan set an elbow against the wagon's backboard. "Monticello is on the way to Albany, so I don't think it's a bad idea. I doubt it would take much time from your trip, anyway. All you would have to do is ask the ticket master whether or not the Aspens placed bets or purchased a horse in the last few days. If they did, chances are, they're still in Monticello."

"Oh, how wonderful. I'll do just that. Thank you, Stefan." Charlotte could only hope he was right about the Aspens' kindness. What would happen if Charlotte approached them, only to be turned away?

She straightened in her seat. *I won't allow it.* She would see the locket delivered. *For Flora.*

CHAPTER 15

The next few days passed in a blur of blue and green as they slowly traveled south. Stefan walked with his new crutch whenever he could, and by the end of the week, he was as proficient with it as he had once been. His shoulder was sore from walking, and his heart was sore from the curious gazes of onlookers, but stares weren't quite so frequent and grating as Stefan remembered. It was as though something Stefan couldn't pinpoint had changed. Memories from the war still hung close in the back of his mind, but a small amount of peace had begun to settle over him. It was a welcome feeling.

Of course, when one was traveling with twin boys, peace was often short-lived.

Stefan had selected a street behind a large general store in the town they were passing through to stop and eat lunch, which both provided the horses with shade and kept the wagon out of the bustling main street. He sat with both eyes closed on the wagon bench and released a contented breath. Birds chirped around him, and carriages clattered down the street in the distance, providing a noise that was nearly constant enough to put him to sleep.

"Mr. Roberts! Mr. Roberts, we should go." Bastian's exclamation jarred Stefan as the boy returned unexpectedly from browsing.

He opened one eye, not bothering to uncross his arms. "And why exactly would we do that? Charlotte is still off purchasing her lunch."

Bastian glanced over his shoulder, his face tense. "Any idea how long that will take?"

Stefan opened his other eye and straightened on the wagon bench. "What happened? Are you boys in trouble?"

Bastian shifted from one foot to the other, avoiding Stefan's gaze. "If we are, you can blame Tom. He never listens."

"And what would I blame Tom for? Where is he, anyway?"

Tom came skidding around the corner as though summoned by his name and hopped into the wagon bed. "We might want to leave."

Stefan looked between the two boys—one who wore a far-too-innocent smile, and one who eyed his brother with a deadly expression. "All right, boys. Out with it. What happened?"

Tom spilled the details on one deep breath. "Bas and I were wandering through the stores when I saw a pottery shop and decided to go in to look around. Things were going perfectly well until, forgetting that my banjo was on my back, I might have turned around. That might have led to the banjo hitting a vase, and...the eventual collapse of the entire shelf. Unfortunately, this shelf might have fallen on top of a fellow who was asking the shopkeeper for directions, leading him to chase us from the store cursing a blue streak and threatening to thrash us without listening to our attempts at apologizing. Thus, the reason it would be in our best interest to leave."

Stefan exhaled. *There goes my quiet afternoon.* Though to be frank, there was little chance of anything being quiet with the twins around. "Very well. But we can't leave without Charlotte.

If the man comes this way, I'll explain." He raised a brow. "Assuming you boys are willing to do whatever it takes to make amends."

Tom grimaced. "Sure thing, Mr. Roberts."

"I'm not sure that man will listen." Bastian joined his brother in the back of the wagon and glanced behind him. "Ah, Miss Charlotte! Quick, get in!"

Stefan swiveled around. Charlotte had returned and stood gazing at them with a perplexed expression, a loaf of bread clutched in one hand. "Should I be concerned?" she asked, waving Stefan's hand off and hefting herself up into the wagon bench. The brim of her hat nearly hit him as she adjusted her skirts and swiveled to face them. "Well? What happened?"

"Nothing that can't be solved with a few calming words." The reassurance died on Stefan's lips when a shout echoed from close by, followed by a stream of less-than-kind words. A greasy-haired man with a bandanna hanging loosely around his neck and rage evident on his face appeared from around the corner. He hadn't yet seen them, but that didn't stop him from uttering all manner of foul things.

"There he is! Drive!" Tom ducked low in the bed of the wagon, trying and failing to conceal himself from view.

Stefan snapped the reins, and Orion leaped forward, jolting the wagon into motion. They raced away from the town and the vengeful man.

Once they were back on the main road, Stefan slowed Orion to a walk and fixed Tom with a hard stare. "In the future, leave the banjo in the wagon if you plan on entering shops. With luck, that will prevent any further catastrophes."

Bastian released a snort. "That's optimistic."

Tom punched his brother in the shoulder, cheer returning to his face. "Don't act like you've never caused trouble. I remember the day you tied Da's laces together while he was at the table."

As they settled back into the rhythm of travel, tall oak and maple trees lined the road, their thick green leaves creating dappled patterns of light upon the ground. The quiet burble of running water denoted the existence of a creek nearby, though it remained hidden from view. That, combined with Orion's slow, plodding hoofbeats, created a pleasant rhythm that was nearly enough to lure Stefan into slumber yet again.

Confounded nightmares. There had been a thunderstorm again the previous night, and as a result, he had barely slept. No wonder Charlotte had called him grouchy. It was hard to be pleasant when one spent every rainy night in a state of agitation.

The urge to sleep was quickly becoming overwhelming, but something else tugged at Stefan's thoughts—Charlotte's words from their conversation in front of the hearth. They had been nagging at the back of his mind for several days, but he hadn't found the opportunity to mention them. *What God does or doesn't do is none of my concern.* She didn't believe God cared, it seemed. So what *did* she believe?

Stefan blinked the tiredness from his eyes and turned to Charlotte. "Did your family read the Bible very often, Charlotte?"

"We did, once upon a time," Charlotte admitted with a sad smile. "I'm afraid our copy was lost in the fire."

"I have our family Bible with me." He hadn't been able to resist bringing it along, if only to take some comfort in the words on long nights. "My mother loved reading it. Her notes are preserved in the margins. She spent many evenings in the front room, where I can remember sinking into a chair of a cold winter night and listening as she quietly read verses aloud." And closing his eyes to cadence of the comforting words.

"My mother was the same way." Charlotte's reply made Stefan snap upright. When had his eyes fallen shut? "I'd love to read your mother's notes, if you wouldn't mind."

Stefan blinked, caught off guard by the request. "Certainly not. She would be happy to know I shared them. My mother always made certain we had time for the Lord while we were under her roof." He shifted in his seat. "Perhaps we should both revisit the Bible. It might have some of the answers to the questions we voiced."

Charlotte returned his smile with one of her own. "Perhaps."

The snapping of a branch cut their conversation short. Stefan's every nerve went on alert. Orion lifted his head, ears swiveling.

"Stefan? Is something wrong?" Charlotte set a gloved hand on his arm.

Stefan jumped at the sudden contact, his heart leaping into his throat. "I thought I heard something."

"That branch? It was probably just a rabbit or some other critter," Bastian said from the back of the wagon.

"Maybe," Stefan murmured, though something felt off, as though they were being watched from the trees.

Another branch snapped, followed by the jangle of a halter. Stefan inhaled sharply as a horse and rider emerged from the woods. The sight might have been innocent had it not been for the pistol clutched in the man's hand. The sound of hoofbeats approaching from behind the wagon told Stefan the thief wasn't working alone.

"Stop the wagon," the man in front of them said, his voice deadly calm. There was something familiar about him, both in the manner he spoke and his dress. The stranger from the stables. Was John the one behind them? Stefan was too afraid to look away and check.

Left without a choice, he steered the wagon to the edge of the road and brought Orion to a halt, his heart pounding. "What do you want? We don't have anything of value."

The man waved his pistol, his blue eyes glinting from

beneath his wide-brimmed hat. "Quiet. Put your hands in the air and don't move." He glanced at Stefan's leg and snorted. "Not that you'd get very far, anyway."

Panic and humiliation coursed through Stefan's mind as he slowly raised his hands, rendering him unable to reach his revolver. Even if he were able, he couldn't disarm both highwaymen in time. As much as it hurt to admit, allowing them to take the horses was the safer option. At least that would give them a chance at survival.

"There's just rope and blankets back here, Hawk," the thief behind the wagon announced. His voice was not John's, but it did sound vaguely familiar. Could it be the man who had chased them from the town? Had he really said there was nothing else in the wagon? As in...not two boys?

Stefan twisted slightly in his seat so he could see the wagon bed and the man sitting on a horse behind it. The thief was indeed the same greasy-haired man who had followed the twins from the store, though his bandanna was now pulled up over his nose and mouth. As for the wagon bed, it was empty, just as the man had said. So where were the boys?

Turning back to the front, Stefan cast a surreptitious glance at the woods beside the wagon. He couldn't be certain, but he thought he saw a flash of red between two of the trees. *Tom.* By some brilliant stroke of luck, they must have gotten away before the men stopped the wagon. He could only hope they would have enough common sense to run for help.

"What do you have 'round your neck, lady?" the first thief said, leaning closer to Charlotte.

Stefan bristled, his fear retreating. "Leave her alone. She has nothing of interest."

The thief's eyes narrowed. "Shut your mouth, or I'll shut it for you. I do what I want."

"It's only a necklace. A silly little trinket, really. It's simple brass that's been made to look like gold." Charlotte shot Stefan a warning look. She was trying to prevent the thief from shooting him, but it still grated to watch her pull the locket from beneath her collar.

The highwayman peered at the necklace and ran his free hand over his neatly trimmed goatee. "Well, I'll be." He muttered the words so low, Stefan struggled to hear. "You had it all along." He made as though to grab for the locket.

The horse that the thief called Hawk was on reared as though suddenly startled, causing the highwayman to scrabble for balance. From behind the wagon, the other thief let out a yelp, as though he was experiencing the same thing. In the same moment, Stefan withdrew his revolver and shot the gun from the flailing man's hand, causing it to fall to the ground.

The wagon bed jolted as the twins reappeared beside the wagon and hopped in. "Go!" Tom cried, clutching the side of the wagon.

Stefan released a piercing whistle, causing Orion to spring into a gallop. They raced away at breakneck speed, leaving the sounds of shouting and cursing behind. A shot whistled past Orion's left flank but thankfully missed. Taking a right at the next fork in the road, Stefan turned the wagon sharply onto a side path. They rode straight through a grassy field, heading for a copse of trees on the other side. Only once they reached the safety of the forest did he slow Orion to a walk. Stefan swiveled around, but the thieves were nowhere to be found.

"Did we lose them?" he asked the twins, trying to calm his shaking hands. "Were they following us?"

Tom shook his head, his chest heaving. "They didn't follow. Maybe they plan on waiting and ambushing us when we get back on the main road." He released a snort. "I can't believe the man from the pottery shop was a highway robber. And I felt sorry for dropping that shelf on him!"

Stefan slumped back against the seat with a sigh, the rush of energy beginning to wear off. "Is everyone all right?" Relief coursed through him as he realized Charlotte was ruffled but otherwise unharmed. Though he had witnessed her in danger once before, seeing a gun pointed at her had frightened him more than he cared to admit.

"We're all right." Bastian's voice was thin but sure.

"You two were amazing. How did you distract the horses?" Charlotte twisted around to look at the brothers, brushing back a flyaway lock of hair.

Tom grinned. "No animal likes having its tail pulled. One short tug did the trick. I'm just glad we didn't get kicked in the process."

"Well, it was incredibly brave. I doubt we would have gotten free without you." Charlotte turned to Stefan, her eyes wide and assessing. "What about you, Stefan? Are you all right? That was some quick thinking on your part."

Stefan glanced at the trees surrounding them. "It got us away from the highwaymen, but I'm not sure where we are now. It might take us a while to get back on track, especially if we plan on avoiding the main road."

"What did they want, anyway? The horses?" Tom looked behind them once more.

Charlotte shrugged. "Valuables?"

Stefan frowned, his mind going back to the robber's words. *You had it all along.* John's conversation from before was rapidly becoming clearer. "No," he said, realization taking root. "It wasn't a random attack, nor did they want the horses. They were looking for something specific." He pointed to the necklace still visible around Charlotte's neck. "They wanted that locket."

CHAPTER 16

Charlotte could only blink in surprise at Stefan's words. "But that doesn't make any sense. Why would they be looking for Flora's locket? It's not *that* valuable."

Stefan's brows furrowed. "All I know is that the thief recognized it. And...and I heard them talking earlier."

"Heard them talking? What do you mean?" Bastian questioned from the back of the wagon.

Stefan shifted in his seat. "When I went to stable the horses the day Tom fell in the river, John was there, and so was the man who ambushed us on the road. They were talking about retrieving something and mentioned pulling travelers over to check. It has to be the locket."

Charlotte removed the pendant from around her neck, tracing the gilded leaves with one finger. So it *was* John she had seen that morning while she was walking through the courtyard. What did he want with dead girl's locket? "I never opened it," she murmured. "It seemed too intrusive, too personal. Flora said she left a note for her mother inside. Do you think the highwayman's desire for the locket is related to that?"

"Perhaps." Stefan nodded decisively. "It's worth a look."

Charlotte eased the lid of the locket open. Inside the hollow body lay a small square paper that looked as if it had been folded several times. Opening it, she quickly scanned the contents. "It's a note to her mother, asking for forgiveness." She sighed. "Poor Flora."

"Anything else?"

"A picture of a lady with black hair that I can only assume must be her mother. Wait..." Charlotte pulled on a tiny corner of paper peeking from behind the portrait. Tugging carefully on it revealed a scrap of folded paper that was barely bigger than her thumbnail.

"What is it?" Tom questioned from behind Charlotte.

"I'm not sure." Charlotte unfolded the delicate paper. "The script is incredibly small, but it looks like a list of names." She handed the scrap to Stefan for inspection.

Stefan's eyes narrowed as he scanned the list. When he reached the bottom, he inhaled sharply. "This name. I recognize it." Then he pointed a finger at the name below it. "I know this one as well. He was executed years ago."

"What are you saying?" Charlotte leaned forward, eager to read the faded names.

Stefan looked up, his gaze serious. He was close enough that Charlotte could make out a ring of faded gold around his pupils, a realization that made her blink. "These men were Confederate spies. After the war ended, a few of them continued to try and revive the Confederate cause. Some chose secretive measures, and others used blatant violence to get their way. Regardless of their methods, they became a danger to the country. The government spent countless hours tracking the guerillas down and putting an end to their misconduct. But the Union never found all of them. Not even close." He held up the piece of paper. "This list could contain the names of some of the missing spies. If it does, it's imperative that it reaches a trusted official's hands as quickly as possible."

"A list of Confederate spies?" Charlotte sat back, shaking her head. "I don't believe it. Why on earth would Flora have such a thing?"

"Well, unless I'm mistaken, this friend of yours would have had to be working as an undercover agent. I knew a few of them during my time in the cavalry. They were very brave souls, and oftentimes they came in unlikely forms."

"Flora, working for the Union?" Could Charlotte's quiet, shy friend really have been a government agent? It seemed far-fetched, but the evidence lay in Stefan's hand. "If so, why give such crucial information to someone she barely knew?"

"The best spies are uninformed spies. They don't have to worry about revealing what they don't know," Stefan said, making Charlotte realize she had voiced her question aloud.

"Yes, but why me? Why not someone better suited to travel? Someone who could handle dangerous people like high-waymen or spies bent on revenge? Someone with more...skills." Charlotte scrubbed at her forehead. There were dozens of others at the hospital who could have taken the locket. Dozens of others who were a better choice.

"Because you were alone and needed something to distract you from the hurt. Because you survived an incredibly deadly event. Because you have a kind heart, and your friend knew you wouldn't refuse her request." Each one of Stefan's points stabbed like a knife in Charlotte's heart. What he said was true, but it didn't make it any easier to understand.

"But then...was our friendship all for nothing? Did she mean only to use me as some sort of unwitting messenger?" Charlotte closed the locket. "I thought she cared." Tears formed at the back of her eyes, but she refused to let them fall.

"I wasn't there, so in all honesty, I couldn't say." When Charlotte's shoulders slumped, Stefan's expression relaxed. "However, I will tell you this. Your friend was most likely willing to die for the information hidden in that locket. For her to give it to you seems like an act of pure trust. In that moment of desperation, she could have chosen anyone else to take that locket. But she didn't. She chose you."

His words eased the hurt but not the panic.

Tom chimed in, his expression bright. "I think it's pretty neat that you get to carry such important papers. You're like the heroines in those dime novels that are always in the garbage cans behind drugstores." Charlotte swiveled to gape at him as he continued. Really? He thought this some grand adventure? "If that list really is important, and we give it to the right people, they might even give us all medals. We could all be heroes!" He whooped, his expression dropping a moment later. "You're still going to deliver it to Kentucky, aren't you? You can't turn back now."

Charlotte frowned, teetering on the edge of an anxiety attack, though there was little she could do to prevent it. "I...I don't know. This whole venture just became far more dangerous. Those men on the road clearly had some sort of knowledge about the spy list. I have a feeling they won't rest until they get it."

"What if the highwaymen are with the Union? Perhaps this friend of yours wasn't working with the Yankees at all. Maybe the paper got in the locket by mistake and they simply want it back," Tom suggested.

Charlotte shook her head, her cheeks flushing with heat. *Oh, please, not now.* "I doubt that's the case. How would they get it behind her mother's portrait without her noticing? It's far more likely that Flora put it there herself. She wanted me to take it to the Aspens. Do you think they know the truth?"

Stefan studied her for a moment before answering, his eyes curious and mildly concerned. "I would guess so. Mr. Aspen is retired from the army, but he still spoke of military affairs on occasion when my father and I visited him. I suspect he still does some work with the government. If we can get the paper to him, I'm sure he'll be able to transfer the knowledge to the proper people. The longer we wait, however, the better chance those highwaymen will have of catching us. If they get the list, it will all be for naught."

Charlotte released a shuddering breath, trying and failing to ignore the white spots that were beginning to appear in her vision. She was rapidly reaching the point of no return.

A gentle hand touched her shoulder. "Are you all right?"

Charlotte looked at Stefan, wincing when she realized his face was slightly blurry. "I'm just having some trouble catching my breath." She focused on her lap, staring at her pale gloves in an attempt to clear her vision.

"Catching your breath?" Stefan's hand dropped from her shoulder. "Ah. I know the feeling."

Charlotte blinked. "You do?"

"Indeed. It never lasts long. Close your eyes and focus on taking deep breaths."

Charlotte shut her eyes, willing her heart to calm and her lungs to stop seizing. Cool wind blew steadily across her face, helping to calm her burning head and relax her tense muscles. After a moment, her heart returned to its normal state, and her thoughts cleared. "I'm sorry," Charlotte murmured, opening her eyes. "That hasn't happened to me in quite some time. Normally, I'm able to stop it before it occurs."

Stefan sat back, his eyes soft. "There's no need to apologize, Charlotte. I understand. You just experienced quite a shock."

"I did." Charlotte raised a hand to her throat. "Something that I thought would be simple turned out to be exactly the opposite." And now she was far from Milwaukee, far from the hospital, and far from everything she had known.

"That's true. So what will you do about it?" Stefan tilted his head. "The choice is yours and yours alone. But, should you decide to continue on, I will do my best to see you safely delivered to Monticello."

Charlotte's heart told her that Kentucky was the right thing to do, but her head argued that turning around would be safer. *Safer for what?* Safer so she could go back to living alone, without anywhere to go? Forever burdened with the knowledge that she'd failed to see her promise through? No. Charlotte took a deep breath. "How do we avoid them? How do we deliver these papers?

Stefan's eyes held a glint of determination and the barest hint of fear. "I don't know exactly, but America's future may be altered if we do not."

$\sim$

"Any sign of them, Tom?" Stefan asked as the boy crept back through the grass to the side of the wagon. The sun was sinking low over the horizon, casting long shadows over the horses' backs as they pawed anxiously at the ground. They had remained at the edge of the field and forest for over an hour, hoping that it would be long enough to draw the robbers away.

Tom reached the wagon and slipped over the side, his brows drawn together. "I didn't see them on the road, but that isn't to say they aren't nearby. They could be waiting for us at the nearest town. What are we going to do, Mr. Roberts?"

Stefan adjusted his cap, pulling it lower on his forehead. "I believe we should err on the side of safety and avoid all towns for the time being." He glanced at Charlotte, noting the pale tint to her skin. Though she was adamant that she felt better, it was obvious she could use a long rest. They all could. "We'll have to find the nearest farm and ask if we can stay for the evening. Then I can inquire if there's a less conspicuous route we can take."

Bastian hugged his knees to his chest. "What if they're watching *all* of the roads? What then?"

"We'll worry about that once we're safe for the evening." Stefan snapped the reins, and they set off toward a small path he had noticed earlier. It turned out to be a narrow and incredibly bumpy road—uncomfortable to travel on, but one that allowed them passage through the otherwise impenetrable forest.

The twins and Charlotte remained silent. How had a simple trip to Kentucky evolved into a race against Confederate guerillas? Troublemakers that he had considered long gone, a problem only the government needed to worry about?

Clearly, Charlotte had known nothing of her friend's involvement, or else she would have been far more hesitant to wear the locket. How cruel that she should have to complete such a dangerous task, but judging by her demeanor, she seemed willing to do it. Impressive.

"I wonder how the highwaymen discovered the note was in a locket." Bastian's pondering broke the tense silence. "They even knew what the locket looked like, because the thief recognized it as soon as Miss Charlotte showed it to him. They must have seen it before."

Charlotte's jaw tightened, her expression flickering with worry. "I'm not certain. Flora had been at the hospital for quite some time before I arrived, so I doubt they would have known about it before that. Or...perhaps they did." She turned, locking eyes with Stefan. "They could have been waiting for Flora to die so they would have an easier time getting to the locket." She ducked her head. "Only, she beat them to it. Flora gave me the locket."

"They must have known enough to guess that whoever had the locket would be going to find the Aspens—thus, the reason they've been patrolling the roads to Kentucky." Stefan snapped his fingers. "That man—Hawk... The hat he was wearing when he ambushed us was the same style the stranger we hid from before wore. I knew there was something off about him. I had a bad feeling about John too."

"If that's true, how many of these highwaymen are looking for us? We don't even know what they look like. For all we know, every person walking or riding along the road could be hunting us down." Charlotte groaned, rubbing her arms.

Tom patted his breastbone, his chest expanding. "Take heart, Miss Charlotte. You have the three of us. We managed to escape those villains once, and we can do it again." He leaned forward. "By the way, that was some fancy shooting you did, Mr. Roberts. You knocked that gun clean outta the robber's hand. Where'd you learn to fire like that?"

"When I joined the cavalry, they taught us how to shoot. We had to have a good aim if we were to hit targets from atop a moving horse," Stefan explained, tapping the revolver at his side.

"You were in the cavalry? Golly. What kind of horse did you ride? Did you wear a fancy uniform with all that gold trim? Did you have one of those special swords they hold out during a charge? What do they call it...a saber? Did you ride into battle? Did you hear the Rebel yell? Folks say it was scary enough to freeze men in their tracks."

Stefan let out a breath and relaxed against the backboard with a smile. Leave it to a boy to come up with an endless amount of questions. Luckily, they were fairly easy to answer. "The horse I rode is right before your eyes, though he was a good deal younger at the time. As for my uniform and weapons, I had both, but they're long gone."

"You mean Orion was a cavalry horse? That's neat. I bet he knows plenty of tricks. Could I ride him sometime?"

Stefan shook his head. "Frankly, I doubt you could even make it onto his back. I'm hardly tall enough to lift the harness onto him."

The path they were on came to an abrupt end, spilling them out into a clearing. Trees encircled the grassy area, providing a safe hideaway from the main road. At the center of the clearing stood a brick farmhouse and a white barn with a sturdy brown roof. Chickens milled around in the grass, pecking the ground in search of worms and other bugs. The smoke rising from the farmhouse's chimney made it clear that the home was occupied.

"Well, I'll be," Stefan muttered, pulling the wagon to a halt. "Shall we see if they'll let us stay for the evening?"

Charlotte lowered herself to the ground and gave the house an apprehensive look. "I hope they're friendly. Our showing up here may come as a bit of a surprise, especially when this clearing was so far removed from the main road. They'll probably wonder how on earth we found it."

"It's worth a try." Stefan dropped to the ground and grabbed his crutch from the wagon bench. "Boys, you stay here and watch the horses. Shout if you see anyone."

The boys mumbled their assent, leaving Stefan and Charlotte to walk up to the door. From the front step, Stefan could hear voices echoing from within the house. He knocked twice on the solid oak door and stood back. There was a scuffling noise from within, followed by a moment of silence. Then the door opened, and a rolling pin descended toward Stefan's head.

CHAPTER 17

"*R*emus, I told you to be home by noon!" The woman holding the rolling pin waved it in the air, forcing Stefan to duck as she nearly hit him upside the head. She halted and lowered the wooden tool, her eyebrows shooting up. "Well, you aren't Remus, are you? I'm sorry. I thought you were my husband. That silly man was supposed to be bringing in firewood, but instead, he's been off fishing all day." The lady perched her hands on her hips and peered at Charlotte and Stefan from behind her spectacles. "Now, who are you two, and what brings you here? How did you find our home?"

Charlotte cleared her throat. "My name is Charlotte, ma'am, and this is my...companion, Stefan. The boys in the wagon are Thomas and Sebastian. We've come a long way and were hoping to prevail upon you for shelter. Only for the evening, you understand. We still have quite a way to go." When the woman frowned, she pressed on. "If it's too much of an imposition, we'd be glad to sleep in the barn."

"The barn? Oh, goodness, no. That would never do. I was simply deciding how best to divide you amongst our rooms."

The woman drew herself up and tucked the rolling pin behind the folds of her brown dress. "My name is Jane. You folks have come upon the Fitzgerald residence."

"It's a pleasure to meet you, Mrs. Fitzgerald. Truly, if our coming is too much of an imposition, we can go elsewhere." Charlotte tugged at the hem of one of her sleeves, desperate to hide the anxiety building in her chest.

"Oh, nonsense." Mrs. Fitzgerald waved Charlotte's words off with a flour-dusted hand. "You two and those lads come straight in. Feel free to put your horses and wagon in the barn."

"Thank you, Mrs. Fitzgerald." Stefan tipped his cap and turned to Charlotte with a quirked brow. "Will you be all right if I go and see the horses settled?" He leaned closer, his voice lowering. "I won't leave if you feel unsafe."

Charlotte cast a sideways look at the woman in the doorway, with her round cheeks and warm smile. "I'll be fine. Thank you, Stefan."

Stefan searched her eyes for a moment before nodding. He used his crutch to swivel and moved off the porch, leaving Charlotte to follow Mrs. Fitzgerald inside.

The interior of the house was painted a rich yellow, with large hearth and cheerful flowers on every windowsill. White curtains fluttered in the breeze like flags, having come loose from the metal rings meant to hold them in place, and the smell of vanilla and some other spice permeated the air. A small wooden cross hung above a dining table at the back of the room, its beams worn and smooth. The home reminded Charlotte of her own in Peshtigo. Her heart ached with melancholy and longing as she lowered herself onto a chair at the table.

"Ilona! Could you please come here? We have guests," Mrs. Fitzgerald called as she bustled about the kitchen, her apron strings swinging back and forth. "Silly girl is probably looking at her beloved *Godey's Lady's Book* instead of weeding the garden as I asked her," she mumbled.

"Coming, Mother!"

A moment after the answering shout, a young woman who looked to be about Charlotte's age entered the room. Her long black hair had been swept into two braids and pinned across the top of her head like a crown. Her hazel eyes appeared kind and surprised as she looked first at her mother and then at Charlotte. "Well, hello, there! How do you do?" She dipped into a curtsy, a bright smile crossing her face.

"I am well, thank you." Charlotte returned the woman's smile halfheartedly, too tired to stand. "My name is Charlotte."

"Ilona Fitzgerald. Are you traveling on your own, Miss Charlotte?"

Charlotte swiped the hair from her face. Hopefully, she didn't look as exhausted as she felt. "Just 'Charlotte' will do. There are three others traveling alongside me. They're seeing to our horses and should join us shortly."

"Oh, how lovely. Will you stay long? We don't get many visitors, and having some company would be nice. Even in town, I hardly have any friends." Ilona plopped down opposite Charlotte and set her elbows on the counter, resting her chin on her hands. "You oughtn't to rush off."

Charlotte couldn't help but laugh. "Oh, I don't know about that. We have a long way ahead of us, you see. We're traveling to Kentucky."

"Kentucky!" At a table near the hearth, Mrs. Fitzgerald rolled and shaped a lump of bread dough, folding and punching it in a manner similar to Charlotte's mother. It was comforting, in an odd sort of way. "What business do you have there? Or are you going to see family?"

"My friend needs to deliver two thoroughbreds to his stables in Kentucky. They'll be competing in the spring races."

While the Fitzgeralds seemed kind enough, telling them of the locket could place them in danger.

Ilona grinned, lifting her head from her hands. "That sounds exciting. Some of the local boys around here race horses, but nothing serious. I hope your friend's horses run well."

"So do I. We very nearly lost them earlier today." Charlotte shivered. "We were attacked by highwaymen. Stefan managed to get us away from them, but we had to leave the road. Hence, the reason we ended up here."

"Oh, how awful!" Mrs. Fitzgerald spun around, holding her dough-encrusted hands in the air. "You poor girl. No wonder you all looked so worn out. You and your group are welcome to stay here as long as you'd like. Those abhorrent robbers have grown worse and worse over the past few months. Why, two weeks ago, they even tried to take the mail from our postman. He got away, but not without a few nasty scrapes."

"Indeed. I heard the postman from a few towns over went missing a week ago. They found nothing but an empty, bloody bag." Ilona drew a line across the table with her finger, her voice rising theatrically. "It looked like it had been slashed through with a knife, or so the girl at the dress shop said."

"You don't say," Charlotte murmured.

Mrs. Fitzgerald clucked her tongue. "Ilona Fitzgerald, that's quite enough of those silly rumors. What did I tell you about believing everything you hear in town?"

Ilona shrugged, her puffy green sleeves rising almost to her cheeks. "It's the most interesting thing that's happened in this sleepy little place, Ma. Can you blame me?"

Charlotte only half listened as realization dawned. Might those looking for the locket have assumed Flora was sending it to Kentucky via mail and began hunting down postmen in search of it? If that was the case, and if what Ilona had said about the bloody satchel was true, it painted a far more dangerous image of the masked men.

Ilona turned to Charlotte and clasped her hands together. "You can share my room while you're here and tell me all about your travels. Where are you from?"

"Oh, a little town in Wisconsin. Peshtigo is its name." *Or was.*

"Peshtigo? That's where that awful fire happened, isn't it? How tragic." Mrs. Fitzgerald shook her head. "A true shame that so many died."

Charlotte winced. "Yes, it is a shame. I lost everything in that fire." Images of Carina and her mother flickered in her brain, hazy in shape. A pang of surprise ran through her at the realization that she couldn't recall their faces as clearly as she once had. It was as if time was slowly erasing them, dimming the features and small imperfections Charlotte had once known by heart. What would she do once they were gone?

The arrival of the twins saved her from having to answer her own silent question. "Hello, Mrs. Fitzgerald." Tom grinned and brushed off his waistcoat, which was covered in a thin layer of dust. "This is a mighty fine place you have."

"Well, thank you, young man." Mrs. Fitzgerald wiped her hands on the towel beside her. "I imagine you must be very hungry after all that excitement today. I have some scones and jam, if you'd like."

Tom bounced on his heels, tucking his arms behind his back. "Ma'am, that's the best thing I've heard all day."

Bastian rolled his eyes but joined his brother in collecting a scone, nonetheless, a smile on his face. The two settled into chairs at the far end of the table and began an animated conversation that was punctuated only by the occasional bite of scone.

Charlotte was so busy watching the boys that she nearly missed the entrance of Stefan. With him was a tall man who must be Mr. Fitzgerald. He was tan, with wrinkles around his mouth that bespoke a lifetime spent smiling. A long string of fish hung loosely over his shoulder, their green scales glistening in the fading light.

"Jane! This fellow tells me you've offered him shelter for the evening. Is that true?" Mr. Fitzgerald asked as placed his straw hat on the coat rack near the door.

"That it is. They were accosted by highwaymen, Remus. I told you the sheriff needs to take action. If he doesn't do something soon, they'll continue wreaking havoc on the roads, and we'll never have a moment of peace again." Mrs. Fitzgerald shook a finger at her husband. A few strands of curly brown hair had escaped her low-hanging bun and bounced around her face.

Mr. Fitzgerald folded lanky arms across his chest. "I'm not the sheriff, love. What he does or doesn't do is out of my control. And what if these folks had been robbers? What then? Letting them into the barn and house without me could have resulted in disaster."

"Oh, phooey. They clearly mean no harm. Besides, if you were home on time instead of spending your day lounging by the creek, I wouldn't have been alone at all."

Mr. Fitzgerald grinned. "I suppose I have no excuse for that." He glanced at Stefan, who had been observing the altercation from the side. "I apologize for suggesting you might have had ill intentions, Mr. Roberts. A man can never be too careful when it comes to the safety of his family."

"I understand." Stefan swept the hat from his head and ran a hand through his hair. "We'll only be here for the evening, anyway."

"But that's such a short time." Ilona rose halfway from her chair. "Tomorrow is Sunday. You could come to church with us before you set off. It won't be out of your way. Also, it's on a backroad, so you won't have to worry about those nasty highwaymen. It connects to the main road several towns down. You'd only have to travel it a short while before getting back on your way to Kentucky."

Stefan looked at Charlotte, raising a brow in question, and she swallowed. Did she want to go to church? How much harm could it do in an hour? "Church would be lovely."

Hopefully, they wouldn't have cause to regret the brief stop before resuming their trip.

~

After dinner, while Mrs. Fitzgerald entertained the twins and her daughter chattered without ceasing to Charlotte, Stefan studied the man of the house. Mr. Fitzgerald seemed content to watch those at the rest of the dinner table, having long ago finished his meal of cooked fish and fresh bread. The look on his face was one of pure peace, and it stirred an itch beneath Stefan's skin. How had Fitzgerald come to acquire a life such as this, with a caring wife and children of his own?

"Where are you from, Mr. Fitzgerald?"

"You can call me Remus, lad. As for where I'm from, I came here from Massachusetts after marrying my Jane. I decided Indiana would be better for farming and raising a family." Remus eyed Stefan. "And you? Judging by your traveling group, you have quite a story of your own."

Stefan tilted his head. "To make short of it, I'm delivering horses to my father's stables in Kentucky. The others in my group have come along for their own reasons. Traveling together was the most beneficial thing for all of us."

"Does your father live in Kentucky, then?"

"No, he's back at our family farm in Illinois." Stefan folded his arms across his stomach. "He isn't well. Hasn't been for a long time."

Remus gave Stefan a sympathetic look. "I'm sorry to hear that. My father buried my mother at eighty-three years of age. They had a long life together, those two. He knew it was going to happen, but I know it didn't lessen the pain."

Stefan exhaled, long and slow. "My father did the same thing, but at a much younger age. He lost a piece of himself that day. Since then, his memory has begun slipping. He's starting to forget who he is. Who I am." It was harsher when put into words. "The doctors say sooner or later, he won't remember a thing. Once that happens, it won't be long."

"Have you nobody else?" Remus questioned softly.

Stefan's jaw tightened, and his next word emerged strained. "No."

"That's a shame. It is good, then, that you are not entirely alone. You have them, after all." Remus inclined his head in the direction of Charlotte and the twins.

"I doubt they'll stay once we reach Kentucky. They have lives to lead, and their journeys extend beyond my father's farm." Though, while it came as a surprise to Stefan, the idea of losing Charlotte and the twins was unsettling. At first, he had found their constant chatter a bit irritating. As of late, however, he somewhat enjoyed the twins' conversation. And then there was Charlotte. Something had changed that night at the inn, and he was reluctant to abandon it.

"I fear I have troubled you. That was not my intent," Remus said. "I only meant to offer you some comfort."

Stefan raised his shoulders in a half shrug, letting them drop a moment later. "I was wondering what would happen once we part ways. There's nothing to tie us together. Once they're gone, I'll never see them again." And he would be alone.

Remus glanced toward Charlotte. "Nothing? Are you certain?"

Stefan nearly choked. "Oh, no. We aren't...we're traveling companions, nothing more."

"But you could be, if you'd ask." Remus gestured to Mrs. Fitzgerald, the corners of his lips lifting. "Take a note from me and don't let a good one get away."

Stefan tugged at his shirt collar. Thank goodness the twins were speaking so loudly. "Now is not the time. Charlotte has much to sort through, and so do I. My father always said a man needed to be right with himself and with the Lord before considering a relationship."

"A right and noble thing. Tell me, what are you still puzzling through? Perhaps I can help."

Stefan blinked. "Well, I suppose I'm still trying to understand why God can allow terrible things to happen in the world. He proclaims Himself to be loving, and yet, He lets terrible things happen to good people." *To me.*

Remus frowned thoughtfully, tapping a finger to his chin. "A common question. Have you read the book of Job, Stefan?"

"Once, long ago."

Remus took one of the candles from the center of the table and set it before them. "Job was a good and faithful servant of the Lord. He was prosperous, humble, and had a good family. In short, he was the last person to deserve punishment." He gestured to the silver candlestick, with its gleaming exterior and ornate design. "Now, Satan noticed Job and asked the Lord permission to cast sorrow upon him. Satan said that if Job was really and truly faithful, taking away his material goods would do nothing to sway his devotion to the Lord. And God allowed it. Satan took away everything that Job had. He took his livestock." Remus waved a hand over the flame, causing it to waver. "His home." He blew on the candle, and the tiny light flickered. "And he took his family." He cupped both hands over the candle, obscuring the flame from view. "Job certainly grieved and even cried out in frustration. He questioned God's reasoning, much as you are doing now. But, though Job questioned God, he never stopped believing."

He lifted his hand, revealing that the flame still burned brightly.

Stefan swallowed hard. While he had heard Job's story before, he had never considered the similarities between the man's life and his own. The revelation was both disconcerting and strangely comforting. "And what did God say in return?"

Remus laughed. "He asked Job a question. 'Where were you when I laid the earth's foundation? Tell me, if you understand.' His words show us the truth of our own mortality." He slid the candle back to its original place at the center of the table. "You see, Stefan, we humans have a tendency to think highly of ourselves and our little lives. What we don't realize is that we have merely a fragmented idea of the world God has created for us. There's no possible way for us to know what His plan is. That plan may include suffering and hardship, but it's happening for a reason."

"A reason?"

"Yes. It may not be the reason you think, but I assure you, it is not needless suffering. He is building you up, preparing you for something that you can't yet see. God has a plan for you, son. You can rest easy knowing that."

"I suppose that makes sense." A reason behind the suffering? He hadn't thought of it that way.

"I can see I've given you something to think about. If I could make any recommendation, it would be to read Job for yourself." Remus tapped the table with one finger. "The Bible holds more wisdom than I could ever hope to give."

"I will." Stefan straightened and adjusted the cuffs of his shirt. "Thank you for your advice."

Remus inclined his head, a smile crossing his face. "Of course. One last thing. Though we are surrounded by the ugliness of the world, you must not forget to look for the beauty. It's the only thing that keeps us sane in these ever-changing times." He chuckled before sobering once more. "You see, Stefan, there is good to be found all around us. You have only to look for it, and you'll discover that it was always there."

Was there anything beautiful left in his life?

"Think about it. You need not come up with a response now," Remus said calmly.

Stefan rose, propping his crutch beneath him. "I will. In the meantime, I'm going to see that the horses get settled in for the night. It's been nice speaking with you, Remus."

"And you as well, Stefan. I'll be praying for you and your friends." Remus raised a hand in farewell, a gesture Stefan returned before exiting out the front door. He would take those prayers. Already, more peace rested upon his heart than he could recall since before the war.

CHAPTER 18

The sizzling of bacon grease drew Charlotte from her slumber and led her to roll over in bed. It took her a moment to recall that she was in a real home and not at an inn or boarding house. The comforting atmosphere reminded her of waking up in Peshtigo.

"Lottie, you're awake! You should get dressed. Church begins in two hours, and your Mr. Roberts seems most anxious to be on his way," Ilona said from the bedroom doorway, a bright smile on her face. She had donned a beautiful pink dress and piled her shimmering hair atop her head in one of the styles from the periodicals she had shown Charlotte the previous evening. The girl certainly loved fashion, and Charlotte's admission that she had worked as a tailor had only spurred Ilona's excitement.

Charlotte lifted herself from the bed which she had shared with Ilona the previous evening. While she would have liked to speak with the young woman more, she had fallen asleep almost the moment her head touched the pillow. "He isn't *my* Mr. Roberts." She scrubbed at her cheeks in an effort to conceal the flush that stole over them. "As for church, I'm afraid I'll have to go in what I wore yesterday. I only have two other dresses, and they're in far worse condition." She began unbraiding her hair, which was still damp from the bath she had taken before bed.

"Oh, but that simply won't do! Let me see if I can find a dress for you. What's your favorite color?" Ilona crossed to her wardrobe.

Charlotte blinked. "Oh, Lona." They'd settled on the nicknames the night before. "You don't have to do that."

Ilona flung the doors open and began sifting through the few dresses inside. "Nonsense. I'm certain I can find something that will suit you. Ah, this should do nicely." She withdrew a lovely dress of soft yellow cotton and held it out for inspection.

"Goodness no. I'd find a way to ruin it."

"I insist. I grew out of it a year ago, and it's been sitting here since. If you don't take it, I'll simply donate it to the nearest charity or use it for scrap."

"Are you certain?" Charlotte brushed her hand against the fabric.

Ilona thrust the garment in her direction. "Very."

Charlotte accepted the dress with a smile. "This is wonderful, Ilona. I've sewn some fine articles of clothing, but I've never had the opportunity to wear one. Thank you."

"But of course! That color should suit you well. Why don't you try it on?"

Charlotte considered the dress for a moment before releasing a breath. "Well, all right. I don't believe I've worn yellow before." With Ilona's help, she carefully slipped the dress over her chemise, pantalets, corset, and petticoat.

After buttoning the dress and tying a yellow sash around Charlotte's waist, Ilona stood back with her hands on her hips. "You look wonderful! Just like a daffodil." She tilted her head, putting a finger beneath her chin. "I do wish I had a bustle to complete the look, but I'm wearing the only one I own. Besides, I think it looks rather charming without it."

Charlotte rubbed her arms, glad the dress had long sleeves. "It's perfect."

Ilona slumped a bit and sighed. "I do wish you could stay longer. Things would be brighter around here if we had some company. But I'm glad you can come to church. Did you attend services often at home?"

"Yes. Before my father passed away, we went every Sunday." She didn't add that she hadn't stepped foot in one since then. Her mother and Carina had continued to attend, but Charlotte had made every excuse not to.

Ilona grinned. "That's wonderful! Now, why don't you come and get some breakfast before we leave? My mother made more than enough food for everyone."

Charlotte allowed herself to be led into the kitchen, where the others were eating breakfast at the table. The twins had been given clean shirts to wear, though they looked to be a few sizes too big. Stefan also wore a fresh shirt and smart dove-gray waistcoat. As Charlotte entered, he glanced up and carefully stood to pull out a chair for her. He had an almost gentle look in his eyes, a far cry from the paranoid man from the day before. Had something changed during the night? "You look… nice," he murmured as she gratefully accepted the seat. "That color suits you well."

Charlotte couldn't help but laugh, though her cheeks heated at the compliment. "Why, thank you, good sir. You look nice as well."

After enjoying a quick breakfast of eggs and bacon, they walked to the barn, where the horses had already been harnessed. The Fitzgeralds had their own wagon, which they had hitched to their horse, Francis.

As the wagons trundled toward the path at the back of the clearing, Charlotte fidgeted with the folds of her gown. How silly to be nervous over something as simple as going to church. And yet she couldn't dispel the feeling. What would the preacher have to say? Would he know she was an outsider in more ways than one?

"You're anxious. Why?" Stefan asked softly. His eyes were fixed, as always, on the road ahead. "Have you changed your mind about church?"

"Is it that obvious?" When Stefan sent her a telling expression, Charlotte released a nervous laugh. "I haven't changed my mind. But what if...what if the preacher knows I'm confused? What if he asks me to leave?"

Stefan's eyebrows shot up. "Why on earth would he ask you to leave? You've done nothing wrong. We all have questions now and then."

"I know," Charlotte whispered, lowering her lashes.

A Bible appeared in the corner of her vision as Stefan placed the worn book in her lap. "I've been meaning to give you that. Perhaps it will bring you some comfort. I know it has for me, especially last night. I read the book of Job."

Charlotte glanced up, meeting Stefan's eyes. "Are you sure? I know how much it means to you."

Stefan lifted a shoulder. "Something tells me you could use it a bit more right now."

"Well, thank you. I can see it's been loved." Charlotte ran a hand over the cracked leather. Opening the front page, she studied the faded handwriting. *Kate Roberts*. So this was the woman who had shared her faith with Stefan. Upon flipping the page, she discovered the marriage and death records. Written in smooth, flowing handwriting at the top of the page was Johann and Kate's marriage. On the other page, written in a hand far sharper and almost stick-like, was the record of her death. Charlotte frowned, running a hand over the names of the woman and her son. *Kate and Franz Roberts.* Gone too soon, just like her own mother and sister.

Stefan cleared his throat. "We have arrived."

Indeed, they were pulling to a stop in front of a small church. The building was made of simple clapboard, with beautiful stained glass windows that depicted various scenes from the Bible. People and wagons milled around outside, and it took a few moments for Stefan to find a place to tie Orion. Once the wagon was secure, he assisted Charlotte down with an appreciative smile while the twins hopped out of the back.

Charlotte hugged Stefan's Bible to her chest and spotted Ilona close to the entrance of the church, already engaged in a spirited conversation with a young couple. It was clear by the woman's bright smile that Charlotte's new friend had no trouble making small talk.

"Shall we go in?" Stefan asked from behind Charlotte's right ear, making a tingle run down her spine. He came to stand beside her with his crutch propped beneath his left arm. He seemed to be standing taller and taller as the days went on, lending him a more confident air—a good change from the tired shell of a man Charlotte had first met.

Charlotte released a deep breath. "I suppose."

Stefan gave her a small smile, one of the first genuine ones she had seen from him. "Don't be nervous, Charlotte. It'll be all right. I'll be here the whole time, and so will the twins. They'll do the talking for us."

True to Stefan's word, the boys were chattering loudly over some trivial matter. She chuckled. "So it would seem."

As they advanced to the door of the chapel, Ilona left the woman she was conversing with and took Charlotte's arm. "Oh, Lottie, I do hope you'll enjoy the service. Will you and Mr. Roberts sit with us? The twins, too, of course."

"I don't see why not." Charlotte allowed herself to be led to the pew where the elder Fitzgeralds were sitting.

As they took a seat, the conversation died down, and the pastor, a kind-looking man, younger than many of the clergymen Charlotte had seen in the past, took the pulpit and opened his Bible. "Romans 8:39 declares, 'Neither height nor depth, nor any other creature, shall be able to separate us from the love of God, which is Christ Jesus our Lord.' Is that not a wonderful thing? To think that God in His glory will always love us, regardless of what may come, is the greatest assurance we will ever have."

Charlotte flipped to the verse in Romans to find the words exactly as the preacher had said. Beneath them, in a faint scrawl, Stefan's mother had written a note. *God of love, God of justice.* Charlotte frowned before leaning over and tapping Ilona on the arm. "Ilona? What does this mean?" she whispered. "Justice?"

Ilona glanced at the Bible. "Oh, it means that God loves us, but because He is just, he calls us to repent our sins. If we are to love Him back, we have to cast off our sins. And the only way to cast off our sins is through Jesus."

Love God back? Charlotte bit her lip. In all the time she had been alone, it hadn't occurred to her that the problem might lie with her own attitude. She had thought of herself as being unworthy of God's attention. Had she not considered God worthy of attention?

"When we hear Jesus knocking at our heart, we're the ones who have to open the door. You have been given the choice to take His gift of love. It is up to us whether or not we accept it." The preacher's words drew Charlotte's attention. "So you see, it is never a question of whether or not God loves us. He loved us enough to send His only son, as John 3:16 says. No, it is a matter of whether or not we accept God's gift."

Charlotte leaned back in the pew. Did God really care about her? She hadn't thought so, not after all that had happened to her and her family. Not after she had been left to fend for herself. And yet, the accusations she had once leveled at God were faint and uncertain, no longer as anger-driven as they had once been.

After the sermon, Charlotte hurried from the chapel with Stefan's Bible clutched tightly in hand. Questions raced through her head, each one faster than the last. She was so buried in her thoughts, in fact, that she jumped when Ilona spoke directly beside her.

"Goodness, Lottie! You ran out of that chapel as though your skirts were on fire." Her new friend stared at her with wide eyes and obvious concern.

Charlotte exhaled shakily and slowed her pace. "I'm sorry, Lona. I was lost in thought. The preacher gave me a lot to think about."

"He's good at that. Last week, he gave a sermon on gossiping. Many of the ladies, including myself, were left with plenty to consider," Ilona admitted.

Charlotte lowered her head with a sigh, studying the vibrant grass around her skirts. "I hope I can find the answers I'm looking for. Being worried and confused is a terrible feeling."

Ilona clasped her hands behind her back, her eyes sparkling with warmth. How was she so carefree and cheerful all the time? "You don't have to worry when the Creator of the world loves you."

Love. Could it be? "Perhaps."

Stefan caught her eye from beside the wagon, where he was waving in her direction. The twins and the older Fitzgeralds were also at the wagons, clearly waiting for their arrival.

"I have to go," Charlotte said, gesturing to the wagons.

Ilona hummed. "So it would seem. I'll miss you, Lottie. I do wish you could stay longer." She folded her arms across her chest, the smile falling from her face.

"What if I send letters? If you give me your address, I can mail them to you every so often. You won't be able to send any back to me until I reach Kentucky, but I'll tell you once I have a mailing address."

Ilona gasped. "To think that I could have my very own pen pal. You can tell me everything that happens on your trip." She pulled a small pad of paper and a pencil stub from her reticule and scribbled down an address, ripped it from the pad, and handed it to Charlotte. "That's the address for our post office. I stop there to pick up my periodicals. I haven't had anyone to get letters from until now."

Charlotte accepted the paper with a smile. "Perfect. Thank you again for your hospitality. For this dress." She touched her skirt, then Ilona's arm. "For your friendship."

Ilona swept Charlotte into a quick hug. "Oh, Lottie, we loved having you. Don't be a stranger, now. I expect to hear from you soon!"

As they pulled out of the churchyard moments later, Charlotte looked over her shoulder at the Fitzgeralds, who were waving from beside their wagon. How was it that she had known them for only a day, and yet felt as though she had known them for a lifetime?

Behind the sweet family, the sun touched the cross at the top of the church, making it glow a blinding white. The image remained fixed in Charlotte's mind for some time—as did the questions that had been raised there.

CHAPTER 19

An hour after they left the church, Stefan allowed himself to relax against the wagon seat, releasing a sigh as the tension in his back eased. It seemed Miss Fitzgerald had been correct about this route, for they had passed only a couple other families on their way home from church...and no highwaymen.

Charlotte sat quietly beside him with her hands resting in her lap. What was she thinking about? The sermon? Miss Fitzgerald? Her eyes had a far-off look to them, as if she was visiting a different time. Perhaps, in a way, she was.

Stefan turned his gaze back toward the road. The sermon had even taken him by surprise, for the preacher's words mirrored the very thing he had spoken to Remus about the previous evening. *Love.* Stefan had always considered the concept to be rather silly. Yet there was nothing light or fluffy about the type of love the preacher had described. The love he spoke of was deep and unrelenting, a commitment that would never dim or sway.

Stefan frowned, shifting in his seat. The book of Job had also caught him off guard. While he couldn't relate to Job in terms of material wealth or livestock, he could recognize the man's struggles and cries of frustration. They mirrored his own angry ramblings and pleas, which had cycled through his head many times. Stefan *had* believed God to be targeting him, allowing him to suffer for some unknown reason. He had even wondered why God hadn't just let him die. It had made him bitter. But Job hadn't lost faith or grown angry. Below God's rebuke to Job, reminding him who was God and who was not, Stefan's mother had written a note. *It is not our place to know the plan. It is our job to live it.*

If God had truly abhorred Stefan's existence so much, he would have died that day along with his brother. And yet, he hadn't. He had survived and gone back home. He had remained with his father after the death of his mother and helped keep the family business running. What would have happened if he had joined Franz in death? Stefan shuddered. It seemed God had kept him alive for a reason, though he still wasn't certain what that was.

Charlotte shifted next to him with a rustle of skirts. What would have happened if he had never found her in Chicago? What would the thief have done to her? If he hadn't been there, something terrible likely would have occurred. *A plan.* Stefan huffed a soft laugh. *Perhaps I was wrong after all.*

"Mr. Roberts?" Tom tapped Stefan on the shoulder, making him jolt and spin around. "I don't mean to interrupt your thinking time, but we're running low on food. We may have enough for..." He paused and spent a few seconds digging through the bags. "One meal. We'll have to stop in a town sooner or later."

Stefan winced. "I'm not certain that's a good idea, considering what happened yesterday. However, we can't avoid civilization forever, can we? If Miss Fitzgerald's directions were correct, we should come upon the main road in a short time. Then we'll find the nearest town and stock up on supplies.

We'll get enough to keep us away from towns for a good, long while." He raised a brow. "We won't be able to simply drive in to town, however. Not when there are highwaymen patrolling the streets."

Tom grinned. "Don't you worry about that, Mr. Roberts. I have a plan."

A plan? *Oh dear.*

~

*A*round two in the afternoon, they reached a stately town with roads filled to the brim with carriage traffic. Shoppers and pedestrians meandered down the portion of the street that wasn't overtaken by vehicles, their faces turned to enjoy the bright sun. Stefan spent a few minutes looking for an escape from the traffic before he spotted a side road that looked relatively unoccupied and turned onto it. He pulled the wagon to a halt behind one of the brick shops and swiveled to face the twins. "All right. You boys know what you're doing?"

Tom nodded. "Clear as day. Quick in, quick out."

Bastian rolled his eyes good-naturedly. "We're only buying bread. We aren't going into an enemy camp."

"True, but it's more exciting when I treat it like we are." Tom jumped from the wagon, causing the thoroughbreds to bob their heads. "I'll race you to the bakery."

The twins darted to the edge of the building and peered around the side, checking for passersby. The road must have been clear, for they crept around the corner and out of sight.

"Be careful," Stefan muttered under his breath.

There was something unsettling about the fact that he couldn't assist the twins, who shouldn't have been put in the line of danger to begin with. Stefan exhaled, frowning at his leg. *Positive thoughts, Stefan.* He couldn't run in to town, but he could certainly bring the wagon around at the first sign of danger.

Charlotte patted his arm. "They'll be fine, Stefan. You don't have to worry so much. They're smart boys."

"I know. But I'm not so much of a coward that I would send children to do my work for me."

Charlotte shook her head. "Why, I don't think you're a coward in the least. Those thieves saw our faces, Stefan. They know I have the locket. If any of us have a chance of getting in and out of town unnoticed, it's those boys."

"True. I suppose they did save us, as well." Stefan tapped his chin. "They're craftier than they let on."

Charlotte rested a hand over the collar of her dress, beneath which the locket was safely concealed. "If only things hadn't escalated so quickly. If only this was still just a simple trip to Kentucky. This journey is nothing like I thought it would be."

Stefan tilted his head. "What did you intend to do after you reached Kentucky? Were you going to travel back to Wisconsin?"

"I hadn't really planned that far. I was more concerned with getting there." Charlotte pursed her lips. A few strands of hair had blown loose from her updo and fallen onto her cheeks, doing curious things to Stefan's stomach. Was she aware of the way she looked in that moment, with her face so bright and thoughtful? "I suppose I was hoping to find some temporary work, perhaps as a seamstress. That would give me enough money to rent an apartment in town." She turned to look at Stefan, the light in her eyes dimming by a fraction. "You know, Stefan, you don't have to continue traveling with me. I can leave and make my own way if it's getting to be too much."

"No," he stated vehemently. "I can't do that."

She rubbed her arms in that familiar habit, and Stefan was half tempted to reach out and stop her, if only to reassure her that she need not be self-conscious. "I feel awful, making you and the twins sneak around on account of me. What if you don't reach Monticello in time for the races? Oh, I could never live with myself."

A few weeks ago, Stefan would have leapt at the chance to part ways with her and return to his peaceful solitude. Yet, the solitude had not been so peaceful as he had first thought. In reality, it had been fraught with anger and that deep sadness Charlotte had first seen in him. Stefan shook his head. "As a former Union soldier, I have a duty to my country, Charlotte. Getting that locket to Kentucky is a matter of national importance, and I intend to do my part in seeing it through." There was another reason, too, one he was too embarrassed to admit aloud.

Charlotte smiled, her shoulders slumping in silent relief. "Thank you, Stefan. It's nice to know that I don't have to do all of this by myself."

Stefan straightened, clearing his throat. "You don't. We'll do what we can to help you, Charlotte. I promise."

Before he could say more, the twins came racing back around the corner, both with pale faces.

Bastian panted, clutching a handful of loaves to his chest. "We should go."

"What now?" Stefan took a couple of loaves so the boy could climb into the wagon. "Did Tom knock another shelf over? Did someone see you?"

"Not sure. Everything was going well until we left the shop. There was a man riding his horse down the road, watching us." Tom shuddered. "He was in the middle of a whole bunch of carriages, but if he hadn't been, I think he would have come over. He wouldn't take his eyes off us for even a second."

Stefan snapped the reins, setting Orion into motion. As they hastened away from town, he turned to face the twins. "Did you recognize the man? Did you see what he looked like?"

"No. He had a hat pulled low over his head." Bastian

frowned. "He was on a white horse, though, and he had a big hat on. Does that help?"

A white horse. Could it be?

"John." Charlotte knew the answer as well as he did. She worried her lip, her eyes wide. "He must be following us. And if he's here, then the other men can't be far behind."

"I agree. I have no doubt he's working with the robber. " But something didn't make sense. Why would the man have pulled them out of the mud if he intended to rob them? It would have been far easier to steal their belongings while they were still stuck. Furthermore, why had he let them go? Charlotte's locket had been hidden at the time, so perhaps he thought they weren't worth searching. That was the most likely reason, though it still didn't quite explain his behavior.

Charlotte tossed up her hand. "I don't know what to do. It's like they're everywhere! How many do you think there are?"

Stefan shook his head. "I don't know. At any rate, we won't be staying at an inn tonight. We'll have to make do elsewhere. It's warm enough to set up a camp if we have to."

Charlotte opened the locket and pulled the list of spies from within. Then she unfolded the paper, peering with a solemn gaze at the names written in faded ink.

"You probably shouldn't open that out here, you know. Someone might see." Stefan glanced up and down the road.

Charlotte frowned, her eyes still trained on the piece of paper. "I know. I wanted to see if there were any Johns on the list."

"Are there?"

Charlotte folded the list and replaced it in the locket. "I don't see one. He could have been using a false name, but he seemed so sincere the first time we met." She shook her head. "I guess appearances can be deceiving."

"I don't trust him." Stefan grasped the reins tighter. "To be honest, there are few people we *can* trust."

It would take the grace of God to get them through whatever lay down the road. And how were they to ensure they were even giving the locket to the right person? Charlotte seemed certain the Aspens were good, but they had thought the same of John and been wrong. Who was to say the Aspens wouldn't also exploit the list? Stefan glanced at Charlotte but didn't voice his fear. They had enough to worry about as it was.

CHAPTER 20

"This should do nicely for the evening." Charlotte turned slowly around in the clearing Stefan had chosen to stop in.

The trees stood like silent sentinels around the wagon, their long boughs creating a thick canopy that blocked out the setting sun. Though woods surrounded the small opening, there was more than enough space on the moss-covered ground to build a temporary shelter. In addition, it was at least a mile from the road, putting them far from any prying eyes. From somewhere among the leafy branches, an owl hooted, the noise strangely comforting...a gentle reminder they weren't alone.

She faced Stefan with a smile. "What would you like me to do?"

Stefan leaned over to look in the wagon bed. "If you'd like to help me get the blankets, we can find a place to lay them down. Boys, I need you to collect any branches and logs you can find and bring them back here. We'll need to get a fire started before it gets dark."

As the twins ran off to complete their task, Charlotte helped

Stefan lift the blankets from the wagon and carry them to a dry spot, where they spread out two and tied the third between the trees to create a roof of sorts.

"Well, I can't say I've ever slept in a house made of blankets," Charlotte commented as she took a seat beneath the temporary shelter. "It's certainly an interesting experience."

Stefan chuckled from where he stood a few feet away. From what Charlotte could see, it appeared that he was rolling rocks into a cluster with the bottom of his crutch, most likely forming a fire pit. "It'll be a first for me, as well. My father was never one for sleeping beneath the stars, though he always said he would like to try. I did sleep outside many times while in the cavalry, but in a proper tent."

Charlotte smiled as a distant memory resurfaced. "When I was very small, my sister and I tried to build a house with our friends. We thought it would be grand to craft a shelter out of sticks and logs, just like the brave settlers. Of course, we didn't account for all the bugs that would also be sharing our little home. We had to call my father out to remove a particularly large spider from our log ceiling. He took one look at it and told us we'd be better off coming inside." She laughed. "I think he was more afraid of bugs than we were."

"What happened to him?"

Charlotte shifted uncomfortably. "He was injured during the war in a manner similar to you. For months, we didn't know what had become of him. We began to fear the worst. But then, just when we had all but given up hope, we received a letter from him. As it turned out, he was alive and coming home. We were so excited." She tugged at the gloves on her hands. "But he came back a different man. Though his leg wounds were gone, I don't believe his mind ever healed. He wandered away into the snow one night." Charlotte shuddered. "My father never returned."

The twins appeared from between the trees with an armful

of twigs each and dumped them unceremoniously into the fire pit Stefan had made, proud smiles on their faces. "Done," Tom announced. "What's next?"

"Very good." Stefan gestured toward the clearing with a nod of his head. "You can do what you would like until dinner is ready. Don't stray too far."

Tom whooped and turned, racing for a large tree near the back of the clearing. "Race you to the top, Bas!"

Bastian jogged after his brother at a much more moderate pace. A few seconds later, the two were clambering up the branches of the tree at a rather dangerous rate.

Stefan hummed thoughtfully, bringing Charlotte's attention away from the boys and their antics. "I'm sorry to hear about your father. War changes everyone, I'm afraid. For some, that change is simply too much to handle." He struck a match against one of the stones and lit the small pile of branches within the makeshift fire pit. "I know many men who turned to pills, drink, and other vices to escape their misery."

"But you didn't. Why?" Charlotte leaned back, studying Stefan. "Even my father, who I thought was strong, succumbed to the horrors of war. How did you overcome it?"

Stefan blew on the tiny flame until it had begun eating at the branches. Once it was burning brightly, he moved from the fire and came to sit on the blanket beside her, making Charlotte's breath hitch. She could smell the scent of smoke and something else on his shirt—a tinge of pine needles, perhaps. It was comforting, but it also did strange things to her heart.

For a moment, they sat together in silence, watching as the horses grazed peacefully and the twins reached the top of the tree. Finally, Stefan spoke. "I can't say for certain, but I saw those men fall into deep, dark holes and use all manner of things to try and pull themselves out." He released a breath. "But none of it ever did. They sank farther into the darkness and eventually gave up all hope. The thing they thought would save them became their downfall. I had my own dark moments, but when I thought of my brother…"

Charlotte rested her cheek in her hand and tilted her head so she had a good view of Stefan's face, outlined in orange by the flames. "You didn't want to disappoint him."

"Yes. I suppose I knew he wouldn't have wanted me to give in to despair. Neither would my mother. They would have wanted me to get back up and live." Stefan leaned back on his palms. "I'm still learning what exactly it means— living—but I'm trying."

"Life. It's a curious thing, isn't it?" Charlotte murmured, staring into the fire. "More often than not, we don't learn to value it until it's too late."

"Yes. In the end, life is a gift. Every minute, every hour is a chance for us to experience the beauty of the world. Whether we take that opportunity or waste it is our choice. I was once willing to give up that gift." Stefan lifted a shoulder. "But I'm finding that my opinion has changed of late." He used his crutch to rise to his feet, glancing down at her. "You were right, Charlotte. The world can be a wonderful place. We simply have to look for the good."

As Stefan walked toward the wagon, she frowned. Could there be any good left in her life? And could this man who tugged at her emotions in surprising new ways be part of it?

$\sim$

Once she was certain the boys were fast asleep on their blanket, Charlotte rolled over and pulled Stefan's Bible from under her arm. She cast a quick glance over at the man where he lay a few feet from the twins. His broad shoulders rose and fell softly in slumber, although every so often, he twitched, mumbling something incomprehensible under his breath. Charlotte smiled as he shifted and released a soft snore before returning to the book in her hands.

As the flames gently popped and crackled, she opened the Bible at random and began to read. The men had kindly given her the spot closest to the fire, so she had plenty of light by which to see the words. The first page she landed on came from a chapter in John. *For God so loved the world, that he gave his only begotten Son, that whosoever believeth in him should not perish, but have everlasting life.* Such simple words, but they held a great meaning. Below the passage, in faded handwriting, Stefan's mother had written one of her notes. *He died for our sake.*

"For us? But why?" Charlotte whispered the questions aloud. Why sacrifice Himself for people who were ordinary and unimportant? People like her? "Why would He make such a great sacrifice and then...and then leave me? Why would He abandon me in my darkest hour?"

It was difficult to admit, but that was the question that had burned at the back of her mind far before the fire ever happened. How could God, who proclaimed to love His children, turn away when one of those very children called out for aid? He hadn't brought Charlotte's father back on that snowy night. Instead, he had let her father die, leaving her family to pick up what remained of their shattered life.

Unlike the fire, the day her father disappeared remained clear in Charlotte's mind. It had been so bitterly cold on that wintery eve. She was sneaking into the kitchen for a glass of water when she heard the arguing voices.

"We can make this right, George. All you have to do is find an honest job and stay far from that train station. We can start over. Think of the girls. They need you. I need you, George."

"The girls want nothing to do with a broken man like me, Mary. They'd be better off if I left."

Charlotte froze in the kitchen, glass of water forgotten. Why did her father feel as though she didn't love him? She had never said or done anything of the sort.

"George, wait! Please, don't go!"

The door slammed shut, leaving Charlotte with the sound of her mother's soft weeping.

The girls want nothing to do with me. Yet it had been Charlotte's father who had left them, not the other way around. "I did love you," Charlotte whispered sadly. "You just didn't believe me." As she spoke the words, a seed of doubt sprouted in her chest, like a thorn poking at her heart. *How is this any different?*

"It's me, isn't it? I'm acting like my father." Realization washed over Charlotte. "I thought it was You who was turning away from me. I thought You didn't care about me." She took in a shuddering breath. "But I was wrong. I'm the one who wandered out into the snowstorm."

For the Son of Man has come to seek and save that which was lost. The verse echoed in the back of Charlotte's head, and hot tears gathered in her eyes as another memory resurfaced, this one of her mother.

Charlotte had been about five at the time of the incident. Unbeknownst to Mother, she'd decided one spring morning to follow her father to work so she could spend the day with him. It had seemed like an excellent idea at the time, and so she had put on her own shoes—which felt like a great accomplishment at five years old—and left the house to go after her father. However, when she reached the forest, she'd became lost among the trees and wandered about for hours.

At last, distantly, she'd heard her mother calling her name.

"Charlotte! Charlotte, where are you?"

Charlotte answered, and her mother came running through the trees. "Charlotte Alice Clarke, don't you ever scare me like that again. You're not to leave the house for a week, you hear? You nearly gave us all a heart attack."

"I'm sorry, Mama. I didn't mean to get lost. Please don't yell like that." Charlotte blubbered, frightened.

Charlotte's mother sighed and tilted Charlotte's head back, brushing the tears from her eyes. "I didn't mean to scare you. I'm not angry. You frightened me, darling. We might never have found you had you not answered my call. How could I have found you if I didn't shout your name?"

How, indeed? During her father's disappearance, through the fire and her friend's death, had Someone been calling her name all that time?

Tears ran down Charlotte's face in earnest as she touched the locket hanging around her neck. She hadn't been led to Flora by coincidence. She hadn't been led to Stefan or the twins by chance. "You've always been there, haven't You?" Charlotte's voice cracked, and she released a soft sob. "All this time, You were looking for me in the woods. But I never answered when You shouted my name, did I? I never responded to the call. I was the one who got myself lost, not You. You were simply trying to find me." She looked up at the stairs that glinted faintly in the gaps between the trees. "Well, I want to be found. I'm so tired of being lost and confused. I'm so tired of mourning. Please, come and find me. Show me the way."

Beloved.

It was a single word that she sensed in her spirit, but it broke some hidden barrier within Charlotte. It was as if her final line of defense had been brought down, leaving her raw and exposed. And yet, at that moment, she had never felt freer. For the voice that had told her she wasn't worthy of God's love and attention, that He didn't care enough to save her, was finally silent. She pushed to her feet, as light as if a weight had fallen from her shoulders. Charlotte swiped at her eyes beneath the star-flecked canopy and laughed...because she would never be the same again.

CHAPTER 21

By the time Stefan awoke the following morning, the fire had dwindled down to glowing embers, and a blue sky peeped through the gaps in the trees. He sat upright and winced when cold dewdrops cascaded from the blanket above him and ran down the back of his neck. The twins snored away beside him, blissfully unaware of the world. Charlotte, too, was still asleep, her back rising in slow breaths from where she lay at the edge of the blanket tent. The sun cast soft rays over her, illuminating her serene face. Her hair pooled around her shoulders like a river of brown tinged with gold.

Stefan swallowed and rose quickly to avoid disturbing the peaceful scene. After locating his hat and securing it on his head, he moved to where the horses were quietly grazing between the trees and set a hand on Orion's back. "Guten Morgen, my friend," he whispered, untying the horse's rope from the tree he had loosely wrapped it around the night before. "Are you ready for another day of travel?"

Orion snuffled at Stefan's outstretched palm, making him chuckle as he led the horse over to the wagon. "I'm afraid there will be no carrots today. Perhaps tomorrow, when we reach Lexington. The markets there are sure to have food." And the horse certainly deserved a treat after all the hard work he had done over the past few days.

After retying the horses to the wagon, Stefan moved to the fire pit and used his crutch to shove dirt over the still-glowing embers. His movements must have been loud enough to wake Charlotte, for a moment later, she sat up with a yawn. Stefan couldn't help but grin at her disheveled hair and sleepy eyes, which focused on him after a few seconds.

"Ah, Stefan. Good morning." Charlotte pushed herself to her feet, fixing Stefan with a bright smile. "Did you sleep well?"

Stefan blinked. While he couldn't say what exactly it was, something about the woman had transformed in the morning light. It was almost as if the harshness hiding behind her eyes had receded, allowing her to really and truly smile. It was... beautiful. Beautiful in the way sunlight twinkled in the morning dewdrops and cast warmth over everything it touched.

Stefan turned away so she wouldn't see his rapidly heating cheeks and coughed, running a hand through Orion's mane. "You seem different today. Different in a good way, that is," he quickly added. "Has something changed?"

Charlotte laughed, the sound like birdsong. "I suppose you could say I took your advice last night, Stefan. I looked for the good, and I found it."

Stefan turned, finding Charlotte a few feet behind him. Her eyes shone with clarity and confidence, a far cry from the uncertain woman he had first met. He smiled. "I'm glad. Happiness suits you, Charlotte Clarke."

Charlotte laughed again and brushed her skirts out so they fluffed around her. "Why, thank you, my good sir. And what about you? How do you feel on this fine morning?"

Stefan tilted his head, gazing up at the bright sky. "I feel...

different. Peaceful, in a way. I'm not entirely certain why, but I like the feeling."

Charlotte began untying the blanket from between the trees. "That's good." She gave the material a shake and folded it, contentment evident on her face. "I suppose we're both improving, aren't we? We're learning what it means to live and be loved."

Love. Stefan blinked. *I suppose we are.*

"Boys, it's time to get up." Charlotte bent and shook Tom gently on the shoulder, causing him to yawn and roll over in bed.

"Not yet, Ma. Five more minutes." Tom blinked blearily at Charlotte. "Oh, it's you, Miss Charlotte. I'm sorry." He staggered to his feet, stretched his arms overhead, and nudged Bastian with his toe. "Wake up, Bas. We have to go." When Bastian mumbled a complaint, he rolled his eyes. "Don't make me get my banjo."

Bastian groaned and pushed himself onto his elbows, raking the curls from his forehead with one hand. "Oh, anything but that. I'm awake."

Stefan snorted in amusement. "That's enough, you two. Grab those blankets so we can get on our way."

The twins hurried to fold the blankets and carry them to the wagon, scrubbing at their eyes as they went. It took only a moment to pack up the rest of the supplies, and with that done, they got back on the road.

After an hour of fairly silent travel, Tom cleared his throat from behind Stefan. "Mr. Roberts? May I play my banjo for a bit? I don't have to." He shifted nervously. "It's just that it's such a nice day, and I thought it might be nice to have a tune to travel along to."

Stefan exhaled. "I have no problem with your banjo, Tom. I'm sorry for overreacting the first time you played it. I...I was a bit on edge that day."

"There's nothing to apologize for, Mr. Roberts. I understand." After plucking a few strings, Tom struck up a gentle tune that seemed to dance around the wagon and swirl with the breeze, taking on a life of its own. The notes rose and fell in a pleasant rhythm that even the daisies lining the road seemed to bob their heads to. Charlotte must have known the tune, for she took to humming along.

To Stefan's surprise, the memories he had expected to flood over him at the sound of the music did not come. The road in front of him remained clear, and so did the soft song. He released a sigh of relief, relaxing back against the seat and letting the sounds flood over him. *Thank You, Lord, for small favors.* It had been a long time since he had been able to truly enjoy a piece of music.

A few minutes later, the song faded away. "Do you want to play along with me, Bas? I'm sure you have your bodhrán stored somewhere in that knapsack of yours. You haven't touched it in a long while."

"I don't care to 'play along,' Tom." Bastian's stilted response evidenced his discomfort. "I sold that drum ages ago."

Tom set his banjo down, causing the strings to hum. "Sold it? Why would you do that?"

Bastian snorted. "Because there are more important things in this life than music. Things like food and clothing. Not that you seem to care."

Stefan frowned but didn't turn around. Bas wasn't normally so irritable, and while he teased his brother, he had never sounded angry. What was it about music that put the boy so on edge?

"You never used to have trouble with music. What changed? You used to love performing with me and Da. We were a trio."

"Are you sure about that, Tom? Or was that just what you wanted to believe?" Bastian ground out the questions in a sharp tone. "Because that wasn't the case. Music destroyed our family."

"What do you mean? We were happy. We were the best musicians in our district," Tom protested. "Da made music his whole life. That's how he succeeded, Bas, and that's how I'm going to succeed too. I'm going to be a fine musician, just like he was."

"You're wrong," Bastian snapped. "He wasn't the man you thought he was."

"He was my father, Bas. That was enough for me. I don't know what happened between the two of you, but I do know he cared about us."

An uneasy silence fell over the wagon, punctuated only by the sound of the horses' hooves. The twins remained stubbornly quiet, though the rustle of fabric drifted from the back of the wagon. Clearly, the issue wouldn't be resolved until someone grew humble enough to make amends.

With a heavy sigh, Stefan pulled the wagon to the edge of a wide field. "Time for lunch." Hopefully, having some food would calm the twins' terse attitudes.

Charlotte quickly procured a loaf of bread from her bag and broke it into chunks, handing one piece to each of the twins. "Here you are. Would you like an apple as well?"

Bastian shook his head and took the bread. He hopped from the wagon, scurrying across the grass toward the small forest to the right. Within a moment, the boy had ducked around one of the trees and vanished from sight.

"I'm going to speak with him," Stefan murmured, holding a hand up to decline the piece of bread Charlotte offered him. "We'll resume traveling when I come back."

Charlotte wrapped the rest of the loaf and put it back in her bag. "Go on, Stefan. He respects you." She pointed over her shoulder. "I'll stay with Tom and the horses."

Stefan used his crutch to lower himself from the wagon and

make his way through the long, waving grass in the field. As he neared the trees, he could only hope Bastian would be willing to talk to him and divulge whatever secret he was hiding. The trip wouldn't be the same if the twins were at odds the entire time.

Stefan followed the faint sound of sniffles to a tree trunk, where a closer inspection revealed Bastian sitting on the other side. Stefan leaned against the trunk. "Hello, Bastian. Mind if I take a seat?"

The boy hugged his arms around his knees, the piece of bread untouched on the ground beside him. His eyes were red-rimmed and watery, though he made a valiant effort to hide them in his jacket sleeve. "No, I don't mind," Bastian muttered, his voice muffled by the fabric of his coat.

"Good." Stefan slid rather awkwardly to the ground beside Bastian and stretched his crutch out in front of him. With that settled, he exhaled and glanced at the branches overhead. The leaves on the trees waved in the gentle wind, creating shadows that danced and flickered every half second. They weren't the only thing moving. "Do you like birds, Bastian?"

Bastian turned to Stefan with a raised brow. "I suppose I like them the same amount as everyone else. Why do you ask?"

Stefan shrugged and gestured to a blue speck hidden among the forest canopy. "There's a jay in the tree over there. It's not often you see a bird so vibrant."

"You don't have to try and make conversation on my account, you know. I'm perfectly fine with the silence," Bastian grumbled, turning away. "You can go back to the wagon if you want. I'll be right as rain in a moment."

Stefan hummed. "I could. But then we'd be missing a member of our party, and that wouldn't be right. Our group wouldn't be complete without you."

Bastian shifted. His normally neat hair had become disheveled beneath his cap, flopping over his head. It made him look far younger than thirteen, especially when combined with his mournful eyes. "Maybe it would be better that way. At least then I wouldn't be weighing you all down with my negativity."

Stefan studied the lush green forest that stretched out before them. "I don't think you're weighing us down. Look around, Bastian. It's a wonderful spring day. I doubt even the most bitter of hearts could ruin its beauty." He glanced at Bastian from the corner of his eye. "Of course, if you *were* feeling disheartened, I'd be more than willing to listen. Others have done the same for me many times, and I've found it to be very beneficial. Keeping your anger locked away will only breed more, until eventually, you can no longer contain it."

Bastian lifted his hands as though fighting for words. "I suppose..." He dropped his arms to his sides. "I suppose I'm frustrated with Tom. I wish he would listen to me when I warn him that he's doing the wrong thing. He isn't always correct, as you know from the incident at the pottery shop. But he always pretends he is. And it gets him in trouble more often than not."

"What isn't he correct about?" Stefan folded his arms across his chest. "I take it this isn't a matter of broken pottery."

"Tom believes my parents were faultless." Bastian tapped his feet on the ground, one after the other. "But they weren't. Tom was everything they could have ever wanted in a son, you see. He was excellent at playing music. He was charismatic. He didn't have this." Bastian gestured to his eyes, the colors contrasting sharply in the sunlight.

"And what's wrong with your eyes?"

"My parents were superstitious. They thought my eyes were a bad omen, and because of that, they ignored me. All I wanted was to prove to them that I could be good at things as well. Things that didn't require me to be the main event of every show." Bastian glanced at the ground. "But nothing I created, nothing I did was enough to appease them." He toed a stick with one boot. "I was always second to Tom."

Stefan pursed his lips but chose to remain silent. He needed a moment to gather his thoughts, for he would only have one chance to reassure the boy.

Bastian plucked at his sleeves. "There was one other thing I discovered that Tom never seemed to learn of. My father led my brother and me to believe he was making money through playing music. We never questioned him, until one day when my mother sent me to take him lunch. I found him at a boxing ring. *That* was how he came home with money. He spent his nights betting." Bastian blew out a sigh. "And my mother encouraged it. It seemed to be working for him...until the night he finally lost it all. I don't believe he gambled after that, but as a result, we grew poorer and poorer. We were forced to move to the slums. The fire happened shortly after, and I never saw my parents again."

Stefan tilted his head, making sure the boy was finished before speaking. "I won't say I approve of your parents' actions, for they certainly weren't good ones. However, I will say this. None of us are perfect, Bastian. We are flawed people who make mistakes."

Bastian nodded. "I know. I don't blame my parents, Mr. Roberts. I know they were only people, just as I'm certain they were simply trying to provide for us. I only wish Tom didn't treat our past like some kind of fairytale. He isn't willing to hear the truth. Even worse, he constantly reminds me of it."

"Have you considered the fact that your brother might simply be trying to remember the best about your parents?"

"Maybe. Tom took their loss rather hard." Bastian hugged his arms around his chest and dug the toes of his boots into the dirt. "For a long time after the fire, he wouldn't even speak about what happened. Even now, months later, he hardly ever mentions that night."

"What did happen that night? How did you manage to escape?"

"Tom and I were separated from our parents in the rush of people escaping when the fire began. In the midst of the confusion, we ran to the lake, where we waited until the fire finally died down. It took a week before we decided it was safe enough to venture back to our old home. We thought our parents might have gone there to look for us, but we were wrong." Bastian's jaw twitched, and his shoulders slumped forward. "Our neighbors later told us that they weren't able to escape the house in time. There was nothing left of our home or our family, and so we took off."

"I'm sure that must have been frightening for you both."

Bastian fiddled with the cuff of his jacket, rolling it back and forth. "It was. After leaving the city, I wanted to find a new place to settle. I figured I could start an apprenticeship and earn enough money to survive. Tom, on the other hand, wanted to continue traveling. He's afraid, Mr. Roberts. He doesn't want to build anything because he fears it will get torn down. But when I try to tell him that, he denies it."

Stefan hummed thoughtfully and laced his fingers in front of him. "I can't blame him for being afraid, considering what happened. However, I can also understand your perspective. Wanting a home and a place to stay is nothing to be ashamed of. What I will say is this, Bastian. You are not your brother. You are Sebastian, a boy who has his own strengths and weaknesses. You don't have to agree with Tom on everything. That being said, getting angry with him for something he doesn't fully understand won't help either. Have you told him how you feel?"

Bastian propped his elbows up on his knees. "No. Every time I've tried to explain it to him, it hasn't come out the right way. I get frustrated, and, well..." He blew a raspberry. "I don't want to make him angry. His enthusiasm can irritate me at times, but I don't want to destroy it."

"I imagine your brother feels the same way about you. He doesn't want to make you angry, but he can hardly avoid it when you won't explain to him why you get frustrated. Take my advice, Bastian. Siblings can be irritating, but they will always be your kin. Talk to Tom. He will listen, because he cares for you." A smile crossed Stefan's face. "I had a brother that was very similar to yours, once upon a time. He irritated me, but in the end, we always reconciled. There was nothing he could have said or done that I wouldn't have eventually forgiven. At the end of the day, I knew I would always have a friend in him."

"A friend. I guess Tom is my friend, even if we do have a tendency to drive each other mad on occasion." Bastian rose to his feet and scratched at the back of his head. "I'm sorry, Mr. Roberts. I didn't mean to slow us down. I promise I'll try to avoid starting arguments from here on out."

Stefan chuckled as he collected his crutch and rose to his feet. "I'm afraid that arguments between siblings, meaningless as they may be, are often inevitable. Luckily, they can be resolved. Will you talk to your brother?"

Bastian inclined his head. "I will. Not here, and not now, but I will."

"Good." As they turned to leave, Stefan cleared his throat. "Oh, and Bastian? One last thing."

Bastian turned back, his face drawn in confusion. "Yes?"

"I'm proud of you, no matter what you choose to do with your life. You're a fine young man, Sebastian."

Bastian grinned sheepishly. "Thank you, Mr. Roberts. It means a lot to hear you say that."

"It's true." Stefan nodded in the direction of the wagon. "Now, why don't we rejoin the others? I'm sure they'll be glad to have you back."

"All right." Bastian took a deep breath, his brows creasing with worry. "I hope they aren't angry."

Stefan patted the boy on the shoulder. "They won't be." If anything, they were probably eager to get back on the road. As they moved from the forest and made their way back through the field to where the wagon lay, however, his heart dropped.

"Mr. Roberts? Why are the horses unhitched from the wagon?" Bastian frowned. "More importantly, where did Tom and Miss Charlotte go?"

A FEW MINUTES EARLIER...

"I didn't mean to make Bas storm off like that," Tom mumbled from behind Charlotte, his voice muffled from a mouth full of bread. "I didn't realize he held such a strong dislike for music. I guess I thought he would feel the same way I did." He hummed. "It seems I was wrong. I'm sorry for that."

Charlotte lowered her pencil and swiveled in her seat to face Tom. "I had the same thing happen on multiple occasions with my older sister, Carina. Sometimes she would get irritated with something I said, even if I didn't intend for it to sound that way. Part of it may simply be that you are siblings, and siblings do have a tendency to get on each other's nerves. However, you also must remember that your brother is allowed to have differing opinions from your own. You'd be wise to ask his thoughts before making assumptions." She winked. "Take it from someone who knows from experience. Bastian will appreciate it."

Tom tilted his head to the side, his eyes full of curiosity. "I didn't know you had a sister. What happened to her?"

"She...well, she's gone," Charlotte murmured, turning back to her letter. "She died in the fire that destroyed my town."

"I'm sorry, Miss Charlotte. Have you been back to your home since then?"

Charlotte twisted the pencil between her fingers. "I'm afraid not. I was injured at the time and had to be transferred to Milwaukee for better care. I received a letter while I was there from a man who discovered the truth about my mother and sister. I left for Kentucky a few months after."

"Oh. I see."

Charlotte bit her lip. "I know it was cowardly of me to refuse to go back. In the end, I suppose I was too afraid. Afraid of what I would find. Afraid of the memories that would haunt me once I was there." She looked away, and her next words emerged faint. "And so I ran as far as I could."

"We all get afraid sometimes. I'm guilty of doing the same thing." Tom blew out a sigh. "I imagine that's why Bas gets so angry with me. He knows I'm frightened and won't do anything to change it. He knows I'm running away."

Charlotte turned, giving Tom a friendly tap on the shoulder. "I suppose it's a good thing we found each other, then." A smile crossed her face. "We won't have to face our fears alone."

Tom returned Charlotte's smile with an earnest grin. "True."

A faint noise drew Charlotte's gaze to the road in front of the wagon. "Tom? Did you hear that?" She leaned over the front. "It sounded like a person crying out in pain."

Tom spoke from behind her. "I didn't hear anything. Perhaps it was Mr. Roberts and Bastian." His voice lowered to something conspiratorial. "Or maybe it was a mountain lion. I've heard they can sound like a person."

There was the noise again. It was most definitely a human

voice, and desperate. Was there someone else on the road with them?

"I'm going to take a look." Charlotte hopped down from the wagon and pushed her hat slightly back. "It could be an unfortunate victim of those awful highwaymen." She pointed at Tom. "Don't leave the wagon until I return, all right?"

Tom inclined his head, his eyes uncertain. "Be careful, Miss Charlotte. Shout if you need help, and I'll be there in a pinch."

"Good." Charlotte began a cautious trek toward the sound, pausing every few seconds to listen. The strange keening noise seemed to be coming from a cluster of bushes beside the road. Suspicion rose within her as she studied the brush from afar. The noise could be a person in need of help, but it could also be a trap. She wasn't foolish enough to walk closer on her own. "Is someone there?" she called, tensing in case she needed to run ba ck to the wagon.

"Help, please!" The faint voice came from behind the brush. "My leg! It's trapped!"

Charlotte crept forward, listening for any additional sounds. "Hang on, sir! I'm coming to help. Don't move."

"I'm not! Please, help."

When she was just a few feet from the bushes, the noises stopped. Charlotte froze along with them. What on earth? "Hello? Are you all right?"

For a moment, the clearing remained silent. Then a voice sounded from behind the bush, this time strong and steady. "You aren't an easy woman to locate, Miss Clarke."

A man in a black waistcoat and jacket and large hat rose from behind the bush. A dark goatee covered the lower half of his face. His eyes were the same blue as Stefan's, but far harsher and colder. *The thief from the road.*

Charlotte gasped and took a step back. "How do you know my name? Who are you?"

"Inns keep records of their customers. It wasn't all that difficult to find who you were once we discovered where you were staying." His slight drawl might have put Charlotte at ease had the situation been different. The man grinned, revealing a set of perfect white teeth—an odd sight, considering his otherwise grimy outfit. "As for my name, you can call me Hawk. I've got a sharp eye, you see." His gaze narrowed as he studied her, making Charlotte shiver. "And right now, that eye has spotted something that belongs to me. That pretty trinket hanging around your neck is my rightful property, miss. I've been searching all over the state for it."

"Stay away from me." Charlotte continued her slow but steady backward steps. "I'll scream."

Hawk snorted. "Your gentleman friend isn't close enough to hear. He wouldn't have let you come out here by yourself if he was." He moved forward another foot. "This can all be resolved in a civil manner if you'll kindly hand over that locket. Give it to me, and you'll never see me again."

Charlotte clutched the locket. She wouldn't be able to outrun the man for long, even if she had a sizable lead. Her only hope would be stalling Hawk until Stefan returned to the wagon and decided to come looking for her. "Why do you care for this locket so much? It's nothing special. It belonged to my dying friend. She simply wanted me to return it to her mother. Would you deny a woman the right to seeing her friend's final wish through?"

Hawk's jaw twitched. "With all due respect, miss, I don't give a hang what your friend wanted. Now, I'll ask you one more time to give me what's mine. If you don't, that child of yours will learn what it feels like to look down the barrel of a gun."

"What?" Charlotte looked behind her and gasped. The horses were scattered across the field with their ropes dragging the ground. Only one animal remained in the road—a white horse, with a dark-coated figure atop it. Tom was struggling frantically in John's grip, his arms and legs flailing. Despite his swinging hands, it was clear that he couldn't get free.

Horror filled Charlotte as John urged his mare into motion and took off down the road with Tom in tow. She turned back around, fixing Hawk with a glare despite the fear growing in her chest. "Tell your lackey to let go of Tom this instant. The boy hasn't done anything to you."

"That imp pulled my prize stallion's tail and dropped a shelf over my friend's head. I won't be letting him go, not until you hand over the locket." Hawk must have seen Charlotte's hesitance, for he sneered. "Let me make the decision easier for you. You have until the count of three. One..." He crept closer. "Two..." Charlotte sent up a silent prayer for safety, clutching her skirts around her. "Three!"

In the same instant Hawk lunged for the necklace, Charlotte whirled and plunged into the woods. She darted in the direction of the wagon, praying Stefan was close by. Branches whipped against her face and tore her skirt as she crashed through the undergrowth, but she refused to slow her pace. The sound of footsteps behind Charlotte were a constant reminder that Hawk wasn't far behind. In fact, his steps seemed to be growing louder by the second.

"Stefan! Stefan, where are you? Help!" Charlotte caught and released a tree branch in the hopes that it would slow Hawk, even if only for a moment. Cursing sounded behind her, informing her that the branch had hit its target. She continued to run, hope rising in her chest as she spotted the edge of the woods. Her heart stopped, however, when something snatched her skirts and held them captive. A thorn bush! Ironic, in a cruel sort of way. "No! Please, not now." Charlotte fought the sharp branches.

The cursing grew louder as Hawk made steady progress toward her.

tefan frowned as a distant shout pierced the air. Charlotte?

"What was that?" Bastian peered around the clearing, concern evident on his face.

The shout sounded again, this one decidedly feminine. It had a desperate quality that tugged at Stefan's heart and urged him into motion.

"Charlotte!" Panic set in as he whirled around. "Where are you?"

The thoroughbreds grazed peacefully a few yards away, but they wouldn't come at his call. He scoured the field, and his heart skipped a beat at the sight of a familiar gray back. "Orion, *hier!*" Stefan let out a sharp whistle.

The horse looked up and cantered over, coming to a halt in front of Stefan with ears pricked and eyes alert. He released a loud nicker as Stefan moved to his side, almost as if he could sense the urgency.

"Come on." Stefan gestured to Bastian. "Get up."

Bastian glanced at Stefan with furrowed brows. "I don't know if that's a good idea. I was never good at horseback riding."

"There's no time. Charlotte is in danger." Stefan cupped his hands to form a foothold, giving Bastian the leverage he needed to heft himself over the horse. Once the lad was safely balanced, Stefan handed Bastian his crutch and carefully lifted himself behind the boy. "Grab his mane with your free hand." Bas quickly did so, and with him settled, Stefan let out a sharp whistle.

Orion lurched forward and headed for the woods at lightning speed. They plunged into the trees, darting around trunks and low-hanging branches as they moved closer to Charlotte's voice. After a moment, Stefan caught sight of her. A figure was running straight at her, but she was unable to move, as her skirts were caught on a bush. Though a hat obscured the man's face, Stefan had no doubt who he was. "Hawk," he ground out. He took the crutch from Bastian's hand and positioned it at his side like a lance. As Orion galloped past Charlotte, the bottom of the crutch caught Hawk dead in the chest, sending the thief sprawling backward onto the ground with a loud grunt.

Stefan brought Orion around with a hand on his mane and drew him to a halt with a sharp command, keeping the horse between Charlotte and the highwayman. "Are you all right?" he called behind him.

"I'm fine," Charlotte responded, though her voice wavered.

Stefan glared down at the highwayman, wishing he hadn't left his revolver in the wagon. Luckily, the man seemed to have lost the gun from his own holster when he was thrown backward, leaving them both unarmed.

"We should turn him in to the police," Bastian said from in front of Stefan. "He's outnumbered."

Orion let out a loud snort, as though in agreement with the boy. Stefan couldn't help but wonder if it would be a crime to let the horse step on the thief just once.

Before he could make a decision, Hawk rose slowly and rubbed his chest, fixing Stefan with a glare. How could one man's eyes hold so much hatred? "You're more capable than I thought, horse boy. As for the police, you could turn me in. However, if you did, you would never see that other child of yours again."

"Tom," Charlotte whispered, her voice shaking. "They took Tom."

Bastian sucked in a breath. "They took my brother?"

Hawk grinned, though the expression lacked warmth. "I did, and I won't hesitate to kill him if you fail to give me the locket."

"You wouldn't kill a child," Bastian said, though his voice betrayed his uncertainty.

Hawk's stare moved from Stefan to Bastian. "What's one boy's life in the face of dozens of others? I'll do what I must to ensure the safety of myself and my friends. If you really care about your brother, why don't you tell your companions here to give me my locket? Otherwise, I'll signal my men to do away with him here and now."

Stefan drew himself upright, trying to ignore the fear that shot like lightning through his chest. "I don't believe you. Your lackeys fled at the first sign of trouble. They aren't close enough for you to signal, nor to give you aid. I would suggest you take my offer and leave while you still have the chance."

The highwayman fixed Stefan with a dark look, his hands clenching. "The next time we meet, Roberts, you're going to hand over that locket. Otherwise, you won't see your child again." He turned and stormed off through the trees. Within a few seconds, the man was gone.

"They really did take Tom." Charlotte moved beside Orion and rubbed her arms with trembling hands, her eyes wide and frightened. "What will they do to him?"

"How could you let them take Tom?" Bastian bowed his head, his shoulders slumping.

Stefan shook his head. "They won't go far. Not when they're so desperate to get that locket. They'll want to be sure we don't try to get rid of it."

"How are we going to get him back, then?" Charlotte laid a hand on Stefan's leg.

"I'm not certain, but we'll think of something." Stefan let out a shuddering breath. "We have to."

CHAPTER 23

The steady clip-clop of the horses' hooves, normally so comforting, now seemed like a death knell as Orion plodded down the road. Charlotte shuddered. How was it that a day that started out so bright and cheerful could so quickly change? Though it was just as sunny and warm, the silence was a chilling reminder that someone was missing, leaving fear to settle in the gap where Tom should have been.

Stefan had not uttered a word since leaving the forest. Not when they had returned to the wagon, not when they had caught the thoroughbreds, and not when they had resumed traveling. His brows were furrowed in intense thought, his mouth set in a thin line. The man was clearly as concerned for Tom's welfare as Charlotte was.

"What are you thinking of, Stefan?" It was a foolish question, but Charlotte couldn't handle the oppressive quiet any longer.

Stefan exhaled. It pained Charlotte to see the tension back between his brows, especially when they had only just begun to relax. "There has to be a way for us to get Tom away from those confounded thieves. Without knowing where they are, however, I'm at a loss. We can't ambush them or sneak into their camp if we don't know where it is. But giving Hawk the locket when he first attacked wouldn't have helped either. He might have killed Tom regardless."

Charlotte lifted a hand to her chest, where that treacherous locket rested. "Perhaps we ought to give them the locket when they next approach us, then. We can make sure Tom is safe and negotiate his return. A list of names isn't worth a child's life, after all."

"But that would be admitting defeat." Stefan's nostrils flared. "It seems so...cowardly. We would be giving them what they want without a guarantee that they'll hold up their end of the bargain. They could still kill Tom the minute they get the locket, and we would be unable to stop them. It's too risky."

Charlotte winced, dropping her hand. "That's true. I wonder if they know we found the list inside the locket. If they did, they may kill us all regardless. They won't want us to spread word of their crimes."

"Indeed." Stefan lapsed back into silence and twisted the reins in his hands.

There had to be *some* way for them to reach Tom, some way for them to separate him from the men holding him captive without giving up the list. Unfortunately, if there was a solution, it was stubbornly evading her mind.

"Charlotte?" Stefan straightened, his eyes brightening. "How important is it for you to get the locket itself to Kentucky? Could you make do without it?"

Charlotte frowned thoughtfully. "Well, I assume Flora was more concerned with what lay within the locket, not the jewelry itself."

Stefan drew the wagon to a sudden halt, causing Charlotte to lurch forward. Luckily, he stuck out an arm and caught her before she fell, gently pushing her back. He set his hands on his knees, determination flashing in his eyes. "I know how we can get Tom back."

"Thank you." Charlotte cleared her throat, heat searing through her cheeks at the sudden contact. "How?"

"We give them the locket and the list of names. You can keep Flora's note to return to her mother."

Charlotte gasped. "But Stefan, we can't give them the list. They'll just take it and leave with Tom."

Stefan shook his head. "That's just it. The thieves believe there's only one list. They'll think they're safe once that list is destroyed."

Bastian sucked in a breath from where he sat in the wagon bed. "So what you're saying is—"

"We'll make more copies of the list." Stefan pointed to the chain around Charlotte's neck. "At least one for each of us. That way, we'll all have a chance of getting those names to the Aspens regardless of what might happen."

"That's brilliant," Bastian exclaimed. "I can keep my copy in my waistcoat."

Stefan sat back and folded his arms across his chest. "When the thieves approach us next, we'll hand over the locket without making a fuss. With luck, they'll be so concerned with ensuring the list is inside that we'll be able to free Tom and get away before they realize what's happened. And if they find the list inside..."

"They won't come after us." Charlotte searched her bag. "I have some paper we can use." She procured a blank sheet and waved it between them.

"Perfect." Stefan grinned. "We should be able to fit three copies onto one page. The smaller, the better."

Charlotte clicked the locket open and carefully removed the list, then handed it to Stefan. He studied it for a moment before nodding. "Let's get to work, then."

They spent the next few minutes copying the names onto

the paper, taking turns using the pencil procured from Charlotte's bag. Before long, they held three copies of the list, though the handwriting varied on each.

Charlotte returned Flora's original note behind the portrait and clicked the lid shut, slipping it into her pocket rather than hanging it back around her neck. She placed her copy of the list into her other pocket.

"Now we can save my brother, right?" Bastian stuck his head between them, his eyes shining with hope. "We just need to find Hawk and give him the locket."

"Not quite." Stefan gathered the reins. "We need to wait for Hawk to make the next move. He'll want to ensure that everything is on his terms, so there's no chance of us catching him by surprise. Our best bet is to make him believe we're complying with his demands, no matter how outlandish they may be."

"How long will it take for him to find us? Who knows what they'll do to Tom in the meantime?" Bastian sat back and released an irritated huff. "We ought to act now, while they're off guard."

"We can't do anything until we know where they're keeping him, as I said. As much as I would love to swoop in and rescue Tom, we'll have to do it their way."

Charlotte turned the locket over and over in her pocket, feeling the engraving of the leaves beneath her hand. Who knew such a beautiful thing could cause such ugliness? "Pray for your brother's safety, Sebastian. That's all we can do for now.

~

That evening, Stefan shut the door to the inn room and turned, freezing when he caught sight of Charlotte sitting on the bed. Why wasn't she in her own room? He had expected a moment of silence to mull over his plans for

Tom, as Bastian was getting food for tomorrow's lunch from the inn's kitchen. "Charlotte? Is something wrong?"

Charlotte exhaled, a sheepish smile crossing her face. "When you spoke with the innkeeper earlier, you told him we were a family."

Stefan inclined his head. "It was safer that way. I didn't want you to write your real name on the hotel ledger." Not after Hawk's admittance that he was checking them.

"Well, because you told him that, he gave me the key for one room. I tried to tell him that we preferred separate rooms, but he left before I could finish. You were getting the horses settled, and I didn't see any sense in disturbing you, so I decided to simply wait here." On the bed. The singular bed.

"Well, then, I suppose I'll take the floor. It's nothing I haven't done before. Bastian can do the same." Stefan lowered himself to the rug and tried not to wince as he put a little too much pressure on his left leg.

"Are you certain? I'm more than willing to find a hayloft to sleep in. I hate to think that I'm putting you out." Charlotte peered over the edge of the bed. "You are the one who paid for the room, after all. It's only fair that you get the bed."

Stefan adjusted his bag beneath him and set his head on it, gazing up at the ceiling with his arms folded across his chest. "No. I'd never make you sleep in a hayloft, Charlotte. It would be horrible manners."

"Manners. Silly of us to still consider them after all we've been through," Charlotte said wryly, sitting back. "We've probably broken at least a dozen rules of propriety by now. I'm certain I'd be called all manner of horrible names if polite society knew."

"So would I. Traveling together, staying in one room, and addressing each other by our Christian names. We're quite scandalous, aren't we?" Stefan chuckled, placing his arms behind his head. "If the society matrons caught sight of us, they'd probably marry us on the spot."

Charlotte hummed from her spot atop the bed. "Most likely."

There was a moment of silence. "I...I suppose some fellow probably courted you when you lived in Wisconsin," Stefan murmured, surprised at the dread that ran through him at the idea.

Charlotte laughed. "Oh, goodness, no. Someone once asked me to marry him, but I turned him down."

"Marry him? Did you know him very well?"

"I suppose you could say I did. We were very good friends at the time, though we never courted. While we got along, I simply couldn't fathom the idea of being married to him." Charlotte released a sigh. "It wasn't that Edwin was a bad fellow. He had a very...loose view of marriage. At any rate, we were better suited as friends." Fabric rustled as she shifted places. "What about you? Did you ever pursue a relationship?" Her voice was tentative, as though she, too, feared the answer.

"No," Stefan admitted. "I never had time to consider marriage while I was in the cavalry. After I was discharged, courting became the least of my concerns."

"And now? Do you still feel the same way about courting now?" Charlotte whispered.

Stefan remained silent for a moment before answering. His heart beat loudly in his ears, nearly drowning out his response. "No."

"I have returned!" Bastian opened the door with loud bang, causing Stefan to jolt. "I brought bread and fruit." He frowned, glancing down at where Stefan lay. "I suppose I'm sleeping on the floor, am I?"

Stefan chuckled, gesturing to the rug next to him. "The lady gets the bed. Now, we should try to sleep. We'll need to be well rested for whatever may come tomorrow."

Bastian grunted and lowered himself to the floor, placing the bag of food beside him. "I hope we hear something soon. I hate to think of Tom out there in the cold with those criminals."

"Knowing Tom, he's probably driven Hawk half mad with his talking." Stefan shifted his bag a little to the left and settled back on it with a snort. "By the time we catch up with them, the highwaymen will be begging us to take him back."

Bastian laughed, though the sound fell flat. He flipped onto his side so his back was to Stefan. "I miss him," he murmured, his voice quiet and a bit unsteady. "If he wants to play his banjo every day after we get him back, I won't stop him."

"We'll get him back, Bastian." *We have to.* Stefan couldn't allow another person he cared about to be lost, and he couldn't allow Bastian to lose his brother. Not when he knew what it felt like.

~

A knock at the door dragged Stefan from a slumber that had, surprisingly enough, been free of nightmares. Scrubbing his eyes, he sat upright and groaned at the twinge in his back. Where was he?

Ah, yes. The floor.

The window cast thin shafts of light over the sleeping boy at Stefan's side, making his hair seem like fire in the warm sun. Bastian was far more peaceful in sleep, absent the worries that had haunted them for the past day.

Stefan frowned as the reason for Bastian's worry resurfaced in his sleep-fogged mind. *Tom.* The boy was still missing. What had Hawk done to him? Not knowing made it all the more frustrating.

The knock returned, this time more persistent. Stefan collected his crutch as quietly as he could and pushed himself to his feet. He made his way to the door and called out without opening it, keeping his hand near the revolver on his hip. "Can I help you?"

"It's a letter for you, sir." At that, Stefan cracked the door open, revealing a young man on the other side. He waved the paper in the air with one hand and tipped his cap back with the other. "The man who left it said it was of the utmost importance."

Stefan's heart picked up in speed. "Thank you." He accepted the envelope with a quick survey of the handwriting on the front and promptly closed the door. "Charlotte," he whispered, making his way to the bed. "Wake up. I have news."

Charlotte yawned and sat upright, stretching her arms overhead. She still wore her dress, though the fabric had become wrinkled. "What is it?"

The sight of Charlotte's sleepy face was enough to distract Stefan for a moment before he recalled the letter in his hand. Taking a seat on the bed, he held the envelope aloft. "I have a letter that may be from Hawk. The innkeeper said it was delivered this morning. There's no name or address on it."

Charlotte straightened, her gaze sharpening on the envelope. "Well, then, open it! We can't afford to delay when Tom's life is at stake."

Stefan peeled the envelope open and reached inside, withdrawing a piece of paper and what appeared to be three tickets. He laid them out on the bed. "Tickets?"

"They're invitations for a dance." Charlotte picked up one of the gilded cards. "For tomorrow evening. It looks as though it will take place in Lexington. Isn't that where John said he was going?"

Frowning, Stefan read the letter aloud. "'To Horse Boy and friends, I dearly hope you have come to your senses and decided to agree to our terms for your child's safe return. In return for your expected cooperation, my friends and I invite you to one of the finest balls in Lexington.'" He forced his jaw to relax and pried his hand from the paper, which was quickly becoming crumpled. "'Wear your best and don't forget a mask. We will see you on the back balcony at ten o'clock. Yours truly, Hawk.'" He bit the name out. "The fool wants us to go to a dance? Not only that, but he had the nerve to sign it 'yours truly'?"

Charlotte tapped her chin. "The ball is certain to attract a large crowd—providing an escape for Hawk should it be necessary. In addition, it's a masquerade. The thieves should be able to conceal themselves fairly easily."

"It still seems like a foolish move to me. Hawk is risking exposing himself in front of a large group of people, and high society people, at that. It doesn't seem right." Stefan tossed the letter onto the bed, disgust coursing through him "Which means he most likely has some sort of plan we aren't aware of. We'll have to be on high alert."

"Indeed. The dance is tomorrow night, Stefan. Will we make it in time?"

"Yes." Stefan leaned forward, resting his elbows on his knees. "For Tom, we will. We'll have to find a place to get clothing worthy of a ball." Preferably something that wouldn't cost much. They were quickly running out of funds, but he would do whatever it took to save the boy—even if it meant skipping a few meals later on.

"Oh, Stefan. I hope this works."

"It will. It has to." Stefan stood and nudged Bastian with his crutch, causing the boy to yawn and mumble something unintelligible. "Wake up, Bastian. We received a letter from Hawk."

Bastian sat up, his expression alert despite his tousled hair and rumpled clothes. "You did? What does it say?"

"We're going to a ball in Lexington. Hawk will meet us there, presumably with Tom." Bastian glanced down at his shabby outfit. "I don't have anything to wear to a dance."

"You don't have to." Stefan folded his arms across his chest. "You're going to stay at the inn with the horses."

"What?" Bastian's eyes widened, his lips parting slightly. "You can't possibly expect me to stay away, not when you're saving my brother." He jumped to his feet. "I even have an invitation!" The boy grabbed one of the tickets and waved it in the air as though proving his point.

"I won't let the thieves take two hostages." Stefan plucked the ticket from the boy's hand and dropped it on back on the bed. "You're staying at the inn, Sebastian, and that's final."

Bastian tapped his foot but remained silent, irritation plain on his face.

Stefan turned and walked to the door, glancing over his shoulder as he went. "I'll be out in the barn, preparing the horses for travel. We need to reach Lexington as quickly as possible if we're to attend that ball."

"All right. Do be careful, Stefan. Come back inside if you see anyone or anything out of the ordinary," Charlotte said, brushing the hair back from her face.

"I will." Stefan cast one last smile at her before leaving.

The stables were quiet in the bright morning, the comforting silence easing some of the nerves that held Stefan's shoulders rigid. As he led the thoroughbreds to the wagon outside, he took a deep breath and watched as his exhale made dust motes swirl in the air. "Lord," he whispered, "I know You can hear me. Please give us protection on our journey today. Let us rescue Tom safely. Please." There was no way they would be able to rescue the boy alone.

Hoofbeats silenced any further attempt at prayer. A familiar white mare drew to a halt in front of him, and Stefan's heart skipped a beat. John. Stefan could have attempted to run back to the inn, but he wouldn't have made it in time. And so he placed a hand on his revolver, eyeing the man atop the horse.

"Give me one good reason why I shouldn't run for the sheriff right now."

John leaned forward in the saddle. "I need to ask you a question, Stefan. It is of the utmost importance that you answer me honestly." His eyes narrowed, though his gaze didn't waver. "Have you opened the locket? Do you know what's inside?"

Stefan adjusted his crutch beneath him, trying not to clench his jaw. It was hard when all he could imagine was Tom's terrified face as the man carted him away. "No." It wasn't necessarily a lie. Charlotte had opened the locket, not him. "All I know is that you took my boy, and I won't be handing you anything until I get him back."

John tilted his head. "I assure you, it is not my intent to harm young Tom, but I cannot give him back without the locket. It is imperative that I have it."

"Then I'm afraid I can't help you." Stefan whirled and took a step toward the inn.

"Stefan, wait."

Stefan froze at the commanding voice and glanced over his shoulder.

John tipped his hat back, raising his hands in the air. "I am not working with Hawk. I simply needed him to trust me. You must understand that. I can't reveal much without putting you in danger, but you have to believe me when I say I am on your side."

"I find it hard to do that, especially considering the conversation I overheard in the stables a few weeks ago." Stefan folded his arms across his chest. "You sounded awfully friendly with Hawk then. You both wanted the locket."

John released an exasperated breath. "I wondered if that horse was yours. I know what you heard, but if you hand me the locket, I promise all—"

Stefan sliced his hand through the air. "Enough. I'm not giving anyone the locket, you hear? Nobody. Especially not the person who took Tom. You can run back to Hawk and tell him I'm not leaving without my boy. The only way he's getting his precious locket is once Tom is back where he belongs."

John fell silent, his head bowed, before finally responding. "Very well. But know this, Stefan." He raised his eyes to meet Stefan's sharp gaze. "I am your friend, and I don't seek to hurt you or your companions. However, there are those who are like snakes among the grass, waiting for a chance to strike. Often from behind. They will kill anyone who stands against them." He shook his head. "Do you really want your friends to be their targets?" Turning his mare's head, he cast one last glance at Stefan. "If you change your mind about giving me the locket, all you have to do is shout. I'll be near." With that, John released a soft whistle, spurring his horse into motion.

Stefan watched until horse and rider rounded the corner of the building. Once he was certain they were gone, he limped inside.

"Are the horses prepared?" Charlotte asked as he entered the room. She had pinned her hair up and packed her bag, which was sitting on the neatly folded bed. She gestured to Bastian, who stood near the room's single window with his own belongings at his feet. "Bastian and I are ready."

Stefan shook his head and lowered himself down next to her carpetbag. "I saw John outside. He rode up and spoke to me."

Bastian glanced over from the window while Charlotte gasped. "What did he say? Did he mention Tom?" Her hand flew up to her neck. "He didn't hurt you, did he?"

"He called himself a friend." Stefan pursed his lips. "I don't know what to make of him, Charlotte. He wanted the locket, but he didn't force me to give it to him. He did warn me that there were others looking for it who would be far less forgiving. I can only assume he meant Hawk."

"Oh, Stefan. This is all so confusing. What will we do?"

Charlotte sank down beside him. "How will we get Tom back and keep the list safe?"

"We need a backup plan. Handing them the locket won't be enough." Stefan considered his next words for a moment before releasing a tired sigh. "John said they'll kill anyone that opposes them."

They sat in silence, thinking hard. Just when Stefan was about to concede defeat, Bastian piped up from where he leaned against the wall by the window. "I have an idea. It's risky, but it might work."

"I'm listening." Stefan leaned forward as the boy pushed off the wall and began pacing back and forth.

"Hawk wants you to meet him on the balcony at ten, but the dance starts at eight, so he'll most likely have Tom hidden somewhere in the building before then. Assuming he brings Tom at all, that is." Bastian bit his lip. "Perhaps this is a foolish idea."

Stefan waved a hand. "Continue."

"Well, if we arrive at the dance when the ball begins, you and Miss Charlotte can look around and try to spot Hawk. If you find him, you can approach him and draw his attention. That will give me a chance to sneak in and create a bigger distraction." Bastian gestured to Stefan's holster. "Then, once the distraction is underway, all you'll have to do is find Tom and get out of the building."

Stefan hummed. "The plan sounds good in theory, but Hawk has other men working with him. They're certain to be keeping a close eye on Tom, which will make sneaking in to get him nearly impossible."

Bastian snapped his fingers. "Not entirely impossible. If the ball is at a high-society mansion, the lighting must surely have a central source." He glanced at Stefan. "Do you have a pocket watch?"

Stefan gestured to his bag, which still sat on the floor. "I do. What of it?"

Bastian began to outline his new plan. As he continued speaking, a smile crept across Stefan's face.

"Bastian, you're a genius. This plan of yours might just work."

Bastian's eyes lit with cautious hope. "You really think so?"

"I do." Stefan lifted himself to his feet and held out a hand for Charlotte. "Come on, Charlotte. We don't have a second to spare."

CHAPTER 24

"Charlotte? Are you almost ready? The ball begins in half an hour." Stefan's voice echoed from behind the bedroom door. The inn they were staying at was a cramped little place on the outskirts side of Lexington, with few amenities except for the bedrooms and stables. While not the most comfortable place, it was perfect for staying out of sight.

Charlotte took a deep breath and adjusted the glittering mask on her face, taking one last look at herself in the mirror above the washbasin. Stefan had helped her purchase a gown of rich yellow, similar in color to the dress Ilona had given her. Though relatively simple in style, the dress's extra fabric required her to use a bustle. It was exciting to finally take part in modern clothing trends, though the bustle was not quite as easy to wear as she had envisioned it would be. Of course, that could be the result of poor manufacturing. Charlotte had made sure to pick the cheapest clothing and accessories she could find despite Stefan's protests. As a result, the contraption stuck to her back end was lumpy and rather wobbly.

There was only one issue with the gown, one that made the bustle problem seem small in comparison—the sleeves tapered off just above her elbows, leaving a gap between the fabric and the gloves that nearly reached her elbows. As a result, a few inches of her scars were clearly visible. Would the ball-goers notice them? What would she say if they did?

Charlotte released a breath, straightening her spine. *I won't be cowed. Not now.* She wanted to stop hiding away, and this would be the first step.

"Charlotte?" Stefan repeated.

"I'm ready."

She opened the bedroom door and exited into the hallway, shivering as a chill stole across her arms. Was it from the cold, or simply nerves? Likely the latter. Luckily, the sight of the man before her was enough to abate some of the anxiety coursing through her. "You look positively splendid, Stefan." Charlotte studied his attire, not bothering to disguise the blush that spread across her cheeks. He wore a black suit, top hat, and domino mask, with a white cravat knotted neatly about his neck. "Is Bastian almost ready?"

Stefan blinked and opened his mouth, but no sound emerged. His eyes flickered with unintelligible emotion. Did the dress not fit as well as she had thought, even though they'd been forced to purchase it readymade? She had thought it a miracle that it sat so nicely on her shoulders.

"Is something wrong?" Charlotte fought the urge to rub her arms. "Is it my hair? I knew I should have pinned it up, but all the magazines say to leave a few pieces loose. These new styles aren't easy to replicate. I'm sure Ilona would have known what to do if she was here."

"No," Stefan blurted, bringing a halt to Charlotte's rambling. "You look...you look beautiful."

"Oh." Charlotte glanced down at her dress, the tips of her ears heating at the compliment. "Well, thank you. Are you certain nothing looks amiss?"

Stefan smiled warmly, his eyes sparkling bright blue from

behind his mask. "You look perfect, Charlotte. I'll be fending off fellows all night. Are you certain you're comfortable...you know..." He gestured to her arms.

Charlotte rolled her shoulders back and inclined her head. "If you have to go into the ball with your leg on display, it's only fair that I should join you. It's easier to face things like this together, isn't it?"

Stefan released a long breath. "It is, but I wouldn't want you to be uncomfortable on my account."

"It's already settled. I'm not going to hide my arms away any longer." Charlotte glanced to the side. "This will be my first dance, you know. Not that I really know how. I've always wanted to attend one, but my family never had the time or the money. Socialites lived in a world that was far beyond our reach." Some of her cheer fell away, and she blew out a sigh. "If only we could truly enjoy it. Do you really think Bastian's plan will work?"

"Nothing is certain, Charlotte. All we can do is try, and I assure you, I will do my very best to bring Tom back safely," Stefan promised, his voice solemn.

"All right." Charlotte ran a hand over the locket at her neck. "To think that all of this started because of a necklace. Had I known what I was getting into, I doubt I would have taken it."

Stefan hummed. "Maybe not. If you hadn't, however, we never would have met. We never would have found the twins either. I have a feeling my life would be far less interesting had that never occurred." He took a step forward, putting him a few inches from her. "I certainly wouldn't have such a lovely lady accompanying me to the dance tonight." He cleared his throat. "Assuming you'll allow me to escort you to your first ball, of course. I may not make the best dance partner, but I promise I'll keep you safe. What do you say?"

Charlotte swallowed, trying to ignore the loud thumping of her heart. Why couldn't she think of anything to say? It was as if words were inadequate to express the riot of emotions inside her. Instead, she leaned forward and brushed her lips gently across Stefan's. The softness of his mouth made her cheeks blaze with heat, and she quickly backed away, a bit breathless. Whatever had possessed her to do such a brazen thing? She didn't know, but she also couldn't bring herself to regret it. "And after the ball?" she murmured. "Will you stay by my side then as well?"

Stefan stood frozen as if in shock, his lips parted ever so slightly, but before he could respond, Bastian trotted down the hall. "The wagon is ready." He skidded to a halt in front of Stefan and Charlotte. "I left the thoroughbreds in the barn and... Is everything all right? You both have the strangest expression on your faces." The boy raised a brow. "Did I interrupt something?"

Charlotte coughed, adjusting her gloves. "Not at all. Shall we be going?"

Bastian nodded, the motion made a bit difficult by the tricorn hat on his head. He had pulled it down over his forehead, completely shielding his orange hair from view. In addition, he had donned a full face mask with a long, hooked nose. It was a bit grotesque but concealed his appearance well enough. They would need him to be hidden from view if the plan was to work.

Stefan cleared his throat, seeming to snap from his reverie, and held out his free arm.

Charlotte rested a hand on his sleeve and fixed him with a bright smile, stifling a smile of her own at the red hue that had crept across his cheeks. *How sweet.* "Certainly. I wouldn't want to be late to my first ball."

With the only man she'd ever want to attend one with.

～

As they pulled to a halt a few buildings down from the mansion where the ball was to take place, Charlotte couldn't help but gape. The homes looked as though they could have fit twenty of her old one inside them. The mansion of their hosts was a stately white, with beautiful pillars that stretched from the top of the winding staircase to the roof. Bushes outlined the circular drive, and neatly trimmed maple trees framed the edge of the expansive lawn. It was unlike anything she had ever seen.

Ladies in furs and shimmering ball gowns ascended the marble stairs on the arms of men with top hats and masks. Finely gilded carriages drove to and from the building, the sort that Charlotte had never had the fortune to set foot in. The faint sound of violins echoed from within the building's ornate doors, a sign of the dancing that was sure to come inside.

Stefan handed the reins to Bastian, who was wedged onto the wagon bench between Charlotte and Stefan, and lowered himself to the ground. "Are you clear on the plan, Bastian?"

Bastian lifted his hand in a salute. "I'm ready. Do you have your watch?"

"I do. Nine-thirty, correct?"

"Correct. All you have to do is find Hawk, locate the room where they're keeping Tom, and keep the highwaymen far from said room. Then we just have to get Tom safely out of the building."

Stefan chuckled, shaking his head. "Easier said than done, I'm afraid. You'll come back out to the wagon directly after nine-thirty?"

Bastian crossed his arms. Charlotte was certain he was scowling, though she couldn't see his face. "I'd rather help you lead Tom out, but I will. I'll have it waiting here by the time you leave the building. Unless you want me to pull up to the drive like those fancy coachmen, of course."

"No. Keep the wagon out of the way so it doesn't draw attention. Move quickly and don't speak to anyone, Bastian. We'll see you in an hour and a half, Lord willing."

Bastian tilted his head forward in agreement. "Sure thing, Captain."

Stefan held out a hand to assist Charlotte in her descent from the wagon. "Are you ready?" he whispered as they made their way up the steps.

"I'm not sure. I feel as though everyone is going to look at us. I'm afraid they'll know we aren't supposed to be there." Charlotte swallowed. "We're walking up instead of arriving in a carriage, after all. And we aren't exactly high society."

"You're right, Charlotte. You don't look like the other women I've seen going in." Stefan adjusted her hand, sliding it closer to his elbow. "You look far better. I bet they don't have pockets in any of their gowns."

Charlotte chuckled and patted the folds of her gown in search of the pocket she had hastily sewn into it. "True. How else would I keep my matches with me?"

"You wouldn't. Make sure you don't lose them." Stefan took a deep breath. "They may be the one thing that saves us tonight."

At the entrance to the mansion, a manservant appeared in the open doorway, his brown hair slicked back and his suit neatly tailored. "Good evening. May I see your invitations?"

Stefan handed the man the tickets and straightened his back. He peered into the foyer. "We were invited by Cliff Hawk. I don't suppose you've seen him, have you?"

The servant shook his head. "I'm afraid I haven't, sir. However, if you're looking to find him, you might consider asking his cousin, Miss Yarrow." He pointed to a blond debutante engaged in conversation with a group of ladies near the back of the room.

Stefan cast a sideways look at Charlotte, who lifted her

shoulder in a shrug. It was worth asking, though Miss Yarrow likely wouldn't be excited to leave her glittering group to talk to them. The girl wore a beautiful white dress, with shining strings of pearls around her neck and elegantly pinned hair. Who else was Hawk related to? How many allies did he have at the ball? Their plan was looking more difficult by the moment.

They crossed to the debutantes, and Stefan cleared his throat. "Miss Yarrow?"

The woman spun around, her expression transforming from surprise to confusion. Her wide blue eyes were the same shade as Hawk's, though her cheeks were rounder and her expression held far less malice. "Yes?"

Stefan sketched a bow. "My name is Stefan Roberts, and this is my companion, Miss Charlotte Clarke. We were invited by your cousin, Cliff Hawk. Do you know where we could locate him?"

Miss Yarrow fluttered her lashes, a smile spreading across her face. "A pleasure to meet you. My cousin does love to invite guests from…" Her eyes narrowed by a fraction as she took in Charlotte. "Unusual places."

Unusual places? Charlotte's cheeks heated. What was that supposed to mean?

"I'm afraid I don't know where he is at the moment." Miss Yarrow flicked her fan open and began fluttering it near her face. "He's been off with his friends the past few days and only returned this evening. Not to mention it's hard to tell everyone apart in masquerade. But perhaps you could escort me to get a cup of punch and I might spy him out on the way, Mr. Roberts."

Charlotte nearly choked at the obvious machination. Perhaps Miss Yarrow wasn't so different from Hawk, after all. Or was it jealousy at the flirtation Charlotte felt? She tugged on Stefan's arm. "Let's go, Stefan. We wouldn't want to keep Miss Yarrow from her conversation."

"Oh, not at all." Miss Yarrow giggled. "But if you find yourself in need of different company, I'll be here."

Stefan patted Charlotte lightly on the arm. "I'm perfectly content with my current company. At least she isn't chasing the coattails of every man who glances in her direction." He inclined his head, though the action was cold and formal. "Have a good evening." He strolled forward, ignoring the woman's outraged gasp.

"Stefan! That was rude." Though Charlotte chastised him, her lips twitched up in a smile. "I imagine that was the most insulting thing anyone's ever said to that girl."

"She could use a few more humbling comments, I think. A woman who pushes others down to elevate herself isn't one I care to know."

They followed the flow of guests down a hallway and through a long parlor before emerging in the far wing of the mansion, where the ballroom lay. Charlotte couldn't help the breath she released as they entered the huge room. "My, but this place is beautiful."

"That it is." Stefan's eyes widened, and he pointed at the ceiling. "Just look at that chandelier. The crystals are beyond anything I've ever seen."

The sparkling lighting fixture truly was grand, hanging dozens of feet above the ballroom. It made Charlotte release a giddy laugh. "To be honest, I've never seen anything like this in my life." If only Carina and Mother could have been here to see it.

The orchestra on the podium near the back wall began a plucky tune, and people drifted toward the center of the ballroom to dance. The rest of the crowd grouped around the dancers, chatting and mingling near the punch and refreshment tables that outlined the room. The French doors to the outside balcony had been flung wide open, letting a breeze drift in and cool the guests.

"Where do you think Hawk would be keeping Tom?" Charlotte asked as they neared the crowd surrounding the dance floor.

"I don't know." Stefan frowned. "I should have asked Miss Yarrow where Hawk was staying, but I suppose it's a bit late for that now. Why don't we start on the left and work our way toward the balconies? If you catch sight of Hawk, tap my arm."

"I will." As they meandered past clusters of people, Charlotte cast surreptitious looks at each and every person. With all the masks, costumes, and finery, it was practically impossible to identify anyone. How could she spot Hawk if she couldn't make out his features? The memory of the thief's cold blue eyes flashed through her mind, and she shuddered. Though he could dress up all he wanted, there would be no hiding those eyes behind a mask.

"Say, what's your name, young man? I don't believe we've met." The voice brought Stefan's and Charlotte's heads around. A portly man approached with a glass of wine perched delicately between two fingers.

"Me? I'm Stefan Roberts, sir," Stefan said, favoring the man with a cordial nod. "My companion is Charlotte Clarke. And who might you be?"

"Barnabus Graham, owner of Graham Mines," the man answered, his chest swelling with pride. "I know everyone there is to know at this event. Everyone of import, of course." He let out a loud hiccup, making the liquid in his glass slosh around. "Which would lead me to believe you are not a person of importance."

Stefan raised a brow in Charlotte's direction, and she narrowly avoided chuckling. The man was clearly far into his cups.

"No, I am not of import. However, we were invited by Cliff Hawk." Stefan adjusted his cravat.

"Hawk? Of course. His father is well known in the mining

industry." When Graham's mask began to slip, he pushed it up. "His company produced a large quantity of lead, making the family quite wealthy during the war. As a matter of fact, they're one of the sponsors for this event. The hosts were so thankful for the donation that they gave the family a private set of rooms in the mansion." The man frowned. "A bit of a waste, that. The head of the family wasn't even able to attend due to a rather nasty bout of pneumonia. I'm afraid it's only the younger Hawk this year. Why the boy should require a full set of rooms, I have no idea, but it's not in my best interest to judge."

"You don't say? That is a shame." Stefan gave Charlotte a knowing look. She nodded her understanding. Tom was most likely in Hawk's rooms. But how to reach him?

"I don't suppose you've seen Hawk around, have you? I'd like to thank him for extending invitations to us." Stefan leaned farther onto his crutch, his voice casual.

Graham tapped a finger under his chin, his eyes narrowing. "I did, but only for a moment. Hawk seems to consider himself above all of us. He might have gone back up to his rooms."

Charlotte tilted her head. "Perhaps we could send a note if we knew where his rooms were located."

"Well, all the rooms have names. The hosts think it's rather whimsical." The man hiccupped once more, and the cup in his hand trembled dangerously. "What was the name of Hawk's room? Something to do with horses and birds. Flying creatures and mythology. A whole lot of nonsense, if you ask me."

"Pegasus?" Stefan suggested.

"That's it. The Pegasus Room."

"Thank you. We'll be sure to send a note. Have a good evening, Mr. Graham. It was a pleasure to make your acquaintance." Stefan tugged Charlotte away and walked toward the stairs, weaving through the crowd. "We have to get to that room."

Charlotte gathered her skirts in one hand to keep pace with

her escort, who had set a rather fast pace considering he was using a crutch. "I agree, but what about..." She drew to a halt as she spotted a tall figure at the back of the room. Though the man hadn't yet caught sight of them, his eyes were clearly visible in the lamplight. They were all too familiar, those eyes— sharp like daggers despite the smile on the man's face. He was scanning the room, evidently searching for someone. For them.

"Charlotte? What is it?" Stefan's arm tightened beneath her grasp.

Charlotte released a shuddering breath. "It's Hawk. He's here."

CHAPTER 25

Stefan shifted to conceal Charlotte behind him. He turned to face her and bent forward so their foreheads were nearly touching, giving the appearance that they were a couple whispering sweet nothings to each other. If it had been a different time, he might have marveled at the way he could make out each of her dark lashes and wondered what it would feel like to kiss her again. Now, however, he could only think of the words she had spoken. "Are you certain?" he murmured.

Charlotte bobbed her head, her breath shaky. "He hasn't yet caught sight of us. Should we hide?"

Stefan glanced over his shoulder. "No. I have a plan. Can I have the locket?"

Charlotte fished the necklace from her hidden pocket and placed it in Stefan's open palm. "What are you going to do?"

"I'm going to confront Hawk and distract him with the locket. While I'm doing that, I need you to locate the Pegasus Room. Once you're certain that you know how to get there, return to the ballroom and wait by the stairs. When Bastian creates his distraction, I'll find you, and we'll run to the room together. We should have about five minutes to free Tom and leave the building before Hawk realizes what's happening."

"I can do that." Despite her unquestioning response, Charlotte stared at him with her eyes wide. "Be careful, Stefan. That man is dangerous. I don't doubt his ability to make good on his threats."

"I will. The same goes for you. Scream if anything goes wrong, and I promise, I'll find you." Stefan gestured toward the staircase, praying that Charlotte wouldn't see the fear in his eyes. "Now go, before Hawk catches sight of you."

Charlotte pressed a hand to her lips and brought it to Stefan's cheek before turning and disappearing into the crowd, leaving a warm spot where her glove had brushed against his skin. Clutching the locket tightly in his free hand, he scanned the crowd. It only took a moment for Stefan to identify the man she had guessed to be Hawk. Though a bird-shaped mask covered his face, there was no disguising the man's cold blue eyes.

"Hawk!" Once the thief spotted him, Stefan limped across the floor, drawing to a halt in front of the man. Straightening to his full height, he studied Hawk with anger rising in his chest. "I didn't take you for a dandy, and yet here you are, formal attire and all."

Hawk snorted, though his eyes narrowed behind the mask. "Having a powerful family does come with its perks, and one of those includes being invited to events such as this." He smirked. "And just where is that lovely lady of yours? I had hoped to secure a dance with her, seeing as you won't be able to do so."

He clenched his jaw. He couldn't let Hawk anger him, or Stefan was in danger of doing something rash. "She decided to stay at the inn and let me come here on my own. It was safer that way."

Hawk tilted his head, his eyes glittering beneath the light of the chandelier. He truly did live up to his name with a gaze so cold and predatory. It might have made Stefan shiver had he not been so angry. "Am I to assume you have what I want, then?"

Stefan opened his hand, letting the locket dangle from his fingers.

Hawk reached out, face eager, but Stefan closed his fist before the man could touch the necklace. "Of course, there are two sides to this exchange. Where is the boy?"

"Nearby. I will gladly return him once you give me the locket." Hawk crooked a finger. "Hand it over. Quietly. It wouldn't do for you to raise a fuss among polite society."

"And what if I did? What would your companions say if they learned that you kidnapped a child?" Stefan kept his voice low. "Your name might even grace the city papers. Why, I can see it now—'Son of Mining Mogul Guilty of Child Kidnapping.'"

Hawk stiffened. "That depends on who they would trust more—a well-respected socialite from one of the largest cities in Kentucky, or a country boy from Illinois. I'll allow you to draw your own conclusions."

A stealthy movement caught Stefan's eye. Turning ever so slightly, he spotted a man making a slow approach through the crowd. A snake striking from behind? John's warning echoed in his mind. From Stefan's other side, another masked figure advanced on him. Though masks hid their faces, Stefan had no doubt who they were. Hawk's lackeys. He was surrounded.

"Well? What will it be?" A smirk crept onto his opponent's face.

Stefan slid his watch from his pocket and made a great show of checking the time. "Nine twenty-eight. I still have half an hour before I'm to give you the locket."

"You'll give me that locket, or you'll never see your boy again. It will be no hardship for me to kill him, you know. That little clack-box hasn't stopped talking since we took him." Hawk thrust out a hand. "Now, Roberts."

The music had come to a halt, and the dancers had left the floor. Behind Hawk's shoulder, the gas lamps on the walls were beginning to flicker. *Perfect.* "As you wish," Stefan said, opening his hand.

Hawk snatched the necklace. "Good man." He let out a sigh as he tucked it into his jacket pocket. "Unfortunately, I cannot return your boy. You see, during his nervous rambling, he happened to mention that my friends and I were 'a lot of no-good traitors to the country.' Now, where on earth would a child such as himself have gotten such an idea? The only plausible explanation I could think of is that you opened the locket." He clucked his tongue. "A true shame. Because you couldn't control your curiosity, I'm afraid I cannot allow you to leave this building alive."

Stefan tightened his grip on his crutch as a drop of sweat trailed down his forehead and the men crept closer. Was it his imagination, or was the room getting darker? "You're nothing more than a greedy, fear-mongering rabble-rouser who's willing to start a war for his own gain."

"My father's business was built on war, Roberts. After all, who else would make the fine bullets that soldiers such as yourself used? Can you blame me, his only son, for wanting to help him succeed?" Hawk took a step closer, his voice dropping to a whisper. "My methods are different, but the results will be the same. The war is only a few years past. I can easily rekindle it with a few well-placed words and misunderstandings. Then my father's business will thrive once more."

"There's no shame in wanting your father to succeed, but there's nothing noble about your actions. Would you really pit men against each other for money?"

"Noble? Who said anything about being noble?" Hawk released a harsh laugh, the sound emerging hollow due to his mask. "I want to start a war, Roberts. There's nothing noble about my actions, and I'm under no impression that there is. I'm not concerned with being a saint. I'm going to get the job done, and if I step on a few toes to get there, then so be it."

Stefan smiled, his temper rising. "I'm afraid I can't let you do that, Hawk." He slipped the pocket watch from his jacket and glanced at it. Ten seconds to nine-thirty. "You're a traitor, and there's nothing I abhor more than traitors."

"I applaud you for trying to do the heroic thing. However, it's a bit too late. Life is far more complicated than good versus bad." His men halted only a foot from where Stefan stood, their faces tensing in preparation for the coming conflict. John, curiously enough, did not appear to be among them.

Before any of them could react, Stefan whirled around and drew his revolver, aiming for the chandelier. *Breathe in, breathe out.* He zeroed in on his target and squeezed the trigger. With a deafening bang, the bullet hit the light in the center of the crystals, exploding the bulb and sending the whole fixture crashing down onto the empty dance floor. As it shattered on the ground, the rest of the lights surrounding the ballroom flickered one last time before going out completely, plunging the room into darkness. *Good job, Bas!*

Screams and shouts echoed as guests panicked and scrambled to find each other. Others rushed for the staircase. The moon cast a faint glow through the balcony doors, outlining the retreating crowd as they tripped and ran throughout the room.

Stefan followed those fleeing in the direction of the staircase, tucking his revolver back into his pocket. People shoved him in their urgency to escape, and several times, he nearly lost his balance and fell. Despite the constant jostling, he doggedly continued on, aware that every second was crucial to Tom's rescue.

"Roberts!" Hawk bellowed from behind, far too close for Stefan's comfort.

Stefan hurried forward, praying that the man wouldn't be able to see him in the sea of people. When he was a few feet from the staircase, a hand grabbed his jacket from behind. Turning, Stefan nearly swung a fist at the person holding him captive before he realized who it was. "Charlotte!"

There was a sizzling noise as Charlotte lit one of her matches, casting dim light over her worried face. "I found the Pegasus Room." Her chest heaved as though she had run a great distance. "We must hurry."

"Lead the way."

Charlotte took off up the stairs, darting and ducking past people, and Stefan struggled to follow. The muscles in his arm ached as he lifted himself up each step. He couldn't let Hawk catch up, even though his body was begging him to slow down.

"This way," Charlotte urged at the top, leading him down a small hallway to the right. The passageway grew darker the farther they went. She struck another one of her matches and held it aloft. "It's just a bit farther," she whispered as Stefan drew abreast of her. "I didn't hear anyone moving or speaking within the room, but we should be cautious. Hawk could have left someone to watch over Tom."

They halted in front of a thick oak door with a small horse carved into the wood. "This is it. The Pegasus Room." Charlotte traced a finger over the plaque above the winged creature, which had the title of the room engraved in brass. "The door is locked."

Stefan grabbed a chair sitting against the opposite wall, placed the back beneath the door handle, and tipped it so that it pulled against the metal. The handle groaned from the pressure but didn't budge. "Charlotte, take over." Stefan waited until Charlotte had resumed trying to pry the handle off before withdrawing the revolver from his pocket and driving it directly down over the doorknob. With a loud *clank*, it finally broke free.

"Let me go in first," Stefan said, readying the revolver in front of him.

"All right." Charlotte ducked behind Stefan as he elbowed the door open. Her skirts brushed the back of his pant leg as he entered the room, scanning for any sign of life. "Tom?"

"I found a lantern," Charlotte said, striking another match. A moment later, dim light illuminated a bound figure that sat like a sack of potatoes against the back wall. A very familiar figure with a head of red hair and a freckled face.

"Tom!" Stefan hurried to where the boy sat, his eyes bright and alert. He untied the ropes from Tom's hands and feet, and when the boy leapt up and ripped the rag off, Stefan took a step back.

"You're here. You really came! Gosh, that rag tasted awful." Tom rubbed at his wrists, fixing Stefan with a shaky grin. "How do you do, Mr. Roberts? Fancy meeting you in a place like this."

Stefan hummed, noting the boy's pale face and rumpled clothing. Despite his brave expression, he was clearly terrified. It was all too understandable, especially considering what he must have experienced over the past few days. "I'm well enough. And you?"

"I'm all right. Those rascals didn't do anything apart from calling me a few choice words." Tom glanced behind Stefan. "Where are they?"

"We can talk later. For now, we need to focus on getting out of here as quickly as possible. The distraction your brother created won't last long, and Hawk is already on the hunt for us." Stefan gestured toward the door. "Come on."

"Wait." The smile fell from the boy's face, replaced by determination. "I know a better way. The servants used a special door to enter and exit the room. They brought me food once when Hawk wasn't around to stop them." He darted to the bookshelf at the far end of the room and gave it a hard shove.

To Stefan's surprise, the shelf swung in, revealing a dark hole where it had once been.

"It's a secret passageway." Tom folded his arms across his chest. "Like in the detective novels."

Stefan moved to the shelf and ducked into the dark tunnel. "Excellent work, Tom. Let's go."

Wooden planks creaked and groaned with every step they took, and thin streams of dust cascaded down from the ceiling on occasion. When Charlotte entered the passageway with the lantern, light illuminated the cramped space, revealing small holes in the planks. Peering through one, Stefan found himself looking into a dim room. "These tunnels must lead to every room in the building," he mused, continuing down the tiny hallway. "By that logic, there should be one that leads to the lobby."

"How on earth will we find the way to the lobby?" Charlotte's voice rose an octave. "We could be trapped in here forever!"

"Shush," Tom murmured from behind them. As they went silent, the faint sound of talking and hollering echoed down the tunnel.

"There you have it," the boy announced, tapping the wall. "We simply have to follow the sound."

"Good idea." Stefan continued down the tunnel in the direction of the noise.

"What exactly did you do to cause such chaos?" Tom asked. "I could hear it from the room Hawk trapped me in. I had hoped it might be you."

Stefan grimaced as he brushed up against the side of the passageway, causing dust to rain down on his suit. "Your brother cut the gas line leading to the lights, and I shot the chandelier. The darkness took the guests by surprise, causing the panic that Charlotte and I needed to escape from Hawk."

"Really? Bastian did that?" Tom whistled. "I wasn't aware he knew that much about lights. I'll have to thank him once we've escaped. Where is he?"

"If he followed the plan, he should be waiting for us in the wagon." Stefan released a shuddering sigh. "If not, we'll be in trouble." It would be impossible to locate the boy in all the commotion.

"And Hawk? What about him?"

"I left him in the ballroom, but he wasn't far behind." A light shown momentarily through the slats in the wood, making Stefan freeze. Luckily, it quickly vanished, and he continued on.

"He's a dangerous man, Mr. Roberts. He threatened to hurt me on multiple occasions." Tom paused, and Stefan thought he heard the boy swallow. "He never did, but still..."

Stefan frowned. "He won't harm anyone, Tom. I'll make sure of it."

Tom fell silent for a moment before speaking. "Thank you both for coming to rescue me. I...I wasn't sure if you would. The locket is incredibly important, after all."

"We would never leave you, Tom," Charlotte said, her voice incredulous. "Our group wouldn't be complete without you."

"Correct." Stefan reached behind him and patted the boy on the shoulder. "We wouldn't have left you in the hands of a highwayman."

"Well, thank you." Tom chuckled, though the sound quavered at the end.

The sound of chatter rose and swelled outside the walls, indicating that they had reached the lobby. Halting, Stefan ran a hand over the planks until he found a thin, square-shaped outline in the wood. "I found a door," he whispered, ramming his shoulder against the wall. The door immediately swung outward, nearly taking him with it. Luckily, Charlotte grasped the back of his jacket, preventing him from sprawling onto the floor.

236

"Goodness, Stefan. Are you all right?" she asked, helping him straighten.

"Thanks to you. Let's get out of here before they find a way to turn the lights back on." Stefan lifted himself carefully out of the passageway and into a small alcove. Once he was certain that Charlotte and Tom were following close behind, he left the alcove and set off through the crowded lobby, heading toward the open door at the front of the room.

Tom sidled up next to him. "Mr. Roberts, I see Hawk. He's watching the exit."

Stefan nodded toward a large group of people migrating toward the door. "Let's get in the middle of that crowd. If we're lucky, Hawk won't see us."

They hurried to join the group, elbowing their way into the midst of the frightened people. As they shuffled up to the door, Stefan held his breath and hoped against all hope that Hawk wouldn't see them. Thankfully, a woman grabbed his arm and started shouting at him, causing him to look away as they passed by.

Stefan let out a sigh of relief as they reached the cool night air. Once down the stairs, they made their way to where the wagon waited along the right side of the road. Bastian was perched on the bench, the reins clasped tightly in his hands and his mask in his lap. He jumped when Stefan hefted himself into the seat. "Mr. Roberts! You made it!"

Stefan held out a hand to help Charlotte up as Bastian joined Tom in the rear of the wagon. Then Stefan snapped the reins and set Orion into motion. Only once they were out of sight from the manor did he slump against the seat with a sigh.

"Tom! You're all right!" Bastian grabbed his brother in a hug.

"I wasn't about to let a couple of thieves get the best of me." Tom pushed Bas back with a grin. "And what about you? Mr.

Roberts said you were the one who turned off the lights. Is that true?"

"It is. Don't you remember the I was helping Mr. Horace install those new gas lights in his store and accidentally cut the line? He wouldn't talk to me for weeks."

The twins launched into a flurry of chatter, their voices overlapping. Stefan could only shake his head in amusement as he focused on the road ahead. Luckily, there were few travelers out so late, and the lane remained mostly clear as they trundled through the city.

Beside him, Charlotte laughed and pulled the mask from her face. "We did it, Stefan. We really did it!"

Her infectious laughter led Stefan to join in. He chuckled, some of the weight lifting from his chest. His heart still beat much faster than normal, as it no doubt would for a while, but at least his head no louder screamed warnings. "We did, didn't we?" He grinned and swiped a hand over his forehead. "I don't believe I'll be attending a ball for a very long time."

Charlotte smiled, brushing the hair from her face. "Agreed. Now we just have to get that list to the Aspens."

"Indeed." And get it to them they would. Assuming they had seen the last of Hawk, John, and whoever else might be looking for the spy list, that was.

CHAPTER 26

Charlotte shifted in her seat and stifled a groan. Everything ached, but especially her back, legs, and shoulders. Upon cracking one eye open, she blinked as she struggled to place her surroundings. The sun cast warm light over her face, and birds chirped from the trees. Why was she outside?

The gentle sound of hoofbeats brought memories from the previous evening. Brightly colored dancers twirling around, rushing to find the horse-engraved door, running through dark passageways, escaping into the night...

Charlotte sat upright on the wagon bench, wincing at the soreness in her muscles. The twinge in her arms was a stark reminder of the long hours she had spent asleep in the wagon. Glancing over her shoulder, she found the twins sleeping peacefully in the back. She smiled as Tom mumbled something unintelligible and pulled the blanket farther over his head. It was good to have him back.

"Guten Morgen. How was your rest?" Stefan asked softly from beside her.

Charlotte turned to face him, noting the exhaustion evident

on his face. The poor man had to have been awake all evening. And if he had dark smudges beneath his eyes, what was her appearance like? She still wore the same gown as she had the previous evening. Her hair had fallen around her shoulders, and her mask and gloves were nowhere to be seen. She must be a real sight. "Did I fall asleep? I'm sorry." She brushed an unruly strand of hair behind her ear. "Some traveling companion I am."

Stefan let the reins hang loosely in his hands. At some point during the night, he had discarded his jacket and cravat, leaving him in his white waistcoat and a slightly rumpled dress shirt. His hair, too, had become mussed, as though the breeze had cast it awry. Though he was in quite a state of disarray, his face was relaxed and happy, a far cry from what it had been the previous night. "There's nothing to be sorry for. If anyone should be apologizing, it's me. I should have let us stay at an inn."

Charlotte shook her head. "It was better to leave the city altogether."

"True. Besides, it's far more beautiful out here." Stefan leaned back against the seat, contentment washing over his face. "No city could compare."

At some point, gently rolling hills and large fields that stretched for miles on either side of the wagon had replaced buildings. The road carved through the bluegrass region with its black fences and black tobacco barns, low stone walls, charming farmhouses, and pastures dotted with cows and horses. Purple- and white-budded trees and waving grasses lined the banks, a cheerful sign of spring and a reminder that they were a long way from Wisconsin.

Charlotte giggled as the thoroughbreds trotted alongside the wagon, nickering back and forth at each other. "This *is* far better. I've never seen anything like it. Have you always preferred the country to the city?"

"Yes. There's too much commotion in the city for my taste. Out here, you learn to appreciate the beauty in the silence." Stefan cast a fond glance at the horses. "That's why I loved growing up at my father's stables. It's also the reason why I want to keep them running after he retires. I don't need them to become more than they already are. I simply want to maintain the legacy my father already created. I want him to be able to step down in grace and enjoy the product of his years spent working."

Charlotte tilted her head. Judging by the spark in Stefan's eye as he spoke of the stables, he cared for them a great deal. "That's admirable." She watched as a white butterfly floated lazily on the breeze, its wings hovering inches above the long grass a few feet from the wagon. "The simple wish for happiness should outweigh dreams of wealth and fame."

Stefan hummed. "Indeed."

Charlotte tipped her hat back, looking up at the blue sky. "I never thought of things that way when I was living in Peshtigo. I used to want more, used to dream of attending balls and finding ways to fit in with the finest members of society." She ran a hand up her arm, feeling the slight grooves in the skin. "Looking back on it, it seems so silly. I thought fine dresses and fancy dances would fill that longing inside me. I was so wrong. I never needed them to be content."

"I said it once before, and I'm saying it now. Joy looks good on you, Charlotte Clarke." Stefan's laugh rumbled deep and low in his chest. "It's far better than any dress or ball gown."

Charlotte returned his smile. "It looks good on you as well, Stefan Roberts."

For a moment, they sat in silence, content with simply being in each other's presence. Then, unable to deny the question that rose to the tip of her tongue, Charlotte spoke. "What now, Stefan? Where will we go from here?"

"We should reach Monticello by the end of the week. Once

there, we'll see if the Aspens are attending the spring races. With luck, we can give them the list. If they aren't there, we'll continue on to Albany."

"I wasn't speaking of the locket," Charlotte murmured softly.

Stefan's eyes widened in realization, and red spread quickly across his cheeks. "Ah."

Grumbling sounded from the back as the twins awoke, making Charlotte sit upright. "Good morning," she called over her shoulder. "Did you sleep well?"

"I slept a good deal better than I did on the floor." Tom yawned and stretched his arms over his head. "At least here, I can move around." He brushed some dust from his waistcoat and glanced around the back of the wagon. "Say, does anyone know where my banjo went"

Charlotte reached under her seat and procured the instrument, handing it back to Tom. "Here you are. We kept it safe for you." She rested her elbows on the back of the bench. "We figured you wouldn't want to be without it for long."

"Not at all," Tom agreed, dragging his thumb across the strings. The grin fell from his face as he studied Charlotte, squinting in the morning light. "Miss Charlotte, where's your locket?"

Charlotte winced and brought a hand up to her neck, which felt slightly barren without the necklace there. "We gave it to Hawk to distract him. You don't have to worry, however. We copied the list onto separate sheets of paper and hid them." She grinned. "Hawk won't be able to stop us, not when we have the ability to continue producing copies."

"But...that locket was important to you." Tom's brows tented. "It belonged to your friend.

"That locket was a piece of jewelry, Tom. While it has sentimental value, the person who once owned it is long gone." Charlotte shook her head. "But you are a living, breathing person. We always would have chosen you over the locket. Besides, we're still giving the list to the Aspens. All is not lost."

Tom sighed, his thin chest heaving in and out, and turned the banjo over in his lap. "I'm not so certain I was worth saving. To tell the truth, I called Hawk a Confederate, and he...well, he guessed that we had opened the locket. He never would have found out if I had kept my mouth shut." He glanced at the instrument in his grasp, his ears reddening. "For that, I'm awfully sorry."

"There's nothing to be sorry for, Tom." Charlotte reached back and gave the boy's shoulder a gentle squeeze, encouraging him to look back at her. "We all make mistakes, especially when we're frightened. We'd never hold it against you. Besides, we had already guessed that Hawk might have known we opened the locket. We're still keeping an eye out for him should he decide to chase after us."

"We'll stop him, won't we?" Tom asked, his eyes filling with hope.

"Yes, we will," Charlotte straightened and glanced at Stefan, who nodded in agreement "Once we reach Monticello, Hawk's time as a criminal will come to an end. If not, it ends in Albany."

But for now, the man was still out there. And though she wanted so badly to be brave for the boys, she wouldn't feel safe until Hawk was standing before a judge.

～

At Charlotte's request, Stefan stopped at the post office in the next town, which turned out to be a small, sparsely populated place that was perfect for avoiding attention. She had explained that she wanted to mail a letter to Ilona, asking the young woman to keep an eye out for the return of the highwaymen. It was a fair idea—even though he doubted Hawk would turn around now.

Charlotte strolled up the stairs to the building looking like a spring flower—a daffodil, perhaps. She had pinned her hair up beneath her straw hat, lending her an elegant air that was only enhanced by the yellow dress she had changed into. The only thing missing from her ensemble was her gloves, a thought that made Stefan smile a bit. It was good to know she no longer felt the need to wear them.

"Mr. Roberts? Mr. Roberts, are you listening?"

Stefan blinked and turned around, finding the twins sitting directly behind him with knowing looks on their faces. "I'm sorry. What did you say?"

Bastian raised an eyebrow. "I asked if you wanted to fetch the food while Miss Charlotte is in the post office."

"Oh. Well, I suppose that would be a good idea." Stefan ignored the question evident in the boy's expression and slid down from the wagon before looping Orion's reins around the hitching post, murmuring a soft command to the horse. He moved to the back of the wagon as the twins hopped down. "I saw a general store a few buildings back," he informed them, setting off in the direction they had come from. "We should be able to get provisions there."

As they ambled down the boardwalk, Stefan's thoughts returned to Charlotte and her quiet words. *I wasn't speaking of the locket.* He knew what she had meant, but he wasn't entirely certain what to do about it. He lifted a hand to his mouth, recalling for not nearly the first time their kiss from the previous evening. She had smelled of flowers and—

"Mr. Roberts? Mr. Roberts!"

Stefan jolted from his reverie and stopped. "Yes, Bastian?"

"We just walked past the general store."

"Ah." Stefan turned around. "Why don't you two lead the way?"

Tom folded his arms across his chest, effectively barring the path to the mercantile. "Mr. Roberts, you clearly aren't thinking of lunch. Your mind is on Miss Charlotte, isn't it?"

Stefan coughed, trying and failing to cover his surprise and embarrassment. "What gave you that idea?"

"Oh, come off it." A smile tugged at Tom's lips. "Bastian and I have seen how you look at her. Just like our da looked at our ma."

Stefan fell silent, trying to formulate an objection. To his surprise, he couldn't find one.

"You love her, don't you?" Bastian questioned softly from beside Stefan.

Love? Warmth spread throughout his chest. The more he thought about it, the more it seemed it could be true. He loved Charlotte's smile and her bright laugh. He loved the way she had taken the boys in without question and had listened to his own story without judgment. And, though it was a bit embarrassing to admit, he had loved their kiss. "You're right, Bastian. I do love her." *Love.* It was the simple truth. He was completely, entirely, undeniably in love with Charlotte Clarke.

Tom's brows shot up. "So what are you going to do about it?"

"I...I don't know." Stefan lifted his shoulders, a sheepish laugh escaping him. "I've never been in love before."

Tom rolled his eyes and huffed a breath. "You've got to marry her, of course."

"Marry! But we haven't even gone through a proper courtship yet!"

"Traditional courtship is meant to give a couple time to learn more about each other." Bastian tapped his chin, a twinkle in his eye. "You and Miss Charlotte have spent the last three weeks constantly in each other's company. I would say that's plenty of time for you to learn about her, and her you."

He pointed at Stefan. "Plus, if you really cared about rules, you wouldn't have let her travel with you in the first place."

Stefan fixed his gaze on the wooden boards below him and cleared his throat. "I suppose that's true enough. But I don't know how to ask. What if she...what if she doesn't feel the same way?"

"I don't think she's given you any reason to believe that she doesn't return your feelings. Has she?" Tom asked.

Stefan lifted his head. "Well...no." As a matter of fact, it had been the exact opposite. Charlotte had chosen to kiss him—not the other way around. She must have felt the same way, or at least slightly.

"Think about it." Bastian's sober expression melted into a grin. "I'm sure you'll come up with something. With the way you're acting, you can't put it off long."

Stefan adjusted his hat, unable to resist chuckling. "I'll find a way to tell her." He exhaled. "Not here, though. The time isn't right."

"And when *will* the time be right, Mr. Roberts?" Tom fisted his hands on his hips.

Stefan shifted and released a breath. "I'll know."

But it wasn't only a matter of timing. What if they didn't deliver the list on time? What if they never caught Hawk? And if they didn't get to the races on time—well, he couldn't marry Charlotte if he had nothing to offer. There were still problems that stood between them and their growing attraction, and until those problems were solved, Stefan would never be able to reveal how he felt.

CHAPTER 27

The rushing of water was the first sign that they were nearing the Cumberland River. Stefan straightened in his seat, straining to see the river through the thick trees and steep hills they were slowly passing through. Flashes of silver and blue caught his eye, accompanied by a faint, rhythmic splashing.

"What's that noise?" Charlotte leaned over the front of the wagon. "Not the water running—the repetitive sound." A few strands of hair had blown loose from beneath her hat, fluttering down around her cheeks and waving with the breeze. She reminded Stefan of a woodland nymph, all wonder and bright-eyed beauty. Was it any wonder that he had fallen in love with her?

Stefan smiled. "I believe that's coming from a paddleboat. They use them frequently around here."

"Will we be taking one?" Charlotte tilted her head to look at Stefan, her eyes glittering in the morning light.

"I'm afraid not. We'll need to find a ferry that can hold the horses and the wagon." Stefan rested the reins on his knee. "If we can't find a place for the wagon, we'll have to sell it and walk or ride the rest of the way. It isn't ideal, but it will get us as far as my father's stables."

"Ah." Charlotte sat back, her face falling. "Perhaps I'll take a ride on one another time."

"You...should." Stefan tried not to choke on the words, though they pained him to say. They shouldn't have. But how could they not, when they reminded him she would be leaving? "They're wonderful. I'll most likely take one on my way back to Illinois."

"On your way back?" Bastian appeared between them, his voice incredulous. He gestured toward the road. "But we only just got here!"

Stefan blew out a sigh and shifted slightly, unable to disguise his discomfort. "I'm aware. The truth is, I don't think I can stay in Kentucky for long after we deliver the locket." Even though he desperately wanted a long break. "I can't leave my father by himself, and I've already been away far longer than I would have liked."

Charlotte hummed thoughtfully. "Have you ever considered bringing him to the Kentucky stable? Perhaps he would enjoy the trip."

"My father hasn't been to Kentucky since my mother died." Stefan shook his head, a frown tugging at his lips. "I don't know if I'll ever be able to make him return. I think he's afraid of the things he'll remember once he's there." *As I was.* They had both run away from Kentucky, though Stefan had once told himself he was doing it for Vater. He rolled the sleeves of his shirt back and avoided the gazes of his traveling companions. "Though, in time, he won't be able to remember it at all. Perhaps that will be a good thing for him." He lifted his shoulders and let them drop. "I don't know. His illness is such a strange thing."

Charlotte tapped him on the knee. "Well, perhaps he may be more willing to move to Kentucky if he knows his son is well-equipped to take over his business."

"Maybe. Maybe not." Stefan watched as a ground squirrel scampered across the road and disappeared into the thick brush on the other side. "My father is a complicated man. On one hand, he begged and pleaded for me to stay home after the war, using the excuse that he needed help with the stables. On the other, he's become tight-lipped about his business. When I try to help, he grows sharp and sometimes even confused." He released a bitter laugh. "It's a sorry state to see him in."

Charlotte pursed her lips, her eyes sympathetic. "Has the doctor offered any solutions? Anything you might do to ease his discomfort?"

"The doctor told me to continue letting my father work until it becomes apparent he can no longer do so." Stefan tipped his hat back, allowing the sun to warm his face. "Then I was to report back to him."

"There must be something more you can do." Charlotte brightened and snapped her fingers. "Perhaps you could bring him back something from Kentucky. Something he would remember fondly. That might help him heal, even if it's in a small way."

"Something he would remember fondly..." Stefan hummed, the idea taking hold. "I like it. I'll think of something." The image of bringing Charlotte to visit his father took shape in his head. What would Vater think of her? He would surely take her in with eagerness, especially once he learned of all she had done for Stefan.

Bastian disappeared from between them, only to be replaced by Tom. "Maybe you should bring us back with you. I could play some banjo for him," he offered, a wry grin on his face. "If he's anything like you, I'm certain it would be a great success."

Stefan snorted. "I'm not certain how he would react to that. He hasn't listened to music in quite some time. He used to enjoy waltzes, however." His father had usually danced with his mother while Franz played the piano. But that had been before... Chances were, the man wouldn't appreciate the music at all now.

Tom whooped and sat back. "I have plenty of those," he exclaimed, plucking a few strings on his banjo in demonstration. His playing was interrupted only when the forest finally opened up, allowing them their first full view of the river. Tom lifted his hand from the strings and said in a low tone, "Woah." His surprise mirrored that of Stefan and everyone else in the wagon.

The river itself wasn't anything unusual—simply a long stretch of murky blue water that ran from one side of Stefan's vision to the other. It was peaceful in the early morning, undisturbed except for the gentle rippling and swirling currents. No, the river wasn't anything Stefan hadn't seen before—but fog had crept over the top of the water, a wispy cloud that seemed to drift along with the current. The sun cast bright beams through the mist, creating prisms of colorful light that shimmered and wavered in the air. The fog would disappear with the rising of the sun, but that in itself made the sight special.

"It's beautiful, isn't it? I haven't been near water in the morning for quite some time." Charlotte's face glowed with happiness.

"That it is," Stefan replied softly. His eyes remained fixed on her as she giggled and said something to the twins. It was beautiful. Very beautiful, indeed. How could he let her go?

As they continued their search for a ferry to take them across the river, the wagon rolled slowly into a small town, the wheels bumping and creaking as they hit rocks and divots in the narrow lane. Stefan winced as they jounced over a pothole and jumped several inches into the air, making the wood groan as they hit the ground. "It would seem that this road is not frequently traveled."

Charlotte made a noise of assent and clamped her hat atop

her head with one hand. "Indeed." Her voice wobbled due to the uneven ground. "I suppose that's a good thing, isn't it?"

"In a way, yes." Stefan narrowed his eyes, staring at the small and shabby community, with buildings that seemed to be falling apart with time. "However, it also means we'll most likely be the only wagon on the road. I don't want to be taken advantage of." He had no desire to run into any additional robbers.

Charlotte released her hand, allowing it to fall to her side. "True. Will we be staying in this area for long?"

"No. We're going to pass straight through once I find the nearest ferry." Stefan searched through the forest for any sign of a vessel on the waters. "I may have to ask someone in town. I haven't seen a sign or any other indicator that there's one nearby."

"Very well." Charlotte leaned back against the seat as they passed the buildings, eyeing her surroundings with an air of apprehension. He didn't blame her.

The streets were nearly silent. Many of the shops were closed, the windows nailed shut and the doors hanging loosely from their hinges. Piles of horse manure and garbage littered the road, the result of weeks of travelers passing through. It was eerie, in a way, to see a place so desolate and empty. Whatever had happened to the little river town must have involved a long and sad story, though it was not one they had the time to hear.

"Ho, there! Who goes?" A raspy voice barked the greeting from somewhere amidst the buildings.

Stefan pulled the wagon to a halt. A man sat on the porch of what looked like a saloon with his feet propped on the lopsided table next to him. His dirty waistcoat and tattered hat had seen better days. His beard, too, could have used a trim.

Stefan lifted a hand in greeting. "Hello. We're looking for a ferry. Do you know of one?"

"Sure, I do. If you continue down this street for a while,

you'll find one." The man pointed toward the other end of town. "Just be wary, traveler. There's plenty of folks around here that would be all too glad to take advantage of you and the missus."

"I will be. Thank you, sir." Stefan tipped his hat.

The man returned the gesture and fixed them with a hardened stare, his mouth thinning beneath his beard. "The best thanks you could give me is to leave this place. We're still trying to clean up after the last group of travelers came through. They looted every building within a mile."

"I'm sorry to hear that. We'll be on our way." Stefan flicked the reins. If leaving was what satisfied the man, he was more than happy to oblige. He had no desire to remain in the little town for any longer than they had to. As they rode away, he turned to Charlotte. "That was odd."

Charlotte inclined her head, her eyes wide. "I feel bad for him, though."

"I wonder when that gang of troublemakers passed through." Stefan frowned. "I hope we won't run across them. I've had enough of highwaymen."

About a half mile from the town, they came to a small clearing with a shack at the center and the river behind. Stefan brightened, noticing the long wooden post that rose from the ground behind the shack. "There's our ferry."

"A pole?" Tom questioned from where he walked beside the wagon. The twins had leapt out after they exited the town, seeming more content with walking along the edge of the forest. "How is that going to help us cross the river?"

"It's not the pole I'm concerned with. It's the rope that runs from it." Stefan gestured to the sturdy rope tied to the post. It stretched taut from the top of the post to a pole on the other side of the river. "The ferry is attached to it."

Sure enough, as they moved around the shack, a large wooden raft that sat in the river became visible. Metal cables attached the raft to the rope above, keeping it from drifting away. At the front of the raft sat a man, his face covered by a straw hat.

As they approached, the man lifted his head, revealing brown eyes that shone with alertness. "Greetings, travelers. How can I help you?" he asked, his voice deep and wary.

"We seek passage across the river." Stefan gestured to the raft. "And it looks as though you might be able to get us there."

"But of course I can. You've come to the finest ferry on the Cumberland River." The man tipped his hat back. "The name is Jack. I'd be happy to take you across. For a fee, of course." He named a price, which Stefan readily agreed to.

Once the money was transferred, Stefan carefully steered the wagon and horses aboard the wooden raft. Though they tossed their heads and rolled their eyes anxiously, they remained still.

"So, folks, where is that you come from?" Jack asked as he reached overhead to grab the rope. He began to pull hand over hand, sliding the raft slowly but surely across the river.

"We hail from the Chicago area." Stefan kept his hand close by his side. Though he didn't suspect the ferryman of intending any harm, the warning from the man from town hung in the back of his mind, making him wary of letting his revolver get far from reach. "We just came from the town north of here. A fellow there said you had a band of ruffians pass through not too long ago. Is that true?"

Jack nodded, his eyes darkening in anger. "Aye, it's true. A group of men looted the place and nearly set fire to our inn. After that, they came here and demanded passage over the river. When I named my fee, they tried to bargain for a lower price. I wouldn't budge." He shrugged. "They got angry and left. I don't know what became of them. Nor do I care." He speared Stefan with his gaze. "Take my word, sir. People like that cause trouble wherever they go. If you see a couple of riders on the other side of the river, get as far off the road as you can."

"We will." Stefan tensed. Surely, this group could not be connected to Hawk and his gang. There was no way they could have gotten so far ahead. *You're being paranoid again.*

"They were an odd bunch." The ferryman wrinkled his nose. "The leader was the strangest of all. He spoke like a gentleman, but he wasn't one. Not when he was dressed like a criminal and cursed worse than a sailor." He ran a hand over his jaw. "Not to mention that locket he had. He had it in his hand the whole time. Kept holding it up to look at it too. It had me wondering if he had some lady back home. I feel sorry for her if that is the case."

The air left Stefan's lungs in one great breath. It couldn't be. But the ferryman's description left no room for doubt. How many thieves carried a locket around with them? Hawk was still after them, and by the looks of it, he had somehow gotten a head start. What were they going to do?

"Hawk?" Tom's face had grown pale, and the boy clenched the side of the ferry so tightly that his knuckles were turning white. All bravado had fled from his posture at John's words. "I thought he was gone."

Jack tipped his head and quirked a brow. "You know the man?"

"He caused us trouble earlier in our journey." Stefan wiped his palms on his trouser legs. "I had hoped he was well behind us." Until Hawk was out of the way, they wouldn't have a moment of peace.

"I'm sorry to hear it." Jack huffed. "Men like that don't deserve to be out on the roads."

The ferry creaked and groaned as it slid onto the opposite bank of the river at an agonizingly slow pace, the wooden boards shouting their protest as they wedged deep into the mud. After a moment of shifting around, it finally ground to a complete halt. Jack stood back, his hands dropping from the rope to his sides. "There you are," he declared in a voice that was slightly out of breath. "Best of luck on your travels, folks."

Tom and Bastian leapt from the wagon and hopped over the muddy bank, coming to a halt on the other side. "Come on, Mr. Roberts!" Tom called. "I don't want to stay by the river for any longer than we have to." He cast a look behind them, fear clear eyes. "We should get to Monticello as soon as possible. Before…"

Before Hawk. The unspoken sentence hung heavy in the air.

"We're coming. Thank you, Jack." Whistling, Stefan cautiously directed Orion onto the muddy shore. The horse stepped hesitantly onto the ground, his ears pinned back as he gauged the situation. After another prompt from Stefan, he pulled the wagon into the mud, working together with the thoroughbreds to trudge across the riverbank. For a moment, Stefan feared they would become stuck again. However, the horses managed to pull them onto the safety of a dirt path after a few minutes of struggle.

"Farewell," Jack called as they rode away. "Keep an eye out for those troublemakers, now. They'll ambush you the moment you aren't looking."

Stefan shuddered. He needed no reminder of the fact that they were still being pursued. Clearly, Hawk was determined to find them, no matter the cost. Stefan glanced into the trees beside them as they resumed travel, searching in vain for any sign that they were being watched. Perhaps they should go straight to the Aspens' home. Would that put the family in danger, though? He grimaced at the thought.

"Stefan? Are you all right?" Charlotte's worried voice cut through the haze in Stefan's mind.

He exhaled, forcing himself to relax. *Don't freeze up now, Roberts. We're too close to give up.* "While I would like to say I am, I'm not. We knew it was possible Hawk would come after us, but I hoped he wouldn't. And that he wouldn't be near so soon."

Charlotte straightened, her eyes determined. "So what if he is? All we have to do is remain out of sight, as we have been."

Stefan wrinkled his nose, trying to keep his irritation and nerves at bay. "I'm so tired of hiding. Just for once, I'd like to be able to walk boldly into town without fear of being seen. Just for once, I'd like Hawk to be the one who has to sneak around like a criminal on the run. I want him to know what it feels like to fear every corner he turns, because he *is* a criminal. He's a selfish, greedy scoundrel who deserves every bit of retribution that's coming to him."

"And it will come." A smile crossed Charlotte's face. "Hawk will face justice, Stefan. In order for that to happen, however, we first have to get that list to the Aspens. And that does mean we must continue to sneak through towns."

Stefan groaned.

"But think of the things we'll be able to do once the list is out of our hands! We can parade through Monticello as though we haven't a care in the world." She laughed. "We can watch the races, ride the steamboats, and take long walks through town. You'll be able to care for your horses, and I'll...I'll find a job, I suppose. We'll never have to think about the list or that monstrous man ever again."

At her hesitation, Stefan cast a quick glance at Charlotte. "Perhaps if you find somewhere to stay in Kentucky, you could invite Ilona to come visit. Assuming... assuming you decide to stay here, of course." *If only you would come with me.*

Charlotte gasped. "But of course! Oh, I'm certain she would love to come and visit. I'll have to tell her all about the ball and our daring escape. She'll think we're heroes!"

"I'm sure she will." Stefan chuckled, some of the anxiety lifting from his shoulders. Perhaps Charlotte was right. Perhaps they would get the locket to the Aspens without further trouble. Perhaps...perhaps everything would turn out for the best.

A loud grinding noise caused the wagon to halt in the middle of the lane. "What was that?" Stefan twisted to peer at the back of the wagon.

"It looks as though one of the wheels has come loose." Bastian crouched beside the back left wheel. His brows wrinkled as he ran a hand over the spokes. "I don't see any cracks in the wood, which is a good thing."

"Are you sure the wheel is loose?"

"Yes. I might be able to fix it, but I would need someone to brace the wheel while I check things out." Bastian straightened, setting his hands on his hips. "Then I can figure out what to do." He glanced up at Stefan, his eyes shining. "Could you hold it for me?"

Stefan knew enough to fix the wheel, but clearly, the boy wanted the chance to show off his woodworking skills. "Certainly." He sighed and turned to face Charlotte, who waited patiently beside him. "You may want to get your lunch out. We're going to be here for a while."

And with Hawk and his highwaymen lurking close by. Stefan could only pray they would be fast enough. If Hawk found them here stranded, what would they do?

CHAPTER 28

"*D*rat. The hub band has come loose," Bastian grumbled.

Stefan took a deep breath and shifted to study the boy without removing his hand from the wheel. The sun, normally so warm and inviting, cast sweltering rays on his back and made him wish they had stopped somewhere with more shade. "What do you suggest?"

"I can fix it," Bastian declared, his face determined. "I've mended a hub band once before. It snapped right off of our milkman's wagon. I helped him fix it, and it never moved again. Honest."

"I believe you." Stefan chuckled, unable to stop himself. "In that case, what would you like me to do?"

Bastian bit his lip, studying the wheel with folded arms. He had thrown his jacket in the wagon bed, leaving him in a gray waistcoat that looked as though it had seen better days. Stefan made a mental note to see if he could find a fresh outfit for the boy once they reached the stables. "Could you continue to hold the wheel steady? I have to find something to secure it to the wagon with. It'll be hard to attach it without the proper tools, but I think I can make do until we reach Monticello. We aren't far, are we?"

"Not at all." Stefan glanced down the lane. "If we can get back on the road within the hour, we'll reach it fairly soon." And hopefully before Hawk.

Bastian released a long breath, relief evident in his eyes. "Good. In that case, I'll return shortly." He raced off to find a makeshift tool, leaving Stefan to hold the wheel and try not to move too much. The boy spent several minutes collecting an armful of sturdy sticks and the extra length of rope from the back of the wagon before returning.

"This should do the trick." Bastian dropped the pile at Stefan's feet. "Would you mind moving a bit?"

"Not at all." Stefan shifted to the side, giving the boy space to work.

As Bastian began to tinker with the wheel, Stefan allowed his attention to wander over to Charlotte. She unfolded one of the blankets on a patch of grass and sank gracefully down, setting the picnic basket on the ground. To Stefan's surprise, she looked up and caught his eye, lifting a hand in a small wave. He waved in return, nearly dropping the wheel he had forgotten was in his hands.

"You really do love her, don't you?" Bastian asked, his head bent over the wheel. He cast a glance up at Stefan. "You can hardly think when you're around her."

Stefan coughed, his cheeks heating. "I suppose it's obvious, isn't it?"

"It sure is. You look like you've just seen the sun for the first time." Bastian reached for one of the sticks. His head blocked most of what he was doing, but it looked as though he had tied the wheel back on with rope and was wedging sticks between the wheel and the wagon frame to hold it in place. "You had better tell her once we reach Monticello, Mr. Roberts. If not, you might lose her forever. Especially if you plan on going back to Illinois."

Charlotte laughed charmingly at something Tom said. Stefan exhaled. "I will. I simply have to find the right time. There's still too much at stake." They had to find the Aspens before Hawk. Not to mention if he couldn't make it to the races on time, the stables would fail. And there was no chance of him weighing Charlotte down with financial problems. Not when she had been through so much.

Bastian hummed, still focused on the wheel. "Can I ask you something, Mr. Roberts?"

"Certainly, Bastian."

Bastian hesitated a moment before looking at Stefan. "What's going to happen to us? To Tom and me, I mean."

Stefan blinked. "What do you mean? You're coming with us to Monticello. That's always been part of the plan. Unless you've changed your mind, of course. Not that we would let you leave with Hawk around."

Bastian bit his lip and reached for another of the sticks he had collected, lodging it against the wheel. "I'm talking about *after* Monticello. What's going to happen to us once you deliver the horses? There's no reason for us to stay once they're gone. Our job was to care for them."

"Oh. Well, I suppose that's true. Do you...*want* to leave?" Stefan had been so concerned with getting the twins to Kentucky that he hadn't given any thought to their fate outside of reaching Monticello. Now that they were nearly there, however, the problem was glaringly clear.

"No!" Bastian twisted, his eyes wide and mouth down-turned. "I don't want to go. I don't know where we *would* go. It's too far to walk back to Illinois. Besides, I don't want to return. There was nothing there for us. We...I want to stay with you and Miss Charlotte."

Stefan's lips twitched up. "Then stay at the stables and help me with the horses. There's a carpenter in town that I'm sure would love to have you as an apprentice. You don't have to leave, Bastian."

Bastian sank back on his heels. "But what about you and Miss Charlotte? If you do go your separate ways, you'll have to go back to Illinois, and Miss Charlotte will leave to find a job." He turned his palms face up. "And what if Tom doesn't want to live here? What if he wants to keep traveling around?"

"I suppose that's something you'll have to speak with him about," Stefan said quietly. "As for Charlotte and I..." His jaw twitched. "I can't say anything before I get a chance to ask what her opinion is. You'd be more than welcome to reside at the stables in the meantime."

Bastian studied Stefan's face, his eyes shining with cautious hope. "Truly? You wouldn't get rid of us?"

"There's no 'getting rid' of you, Bastian. You aren't items to be tossed aside. You can stay as long as you wish." Stefan winked. "Unless you get tired of caring for horses, of course."

"As long as I wish..." Bastian pushed his sleeves back, a smile crossing his face. "That sounds nice. Thank you, Mr. Roberts."

"Of course, Bastian." Stefan returned the boy's smile.

"And what about you? What will you do once you deliver the list?" Bastian refocused on his work on the wheel. "Will you go straight back to Illinois? Or will you stay in Kentucky for a little while?"

"I'm not entirely certain." Stefan leaned against the side of the wagon. An image of a farm came to mind, with two red-headed boys running through the stables and a beautiful woman waving at Stefan from the porch. He tilted his head back to study Charlotte. *Yes.* That would be a fine future.

"What about your hopes of taking over your father's business? Will you give it all up?"

Stefan turned back to the boy. "That will depend on my

father." And on his condition by the time Stefan got back to Illinois.

Bastian snapped the hub back into place with a triumphant "aha!" before twisting and fixing Stefan with a pointed look. "With all due respect, Mr. Roberts, how is that any different from what you told me? You said I should talk to Tom about my dreams. You said I should be proud of what I do. But what about you? Why don't you talk to your father about taking over the horses?" He rested his elbows on his knees. "Maybe talking to your father about his memory would make him listen to you."

"Perhaps." Stefan brushed his hair beneath his cap. "I...I simply don't know how." How was one to tell one's father that his memory was slipping? That he was no longer fit to care for the business he so loved?

"I'll speak to my brother if you speak to your father," Bastian offered. "That way, we'll both be held accountable."

Stefan held out a hand to the boy. "Very well. It's a deal."

"Good." Bastian grunted, using Stefan's hand to heft himself to his feet. "The wheel should hold us until we reach Monticello. Tom and I will walk just in case."

"Perfect. Thank you, Bastian." Stefan waved to signal Tom and Charlotte over.

The sound of cracking twigs prevented Bastian from responding to Stefan's gratitude. Turning, they both searched among the trees for the source of the noise. The hair on the back of Stefan's neck rose, a sure sign something was amiss.

"Did you hear that? It sounded as though someone was walking through the trees." Bastian spoke in an intense whisper, his eyes darting back and forth. "Do you think it's him?"

"Maybe it was a squirrel." Stefan's rapidly beating heart told a different story.

The snapping noise sounded again, accompanied by a horse's snort. A white stallion appeared between the trees, heading straight for the wagon. Stefan sucked in a breath. A familiar man sat atop the horse—one he couldn't make head or tails of. "Get behind me." He waved Bastian behind him and set a hand on his revolver.

Tom released a yelp from across the clearing, and when Stefan glanced back, the boy had moved to stand in front of Charlotte. His face was pale, but he remained before her as the rider approached. Charlotte, for her part, was on her feet and staring at Stefan with fear plain on her face.

"Stefan." John drew his mount to a halt in front of Stefan. The mysterious man peered down at him, his dark eyes unreadable. "I've been searching for you, my friend. I bring news."

"What sort of news? News pertaining to the highwayman from the river town, perhaps? I suppose you weren't among their group." An accusing note crept into Stefan's voice.

John's face creased into something that looked almost like remorse before smoothing back into a calm expression. "I may have been a member of their party, but I did not partake in their activities. I came looking for you because they made mention of something you'll find important. He reined his mare back, causing her to toss her head. "They were traveling to the residence of one Johann Roberts. They said they had business there."

"My father's stables." Stefan's heart dropped to his toes. "Do they know where the stables are located? Do they intend to destroy the buildings?"

"I doubt they will harm anything if you are not there." John shifted in his saddle. "But you would be wise to avoid the stables for the time being." He raised a brow. "They have quite the vendetta against you after what happened at the ball. Stefan, this could all be solved if you would only give me the list. I know you have it, and I know you've seen it. If you hand it over, I assure you, these problems will leave. You need to trust me."

"Don't trust him, Mr. Roberts! He's bad like the rest of them," Tom called from across the clearing. "He's the one who took me. He gave me to Hawk!"

Stefan swallowed. "If you really are on our side, explain this plan of yours."

"I'm afraid I can't do that. Nothing can be revealed until Hawk is gone." John rested a hand on his horse's neck, for she was shifting nervously.

"Then the list stays with me." Stefan rolled his shoulders back, stretching himself as tall as he could.

John studied Stefan for a moment before smiling, his teeth glinting white in the sun. "Feeling brave, are you? Very well. I won't stop you if you're so desperate to complete your mission. Perhaps then you will believe me." He pointed at Stefan. "But be careful, my friend. You aren't safe yet." He gestured toward the lane. "Hurry on. They will come looking for you before long."

Stefan straightened and returned to the wagon as quickly as he could. "Come, Bastian. We should go."

Bastian frowned, still watching John. "But...what if he's lying and they didn't go to the stables, after all? They could be waiting up the lane. He could be setting a trap. He already did once."

Stefan hefted himself onto the wagon bench and held out a hand for Charlotte, who had run up to the side of the wagon. He kept his voice low. "I have a plan."

Charlotte joined him in the vehicle, her widened gaze seeking John, who had moved to the side of the road. "What about him? What if he follows us?"

Stefan flicked the reins, and the wagon rolled unsteadily past John. Stefan didn't look back. Only after they turned a bend did he answer Charlotte. "I know you're all afraid, but you have to trust me. We're too close to turn back, and going to the stables would put us at more risk. We'll head straight for the racetrack and pray the Aspens are there."

And if John decided to follow them? Well, that would put his "friend" statement to the test.

Charlotte studied his face before sinking back against the bench. "All right, Stefan. I trust you."

That felt mighty good.

CHAPTER 29

"I don't believe it." Charlotte gasped, leaning forward. "We're here!"

Monticello spread before them, full of life. While it wasn't nearly as big as Milwaukee, it seemed like the perfect blend of man and nature. The dirt streets were swept clean of manure and debris. Trees poked through the cracks between the buildings, providing a hint of greenery in a brick-filled landscape. Stagecoaches and wagons rolled along the main road, filled with chattering people dressed in colorful dresses and casual suits.

As they joined the caravan of vehicles, Charlotte spotted a mill, a tavern, and even a stately courthouse that fairly dwarfed the buildings around it. Birds observed her from the tops of buildings, tilting their heads to and fro as they fanned their wings to catch the warmth of the sun. It was hard not to be excited, even with the worries that still hung heavy over them. She turned to Stefan. "I'm surprised your father is so averse to visiting. I would travel here often if I was in his position."

"This place was filled with soldiers a few years back." Stefan glanced from one side of the street to the other with wary eyes.

He clearly wasn't as thrilled by the town as she was. Not that she blamed him, with Hawk so close at hand. "Monticello seems to have picked itself up, however. It certainly looks better than the last time I was here."

"Where are your father's stables?"

"They lie to the west a few miles." Stefan gestured in the general direction with one hand.

Charlotte inclined her head. Good. If Hawk had really gone to the stables as John said, it would give them a head start to finding the Aspens. "Will we be visiting them after all this is done? To make sure they're safe?"

Stefan's hands tightened on the reins. "That depends on the Aspens. If they're at the races, we will. If not, we'll have to go straight to Albany."

Despite his casual tone, worry shadowed his face. Charlotte reached over and took his hand, giving it a reassuring squeeze. "We're nearly there." She offered what she hoped was an encouraging smile. "Then we can put all of this behind us."

Surprise flitted across Stefan's features, though he didn't withdraw his hand. "I know. I'm just worried about the stables. I fear they'll destroy the buildings—or worse, hurt the stable hands and the horses."

"Oh, Stefan. I'm so sorry." Charlotte withdrew her hand and blew out a sigh. "I wish there was more we could do, but I suppose getting this list to the Aspens is the next best thing."

"Certainly." Stefan steered the wagon onto a side street, heading for a large, grassy clearing at the edge of town. "And this is the place we'll start looking for them."

The racetrack was, in fact, nothing more than a large field with colorful flags to denote the path the horses were meant to take. A fence surrounded the area, with two gates serving as entrances, one at each end. Despite the small size of the venue, dozens of spectators surrounded the track, all intently focused on the thoroughbreds thundering in a circle.

Charlotte's eyes widened. "I didn't realize the races were happening now."

"They run from mid-May to the end of June. The earlier races are usually more populated than the later ones—hence, the crowd." Stefan gestured with his head to the thoroughbreds, who walked peacefully beside the wagon. "Lake and Persnickety aren't set to run until next week."

Charlotte scanned the people around the track, and her gaze quickly landed on several men who stood to the side of the field holding white placards. "What are those men doing?"

"They're bidding. Owners take offers as soon as their horses are done racing." Stefan was also looking through the crowd, his gaze attentive. "Other times, they take bets on who the winning horse will be. If their horse wins, they keep the money. If not, they pay. It's a lucrative industry for the honest businessman but an endless pit for the foolish one." His jaw twitched. "These animals deserve better than to be sold off to a greedy gambler with no sense of care. There are some men who would run them into the ground for a cent. I would never let that happen to my father's horses." He straightened, his eyes fixed on someone in the crowd. "Well, what do you know? Burnsby! Over here!"

One of the men turned from the racetrack, his face brightening when he spotted Stefan. He hurried over to the wagon. Tilting back his flat cap, he looked up at them with a wry grin that spread across stubble-covered cheeks. "Roberts! It's been a long, long time, my friend! I didn't expect to see you or your kin here. I thought your stable hands would go to the Lexington or Louisville derbies. That seems to be where everyone else is headed this time of year. They say there's something big in the making, you know. Rumor has it there'll be a new race in a few years that'll put this to shame."

"I decided to stay local this year." Stefan leaned down to shake the man's hand. "My father hasn't been to the Kentucky stables in a long while, as you well know. I thought it was about time I checked in on them and made sure things were running as they should be."

"Running, eh? They're running, all right. I think one of your Kentucky horses is on the track right now. You don't have anything to worry about." Burnsby released a hearty laugh, turning his gaze on Charlotte. "And who is this lovely lady?" His eyes widened as he glanced behind them. "Oh, and two lads, as well! Why, Roberts, you have a veritable caravan with you. It seems you have quite a story to tell."

"This is Miss Charlotte. The boys are Tom and Sebastian," Stefan said, a soft smile crossing his face. "Charlotte, boys, this is William Burnsby. He's the ticket master I mentioned earlier."

"You mentioned me? Why, I ought to be honored." Burnsby sketched a pretend bow, his eyes sparkling with mirth. "I'm right pleased to meet you, miss, and the boys as well. For what it's worth, I'm not certain what you've done with Roberts, but I applaud you. He looks a sight healthier than the last time he was around. I always told him he would be better off with a family. It's good. Very good, indeed."

"Oh, we're not family." Warmth flooded Charlotte's face. "Just friends and traveling companions."

Burnsby turned to Stefan, his brows rising beneath his cap. "Well, you'd better hurry up and marry her. I doubt you'll find another lady that'll put up with your grouchy attitude."

"Burnsby, I need to ask for a favor." Stefan cut the man's ribbing off by leaning forward, his eyes serious. "I need to know if the Aspens are here. If not, I need to know if they have tickets for any of the upcoming races."

Burnsby scratched his head and glanced up at the sky. "The Aspens? I might have seen them. Let me take a look." He dug one hand into his pocket and withdrew a wad of ticket stubs. "Aspens...Aspens...ha! You're in luck, Roberts, fine luck, indeed. Old Mr. Aspen bet on a horse that's set to run in the next race.

They'll be watching somewhere in the crowd. I couldn't tell you where exactly, though."

"We can find them. Thank you, Burnsby. I owe you." Stefan released a relieved sigh, sitting back on the bench.

"You can pay your debt another time. Go and enjoy the races with this fine lady, or else I might just ask her myself." With a wink, the ticket master darted back into the crowd, shouting something about placing money on the next race.

"He's always been an interesting fellow. A bit rough around the edges, but kind, nonetheless." Stefan glanced around. "Now we need to locate the Aspens before they leave."

"What do they look like? We could split up and search the crowd for them," Charlotte suggested, lowering herself from the wagon.

Stefan shook his head as he joined her on the ground, wrapping Orion's reins around a nearby post. "No. That's asking for danger. We don't know for certain where Hawk and his men are. They could be somewhere in the crowd, waiting for us to split up. We'll search together."

The twins appeared beside them, their faces full of eagerness. "I can't believe we're at an honest-to-goodness horse race!" Tom's eyes flashed with excitement. "They've started to line the next horses up. Who do you suppose will win? I like the look of that tan one."

"I'm not sure, but there will be time for enjoying the races later. Right now, we need to focus on finding the Aspens. More often than not, the spectators gather around the finish. Why don't we start over there?" Stefan pointed toward where a line had been scratched in the dirt of the track.

"That's as good a place as any." Charlotte hoisted her skirts and set off for the track, sidestepping the piles of manure that dotted the ground.

Before long, they were immersed in a crowd of people and surrounded by the smell of cigar smoke and roasted peanuts.

Ladies fluttered fans in front of their perspiring faces, while fellows stood on tiptoe and craned their necks to see over each other. Charlotte attempted to squeeze past one such man and was instantly elbowed in the side. "Goodness!" she exclaimed, rubbing at the sore spot. "Has everyone lost their sense of manners?"

"It would certainly appear so, wouldn't it?" Stefan took her hand, cutting a path through the crowd by waving his crutch in front of them. The twins hung close at their backs, chattering with each other. Stefan bent to speak close to her ear. "The older Mr. Aspen is a short man with white hair and a monocle. His wife stands a foot above him, with black hair and a mole on her chin. I imagine they're probably dressed in something that most of the people here couldn't afford, so they should stand out."

Charlotte straightened and scanned the crowd. Unfortunately, it was nearly impossible to distinguish one person from another through the haze of smoke and moving figures.

Stefan narrowed his eyes and attempted to peer over the shoulders of the men standing next to him, though they were a good few inches above his height. "I don't see them," he called over the noise of the crowd. "Perhaps we should check the other side."

"Hang on just a moment," Tom said from behind them. Without preamble, he leaped onto Bastian's back, scrambling up so that his knees balanced on the skinny lad's shoulders and his hands rested on his brother's head.

"Tom!" Bastian gasped as he staggered from side to side and clutched at Tom's knees. "A warning would have been nice!"

"Quiet, Bas. I'm looking around." Tom scanned both sides of the track. "I think I see them, Mr. Roberts! They're right next to the finish line. Mrs. Aspen is wearing a bright blue dress and a large hat. It's hard to miss."

"Excellent work, Tom. Let's get that list to them, and quickly." Still grasping Charlotte's hand, Stefan made his way through the crowd, dodging the flailing arms of spectators. After a moment of struggle, they emerged on the other side of the track, where a blue-clad figure and a stout man in a black suit stood near the finish line.

Charlotte cast one last glance around to assure they weren't being watched before moving closer to the pair. "Mrs. Aspen?"

The woman turned, her enormous, flower-covered hat wobbling dangerously. "Yes?"

Charlotte resisted cringing at the scrutinizing looks of both Mr. and Mrs. Aspen. Her dust-covered ensemble must not be to their liking. Hopefully, they would hear what she had to say without paying too much attention to her worn appearance.

"Can we help you?" the man, presumably Mr. Aspen, asked. Though small in stature, he had an imposing look about him, a testament to his power and wealth. His white mustache quivered as he studied them. Trying to place them, most likely.

"Mr. Aspen? It's me, Stefan Roberts. I believe you know my father, Johann Roberts. You bought horses from us on several occasions." Stefan stepped forward, extending a hand. "And allow me to introduce Miss Charlotte Clarke, my traveling companion."

Mr. Aspen's eyes widened in recognition. "Stefan, my boy! I didn't recognize you dressed as you are. How have you been? Is your father here?" He let out a chuckle. "He always has the best stories. I haven't heard from him in quite some time."

"I'm afraid not. We've come on different business this time." Stefan nodded to Charlotte, his eyes beseeching. "Go on, Charlotte. Tell them. I'll keep watch."

Charlotte stepped forward and took a deep breath. It all came down to this moment. "A few months ago, I became friends with a woman who was very ill. As she neared the end of her life, she asked me to deliver a message to the Aspen residence in Albany, Kentucky. She said her name was Flora, though I suspect her full name was Flora Aspen."

Mrs. Aspen's face turned deathly white. "Flora? You say she is...ill?"

"I'm afraid she has since passed on." Charlotte winced at the woman's stricken expression. "I'm sorry to be the bearer of such bad news. However, Flora wanted me to give you something. Something that was very important to her, and that she thought would be very important to you." She reached into the pocket of her dress, searching for the list. The paper brushed against her hand, and she grasped it, holding it out.

The page fluttered between her fingers, a world of secrets recorded on one small note. Charlotte swallowed, waiting for the woman to take it. Waiting for her journey to end once and for all.

Mrs. Aspen reached out, her brows furrowed.

A gunshot rang through the air, making both of them jump.

"It's all right," Stefan said from beside Charlotte. "That was just the signal to start the next race."

"Oh." Charlotte laughed nervously. "Sorry."

A cry sounded from behind them. Charlotte turned to where the twins stood at the edge of the track. Bastian was staring blankly at his side, where a patch of red spread quickly across his shirt. Before she could blink, he crumpled.

Tom dove to the ground beside him, his pale face shooting up a moment later. "Someone get help! My brother's been shot!"

CHAPTER 30

*H*orror filled Stefan as Bastian dropped to the ground, clutching his side. Charlotte and Tom quickly knelt beside him. Around them, crowd members cried out and glanced around in horror. Several of them started rushing toward the gate behind Stefan, though those on the other side of the track had yet to realize what had happened due to the noise.

Charlotte glanced up at Stefan. "Stefan, what should we do?" Her voice wavered.

Stefan blinked, the shock of the moment wearing off. "Here." He began tugging at his pinned-up trouser leg. Freeing it, he motioned for Tom to draw closer. "Tom, I need you to rip the bottom of my trouser leg off, enough to make a compress for Sebastian's side."

Tom nodded, his freckles dark against his white face. With shaking hands, he set about tearing the bottom half of the pant leg off. He held the torn piece of fabric aloft a few seconds later. "What now?"

"Press it firmly into your brother's side and don't let go." Stefan whirled around, finding a very concerned Mr. and Mrs.

Aspen standing behind him. "I need you two to find the sheriff and the doctor. Quickly!"

His sharp command seemed to snap the couple into action, and they hurried away. Stefan scanned the spectators across the track, most of whom had heard the frantic shouts and turned to exit through the gate on their side of the field. The horses thundered around the track, their hoofbeats matching the pace of Stefan's heart as he assessed the faces in the crowd, searching for the one he knew must be there. "Where are you, you coward?" he whispered.

Another gunshot rang out, and a patch of dirt flew up from a spot near Stefan's feet as the bullet landed next to him. He jolted in surprise and searched in vain for the source of the shot. His eyes landed on a tall figure standing stock still on the opposite side of the track, a stark contrast to the fleeing crowd. A figure with a pistol clutched in one hand. The man slid his gun into his jacket before spinning and plunging into the sea of people.

Stefan gritted his teeth and charged around the track, elbowing his way into the group. Charlotte's fearful cry sounded behind him, but he continued forward. He was finished with running and hiding. He was finished being afraid of every noise. Hawk wasn't going to leave the track unless it was in cuffs.

Luckily, a cluster of frantic women blocked the shooter's exit and forced him to dodge and duck around them, giving Stefan time to catch up. He looped in front of the man and drew his gun, forcing Hawk to halt. "I thought you were cowardly before, but shooting a child has to be the lowest thing of all." Stefan glared into the villain's cold blue eyes as he approached. How could anyone have so little care for another's life?

Hawk's gaze flickered to the exit behind Stefan. "I did what I had to in order to survive. The authorities would never let me go free if they discovered my name on that list. Had you simply given me the locket and gone on your way, none of this would have been necessary." As Hawk edged ever so slightly toward the gate, a flash of light drew Stefan's attention to the man's waistcoat pocket, where a chain glinted in the sunlight. The locket. "Judging by the conversation you were having with the Aspens, you didn't learn your lesson. If only you had brought the horses to Kentucky and left dear Miss Clarke alone."

"I'm no fool, Hawk." Stefan shifted to block the man's escape, keeping the gun trained on the thief. "And I wouldn't leave Charlotte to the likes of you. Now stay where you are."

Hawk shrugged, a smile tugging at his mouth despite the desperation clear on his face. "Come on, Roberts. We both know you won't shoot me."

"What makes you so sure of that? You just put a bullet in my boy. You kidnapped a child and threatened to kill him if I didn't comply with your demands. You've admitted to being a traitor to your own country, a crime for which you could hang. You're scum of the lowest sort, and the only mercy I'll extend to you is a prayer that God saves your soul." Stefan took a step forward. "The world will know of your treason one way or another. You can accept your defeat like a man or run like a coward, but you aren't leaving this track free."

Hawk sneered, though Stefan didn't miss the hint of unease in his eyes. "Oh, Roberts. I would never run from a fight."

Before he could blink, the man lunged, kicking Stefan's supporting leg. He struggled to adjust his crutch and his grip on the revolver in time. Just when he regained his footing, Hawk's fist flew at his face, and Stefan narrowly leaned sideways in time to avoid being hit upside the head.

"What's wrong, Roberts? Can't fight, can you? I guess it's different when you're not on the back of a horse." Hawk taunted, swinging his fist again.

Stefan hopped back as people from outside the fence

released shouts and screams. Why wasn't anyone helping? If they were too scared to step in, perhaps he could use their attention to his advantage. "You're becoming quite the attraction, Hawk," he said, keeping the gun trained on the man. "I wonder what they would say if they knew the truth?"

Hawk's eyes flicked to the crowd. "We've been over this, Roberts. Everyone in Kentucky respects me. They know who I am. You, on the other hand, are a no-name country boy. Who would believe you?"

"You're wrong, Hawk. I spent half my life here. If I had to wager a guess, I would say it's you who's the outsider." Stefan raised his voice. "Ladies and gentleman, if I could have your attention—"

"You won't say a word, or my men will shoot that woman of yours."

Stefan froze. "You're lying."

Hawk straightened, the mask of cool arrogance falling back onto his face. "When have I ever lied? You'll let me leave this place, or I'll give the order."

Stefan hesitated. *Lord, help me. What should I do?*

A shout rang out from the opposite side of the track, near the second gate. Stefan struggled to see around Hawk, who whirled around himself seeking out the source of the noise. Another fight seemed to be breaking out at the back entrance to the track. Four men were struggling, one with a pistol raised high in the air.

Another commotion broke out behind Stefan, where a man shoved his way through the crowd, a gun lifted toward Stefan's back—until a horse and rider parted the sea of people and blocked his path. John!

He gave Stefan a nod. The message was clear. His distraction wouldn't last long.

Turning back to Hawk, Stefan adopted what he hoped was

a confident expression. "It seems your men won't be able to help you, Hawk."

Hawk faltered before tipping his chin up. "No matter." He whipped the pistol from his jacket and pointed it at Stefan.

The world slowed. As the hammer clicked, Stefan drew his own revolver and fired. The bullet landed true, and the gun flew from Hawk's hand. Stefan lowered his smoking weapon.

A shout stopped Hawk from diving for his pistol.

"Roberts!" Burnsby appeared beside them. "What's going on here?"

"This man, Cliff Hawk, just shot one of my boys." Stefan gestured at his nemesis. "He's been chasing us from the time we left Chicago to the minute we reached this track. He's a traitor to the state, and he deserves to stand before a judge."

Burnsby faced Hawk, who straightened with a deceptively sheepish look on his face. "Is this true?"

Hawk shook his head, his eyes glinting. "Not at all. Roberts has spread misinformation about my good character in an attempt to ruin my family name. It is *he* who should be in jail."

Burnsby frowned, glancing back at Stefan. "Roberts has never been anything but honest, sometimes to a fault. I have a hard time believing he would say something accusatory unless it was truthful. That being said, I can't rightly believe either of you without some proper evidence. Do either of you have a way to prove your accusations?"

"Look at the other side of the track, and you'll find my evidence lying on the ground with a compress on his side." Stefan pointed toward the spot where Bastian had fallen.

"You can't prove I was the one to shoot him," Hawk retorted. "There were numerous men here with weapons."

Stefan snatched a paper from his waistcoat. "I have evidence that can put your doubts to rest, Burnsby. This is a ransom letter I was sent after one of my children was kidnapped." Thank goodness he had kept it. "Tom can attest to the fact that Hawk took him. He's a kidnapper and a blackmailer, if nothing else."

Burnsby took the letter and studied it with widening eyes. "Well, I'll be. It is signed with his name. You said your boy can attest to the fact that it was this man who kidnapped him?"

"Absolutely."

Burnsby turned back to Hawk. "Sir, you're going to have to come with me. I would recommend walking along nice and easy." He moved forward with hands outstretched, ready to rest an arm on Hawk's shoulder.

"I'm not going to jail." Hawk's fist snaked out, hooking Burnsby in the jaw with enough force to send him to the ground. Before Stefan could react, Hawk swerved around his friend's prone figure and headed for the gate.

"Stop that man!" Stefan lunged after Hawk.

To Stefan's relief, a few men moved to block the gate, their arms outstretched to catch Hawk. The thief was forced to skid to a stop and spun to face Stefan, his expression animalistic. He was truly desperate now, and there was no telling what he would do to break free.

Before Hawk could make a move, however, a man tackled him from behind and pinned him to the ground. They scuffled for a moment before the black-coated stranger punched Hawk in the head, causing him to fall limp. By the time Stefan reached them, the fellow had placed silver handcuffs around Hawk's wrists.

Mrs. Aspen emerged from the crowd and drew to a stop beside them, her face fraught with worry.

"I owe you thanks, sir." Stefan gasped, trying to draw air into his constricting lungs. "That man is a criminal."

"So I was told." The newcomer sat back on his knees, giving Stefan a view of the silver star on his chest. "Sheriff Mullins at your service. This man shot a child?"

"He did. Hawk was also party to kidnapping, blackmail, and

treason. I have evidence that can prove each of my accusations." Stefan relaxed by a fraction.

"That will be proved inside a courtroom, given that you are able to produce all the evidence you say you have." The sheriff straightened, gazing down at the unconscious man. "In the meantime, I can handle things. Thank you for your help, Mr...?"

"Roberts. Stefan Roberts. I'll be staying at my father's stables."

The sheriff tipped his hat. "Well, Mr. Roberts, you are free to get back to your family. I'll stop by your place soon to collect your statement. I'm sure you want to check on your boy."

"I do. Thank you, sir."

Stefan cast one last glance at the man who had caused him so much strife over the past weeks. *It's over.* The realization hit him like a shockwave, causing him to sag in relief. He released a shuddering breath that contained all the worry and fear that had plagued him. *It's really over.* Never again would Hawk hurt someone he cared about.

"One more thing, Sheriff." He bent and grabbed the chain peeking from Hawk's waistcoat pocket. With a tug, the locket rested in his palm. Stefan closed his fist around it, the cool metal a balm for his heated skin. "This belongs to someone else."

The sheriff lifted his shoulder in a shrug. "Very well. I don't think he'll be needing it anymore."

Stefan hurried around the track, not stopping until he reached the place where Tom and Bastian sat on the ground. A white-coated doctor knelt beside them, directing a crew of men with a stretcher.

Charlotte stood to the side with her arms wrapped around her middle. As Stefan came within a few feet of them, her face brightened with relief. She rushed forward and wrapped her arms around him. "You're all right. Thank the Lord, you're all right. I was so afraid when I saw you two fighting."

Stefan smiled and dropped his crutch so he could embrace her with both arms. "I'm all right. Hawk was arrested. He won't hurt us again."

Charlotte released a shuddering breath and tipped her head back to look at him. "I don't care about Hawk. I was so worried about you, Stefan. I thought he would kill you."

"I'm safe. *We're* safe." Stefan glanced over at the twins. "How is he?"

"The doctor says the bullet grazed him. He'll have an impressive scar, but he'll live."

Stefan exhaled, relief flooding through every vein. *He'll live.* He hadn't failed Bastian, after all. "I have something to return to you." He backed away enough to open his palm and reveal the locket.

Charlotte gasped, clutching the locket to her chest. "Oh, Stefan. Thank you." She hugged him again, setting her head against his chest.

Stefan wrapped his arms back around her. "We did it, Charlotte. Brought Hawk to justice, and now you can complete Flora's mission."

She raised a shining face to him. "And then we have the freedom to choose our future."

Their future...

Did he dare hope she pictured him in hers?

CHAPTER 31

Green fields that stretched as far as the eye could see surrounded the Roberts estate, rolling and dipping like gentle waves in a valley between towering hills. Horses dotted the meadows and raised their elegant heads to gaze curiously at the wagon as it drew to a halt in front of the house at the center of the clearing. To the left and right were what Charlotte assumed to be the stables, long buildings with sturdy posts and large doors.

A low moan came from the back of the wagon, reminding Charlotte of the purpose for their hurried ride here. "We should get Bastian inside." She lowered herself to the ground and rushed to the back of the wagon.

The doctor looked up where he sat beside the boy. "Do you have a first-floor room we could place him in?"

"Yes. The second room on the right is an empty bedroom." Stefan came to stand beside Charlotte. "Do you need help with the stretcher?"

The doctor gestured to Tom, who clambered down from the wagon and stopped beside them with tented brows. "I have young Tom here, and he's promised to help me."

"All right. The staff will see you settled." Stefan motioned for Charlotte to join him on the drive.

She drew closer to him before glancing back at the twins and the doctor. "Don't they need our help?"

Stefan shook his head, exhaustion plain on his face. "The doctor patches up our jockeys when needed. I trust his judgment. Besides, we have another matter to deal with."

He pointed toward the driveway, where a carriage pulled by two black horses approached at a rapid rate. The driver tugged on the reins and brought the carriage to a halt a few feet from where they stood. A second later, the door flew open, and Mr. and Mrs. Aspen descended from the vehicle before advancing toward them with worried expressions. The feathers on the lady's hat fluttered with every step. "Dear heavens. Is that little boy all right? Everything happened so fast, we never finished speaking. And I must know about Flora."

"Genevieve, do calm down." Mr. Aspen patted her arm, though his voice contained a hint of fear. He glanced at Charlotte, his brown eyes shadowed beneath his thick white brows. "You did mention our daughter, did you not?"

"I did. I'd be more than happy to explain inside." Charlotte turned to Stefan. "Would you lead the way?"

Stefan swept his arm forward, a lock of hair falling over his forehead. "Certainly."

The door swung open as they approached, held by a stocky man with blue eyes and a dark beard. "Mr. Roberts, sir. It's good to see you back," the man said, reaching a hand out to shake Stefan's. "I directed the doctor and the boys to the closest bedroom. What happened?"

Stefan glanced down the hallway to the right, where the faint echoes of talking could be heard. "Very good, Howard. I'll explain everything once I'm finished here."

Howard's gaze roamed over Charlotte and the Aspens. She could only imagine what he was thinking. They made for a quite a sight, after all—two boys, a travel-worn young woman, and a pair of socialites. "Very well. Would you like to take your company in the parlor?"

"Yes, that will do nicely." Stefan touched her elbow gently, a half smile on his face. "This way, Charlotte." He led her and the Aspens into a parlor where a large piano sat against the back wall. Though the keys were dusty, they were well-worn. Who had played the instrument? Perhaps the brother Stefan had spoken of. The rest of the room held an assortment of furniture, including a couch and a cluster of worn chairs.

Stefan directed Charlotte to one of the chairs and showed the Aspens to the couch before sinking into the seat beside her.

Charlotte faced the Aspens, who regarded her with a mixture of confusion and hope. "I suppose you'd like to know why we came all this way to find you." She reached into her dress pocket and withdrew the locket. Holding it out on her palm, she waited for Mrs. Aspen to take it. "This belonged to your daughter. She wanted me to give it to you."

For a moment, Mrs. Aspen simply stared at the locket with wide eyes. Then, she sagged against the back of the couch. "So it's true. My poor, poor Flora." She lifted a trembling hand to her head, rubbing at it as though the gesture could rid her of her sadness. "I never got to say goodbye."

Mr. Aspen took his wife's hand and drew her closer. "Oh, Genevieve."

Charlotte looked to Stefan for help. He gestured toward the couple, his eyes encouraging as he spoke softly. "Tell them what you remember of their daughter. It will bring them comfort."

Still, Charlotte struggled to find words. How did one comfort grieving parents? What would she have wanted to know if someone had been with her mother and sister before they died?

"I didn't know Flora very long," she finally began. "Not nearly as long as I would have liked, anyway. For the time that I did know her, however, she was as kind and lovely as any woman could ever hope to be. She was incredibly cheerful, despite being in a situation most people would be depressed about. She...she loved the sky and the clouds and always chose a bed near a window." Charlotte paused, a wave of melancholy washing over her as she recalled the hospital and the dreary memories that came along with it. "She was a bright spot in a dark place. Towards the end, I painted a sky and hung it above her head. I can only hope that it brought her some measure of peace."

"She always did love being outside," Mrs. Aspen whispered, a large tear running down her face. "I used to scold her fiercely for spending so much time in the sun without a hat. I told her she would get horribly burnt. She never listened, of course. She was quiet but oh so stubborn."

"I can see that." Charlotte allowed herself a smile. "During her last few weeks, she asked me to bring you this locket. She told me she had made a terrible error and wanted to resolve it before she passed away. She wanted to make amends with you, Mrs. Aspen."

Mrs. Aspen sniffled and procured a handkerchief from her sleeve to dab at her eyes. "There wasn't anything to forgive. I wasn't mad at her. I might have been terse in the beginning, but I could never stay angry at Flora. She was too sweet for that."

"That she was. I don't know what transpired between the two of you, but Flora seemed genuinely remorseful. There's a note in here that should explain most of it." Charlotte swallowed. "However, there was another reason she wanted me to bring you the locket. You see, Flora was carrying something with her that she thought would be very important to you, Mr. Aspen." She waited until Mr. Aspen looked at her to continue. "Stefan and I have come to believe that your daughter was working on something far greater than she ever told you or me.

I'll allow you to look at it for yourself." She held the locket aloft, waiting for one of the Aspens to take it.

After a moment of hesitation, Mrs. Aspen accepted the necklace with trembling fingers and carefully clicked the lid open, causing the note to fall into her lap. "I gave her this locket on her sixteenth birthday," she murmured, tracing the portrait within. "We were going to send her to boarding school, and I thought she might like something to remind her of home. I had put a bit of rose petals on the inside, to remind her of the gardens she so loved." She lifted the tiny piece of paper from her lap and unfolded it, scanning the pencil-thin words.

Mr. Aspen picked up the locket and examined the interior. "What was it Flora wanted me to have?" His voice sounded far more vulnerable than Charlotte would have expected from such a callous man.

"It should be behind the portrait."

Mr. Aspen carefully extracted the piece of parchment from behind the portrait and unfolded it, his brows furrowing as he studied the names written upon it. "I don't understand. Is this...?"

"A list of Confederate spies and guerillas." The voice came from the doorway, causing everyone to jump. A man entered the study and removed his hat, revealing a familiar set of brown eyes. *John.* Charlotte gasped. He must have followed them from the track.

Stefan leapt to his feet and moved in front of Charlotte, though he kept his gun tucked away. "What are you doing here?"

John continued on as though not in the least unnerved by their reactions. "They're tricky creatures, guerillas. Some were caught during the war, but many escaped and have been continuing illegal activities since then. They would revive the Civil war for their own personal gain given the choice. One person on that list you'll find of interest is Cliff Hawk, son of the lead-mining mogul Lars Hawk. You may have had dealings with him in the past."

"You didn't answer my question. Who are you, really?" Stefan took a step forward, his shoulders drawn back and his voice firm. "You worked for Hawk, and yet you helped me back at the track. Why? And what are you doing here now?"

John straightened, placing his hat back atop his head. "I did try to tell you that I was on your side, but you didn't believe me." He shook his head. "No matter. I understand your hesitance, and now that Hawk has been captured, I can explain." He sketched a half bow. "My name is John McAllen, special agent of the United States military. I was part of a network during the war that collected and distributed information to Union officials."

Charlotte sucked in a quiet breath. *A spy.* Had he known Flora?

"I know of you through common acquaintances." Mr. Aspen raised a brow. "What business did you have with my daughter?"

"Three months ago, I was given the task of uprooting a network of former Confederate spies causing trouble in Kentucky and the surrounding states, the head of which was suspected to be Cliff Hawk. In order to do this, I needed to go undercover and gain Hawk's trust. Doing so allowed me to collect the evidence I needed to incriminate him. I almost had enough, though Hawk was a sly one." John glanced at Charlotte over Stefan's shoulder. "And then I learned of the list, one that had been made by a fellow agent named Miss Aspen and went missing soon after her death. Hawk was desperate to get that missing list, and I suspected it was the final piece of evidence I needed. With it, I could bring down not only Hawk, but his entire ring. I decided to stay undercover in the hopes of getting to it before him. Of course, maintaining his trust also meant doing things such as assisting in the kidnapping of your boy, which I sincerely apologize for. I never would have allowed Hawk to harm him. He was deeply suspicious of me and would have killed me if he discovered who I was."

Stefan's posture relaxed slightly. "When did you realize we had the list?"

John chuckled. "After Hawk ambushed you the first time. He was livid you managed to escape and wouldn't stop ranting about it."

Stefan opened his hands. "Why didn't you just take it from us?"

John adjusted the collar of his jacket. "I made inquiries about you and Miss Clarke soon after you escaped Hawk, which is when I discovered your connection to Miss Aspen, as well as your intentions with the list. I then confronted you in the hopes that you would relinquish it, though you didn't trust me."

Stefan grunted. "Understandably."

"Yes." John flashed a brief smile. "After I failed to get the locket from Hawk in the days following the ball, I decided it would be best to keep you and your copies of the list safe from afar. The most important thing was getting it into the hands of a government official." He gestured toward Mr. Aspen. "Which I knew Mr. Aspen was capable of doing. I simply had to follow along and make sure you remained on the right path until then. What I didn't anticipate was for Hawk to attack you. However, his getting himself arrested proved convenient for me."

Charlotte exchanged an amazed glance with Stefan before turning back to John. "All along, we were trying to evade you, and you were trying to help us."

He gave her a patient smile. "And now you understand why I needed the list."

Mr. Aspen shook his head, looking at the list with an expression akin to wonder. "My own Flora, working for the government. I don't believe it."

Mrs. Aspen's eyes shone with unshed tears. "She always wanted to have some part in the war effort. I told her that her position was at boarding school, getting a proper education. It was a great matter of contention between us. One night, it got so bad that she ran away. I thought she would come home after a few days, but she never did. I never saw her again." She sniffed, wiping at her eyes with a handkerchief procured from her reticule. "I never knew what happened to her. I suspected the worst. We looked high and low, but we never would have guessed that she was working for the government." She smoothed the letter. "My Flora was a hero."

"She truly was. If I'm not mistaken, that letter could put multiple criminals in prison." Charlotte cast a glance at John. At his nod of approval, she continued. "Flora's work may have saved this country from another war. For that, you should be extremely proud."

Mrs. Aspen continued to dab at her face, tears running freely down her cheeks. "Thank you. Thank you so, so much. I know my Flora would be everlastingly grateful to know how much you cared about her." She leaned forward, crumpling the handkerchief in her hand. "Do you know the hospital where she passed on? Perhaps we could arrange for a proper funeral."

"Not a hospital, but a church." A smile flitted across Charlotte's face. "She had the very best care there. I'll write down the name for you."

"And I'll see to it that the list is delivered into the proper hands," John interjected, stepping forward. "I assure you, it will be safe with me."

Charlotte looked between Mr. Aspen and the agent, noting the way Mr. Aspen glanced at the list with apprehension. "What you do with the list is your choice, Mr. Aspen. I've dealt with enough strife because of it."

After a moment of hesitation, Mr. Aspen passed the list to John. "I have heard the name John McAllen in my social circle on more than one occasion. If my friends think highly of you, I trust you to complete my Flora's mission." He turned to look at Charlotte. "It's what she would have wanted."

John took the list and tucked it into the inside pocket of his jacket. "Thank you, sir. You did the right thing. If I was a more powerful man, I would give you all medals for the service you've done. Unfortunately, I'm not. All I can give you is my gratitude and a promise to see the rest of the mission through." He tipped his hat. "Good day, ladies and gentleman." With that, the man strode from the room, leaving them in silence.

After a moment, Mr. Aspen sat back. "I hope I made the right decision." He released a long sigh. "I want Flora to rest easy. I want her to be proud of us."

Charlotte inclined her head. "She loved both of you more than you could ever imagine. Even when she knew there was no chance of her going to Kentucky again, she never stopped wishing she could reconcile." She smiled. "And now she has. Flora is finally home." And her promise was, at long last, fulfilled.

CHAPTER 32

As Charlotte spoke with the Aspens, a gentle expression on her face, Stefan caught her eye and gave her a nod.

"Go," she mouthed, waving a hand toward the door.

Stefan made his way back through the foyer and to the bedroom where the boys had been taken. He smiled at the sight of them fast asleep on the bed next to each other. Bastian's face was peaky, but he at least looked comfortable in his rest. A note from the doctor on the nightstand assured Stefan that the man had borrowed a horse to ride back into town to fetch more medication, with the promise to return shortly. After casting one last look at the twins, Stefan left them to their rest.

Outside, the wagon sat in the middle of the drive. A few stable hands had untied the thoroughbreds from the back and were leading them into the stables, but Orion remained at the front of the vehicle. Stefan walked closer and stroked the Percheron's nose. "Thank you for being patient, my friend. It has been a long time since we were last here, hasn't it? I suppose you'd like to visit your old stall and get some fresh oats."

Orion bobbed his head and released a loud whinny, as though agreeing with Stefan's statement.

Stefan handed the nearest employee, Howard, Orion's reins. "Thank you for taking care of the horses." He released a sigh. "It's been quite a day." Far more than a day, in fact. Had it really only been a few weeks since he had set out from home? It felt like an entire lifetime had passed.

Howard inclined his head, the lines around his eyes becoming more pronounced with his smile. "We missed you around here, young Roberts. It's good to have you back." He paused, working his jaw. "I...don't want to force you, but if you're wanting to visit your family, their spot under the oak tree looks beautiful this time of year. I could give you a ride."

Stefan exhaled. "I can walk. Thank you, Howard. I think I will go and see them."

With a nod of gratitude, he left the hand with the horse and made his way across the yard, heading for the oak tree behind the house. There he had spent many summers, reading books or napping in the warm sun. Now, however, the trunk of the tree sheltered two marble headstones, each as polished as they had been on the day Stefan left them. Somebody must have kept them clean. Howard, most likely. He had been a member of the stables for as long as Stefan could remember.

He approached the stones hesitantly, unsure of what to do or say. What *was* one to say after so many years of absence? At length, he lowered himself slowly to the ground, putting him face to face with the names carved in the marble. He reached out and traced both of them. "I'm sorry," he murmured, allowing his hand to fall to his side. "I'm sorry I didn't visit sooner." He released a sigh, studying his ragged trouser leg. "I'm no better than Vater, am I? I thought I was staying away because I was helping him. That I was doing the right thing. To tell the truth, though, I was afraid. But there's nothing here I need to fear. Not anymore."

Stefan glanced back at the house. "I thought the bad memories would ruin this place. But home can't all be good memories, can it? It's a mix of the happy and the hurt, the joy and the sadness." He turned back to the graves. "But I'm here now. I brought some friends with me, as well. I wish you could both have met them. I know you would have loved them as much as I do."

He removed his hat and swiped a hand through his hair, a smile twitching at his lips. "Charlotte is the most beautiful woman I've ever met, Mutter. She's kind and understanding and..." He chuckled. "I can't fit her into words. I just know you would have loved her." He faced Franz's headstone. "And you would have loved the twins, Franz. They remind me of you. There never would have been a quiet moment in the house again. But that won't happen, will it?"

Wind blew through the leaves of the oak tree, making the dappled patterns of light on the ground flicker and change. The horses nickered from across the fields. Two thoroughbreds, perhaps Lake and Persnickety, raced each other, tossing their heads in pure excitement.

"Remus was right," Stefan whispered as he surveyed the property. "There is good in my life." He glanced back at the graves. "I know you and Franz are happier now than you ever were here on earth. I'll meet you both again when the time is right. But, for now, I'm going to enjoy the gift I was given. I'm going to live, Mutter."

And never before had he been quite so excited about it.

～

Charlotte waved from the front porch as the Aspen carriage pulled away. "Goodbye, Mrs. Aspen! Do come and visit again soon!"

Her friend's mother fluttered her handkerchief in the air, a smile gracing her lips despite the tears she'd so recently shed. "We will. Farewell, now."

With that, the carriage trundled away, leaving Charlotte alone. She swiveled, gazing out over the lawn in search of Stefan. It didn't take her long to spot him, as he was approaching from a few feet away.

"How did it go?" he asked, stepping onto the porch. "Is everything all right?"

"Yes. They took the locket and the letter with them. Mr. Aspen said he'll listen for news of Hawk and the other marauders over the next few weeks. Once the court sees the evidence that John has collected and hears what we have to say, I believe the world won't see Cliff Hawk again for a long, long time."

"Right." Stefan hummed, resting his back against the house. "We did it, Charlotte. We really did it."

Charlotte rubbed at her eyes. Goodness, but she was tired. She had several weeks' worth of sleep to make up for, after all. "We did. I can't believe it's all over." She moved closer to Stefan and nudged his side with her elbow. "And now we can finally be normal people. We can live out our lives and raise families until we're old and boring."

Stefan laughed, the sound rumbling deep inside his chest, and returned the nudge. "I don't think we'll ever be boring, Charlotte. Not after this."

Charlotte giggled. "True. Shall we go and check on Bastian?"

Stefan pushed off of the wall, his expression changing to something more sober. "Yes. Though they were sleeping when I looked in on them earlier, so don't make too much noise."

As they entered the house, Tom appeared from the side room, his hair disheveled from sleep. "Mr. Roberts, Miss Charlotte, come quick! Bas woke up!" he exclaimed, his expression filled with excitement.

Charlotte hurried to the guest bedroom, where she was met with the sight of Bastian sitting up in bed, his face pale but alert. "Bastian!" She darted to the side of the bed and embraced the boy in a tight hug. "You scared the living daylights out of us." She smoothed the red curls back from his forehead. "You aren't allowed to do that ever again, you hear?"

Bastian smiled sheepishly, his expression still tight with pain. "Sorry, Miss Charlotte." He glanced down at his side, his brows tenting nervously. "The doctor said I'll have a scar on my side. Do you think it'll be bad?"

Stefan lowered himself so that he was sitting on the edge of the bed. "Don't worry, Bas. It can't get much worse than mine." He gestured to his leg with a good-natured laugh. "What you *will* have is quite the story to tell."

Bastian shifted, wincing. "Tom told me what you did, Mr. Roberts. It was brave of you to go after Hawk and confront him. He told me the sheriff arrested Hawk. Is it true he's gone for good?"

"It's true." Stefan ruffled Bastian's hair. "Hawk and the other men with him are going to prison, once they're captured. I can't imagine the elder Hawk will be very happy when he learns what his son's done."

"No, I don't imagine so." Bastian looked down at his hands, his shoulders drooping.

Charlotte frowned. "Why so melancholy, Bastian? Would you like something cool for your side? I'd be more than happy to wet a rag for you."

Bastian's jaw twitched, and he shook his head. "No, it isn't that. It's simply that...we're here. Our journey is over. You don't...you don't need us anymore."

"Why, Bastian. Why would you ever think such a thing?" Charlotte leaned forward and rested a hand on his shoulder. "Of course, we need you. You and Tom have brought so much light and life into our lives. We wouldn't have made it to

Kentucky if it wasn't for you two. We would never send you away."

Bastian glanced at Tom, who stood silently at the side of the bed. "But Tom said he wanted to continue traveling," he whispered.

Charlotte looked to Tom, waiting for his response. For a moment, the room remained silent. Then, with a shake of his head, the lanky boy released a long breath and crossed his arms. "I guess I did want to travel around once upon a time. I thought I would be happier if I didn't have anything tying me down. But, over the past few weeks, my opinion has begun to change. Besides, someone reminded me that my opinion isn't the only one that matters." He fixed his brother with a smile. "I'm more than willing to stay. Assuming we're welcome, of course."

Stefan held out a hand, which Tom shook. "You're always welcome here, Tom. We could use a fine young man like you in the stables." He coughed lightly. "Say, I have a piano that hasn't been touched in years. I don't suppose you'd like to learn how to play it, would you?"

Tom grinned. "Mr. Roberts, I do believe you read my mind."

Charlotte caught Stefan's gaze from over the boy's head, noting the serious look in his eyes. She could only imagine what he was thinking, for her own thoughts were racing. The boys' futures were secured, thank goodness. They would never have to worry about food or shelter again. Stefan would make certain of that.

But what about her?

❧

The sun had begun to sink by the time they made their way out for dinner that night, the yellow light casting brilliant colors over the yard and pastures. The cook offered a light meal al fresco for Stefan, Charlotte, and Tom. Though they assured Bas that he could take his supper on a tray, he insisted on accompanying them and made his way slowly outside with his brother's assistance. Charlotte made sure to stay close to the house and arrange the picnic blanket in a way that would give them an excellent view of the gold-dappled fields. Was it any wonder Stefan's father had chosen to build here when the land was wrapped in such beauty?

Soon as he finished his meal of sandwiches, fruit, cheese, and pickles, Tom hopped up. "I'm going to try and climb one of those trees. If you hear a crash, you'll know it didn't go well."

Charlotte winced and set her cheese down on the picnic blanket. "All right. Be careful, Tom. I'm not going to climb up after you if you find yourself trapped."

Stefan chuckled from close behind Charlotte, making her jump. "Neither will I, I'm afraid."

"Bah. I won't need help," Tom said, waving off their concerns. "Watch me, Bas. I wager I can make it to the top of that maple tree before you can count to sixty seconds."

Bas laughed from where he sat on the picnic blanket, pale and shaky. Despite his weak appearance, he had a smile upon his face. "You're bluffing. You won't make it past the first branch," he called to Tom as the boy raced to the nearest tree.

Charlotte smiled. "I think Bastian will be all right," she whispered to Stefan. "He already seems far better than he did two hours ago."

"He's a strong lad. This won't keep him down for long." Stefan watched the boys shout to one another, an easy smile on his face. After a second, he stood and looked down at her. "Will you take a walk with me, Charlotte? We have some time left before sundown, and I'd like to enjoy the day."

"Of course." Charlotte accepted his offered hand and lifted herself upright. Her heart thudded noisily in her chest, so loud that she wondered if Stefan could hear it. "I'd love to walk with you, Stefan."

They set off at a slow pace through the wildflower-dotted grass, with no real destination or stopping point in mind. Charlotte inhaled a deep breath as they ambled along, enjoying the feel of Stefan's arm beneath her hand. What was she to do now that the locket was delivered? Was there really a chance that she might never again see Stefan or the twins?

"It feels as though summer is growing closer by the day, doesn't it?" Stefan tipped his head upward. "The sun no longer hides behind the clouds, and the birds are beginning to nest."

"Certainly. Though I must admit, I'll miss spring when it's gone." *Because now it reminds me of you.* Charlotte gazed down at the folds of her dress, hoping Stefan wouldn't see the defeat in her expression.

A hand appeared in her vision as Stefan plucked a few wildflowers from the grass. "A lady should never be without flowers," he murmured, handing her the makeshift bouquet.

Charlotte accepted the flowers with a smile and gave them a sniff before holding them close to her chest. "Thank you, Stefan. They're lovely."

They fell into an awkward silence, both seemingly unsure of what to say. What *was* there to say, when the threat of parting hung over them?

Stefan cleared his throat. "Charlotte? I've been thinking."

"Thinking about what, Stefan?"

"Thinking about what you said before the dance. You asked me if I would stay by your side even after the ball was finished."

Charlotte swallowed as her heart began to pick up in speed once again. "I did say that, didn't I?"

"You also mentioned that society matrons would try to marry us on the spot once they caught sight of us." Stefan coughed. "And...well...I couldn't help but wonder if they wouldn't be right."

Charlotte stopped in the middle of the field and tilted her head, squinting up through the sunlight at Stefan's face. A patchy blush had begun to spread across his face. Could it be? "Stefan Roberts, did you just suggest that we marry?"

Stefan looked at the ground, the red in his cheeks deepening. "That wasn't how I imagined myself saying it, but...yes?"

"You want to marry me because of what the society matrons might think?"

"No!" Stefan grimaced. "I'm no good at this. I've never..."

"Never proposed to anyone?" Charlotte laughed, letting her hands drop to her sides. "I suppose that's a good thing."

"Confounded emotions. I could never figure out how to put them into words," Stefan mumbled. "My brother always said he would marry before me because I wouldn't be able to get the words out of my mouth. I guess he wasn't entirely wrong."

Charlotte grinned, joy coursing through her like blinding light. Stefan wanted to marry her! "Feelings can be tricky, but I think that's the thing that makes them wonderful. There's nothing as amazingly complex or beautiful as human emotion, even in its messiest form."

"If only they weren't so hard to express." Stefan chuckled. He turned to Charlotte, and she looked into his eyes, eyes that matched the clear sky above. "The truth is, you amaze me. After everything you went through and all the horrible things you saw, you could have easily chosen to lock yourself away from the world. And yet, instead of hiding, you decided to journey all the way to Kentucky for your friend. I...I thought you were beautiful from the start, with your compassion and your bravery and even your old dresses with pockets. But..." He swallowed, a smile spreading across his face. "You're even more beautiful now. There's a light in you that wasn't there before, Charlotte. It's as if you took what was already good within you and turned it into something even more beautiful."

"God did that. Not me." Charlotte glanced at the waving

grasses at her feet, a flush spreading across her cheeks. "To be honest, I thought my life was ending. But traveling with you and the twins gave me hope that I might have a good future. And now I know I don't have to worry about that future." She looked up with a smile. "Thank you for not giving up on me, Stefan. I worried you might turn away when you saw how hard-headed I had become, but you didn't."

Stefan shook his head. "You say that as if I'm perfect. I'm not, Charlotte. You helped me as much as I helped you. I was broken, frightened of what the world thought of me, and then you came along and showed me that I didn't have to be a shell of a man. You encouraged me to stand tall and proud. Just like you, I thought my life was hopeless. In truth, there were blessings all around me. I've simply refused to look at them. But I'm looking at them now."

He took a step closer, making Charlotte's heart jolt in her chest.

"I can't fathom the idea of living my life without you." Stefan reached into the pocket of his trousers and withdrew a small box. Cracking it open, he held it toward her, his gaze earnest. "Charlotte Clarke, I love you. I can't get down on one knee, and I can't dance with you like the other gentlemen can. But I promise to love you until the day I die. So, Charlotte, what do you say? Will you marry me, *mein Herz*?"

Cradled within the box in Stefan's hand was a thin golden band, empty of gems or stones. Though the ring was simple in style, it had been engraved with beautiful flowers, the sort that only appeared in spring. *Spring.* The season of new beginnings, and Charlotte's favorite time of the year.

"I bought it while you were mailing your letter to Miss Fitzgerald," Stefan explained softly. "It reminded me of you."

Charlotte smiled and reached up to cup both sides of Stefan's face. He gazed back at her, his eyes tentative and uncertain as he waited for her response.

"Yes, you wonderful man. I will marry you." Charlotte bobbed her head as tears sprang to her eyes. "I love you, Stefan Roberts." She buried her face in his chest, unable to prevent the laugh of pure happiness that escaped her.

Stefan released a great sigh as his arms enfolded her, surrounding her with warmth and strength.

"It's about time! Now put the ring on!" The shout rang out from across the clearing, followed by a loud cheer.

Charlotte looked up just in time to see Tom waving wildly from the top of the maple tree. Her gaze moved down to where Bastian watched them from the picnic blanket with a matching grin on his face. She laughed. "Those boys knew precisely what was happening, didn't they?"

"They encouraged me to move forward with it," Stefan admitted, a chuckle rumbling through his chest. "I decided it was time to put them out of their misery."

"Oh, really? Is that the only reason you proposed to me?" Charlotte teased, backing away.

Stefan grinned as he slid the ring onto her finger. "No. This is why." With that, he swooped in and kissed her.

Though she couldn't explain it, the kiss was like starry nights and fresh flowers and everything else she loved. All other thoughts fled, and she found herself wishing it would never end.

All too soon, Stefan backed away with a half smile on his face.

"Oh." Charlotte cleared her throat as some of her wits returned. "Well, I could get used to that."

Stefan laughed. "You had better. I plan to do it often."

As they made their way back toward the picnic blanket with their fingers entwined, Charlotte tilted her head, studying the ring that now flashed on her finger. "What was it that you said to me when you proposed? *Mein* something."

"Mein Herz. It means *my heart*. It was what my father called my mother." Stefan glanced at their interlocking fingers, his eyes sparkling with pure joy. "I thought it only fair that I continue the tradition. It is true, after all. You are my heart."

Charlotte smiled, warmth spreading throughout her chest. "'My heart.' I like the sound of that." For in those two words was a story of a long battle and a hard-won victory. It was a story of loss and healing. But most of all, it was a story of courage. And with the knowledge that the man beside her loved her, courageous she would stay.

EPILOGUE

December 1872

The front door slammed open, making Charlotte jump from where she stood at the stove, a pot of bubbling soup before her. "For goodness' sake, boys. Mind the door. The wind will rip it right off the hinges."

Laughter sounded as the twins appeared in the kitchen threshold, their hair ruffled. "Sorry, Charlotte," Tom apologized with a sheepish grin. "We were having a snowball fight."

Charlotte huffed, trying and failing to keep the grin from her face. "Well, you had better go wash up before dinner. The two of you look as though you went for a swim!" The lanky boys were fairly drenched.

"We do have good news," Bastian chimed in. "The mare finally had her foal. Stefan wants you to come out and see it."

"Well, I do believe I will." Charlotte set her spoon on the counter and moved to the front door, slipping her muck boots on. It wasn't very ladylike to be tromping around in them, but Stefan had assured her he didn't care. She descended from the porch and waded through the snow, not stopping until she reached the stables and slipped inside. She peered down the hallway. "Stefan? Are you in here?"

"Back here!" the voice she so loved called, followed by the sight of a hand waving from the back stall. "Come see the new foal."

Charlotte hurried to the stall door and peered over the edge, a smile splitting her face as she took in the sight before her. "You're going to get your new trousers all dirty, you know."

Stefan grinned from where he sat on the hay-covered ground. "It hardly matters now. Just look at her, Lottie. Isn't she beautiful?"

Charlotte studied the little foal that slept on a bed of hay with her mother standing quietly beside her. Her dark coat was reminiscent of Lake, though she had four white socks and a little star on her head. "That she is. Have you named her?"

"Not yet. I was thinking you could." Stefan lifted himself to his feet, his weight balancing evenly on his new wooden leg. "Do you have any ideas?"

Charlotte hummed, tapping a finger beneath her chin. "How about Spring's Dance? It'll remind us of the most cheerful season in the year."

"Spring's Dance. I like it." Stefan leaned over to kiss Charlotte. "I'll have to let you name the horses from now on. You're a natural."

Charlotte waved him off with a grin, warmth spreading across her cheeks. "Oh, hush. You're flattering me." She glanced down at his leg. "How's your new prosthetic? Bastian did a fine job on it."

Stefan nodded and pulled his pant leg up so the warm oak glinted in the lamplight. "I couldn't have asked for a better early Christmas present. The boy is certainly talented. The carpenter in town is thrilled to have him as an apprentice, just as the new restaurant owner was all too happy to have Tom play music for his opening dance. Those boys are going places." He tilted his head, leaning back on the stall door. "And how are you? Are you cold?"

Charlotte fitted herself into her favorite spot beneath Stefan's arm and exhaled, enjoying the warmth that radiated from his coat. "I was, but not anymore. Have you heard from your father?"

"Priscilla was confident he'll be ready to travel by next year. In the meantime, however, we'll most likely have to go to Sycamore and stay with him." Stefan frowned. "I don't want to endanger him in his fragile state."

"It'll be all right, Stefan. We'll sort things out," Charlotte said reassuringly, looking up into his eyes.

Stefan paused for a moment, clearly in thought. "You know, if we do go back to Sycamore for Christmas, we could make a short journey north. It wouldn't take all that long—a few extra days at most by train." He shrugged. "But only if you want to."

Charlotte stepped away from Stefan. Journey north? Did she want to go back to the place she had fled from all those months ago?

Stefan studied her with a knowing look. "You wouldn't be alone, Charlotte. We would be with you every step of the way."

I won't be alone, will I? Charlotte nodded, calm washing over her. "I know."

Stefan leaned against the stall and drew her closer. "I would never force you to do something that causes you anxiety. I was in your very position not so long ago, as you know. However, coming back here made me realize that the memories I had were just that—memories. History. Echoes of long ago. It didn't make them any less hurtful, but it did give me a measure of peace." He glanced down at her, his eyes full of sincerity. "I think it could do the same for you, if you were willing."

"I never did discover whether or not they were properly buried," she murmured. "It's a shame to think of them not having a grave." Shadowy memories of Carina and her mother flickered in her mind, of their smiling faces and bright laughs. "Let me consider it for a while," Charlotte finally settled on saying.

Stefan placed a gentle kiss on her forehead. "The choice is yours, mein Herz, and yours alone."

Charlotte hummed, a smile softening her lips. "Thank you, Stefan." She pointed toward the door. "I'm going to return to the warmth of the house. It's getting a bit cold out here."

"Go. I'll join you in a moment. I need to make sure these two are settled."

After waving in farewell, Charlotte hugged her arms around herself and trudged back through the snow to the house. She walked through the kitchen without removing her boots, not stopping until she reached the bedroom she shared with Stefan. There she opened the top drawer of her nightstand and collected the crumpled envelope she had placed there months ago. Charlotte viewed the return address at the top, written in ink that had faded over time. *Marinette.*

"What would You have me do, Lord?" She bit her lip, indecision warring in her mind. "Should I return to Peshtigo?"

The answer came to her softly, a gentle word spoken in the back of her mind.

Charlotte glanced at the envelope once more before nodding decisively. "Very well, then. I trust You."

She moved to her writing desk and slid into the seat. After pulling a clean sheet of paper from one of the drawers, she set it in front of her, along with her pen and ink. By the time Stefan returned from the barn, a sealed envelope lay in front of her.

"Have you made a decision?" He came to stand behind her and placed his hands on her shoulders.

Charlotte leaned back to look at him. "Yes."

As she gazed into his eyes, so full of love and happiness, she smiled. Regardless of what happened in Peshtigo, she would be happy. For Charlotte Clarke was no longer alone. And she never would be again.

The End

Did you enjoy this book? We hope so!
**Would you take a quick minute to leave a review where you
purchased the book?**
It doesn't have to be long. Just a sentence or two telling what
you liked about the story!

Love Christian Historical Romance?
Looking for your next favorite book?
Become a Wild Heart Books insider and receive a FREE ebook
and get exclusive updates on new releases before anyone else.
Sign up for our newsletter now.
https://wildheartbooks.org/newsletter

Hello, reader! I hope you enjoyed following along with Charlotte and Stefan on their trek to Kentucky. Their journey took a lot of planning, especially when it came to estimating how far they would travel in one day. After researching how long it would take for their journey using a horse and wagon, I can safely say I'm glad I have a car!

As with the first book, much of Charlotte's story is rooted in the Peshtigo Fire. At the same time the Great Chicago Fire began, residents of a Wisconsin lumber town called Peshtigo found their town being consumed by an inferno. Witnesses described what appeared to be a "wall of fire" descending upon them, accompanied by winds nearly as strong as a hurricane. The terrified citizens had only a few minutes to seek shelter in open fields, root cellars, and the Peshtigo River before the firestorm roared through. Many burned where they stood, while others drowned in the bitterly cold waters of the river. By morning, the fire had died down, leaving behind a charred wasteland. Those who survived the night walked to the nearby town of Marinette, which had been only partially damaged by the flames. Once there, they waited until help arrived from Milwaukee, Green Bay, and the surrounding cities.

An estimated one million acres of land were completely razed over the course of the night, and over 1,200 people lost their lives. This makes the Peshtigo Fire the deadliest wildfire in American history. The origins of the fire are still unknown, though historians suspect it was most likely caused by a combination of dry conditions, high winds, and controlled burns. Loggers and farmers often piled up large amounts of slash— leftover tree and agricultural material such as branches, logs, and dead plants—which they would then burn to clear land. Although these fires typically died out quickly, it is possible that one rekindled and rapidly grew out of control.

Cliff Hawk and his gang of ruffians are based on a combination of spies and Confederate guerillas. Spies were used by both sides of the American Civil War to gather information on the other side and oftentimes came in unlikely forms, such as with Flora. Guerillas were unorganized bands that caused havoc not only for the enemy forces but among communities by raiding, assaulting, and even murdering individuals. The sporadic and irregular nature of their attacks made them effective at sowing confusion, but they were eventually deemed too violent and had mostly disbanded by the end of the war. Hawk's gang is a little more organized than the typical guerilla group, but their underhanded tactics are similar.

While the fictitious spring races Stefan goes to take place in Kentucky, the actual Kentucky Derby wasn't first run until 1875. It, along with the Preakness Stakes and the Belmont Stakes, went on to form what is now known as the Triple Crown races. Only thirteen horses have ever won all three races, beginning with Sir Barton in 1919 and finishing most recently with Justify in 2018. If you would like to see more of Charlotte and Stefan, feel free to visit my website at avrieswan.com or check out my Instagram at @avrieswanwrites. I hope to see you there!

ABOUT THE AUTHOR

Avrie Swan is a Christian author and avid reader with a love for all things historical. Having grown up exploring antique stores and museums, she eventually decided to combine her interest in history with her love for writing and began working on her first full-length novel at the age of fourteen. She especially enjoys writing stories that focus on themes of family, faith, and growth through difficult times.

When Avrie is not writing, she is watching old movies, collecting antique books, and hunting for agates. A native Wisconsinite, she enjoys spending the cold winters indoors with her cat on her lap and a good book in her hand.

When Rennie must escort a little girl to her parents' home in San Francisco, John is forced to alter his plans to travel across the country with them. But the journey proves far more adventurous than either of them expect.

~

Ranger to the Rescue by Renae Brumbaugh Green

Amelia Cooper has sworn off lawmen for good.

Now any man who wants to claim the hand of the intrepid reporter had better have a safe job. Like attorney Evan Covington. Amelia is thrilled when the handsome lawyer comes courting. But when the town enlists him as a Texas Ranger, Amelia isn't sure she can handle losing another man to the perils of keeping the peace.

Evan never expected his temporary appointment to sink his relationship with Amelia. Or to instantly plunge them headlong into danger. But when Amelia and his sister are both kidnapped, the newly minted lawman must rescue them—if he's to have any chance at love

A Heart's Forever Home by Lena Nelson Dooley

A single lawyer whose clients think he needs a wife.

A woman who needs a forever home...or a forever family...or a forever love.

Although Traesa Killdare is a grown woman now, the discovery that her adoption wasn't finalized sends her reeling. Especially when her beloved grandmother dies and the only siblings she's ever known exile her from the family property without a penny to her name.

Wilson Pollard works hard for the best interest of his law clients, even those who think a marriage would make him more "suitable" in his career. And when the beloved granddaughter of a recently deceased client comes to him for help, he knows he must do whatever necessary to make her situation better.

As each of their circumstances worsen, a marriage of convenience seems the only answer for both. Traesa can't help but fall for her new husband—the man who's given her both his home and his name. But what will it take for Wilson to realize he loves her? Will a not-so-natural disaster open his eyes and heart?